MY NAME IS A KNIFE

MY

NAME

ALIX HAWLEY

IS

A

 *Vintage Canada*

KNIFE

PUBLISHED BY VINTAGE CANADA

Copyright © 2018 Alix Hawley

Published in 2018 by Vintage Canada, a division of Penguin Random House Canada Limited,
Toronto. Distributed in Canada by Penguin Random House Canada Limited, Toronto.

www.penguinrandomhouse.ca

Vintage Canada and colophon are registered trademarks.

Library and Archives Canada Cataloguing in Publication
Hawley, Alix, 1975–, author
My name is a knife / Alix Hawley.

Issued in print and electronic formats.
ISBN 978-0-7352-7329-0
eBook ISBN 978-0-7352-7330-6

1. Boone, Daniel, 1734–1820—Fiction. 2. Boone, Rebecca Bryan,
active 1755—Fiction. I. Title.

PS8615.A821M92 2018   C813'.6   C2017-907358-3
                                              C2017-907359-1

Text and cover design by Five Seventeen
Cover image: (painting) *Portrait of a Woman*, Marie Wandscheer, 1886.
Rijksmuseum, Amsterdam.
Interior image: (dirt texture) © texturelib.com

Printed and bound in the United States of America

10 9 8 7 6 5 4 3 2 1

Penguin
Random House
VINTAGE CANADA

For Theo

REBECCA

NOW I AM READY to tell the story of Madoc—

Before he went mad, this Madoc grew up in a bloody house, with a bloody family. You will have to imagine how they looked, I cannot tell you. It was hundreds of years ago, not here.

He was a prince. His father had two wives, as some kings do, and many fierce sons who loved fighting. Once the old king died, they were all ready to go to war for the crown.

Each queen wanted one of her own sons to be the new king, but their hearts ached over the bloodshed. Each of them cried in her castle, and Madoc heard his mother's weeping. Then he took off his armour and left it in a field. He gathered his wife and children, and one hundred other people, and had all of them singing at the shore as ships were built for them: *Praise Madoc, our sailor prince and saviour.*

They sang for hours.

This pleased Madoc. He loaded his new ships with gold, food and fine clothes for everyone. And he went up to the castle and kissed his mother's tears away. He said she must come with him to a new place, a beautiful place. She smiled then and said she would live out her days wherever he took her. So Madoc led her down to the shore and named his first ship for her, the *Queen Christian*. He gave its figurehead a gold crown with a pearl as big as a fist—and they sailed into the west for many weeks, through windless days and gales.

They met with monsters.

One was a dragon. Its fiery breath burned the mast and sails of one of the ships, and the people on it had to swim for their lives. Madoc rescued them and his wife gave them wine.

Some others were lost when a storm broke up more of the ships. One of them was Madoc's own son, the most beautiful of the young men. He had the blackest hair you can think of—

No one can think of it—

They could not reach him as he tried to hang onto the broken mast in the waves. Madoc's wife, the young man's mother, wept for him as he cried out for help, drifting farther and farther away. His voice stayed in her ears.

She did not watch as his poor body gave up at last and vanished into the ocean.

Soon another monster came in the night, blowing a poison at the last ship that sent many of the people into a heavy sleep. They were not dead, but could not be woken, though Madoc tried lowering them on ropes into the sea and blowing trumpets into their ears, and their little children cried and touched them.

Madoc said they must carry on, and that he was their king now.

But he was mad, in a quiet way. He thought all the time of his armour, which must have rusted in the field by now. He stopped sleeping altogether, and sat staring. His wife watched him. No one knows her name, it is lost, and what was she queen of, in the end?

The ship sailed on, until they came to a shore where the sun was just rising—

Daniel, you always began stories to the children that way—*Now I am ready to tell.* The children still ask for this tale of yours. When my son Jamesie was little, half asleep and sitting on your feet before the fire in our first house, he asked all about how the ships were built, what they were made of, what the monster's poison was. He loved to know things. He was full of questions. *Why, why.*

Jamesie is gone now, more than two years gone, and in his grave somewhere.

You told him you'd heard it from your uncle, another James, who taught you at the school you ran away from time and time again. And you have run from us. You are gone too. Months now. I hardly think of you any longer.

The fire in my house is low. I sit watching the embers. Upstairs, my youngest boy Jesse is awake, calling me. He will wake the others.

When I go to him he blinks at my light and asks for Daddy's Madoc, the way Daddy tells it. Again. Do you remember this, Daniel? It is a story about you, but not all about you—

PART ONE

DANIEL

THE
BLOODY
FAMILY

I

June 1778

MY FEET ARE SKINNED, I can run no more, I am sorry for it.

I lie gasping on my belly in the cane and the mud. I cannot run back. The sun beats me hard on the side of the face. My eyes burn, gnats come in a cloud for them. All night I have lain here. Two days and nights I have run, and behind me is so much, the grassy smoky scent of her skin, the sleeping mat in our house, the bark walls letting the night through. Her eyes with creases round them like stars. And my Shawnee father's eyes also, black as black, looking for the son he took to replace the one we killed, but I am gone.

If they left straight away, if they kept to the Bullskin Trace, they will be no more than a day behind. If my father took time to gather more warriors and supplies, if he sent perhaps first to Detroit for British help, they will be some days yet. Perhaps some weeks, perhaps a month if luck holds, if I have any luck left.

My guts stir, they will not hold, they go liquid. The river gagged me up miles from where I set out to cross. I limped a few miles more before I could go no farther. The fort, my fort, the dreadful place with my name, it is not far from this great canebrake that has snagged me. If it is still there and has not been burned to nothing.

Hold your guts in you ape. Now look. In my mind I see the gate, I see myself walking straight up to it. I know just how I appear, filthy and starved, my gun wet and dirty, my hair all plucked but for the warrior's lock plastered down the back of my head now, my shirt lost, my feet swelled dead white with water and beaten into platters from running. *White Indian*, they will say. Or perhaps only *Indian*, with a bullet as a further greeting.

Rebecca, I am near to you and the children now, whatever state you are in.

A gnat in my ear-hole. Mud in it. I pull my cheek up out of the sucking riverbank and crawl backward into the shallows to clean myself in some fashion. My hands ache. They are not young. I wash out my scratched eyes, I take a little water to ease my cracked tongue. I pick up the gun, I crouch hidden in the cane and I listen.

A hum. A patter. Footfalls.

Someone just downriver, up the high bank above the cane. I muster my voice and I cry out *Hey*, but it becomes a long cough.

—Who is it?

English. No soft-singing Shawnee. The snap of a gun lock, a hard yell, *Here,* the charge of legs running. My dried lips say:

—Wait—

—Where are you? Answer.

—You know me.

—Who?

I cough again, I say it. I say my name, my old name, though I hardly want it in my mouth:

—Boone.

A hesitation. I cannot see the man but I know he has stopped. I hear him rummaging about himself for a moment. Then very careful he speaks:

—You said Boone?

—Yes, yes. Do not shoot me for God's sake.

He crashes down the bank into the canebrake like a great mad dog. I do not move. His gun shoves through the stalks at me, then his face with a lead ball between his teeth.

—Flanders. Flanders.

My daughter's husband, still spare and swarthy and long-necked as a baby bird, as though no time has gone. He spits the lead into his hand and says:

—Jesus, Sir. Bless me. Christ almighty.

—Rebecca—

His face is all astonishment, though it tightens now. My head booms. I say:

—And—your wife.

I cannot force my girl's name past my teeth. Jemima. So many times I have seen her dead in my mind, her and my wife and all the rest. Flanders says:

—Jemima is up at the fort.

—The fort.

—We are not far.

I laugh, though my laughing is only panting, I say:

—I know where we are. It is standing?

Flanders crouches to hear me and says it is. He looks up the bank now. I hear them also, quick steps coming along from where the fort is. They will have heard him yell. Down they crunch through the broken cane. All eyes, all faces I know, boiling up with rage, swelling with it like dried fish in a pot. Dick Callaway is first with his flattened-down hair and his old militia jacket. As soon as he sees me his gun nuzzles at my ear. My own gun is no use, it is wet, and a makeshift thing. I force myself to speak:

—How do, Dick. In a red coat too.

—You bastard, back here alive?

I am struck with another fit of coughing. I manage to say:

—Am I alive?

The gun butts my cheek.

—What did you say, Boone?

I can do nothing but laugh again and cough as others arrive and stand gawping. Flanders crouches to thump my back and haul me upright. Dick has not lowered his gun, his grey eye glinting like a pearl out of the dull squinting flesh round it. I breathe in, but he says first:

—None of your lies.

He twists the gun and bangs my ribs with the stock very clumsy but hard enough. Flanders drops his thin arm from mine. My lungs rattle and before I fall the words burst from them:

—Tell her, tell my wife I am here, tell her they are coming, tell her what they are going to do—

THIS SMELL STRIKES MY NOSE and the back of my throat with the worst sort of familiarity, when you think you have forgotten a thing but find you have not. Dirt, dung, cooked meat, hair.

I stand wet in the back gateway of the fort with the river behind, Flanders propping me up. Old Dick and the rest are talking on back at the bank. The big front gate across the fort from us is wide open with no one watching it. Anyone about is watching me, as I can tell. And what I see hurts me.

I take a step inside before Flanders tightens his grip on my arm. Boonesborough. Still the rectangle we laid out, the idea of a rectangle at least, though nothing here is straight. The cabins still along the walls, some with windows broken. The stockade fencing between some of the houses coming down in places, and wide open on the east side. The shingle roofs gone grey and loose over the winter. Powdery heaps of dust round the hole that should be a well but is no well. Another hole next to it, just as dry.

An old cow rubs its chin against a broken section of paddock fencing in the middle of the fort. Still broken. Its bell clanks in unmusical fashion. Flies suck at its eyes and it does not blink.

Oh Christ, this place. I cough again and I say slow:

—All these months—what have you all been doing?

Flanders warns me with a small shake of his head. Old Dick at my back sends an elbow to my side and I fall forward, Flanders catching me before I tumble to my knees. Dick is not so old, he only acts it, but he is not accustomed to hitting. He rubs his shoulder and cannot bring himself to look at me, he is angry I have made him do it twice now. He says:

—What have *you* been doing all these months?

Others are coming. White-headed Billy Smith appears out of his cabin saying Who is this now—but Old Dick turns to Flanders and says very tight:

—I will decide what is to be done with this person. Put him somewhere and keep your gun on him.

Well. This is all the announcing I get. Dick has had enough of striking me for now, he strides to his house in the little row beside the paddock. He chose that place for his children's safety, away from the walls, though there are not half enough walls here. A crack gapes in his door when it bangs shut. He has put up a flag on a pole on his roof, it twitches in the breeze.

Flanders holds me where I am. The others mill about, they are not easy. Billy Smith keeps where he is in his doorway. Not a word, nothing, even from the hobbled horses. John South's old wife stretches out her window to bob her neck about as though she is taking sips of wind. Flanders moves an inch from me.

And Squire.

My brother in the doorway of his gunsmith shop, between his house and Callaway's. I know him even with the light going and my eyes so poor and full of dirt. All his life I have known him and his slouched outlines. Squire—

I limp a step or two towards him and the pain of my torn feet stabs up my legs again. Flanders takes my arm back very gentle, I stop for his sake. My brother does not move. The silence is hard and thick, Squire, even from you.

All I can do is cough and cough and sit my arse down hard on the ground. When the fit stops, I try to stand, but I cannot do it. Flanders is watching the other men, uncertain. All the faces stare like crows over bones but not your face, Rebecca, not yours. Where in Hell are you? God damn it all, I will find you and you will hear me.

—What have you done with her, you sons of bitches?

Flanders speaks into my ear but I throw him off, I drag myself across the fort through all the shit. No graves, no markers. A horse nickers and blows warm on my arm. I will not feel any ghost of yours, Rebecca, no cold breath on me. Have they made a prison house, have they put you there because of me? Have they made a burying ground outside?

No one stops me, they only watch. Let them watch me. I get to the front gate, I stand holding myself up and looking out over the flat, the darkening fields of corn and flax and the rest. The great elm on the left, the elm I once thought was a sign that this was a good place. And the sound of the spring, which is the only sound. And stumps, still not dug out, with the look of wicked little creatures from one of your fairy tales, Rebecca. I ran here hardly stopping, I ran from them, I ran for you, to tell you they are coming.

Nothing moves over the bare ground or the fields or little orchards, nothing in the meadow beyond these, all the way to the line of the forest. There is nothing. No one else comes. With the last of my strength I hobble back into the fort with everyone gawping and whispering. Old Dick visible in his window, unsure of what to do with me. And Flanders taking my arm again:

—Sir, Dan, wait.

I do not wait. I shake him off, I get myself along the wall to my cabin door. I go inside and suck in the air. The window is broken but the smell in here is its own, empty, overlaid with a whiff of cat. Nobody. Nothing, nothing.

Until a body is throwing itself at me from the doorway behind, crying and snatching at my arms. I stagger—

Not Rebecca. Not my wife. Almost her, in this dimness. But I know my daughter, my girl Jemima, with her mother in her face. Her black eyes swim and swim, they are as black as Rebecca's, they do not leave mine. She twists my skin in her fingers as if testing it is real flesh:

—Daddy Daddy, you are here—

Daddy Daddy—how many children have called me in this way. But I will not think of other children. Here is Jemima. Here I am. Home.

Crying and laughing my girl collapses onto her knees with one arm tight about my leg. *Daddy.* A streak shoots past us. At once I am laughing and crying with her:

—Well my girl. Old Tibby is still here. Or was.

The cat is quite gone out the door. Flanders is a shadow there with his gun, he keeps his eyes on me and not on wherever Tibby ran to. Jemima rubs away her tears with the back of her hand, impatient with them. I say:

—And where is your ma?

—Oh—

She pulls something from under the dried-up straw pallet on the bed. A paper, folded and gummed with a knot of pitch. She hands it to me, watching my face very close. She says:

—She told me to give it to you when you came back. I knew you would come, even if she did not.

I peel back the pitch and hold the paper to my eyes, and here is what meets me:

My brothers have read out the newspapers that tell of your capture by the Indians and call you a Famous Partisan. There are drawings of you that do not look a thing like you.

*If you are alive, you ought to know that we are all right.
I hope to be living when you read this letter. I have no
way of knowing if you are. I do not care any longer. I will
not wait.*

When you did not return from salt making, and we got word
*you had been taken captive, I kept a lamp in the window for you
until we had not enough tallow to justify it. But perhaps it was
my son I left it lit for.*

My daughter will give you this letter.

Rebecca's words, her hate, striking my brains. No greeting. No signature.

My daughter. *My* son.

My son. I do not wish to see it but I do. Jamesie stuck through with arrows like a saint in a thick old book, all wounds. They were still in his body when I found it, Cherokee Jim put them there for me to see, as I know well enough. The man who told me not to come to Kentucky. To stay where I was in Carolina with my children. *A good place. To stay.*

Thinking of this murderer's words and name, his false English name, my brains hiss in my head, my eyes dry and shrivel, my legs go stiff and again I see my boy. His eyes frozen colourless and his plait covered in frost and earth. I dug him up to look at him and his wounds and I buried him again.

I did not find the murderer, Rebecca.

Well. The words are yours but written in a man's hand, carved hard into the paper as if into bark. Is it a Bryan hand? You were born a Bryan, you have always been a Bryan at heart, though I made a Boone of you in name, and the son and daughter are mine, they are Boones! See one of your brothers penning the letter for you at this table in my house, smiling into his little beard.

Or my brother's hand. Ned's hand——

I sink down onto the rough tabletop. To my daughter, *my* daughter, I say:

—Where is she? Your mother?

Jemima comes to squeeze my wrists. She says:

—Gone back to Carolina.

My girl, you were always so frank. I say:

—When?

—A little time after you were taken. Israel went, and Susy too with her baby, and some of Ma's brothers.

Israel. My next son after Jamesie, my dead boy. Susy, my oldest girl, whose name the men make free with as if it were a ball to toss back and forth. Gone for months now.

I look again to Jemima's face, it shines in the darkening room:

—The other children?

—Went with her. Daddy—

I crunch the paper in my fist and I crunch Jemima in my arms. My daughter. The only one left here. Her cap beneath my chin has the faintest whiff of Rebecca's old bayberry soap. Old cleanness. I had thought that lost to me too. Some six months I was gone. Jemima, I know now that it was my brother Ned who made you, the first time Rebecca thought me lost for good, but you are mine. And you at least are here.

She is thinner but strong. Her shoulders rise, she begins her fierce crying again. Between her sobs she says:

—I stayed. I was waiting for you. I made Flan write a letter to the Indians, I told them not to touch a hair of your head or I would kill them all. But I did not know where to send it, Daddy. And your hair—

She feels the shaved sides of my head. And here is the past again crashing ahead, things I do not wish to think of. Sweet hands knifing off my hair. Grass-smelling and somehow silky in the palms in spite of all their work. In my mind her lips part, a word is coming.

But I do not know which word, which tongue. And I ran from her as well as the rest. Methoataske my wife, will you come with them from Old Chillicothe town, will you insist on leading the march with a skull-cracker in one hand, your shaving knife in the other, out of pain that I ran? And Eliza behind you, fierce as fierce. Your daughter. She wanted me for a father, she wanted my help. Another lost child of mine.

I close my eyes to them both. It is all I can do now, I will keep them hidden. To my girl I say:

—Jemima, letters mean nothing. It would not have helped.

Her voice goes sharp:

—It would have helped. Everyone said you were dead or gone to live Indian forever. I knew you were alive, I knew!

And what I am to say in the face of such belief, I do not know.

⌣

Jemima brings back some jerked meat and the cat and a fat-lamp, and crouches in its spitting circle of light. I cannot eat. I ask for ink and paper, she runs and begs these from one of the neighbours, without saying it is me who wants them. Her eyes do not leave me, but when Flanders comes in, I tell her she ought to get some sleep, and after another embrace she goes next door with him for the night. I hear her through the wall. *Stop it. Daddy will not go anywhere. You do not have to guard his door.*

I sit at the table with the paper. The lamp sizzles. The fort is quiet but for a few of the horses nickering. I think Old Dick might come for another look at me but he does not, no one comes.

I look at the empty page and I write:

Dear WIFE

I have not written a word in months. My hand is stupid as a child's, the quill bites the bone of my thumb. The pain in my feet and my eyes hammers at me. I crawl over the dirt floor and feel about under the bed and the pallet for something else of hers, something better. A tin bowl dented in. A beetle husk, bones of a bird or mouse. Dried leaves, dried catshit. Quite a witch's recipe. And a small scrap, tucked under a bed rope, it comes away when my fingers find it and pull.

In the circle of light, it is yellow as egg yolk. Rebecca's. She has always had it, it was something of her mother's, some bit of silk. She only took it out of her workbox and showed it to me the one time, her eyes shining in a private fashion. She rubbed it between her fingertips as if she were a sleepy child with a bedsheet. Well. Her ma must have been very fine, I do not know.

Our Jamesie, my Jamesie, was not a lover of sheets. He said he liked to be cold, do you remember it, Rebecca? Well I am sure you do. Yet Squire buried him wrapped up tight in one of our wedding sheets. I wrapped him again after I checked his grave and made it a better one. All I could do. He is all right, out of this life. But what do you think you are doing, leaving yours? I am your life, this is your life. I left everything for you. And so I will tell you here first, before I tell anyone else. You know well enough that the Shawnee will not leave me be after I ran from them. I know too much now of their country, their towns, their ways. They made me one of them, I am one of them. They will come soon. They will find me, and then we will see what they will do.

3

My compliments to you. I wish only to oblige you in your wishes.
Is this what you wish to hear? That I will be scalped, burnt slow,
ripped to shreds, fed to dogs? That I will have to first look my
Indian father in the face?

I DO NOT FINISH this letter. I do not add, *And perhaps my Indian*
wife also. How can I tell my wife of my other wife?

I will write, I will tell you what I have done. But not yet.

I lie on the bare bed, it sags beneath me. I sleep hard. I dream
of a deer. In the dream I shoot it in the gut and it wanders off leaking blood. I chase it through the woods the whole day until I find it
at twilight lying at a campfire, where it turns into a woman when
it sees me. It is you, Methoataske. I believe it is.

I sit with her at her fire and she talks some, telling me things of
the invisible world. Animals, tracks, marking, signs. Things I have
always known how to see. And things I have not seen. Ghosts in
everything there is, even in spoons. *Manitoc.* She once told me this
word, but said it was not the same as the word for ghosts. She could
not tell me just what it meant. Only that she saw them, anyone could
see them if they knew how to look. My ghosts were people, they
were different, they seemed poorer. I told her so and she smiled.

Her daughter, my daughter, played with spoons. She named one after herself. Eliza—

Do not think of them. Do not think.

My heart is tired. I cannot think of them in another life. I do not feel my old ghosts now as I lie alone in the cabin. Not my boy, not my brother, not my old daddy and ma, not the men who came out here to look about the country with me, not the other prisoners dead at Detroit where I left them. And not anyone else dead through my fault. They will not speak to me now after all I have done, they will not help me.

There is too much to think of. How we are to get out from beneath all of what is coming. How I will save everyone who does not want my saving.

I turn myself over on the bed and stare at the chipped wall. I do not wish to think of Martha but I do. When I had to stop and sleep an hour on my long run back to this place, I dreamt of her. Rebecca's sister, like her but not so settled in her skin. Her narrow hips and white thighs against earth and flattened young corn, as I saw her once. Her mouth opening, the *V* between her legs opening. Her endless want, the way she was before I left. Now I know what she was about, trying to keep me from knowing that Neddy, her husband, had fathered Jemima on my wife. I pulled away and she gripped me with her limbs and her insides. *Stay. Stay.* Even in the dream I knew enough to go.

She is here though. I heard her voice outside before night fell entire, talking low with some of the other women. Much later I hear her knock in the dark and say my name soft through the door. *Daniel, Daniel?* She makes a great question of it, asking everything of me. I do not reply and she goes away, but I know it is only for the time.

Methoataske did not ask me to stay. She never asked. Always quiet when we lay together on our sleeping mat. Gentle arms and hands, at times a gentle laugh. I loved to hear it. I wish she had asked me. I do wish it, Methoataske, though I do not know how I could have done it.

I ran from you and my Shawnee life to save this place. I close my eyes.

⌣

I wake with my brains knocking against my skull, and I have to empty my sick bowels into the shallow bowl from beneath the bed. I am filled with a panic to get outside. As I hobble into the grey dawn with the stinking bowl, Jemima hears my door opening and is beside me before I know it. Flanders comes out rumpled with sleep, and she sends him in again. She has her buckets with her. Bold as she ever was, she says:

—Come out to the spring with me.

I point at my raw feet and I say:

—I cannot get far in this state. Seems I am quite at your mercy, my girl. You will have to help me.

She laughs her clear ha ha as I set down the bowl:

—I will get some water for you too, poor prisoner Daddy. And you might get a crust of bread. If we had any bread.

Prisoner. Perhaps I am one again. Off my girl runs with her buckets, she aims a smile back at me. Flanders pokes his thin neck and his gun from the window and he gives me a cautious nod. Other women are coming from their cabins with their own buckets now. They stop for a long look at me, my half-naked state and my half-shaved head. One says my name loud. *Daniel Boone.*

Old Dick's sturdy little daughter Kezia gives me a dog-eye. I nod and I say:

—How do, ladies.

They are surprised at my voice. Now the girl's mother Elizabeth Callaway emerges across the way and tells them to come, and off they all gaggle into the dim morning. One of them says *prisoner*, but not in Jemima's laughing fashion. I may be one today, if Old Dick has his way. *Did you see him. Look at him. Look. Half Indian and half dead.*

Martha is not among them. Nor have I seen any sign of Ned yet. Well. They will keep. None of my difficulties flies off easy, as I know.

I follow slow to the big front gate to watch for what may be coming. When she has her water from the spring, Elizabeth sends Kezia hurrying back to the house with it, and sets to calling the children to her school beneath the great elm just beyond the walls. She stands in the front gateway with her arms crossed but pays me no heed. The children dart looks at me as they run past, out to the tree. Once she has them sat down she stalks the line of them before she flattens her hand upon her thin chest and says:

—Children, pay no mind to the prisoner lately returned from the Indians. Now. Heart and stomach! Heart! And! Stomach! Who said it?

One of the boys raises a hand, but quick enough she answers herself:

—Queen Bess said it at a speechmaking. She was the daughter of Henry Eight. She had red hair and no beauty, but she gave a fine speech before her army as the wicked Spanish came in their ships to attack her land. She had the heart and stomach of a man, and so she said, and so she and her men won the victory.

The boy pipes up quicker this time, it is my brother Squire's boy Moses sitting with his chin on his knobby knees:

—What happened to the wicked enemy ships? Did they come back?

Moses, if you knew what was coming.

I lift my arm, but I cannot get enough words from my throat before I cough and cough again. Moses and his little brother Isaiah turn to see, Elizabeth gives a loud set of claps and refuses to look at me. She does not know what is coming, she knows nothing.

Two of the younger men are making their way in my direction
from Old Dick's place, they are unhurried but coming straight.
One is John Holder, married to Dick's daughter Fanny. His sleek
narrow head is like an otter's, he is tilting it at me. The other is
copper-haired Alexander Montgomery with fringe all over his
hunting shirt and a broad smile on his face. Well I have no need to
hear their thoughts just now. I turn and limp back to my house,
where the stinking bowl still sits outside the door. Before I have
shut myself in, Jemima appears, slopping water with her quick gait.
She holds out a bucket:

—Here you are. Flanders says you ought to stay in for now, for
Colonel Callaway's sake.

—You are always in a hurry, duck.

—What is there to wait for? You ought to sit down, from the
smell of your pot.

Her nose wrinkles as she looks behind her to where Holder and
Montgomery are outside. I shut the door and I say low:

—Leave it for those two. Listen now, we will have to wait some
time but I do not know how long. You will be my eyes today. Any
sign outside?

—Of what? We have not seen a buffalo in weeks.

—Indians. Shawnee, Cherokee. Or British, for that matter.

She is holding her nose now and creasing up her brow, and I
am struck by a memory of the egg-headed English governor,
Hamilton, at Fort Detroit doing the same when he promised safe
passage for my people, if I would only give up my ridiculous fort
and my ridiculous claims on his Indian allies' land. We should all be
quite safe, go and live as British again within his walls, which are
true walls and not the sorry fallen-in ones we have here. Well. In
Jemima's ear I say:

—Did you see anyone? Anything at all?

She shakes her head:

—Next time I will take the gun with me. Though Flan used up most of our shot trying to hunt this winter. I am a better shot, Daddy, likely better than you now.

—I believe it, my g—

I cough before I can finish the word right. She laughs, she says:

—Your girl, I know I am, poor old man.

Jemima, I am sorry for it, and for all you have endured because of it, but I say:

—Do not forget it. Say nothing for the time. And be on the watch for any movement —

—I know what to look for.

Her eyes burn black. Rebecca's eyes made young again, no hate in them, no cloud. She leaves me, singing loud. I hear young Holder and Montgomery tell her good morning. They do not knock, but they wait for a time listening. I know Old Dick has sent them spying. I give them no satisfaction, I only set the stinking bowl outside my door, then I go in again and hum a Shawnee tune until my throat cracks and I finish with a great chorus of hacking.

I have to lie down though I do not wish to do it. I go on coughing and puffing like a bull for a time, I have no tobacco to soothe myself with. Through the broken window I can still hear Madam Callaway going on about Henry Eight, fond of listening to her own knowledge. I do not hear any of the children answering, though I can see them in my mind, sitting on the bare ground under the elm, where anyone can see.

Squire's boys there—

I must say it, there is no way not to say it. I know this. If anyone will listen to me.

I get up. Flanders or Jemima has left my poor makeshift gun on the floor next to the bed. I take it up, I break the stock off to show just how harmless I am.

With both pieces I hobble over to my brother Squire's gunshop. He is in the shadow at the back of the building, trying to get his fire lit. But he looks up from snapping his flint, his face all bony hollows. I do wonder just how bony I look, my rib cage feels set to shove off through my skin. Bright as I can, I say:

—How do, gunsmith. I am in want of many things. A shirt is one. But particularly a new gun. I restocked this barrel with a limb I found on my way back here. Best lock I ever had in my life. I was in a hurry but it works well enough.

He says nothing. He has never been one for talk. At last he scratches his cheek and he says:

—Who gave you the barrel?

—My Shawnee family.

—Your Shawnee family.

—Yes.

Squire's mouth thins and stretches. I feel mine do the same, as though I were his broken mirror. I think to tell him more but I do not do it. After a time my brother says:

—You have another family, as you may recall.

—I do, or perhaps I did. My wife and most of my children are gone.

He gives his head a slight shake. To him I wish to say, *Squire, I thought it was you, I thought you had been with my wife, I had thought you were Jemima's father until I heard the truth. I did learn some things when I was with the Shawnee, ha.*

It is a long sharp splinter between us, though we never talked of it. Squire did not give Neddy up. I see him and Ned as small boys sitting quiet on the bench in Meeting and swinging their legs. They were close when they were young, though Neddy and I were always closer in looks. *He looks so much like you.* Ma's words. My wife Rebecca's words also, after I came back the first time. *I thought you were dead.*

I hold out the gun pieces. Squire takes them, he fingers the lock and reaches for the grease on his shelf. His eyes take their usual interest in how a thing is made. When he runs his hand down the grain of the stock, his fingers shake. I say:

—You are ill, Squire?

He says:

—Ague. Comes and goes. I am all right. Cannot do so much work as I would like here.

—I see that.

His eyes stay on the gun's lock. He moves its parts, he says:

—No worse than most.

—Well. I thank you for that opinion.

He holds the barrel up to his eye:

—Trade garbage. English.

—Yes. They are still making friends in the wilderness.

—What did they trade you for?

Squire's eyes are flat and shadowed. I hold out my empty hands and I say:

—I ran. I left.

—Time you did, was it?

—It was.

—And they did not chase you.

—No. Or not far. I kept to streams after the horse they had given me wore out. You can see the great beauty of my feet.

I thrust one out at him. It has the look of a skinned creature, with the old bullet scar on my ankle a sicker white. He says only:

—They gave you a horse too? What did you give them?

—Squire—

—It is only that we heard you had given all of us away.

He sets down my gun barrel and kneels once more before his

sputtering fire. I could tell him about my wedding horse, my wife, all my gifts. My guts churn up again. I say:

—Squire. There is no truth in that story. Tell me you do not believe it.

He looks at me hard. He says:

—Then what was Johnson talking of? He left for Harrodsburg after he got back here. Said he would not live in a place with your name after what you had done to those men with you, and to us here.

—You believe what Andy Johnson says? He played a madman the whole time the Shawnee had us. I believe he *is* half mad, hairy creeping bastard. He did not know what I was about. Harrodsburg can have him. It has had its share of Indian trouble too. Perhaps they will sell him back to them.

Johnson, Pekula the Shawnee called him, their Little Duck, all mad stupid prancing, who ran off sly one night months ago. Squire shakes his head again. He does not like to be perplexed.

—Squire.

He turns his back. A line of sunlight is just inside the shop now. He squats, his thin legs tremble slightly as his heels lift. His moccasins are patched and patched, the soles of his feet must be near as bad as mine. His shoulders round as he says:

—Dan, I am glad you are all right. But I do not know why you are here now after so long.

—To tell you what they are planning—that is why I am here. Look at the state of me. I need your help—

He puts a hand up. I say:

—Listen now, the rest will not listen. There will not be so very much time.

—Dan, I cannot hear anything more from you now. There is food to get. I have children here. We lost one while you were gone. I cannot take them anywhere other, but at least I can hunt.

This cuts me down to my ribs.

23

—You lost one?

—Born dead in April. No midwife. Rebecca was already gone.

—Well. Well Squire. Is Jane all right?

He only crosses the little shop and takes up a long gun from where it leans against the wall. Looking down its barrel he says:

—There will be no more dead children. I will see to that.

I say:

—I will hunt with you, give me a horse—lend me a horse and a gun and I will promise you whatever game there is to get. You know how Kentucky game feels about me, no matter my condition.

I force a laugh from my rotten lungs, but my brother only gets his powder horn and shakes two bullets about in their pouch, then turns it out empty as if to show me how poor I have become.

⌣

The sun sits just above the wall. A clear day it will be, bright and fine. Birds call from the trees past the fields beyond the stockade gap. The women chatter as they go about their business. My name pokes up like weeds through their talk again and again. *Boone, Boone.* I drag myself off towards my cabin. I will think of what to do, my brains will grind to work again.

I suppose I will have to hunt somehow, if only to feed myself. I think of setting a fish line at the river so I will not have to hobble far, though in truth I would like to get Jemima and hobble as far as it is possible to go from this place. I am hungry, hungrier than I have been since the Shawnee marched us half starved through the snow for days to their town. On my run back here I smoked the tongue of the buffalo I killed, I meant it for my youngest boy Jesse, but I lost it along with my shirt when the raft I made to cross the Kentucky was tugged away by the current. I did manage to keep hold of the gun in the water, but what use is it to me now? Squire.

—Why is no one watching him?

The voice is cool at my back. I know who it belongs to, so I do not turn. My spine hardens and I limp on as best I can.

—Just as well, I will ask you before everyone, as you are out. Where are the rest? We sent more than twenty of you to get salt, and by God I see only you back.

I carry on in my limping. But Dick Callaway only speaks louder so all may hear:

—Boone, you will tell me now what you have done with my nephew and the others.

At this I face him. His grey hair is greased back hard from his unhappy forehead, his wide shoulders are raised. I say:

—Whatever your nephew did, he did himself.

Even as I say it I see young James Callaway's angry face, always red like his red hair. Rooster, the Shawnee called him, Napeia. Impossible young man, impossible prisoner, refusing all they asked, fighting them whenever he could. No one would adopt him as their own. Chief Black Fish, my Shawnee father, sold him to the British, who can blame him? James Callaway is dead, hanged at Detroit and buried there, I am sure of it. And I could do nothing.

Old Dick's face is pained but he goes on in his measured fashion, as though he has waited all his life to say this to me:

—It was your command he was under, Captain Boone. You had charge of those men, and what did you do? Gave them to your Indian friends, very nice indeed.

The words fire out of his mouth: *Captain. Nice.* He thumbs the corner of his lips. Here is why he did not kill me outright, wanting to say his piece to me before everyone. The women stand in a tight little fist to listen. A few children run to their mas, a cow lifts its tail and shits in lazy fashion not far from Colonel Dick. Billy Smith comes with his white head and his hands raised, saying, Now boys—

But Dick has not finished. He walks slow at me with his hands behind him:

—You sold them, we all know it. You are no captain, your title is worthless. You ought to be hanged.

—Where did you get your title, Colonel?

Dick is one who loves titles and marching about. And outranking me. Before he can answer I hold out my arms:

—Go on. Here I am at your service. There is surely still a length of rope to be had even in this place.

I feel myself quite Christly in this position. I cock my head at him. In spite of his attempts to keep himself cold, his grey eyes bulge with blood. He holds himself unmoving just before me, all shiny face and patted-down hair. Many of the men are gathering now also, and a rumble of talk rises. We might be on the stage, in this position. When I grin at this thought, Dick grips one side of my neck, his hand is very glad to find it:

—By God I will do it, you son of a whore, but not before you tell us just what you did!

In the edge of my eye I see Squire coming in the back gate. He has his gun but no meat. This makes my arms drop and my strength rush from me. Old Dick tightens his hold. Billy Smith has come up beside us saying:

—Peace now, Dick.

I jerk my head away, I step back. Everyone goes on standing about. Well I will give them a speech for their trouble:

—Billy is right, I am back alone.

I look up until my sore eyes shut themselves against the blue. The talk starts up again, the low vicious hum of it. I say:

—I did sell the rest after the Shawnee caught us at the Blue Licks, but I sold myself along with them. You wish to know why? It is because they would have come for you.

—Goddamned lies!

This from Dick of course. I say:

—You are correct, Colonel, and you are lucky too that I am an excellent liar. The Shawnee believed every one of my tales of the fort being in sound condition, too strong to take, and full of brave fighters.

I bow in his direction. I bow in the direction of the hole in the stockade. A low groan bursts from him:

—You left us without enough men to keep the fort in order, and many were sick all winter and spring.

—Is that your tale, Dick?

Quick he is pointing at me, looking round for agreement:

—Look at this brave man, brave enough to save his own skin. Going over to their side and laughing like Judas. Ha ha ha ha.

My heart bangs in my throat with the beat of his furious false laugh. I say:

—I saved everyone. As many as I could. Most are alive, adopted into families. The Shawnee would have slaughtered the lot of us otherwise. Blood all over the snow at the salt licks. A fine picture.

Most are alive. I see graves, I see a tangle of corpses of all sorts, I see the smile of my Shawnee wife, the faces of my children, my boy Jamesie now dead, Squire's baby.

—God will be your judge.

This from Elizabeth Callaway who has followed the children fleeing her school teaching. She sets her long chin at me, and I say:

—God is not here. I am here! What I did saved you, and you, and you, and the rest!

The women draw themselves together like a mouth readying to spit. Dick stalks to his wife's side:

—Boone, I judge you before all these witnesses as a coward and a traitor.

Billy Smith holds up his hands, Dick nods at his own pronouncement. Elizabeth clutches his arm, the other women scatter slow as geese. I step back with my legs throbbing. I must speak now, I know it, though my chest sags at the thought. I raise my hands like Billy and I say:

—Listen to me. We must build up this place. All of us must. As it is, it will not withstand a single one of them if they come. They may come. This is true, it is the truth.

Elizabeth cries:

—How can we believe anything you say? Why would we? Look at you!

—What choice have you got? I know them better than anyone here does. I now know their winter towns and the routes to them. I know the British fort at Detroit, come to that. I know many of the chiefs, Shawnee and Cherokee. Black Fish adopted me as his son.

My breath catches, if there were a way to take back the words and make them private again I would do it.

—Gained a few relations for yourself, Daniel.

It is Billy Smith who says it. The rest are shocked and silent. My Shawnee wife, my father and mother and sisters sleeping in their bark houses. I cry:

—I know it! Come to think, the colonel here is my relation too, with his nephew Flanders married to my daughter. Quite a happy family we all are.

My daughter. At these words some of the men smirk, some of the remaining women look at me sideways. Dick sets his mouth. Old talk, old tales, they are never gone. But Jemima is mine. She is beside me now, staring down the rest. I go and pick up a chunk of log fallen from the stockade, I jam it hard into the ground and I say:

—Well. Here I am, so now you must take me back.

I find a hammer in Squire's shop and I take it as he watches. I go out and I begin to repair the hook for the bar on the front gate. No one else will start and so I will do it.

The rest go on doing little, puttering about, no one guarding either gate. A few young men up in the one good corner blockhouse, aiming their guns at nothing. A few women in the fields and the young orchards. My old friend William Hill had plans for these, when we were young men, when this was new country. His bright dreams of peaches and easy game and Indian maids all over Kentucky. *Oh the Indian maids.* So he would sing. Hill, the plague of my life since we were boys, always wanting to write stories about me, to marry me off, to take my life over for me. Dead at Detroit too through my wishing it. But I will not think of him now. I will not think of being young.

At noon I stagger indoors. My whole head burns, the skin of my back is sunburnt, my mouth has a queer taste. I recognize I am half starved. Jemima comes in with a shirt and a bowl and Flanders behind her. She says:

—Here. Put this on. And this is for your feet.

I sit and pull Flanders's linen shirt over my head, it is long in the arms but it will do and I am glad to have it. My girl begins to poultice me up. The oak ooze spread over the sores and torn blisters on my feet has its old bitter smell, it is an odd comfort, it makes me think myself in the woods again alone. I dab a little of the ooze onto my fingers and swallow it to settle my shrunken stomach. Flanders says quiet:

—Quite a talk you gave everyone.

The oak is sharp as old vinegar, I gag on it and I laugh. Jemima says she will put a heap of it in everyone's water buckets tomorrow morning, that will lay them all up in bed for a day or so and teach them their lesson. I catch at her sleeve and I say:

—They do not understand, duck. The Shawnee will be here soon. The scouts are likely here by now. I have not said so to everyone yet so as not to start a panic, but this fort is no fort—

My girl is a lover of danger, always the child to throw herself laughing off a horse into the depths of a river. Taken by Cherokee and Shawnee, gone for days, and bold as could be when we found her, while my body near gave out with relief that she was not dead like her poor brother, my Jamesie. She stands now and bounces up onto her toes just as she did then, calling *Daddy Daddy* through the trees.

I look Jemima in the face, it is all I can do. How many times have I seen you dead in my mind? How are you still so full of life?

I grab hold of her wrist and she is talking still:

—Daddy, I will watch, I watched for you all the time. I saw nothing today, but I will keep looking.

Flanders takes her hand from me. The apple of his throat bobs as he says:

—Sir, we nearly lost her to Indians once. I have to tell you I will not let it happen again.

—No one wishes anything bad to happen here, Flanders. We will parley. We will make things right with them. How, I do not know yet.

Jemima shakes him off and he says in his thin fashion:

—That is fine. Only you ought to know that I will not let her go again, no matter how many I have to kill.

4

SEE MURDER, see all manner of knives, guns, tomahawks, axes, ball clubs, plain clubs. See the shine on all of them coming straight down at your face before your eyelids can shut themselves. See all faces turned to mash, all skulls staved in like ice on water, all limbs broken into letter *V*s.

But *V* is for *victory*, it was the first letter I learned to write, at the table in my older brother Israel's little house in Pennsylvania. His wife taught me before she was dead and my brother was also. A long time ago, I can hardly count how long.

Now what is there to write? I cannot sleep. I line out *1, 2* and *3* on my forearm with my finger. How many days have we got? I count and count in my mind like a schoolboy, but there is no fathoming it, and my brains are still fatigued, perhaps they are full of mud also. It could be tomorrow the Shawnee come. But I do not expect so. An army takes time to travel, even a quick-moving Indian army. Black Fish, my father, I know you, I know this. Again the idea of murder comes into my mind. I want none of it, though perhaps you do now. Perhaps you wish to start with mine.

Can you forgive me? I do not know if you can.

I turn over on the bed. Let us say we have a month. Think of a month and what can be done.

There is food to think of, and I do think of it. All night my stomach roars its complaint. Jemima brought me cooked green corn and green onion. Wholesome, I will say, if not much to go along on. The plantings have taken hold, at least. The corn is getting higher, the people here were not driven to eat all the seed over winter.

Green corn has never been to my liking, it is small hard stuff and always pricking up its ears on the stalks to see how I will get out of this or this or this.

We have some food then.

What else? I have one poor bird club to my name, I made it as I ran, and my gun barrel. How many guns here are working? Squire, you will have to speak to me. Everyone will, I will see that they do.

—

Bang bang bang bang bang. And bang again.

I stand beneath the great elm outside the walls. Day is just cracking over the hills across the river, the fort is still quiet. Elizabeth, I will be schoolteacher today. I have stolen the bell from the thin cow roaming about and I bang at it with my little club without stopping.

Billy Smith is the first to come out through the gate, his white hair is startled, his white legs look ghastly beneath his nightshirt. He says:

—Dan, what is this for?

I bang on, and I call as loud as I can:

—Billy, you are Major Smith, are you not?

—I was, yes. I have my militia papers.

—Then you still are. I was appointed commandant of this fort before—I left. And so I may appoint you to that position now, if you will have it.

His eyes drift like clouds. He says:

—Colonel Callaway is the ranking officer—

At this Dick appears with his hair already wetted, grim as if summoned out of his wife's loving skinny arms. He says:

—What are you doing out? And at this hour?

Elizabeth is behind him with Kezia, angry as her father is. I strike the bell again and again until more people come wincing and squinting towards me. To Billy I say:

—That is so, Major Smith! But I have the right to pass my commandant position to you. I know you are a sensible man and a kind one. The rest of you may think what you like of me, take away my captaincy if you wish. But listen first.

Billy shakes his white head:

—Dan, you may stop that noise.

Dick puts his hand to his forehead and says something loud but I do not hear, I do not choose to stop my banging until he is quite done, at which time I yell raw-throated:

—I have come back to tell you that a war party is already on the way. It will be led by the Shawnee who captured me and the other men.

—Where are the other men?

This from the round little wife of William Hancock who is still gone. She gazes very earnest at me but I will not think of him or the rest. I yell on:

—They may have Cherokee and Wyandot friends with them, and likely some British. What they will do here, I do not know. I do know much about their ways and I do know they are not pleased with our presence.

One of the young men yells:

—Are they pleased with you?

Simon Kenton is a big fellow and a clever one, he is grinning. I laugh and I say:

—I will ask them when they come.

Old Dick gets his words in now:

—He speaks Indian. He will tell them all there is to tell, and in their own tongue, very nice.

I bang the bell and I shout:

34

—I do speak Shawnee very well, they complimented me on it more than once. And we have no secrets from them, which is not my doing, lest you ask. Their scouts are likely near us already. What secrets do you have, Colonel? You may tell us all, we are your friends.

A small laugh snakes over everyone. I see Kenton smirk. Dick is cooking up a retort, but I say:

—You have no need to be my friend to know that the state of this fort is no joke. When they come, I will talk my best with them, but we must at least make ourselves safe from harm and show our strength. Major Smith, I ask your permission to have all of us put this place in order. I do not know how long we have, perhaps a month. And look round you.

The daylight lifts as I say this. Quite a splendid effect, I will say. It spills gold over the broken stockade, the weak gate with its missing logs, the corner bastions only half built, the well that is no well at all, the dotted heaps of cowshit. All shit, covered in gold. Look.

Billy Smith is blinking against it all. I say:

—I beg your opinion, Major.

He twists his beard. He has always looked older than his years but here he looks quite a Father Time. Very slow he says:

—Boone—Captain Boone—is quite right. I accept the commandant position. We ought to make ourselves safer here, no matter what is to come. It will do no harm.

Old Dick has his hand over the top of his head now and is watching Billy Smith very close. Billy in his nightshirt joins me beneath the boughs of the elm. Some of the other men follow, a parade of white shirts, some so worn their backsides show through. I call:

—Jemima. Bring your scissors.

Quick as a cat she darts back into the fort and out again with her dark plait flying. She comes to me with the scissors. Flanders is behind her, others also, though Dick remains where he is, flat-faced and thinking his own thoughts. The air is not easy, no one is easy, but here they are.

I kneel. I tell Jemima to cut off the lock of hair, my last, the one the Shawnee leave their warriors on top of their skulls.

One thick snip and the hair falls in a black curve on the ground. I think of Methoataske my wife cutting off the rest so long ago in the icy river at Chillicothe. The women stand some distance off but they watch just as the Shawnee women did.

Martha is there with two of her girls, gulping me with her great eyes. No Ned. Well. I do see Squire with his wife and his knob-kneed boys standing in a small row to one side. I get up and I shake my shorn head and take a breath. They all wait, they listen.

Build the corner bastions higher at the front of the fort. Finish the two on the back side so we can see them if them come from over the river. Get roofs on them. Cut gunslits in the walls and in the bastion floors where they overhang, do not make the slits too big.

Clear the brush close to the stockade. Cut down more of the trees.

Build out the east end, close it all in and get more of the cattle inside, and any hogs we can catch in the woods. Find something to feed them. Find something to feed us.

Fix the front gate, which has the look of an old woman's mouth. An old whore's mouth, I will say it before anyone else can. *Your sister is a whore. Your wife is a whore. Your daughter is a whore.* I have heard it enough in my life.

Dig a goddamned well, God damn it.

These things I tell them to get to first. I feel myself quite a schoolmaster with a set of slugs to teach, I have to line out every step before they begin. Dick does not like it but he feels the rest listening to me for the time, so he goes along. For ten days I drive them hard, we are hard at it as soon as dawn shows itself. Major Billy thinks on all I say and agrees to it. I know I have him now and I am glad of it, he is a good man. Most respect him if they do not respect me, and so they work. Old Dick cannot argue with work.

My guts go on worrying. How many men have we got? Some fifty, if we count the black men here, and all the older boys who can shoot. I send a few of the young hotheads out scouting, and big Kenton with Nat Henderson's black man London to Harrodsburg and Logan's Fort asking for support. They are both quick riders. I watch them go into the afternoon, hoping we will see them again, and the horses, we have none to spare. My breath and my feet are still all wrong, but I work and work.

We set the children free from Madam Elizabeth and her speech-ifying. I post the younger boys to stand watch in pairs along the river and the fields, they are not to go too far. I have Jemima set the little girls to making bandages, though there is not much cloth to be had. Squire's small wife Jane does not look wholly well but she says she cannot sit still. She has a few women try their hand at weaving nettles with the underbelly wool of the buffalo skins we have got, perhaps it may work.

I watch, I watch everything, even when I am not on guard duty in a bastion or at a gate. With their mothers the bigger girls keep at the crops and at hauling water from the spring to fill every bucket and pot we have. Even piss pots? unhappy little Kezia Callaway barks at me, and I say, Yes those also. She huffs off through the gate all incredulous to tell her daddy. Colonel Dick is keeping himself to himself, patrolling close to the woods on his fine heavy bay gelding. Perhaps he may shoot something useful, such as his leg.

Each day I watch. I watch until I am half blind with it. But I see nothing, no tracks, no scouts.

By the tenth day we have made some progress, though the bastions are not near done and the stockade is still open at the east end. The men are slowing with the heat, their trust in the work is low. The complaints and the questions grow louder. *What is this all in aid of? Why the hurry? We ought to go after them before they can get to us. I did not come out here for this.*

What did you come here for? Why did I lead you here, why did I open this place? This I think but I do not say it. I work. The stockade building is very hard. We fell tall pines, then limb them and haul them to the fort by rope and cow, we have no good oxen left.

I am not strong, I am not as I should be, but I work in the shadow of the wall where I hack my hardest at the log ends with an axe to make points before we heave them upright. When we have another up and steady in the row, I kneel a moment to stop my head swimming.

Squire is beside me. He takes up my axe and chips at the log to finish off its spike, though he looks as weak as I do. I say:

—Not enough days. Well into July already, and the dark comes faster each evening.

—Dark for them too. Less time for travel every day.

—Time is not the same for them.

Squire gives me a queer look as he chops, a pine chip flies at my face like a wasp. I rub at my cheek and say:

—I thank you for that. Get back to your shop, we need guns that can aim just as well.

Amusement visits his face for a moment. I say:

—I have much to thank you for in truth. For burying Jamesie for me. And for Rebecca.

His eyes go dark. He keeps chopping. I say:

—Jamesie was a better axeman than either of us.

He says in his quiet fashion:

—He would have been a good man.

—Yes.

Well. *Would have been* seems to me the saddest string of words there is. The future that cannot be. The dream of it. Some part of my mind is always dreaming it.

The sun is crossing the top of the elm now, it is always rolling across the sky. I take the axe back and set to work again. The men shout out, near ready for this log to be hoisted into its hole. The point is ready for catching at the belly of anyone who tries to get over the wall. Feeling quite queer and dizzy I stop and I say to Squire:

—I owe you my apologies also. I thought something of you that was not true. I know it was Ned with Rebecca.

Squire stands and takes up the end of a puddle of rope to loop round the log. He says:

—You ought to go and see Ned. Been very sick too, still in bed with ague.

—I ought to.

But I do not go. I shout for the party bringing the next log to hurry themselves, we do not have time, there is no time here.

⌣

The evening is dry and clear and so we work on. I am hacking out a narrow porthole in the new stockade wall when Squire's boy runs up panting so hard he cannot get a word out. I put my hand on his shoulder, it sticks with the sweat there:

—Moses, what is it?

He swallows air. A tiny bat flies round his head as though it would kiss his cheek. The thin bare skin of its wing brushes his face,

he swats at it and tears off running. He looks behind to see if I am
following. I do follow as quick as I can go. He runs round the back
wall towards the riverfront, where he leaps up onto a stump. His
little brother Isaiah is there gawping, and Moses at last breathes out:

    —Look.

He watches my face, he knows I see. The shadowed shape of
a man across the river, kneeling in the open at the water's edge.
The face of my father Black Fish comes into my sight as faces do
out of trees sometimes, out of leaves or streams. Invisible until
you go looking.

    Who? In the dimming light I see this man's straight posture and
light skin, the one dark lock of hair atop his head as mine was, his
parts are hanging, he is quite bare. For a moment I think it is my own
self, my past self from before any of this happened, walking naked up
out of the river to meet me here again and tell me what to do. I cry
out in Shawnee. *Keela.* You.

    The man freezes. I shout for the men on guard duty and in a
moment two come at a trot with their guns. Moses and Isaiah have
their thin arms about each other now, and Isaiah twists back to look
to me.

    It is beginning, it is now, we are not ready—

    The guards holler for the gate to be shut. Before it is done,
Major Billy comes out with his gun cocked and I say:

    —Do not shoot, Billy. Not yet.

    He calls:

    —Who is it?

    The man across the water has no gun. He is not quite so tall as
Black Fish, he is narrower, so thin he looks unfleshed. Who is he?
He staggers into the water with his hands up, then falls flat as if his
bones have given him up. I expect no answer from him. But he lifts
his head and yells quite bold:

    —William Hancock. I am no Indian.

Hancock. My heart gives a great leap and hangs high in my chest, it does not know what to do next. One of my fellow captives, adopted at Old Chillicothe town by the Shawnee who called himself Captain Will, who was kind to Hancock and to me. Though he once told me every man and horse in Kentucky belonged to him and I did not believe it, I did not listen. He told me to go home.

40

I call:

—Hancock.

He has got himself to his hands and knees, his head is hanging low, but I hear him clear:

—Boone. Ha. So you are here.

Major Billy tells the guards to get the canoe and go over to him. These men toss me a look as they push off the bank into the blackening water. Others have come out the back gate and stand silent along the river. There is only the dip and splash of the paddles as the canoe returns, and the bullying question of Kezia Callaway, who has run away from her ma and got out of the fort: *Who is it? Who is it?* Colonel Dick pulls her to him and keeps his arm about her. He is watching hard.

The guards have to lift Hancock out of the canoe, and nearly tip him over into the water. He rights himself, he is a skeleton tottering up the bank at me. He stretches his arms high, and says:

—I give myself up. Though Boone owns me. And all of you.

He turns to the rest and he gasps:

—This Boone promised them the fort. Promised everything there is.

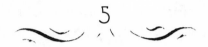

5

*Mr. Hancock who arrived here yesterday informs us of British
and Indians coming against us to the number of near four
hundred, whom I expect here soon. If men can be sent to us it
would be of infinite service. We are all in fine spirits, and have
good crops growing, and intend to fight hard.*

*I do not recall promising everything there is. If I did it was
only*

*The goddamned people here do not use their goddamned
ears*

Please tell my wife Rebecca Boone that I am
Fine spirits!
Four hundred

THIS LETTER I WRITE in my brains first. I lick the ink off the nib
and look at the empty paper. There is no sense to it, to any of it.

Four hundred coming.

Some sixty men here, if Kenton and London return from
Harrodsburg and Logan's Fort with more very quick. And one
further, if Ned recovers from his sickness. If he does not recover,
my Fate will be fixing things for me again, no matter what I want.
But I will not think of Ned, living or dead.

Some two dozen women and children.

Numbers race all through my blood. I will write them down and send them to Virginia in hopes their army will be moved to save us, and perhaps first save me from the people here. I wish to write: *I only promised the fort to stop the Shawnee attacking it outright and killing everyone, I bought us time and what is better than time?* But there is no time now.

I write. I blot the page with ink spots like a rash, but I do not try to beautify it. No time, no time, the lack is all I can think of. I give this letter to young Alexander Montgomery, the brash copper-headed fellow, I tell him to ride hard with it and get back as fast as fast. Off he goes into the dusty sunrise without thinking to argue with adventure, or with me.

Colonel Dick has sat in talk with Hancock all night. I see him come out into the morning and hand his own letter to another young man who he sends off into the morning on his own best mare. I do not care what he has to say about me in his lengthy fashion. *Daniel Boone saith this and William Hancock saith the other and Daniel Boone ought to be hanged drawn and quartered.* I have heard enough of it from Flanders, who Dick had sit listening with Billy Smith and others. Hancock told them the Shawnee plan is to offer us the king's flag again, and if we do not want it, they will batter down our fort with their swivel guns from Detroit. I am tempted to laugh out, I say:

—Artillery just for us? How will they get swivel guns through this wilderness?

Flanders looks as though he has been slapped. He says:

—They will live on our stock and crops till they starve us out, Hancock said so. He heard all their talk at their big council.

—Well Flanders. I did tell you they were coming. Now we know it will be soon.

He nods his birdlike head and sets his lean jaw. I go on:

—Did Hancock say anything more?

—About what?

—About me.

Flanders looks off to see who is passing at the cracked window. Belief in me is washing away. I rap his forehead with my knuckle, he pulls himself up tall and leaves my cabin. The cat comes in and pisses in a corner before swishing out again with its tail up like a whiff of smoke.

Hancock's wife Molly opens her door, she is all surprise, but she is a short round woman with a nose too small, and always has a look of surprise about her. Perhaps it is God she is surprised by and what He has failed to do here. Her husband often used to lead the Baptists among us in their prayers by the river. I have seen no praying since I returned.

—Mr. Boone? Captain?

Molly's fingers twitch about her cap. She does not know what to call me. In truth I do not know what to call myself. I say:

—May I come in?

She twitches further and sticks out her teeth but she says I may, and so I do with my poor guard Flanders at my back. A pot sits above the fire, it smells of a bone boiling. I say:

—For the starving invalid. I know how he feels.

She smiles and then drops her smile quick as I take up a bowl and fill it. I carry it to the bed where Hancock lies pale and flat as an old book left open. Well well, I can read.

—Hancock. William.

He opens his lids and looks about him as if he thinks he has awakened in Heaven at last. His eyes fog over quick enough when they settle on me. I say:

—Eat this, it will help you. Then we will talk.

He sits up in his odd springing fashion, the bed shakes and the bowl slops. He says:

—Poison!

I laugh:

44

—You had best ask your lady about that, though I have been poisoned myself enough times to know this soup is all right.

His wife hurries over and takes the bowl from me with her mouth knitted up tight. I say:

—All right, it is all right, I have not touched the broth. Hancock, you must tell me exactly what you know.

His warrior's lock falls over his forehead, he tugs at it. He says:

—Why should I speak to you ever again? I told Colonel Callaway and Major Smith everything.

—I know it. And I can see you are ill. It is a long run from Old Chillicothe.

—It is that! You ran off just as you liked! You sent them into such a spin, I knew they would kill the rest of us you had left behind you. I had to wait until that Indian, that flat-faced young one who called himself my father, was asleep. I ran naked out of that dirty hut with nothing but a handful of dried corn I snatched up from a basket. Nothing more! I could have died fifty times in those woods, I was seven days lost in the wilderness, like our Lord—

—Captain Will was the name of your father there, Hancock.

The muscles in his jaws clamp. If he could bite me, he would. Instead he looks all holy to the ceiling and he says:

—It was only God saved me. I lay down to die and I saw the name of my true father, Hancock, carved into a tree above my head, so I knew the fort was near. Praise to Him.

—You have never been a woodsman. Christ was not much of one either, it seems. Perhaps God meant that tree for your head- stone.

I give him a hard smile, and he says:

—I did not think you would come back here. Why did you run off, when you liked it there so much? How could you go about whistling and contented for months and months in such a dirty place, among such a parcel of Indians?

At this he lies down again, his long skeleton chest heaves. 45
Flanders gives me a nudge and says soft:

—Sir, he is not well.

—I know he is not, I can see that. I will only trouble him to ask what else he knows, anything at all that might help us if Black Fish sets out for here.

Hancock flashes his teeth to the roots, he is quite a death's head, but he is loud as ever:

—Your Indian father? You are concerned for him?

—Hancock—

I stand, the bed rocks. I see the slow shine find its way to the dull surface of his eye. He knows of my Shawnee father and mother and little sisters. And of my wife and child. It disgusts him more than anything else, as I can see. Perhaps so much he cannot bear to speak anymore of it. He looks sick in his guts.

I hold myself still. My Shawnee life is mine, it is sunk and closed up, it has no place here. I tell him very soft:

—Perhaps you will pray for me, William.

His eyelids flicker in bafflement. Round little Molly is all nerves now, bustling about the bed. To her I say:

—We will go now. Keep him quiet. Let him sleep as much as he can.

But Hancock springs up once more like a Punch puppet. He says:

—You will see them all again, Boone. Twelve days. They are coming and it is your doing.

Twelve days. Quite like waiting for Christmas, in some other world. *Now the joyful bells a-ringing, All you mountains—*

Rebecca sang this sometimes at Christmas. But she is far off as snow now. I sit sweating as the day heats. I do not know what words come next, I have forgotten her songs. She has forgotten me, she said as much. For the time I will forget her as best I can. I do not have much choice, do I.

My feet are not so swollen, a small gift. I walk about better and I see what is still to be done. The sky is the dry sort of blue that means a stretch of fine weather. I suppose this is a gift also, though I do not know what we will have to pay for it.

The talk of me spreads like ripples from a fly fallen in a jar of milk. Most comes from Hancock, who has not died but is still ranting from his bed to anyone who will sit and listen. *Boone promised everything to the Indians.* He says it again and again as though it were true, but it is not true. It was not true when I said it.

With Major Billy Smith I am able to keep order though I feel unrest all about. Hancock, go on praying for me if it will keep you talking of my family at Old Chillicothe. No one will believe you. I hardly believe it myself, so far off it seems now. His mind is occupied with my promises and my soul, at any rate, and everyone thinks only of the Shawnee coming. And so work carries on. One relief.

It is a hot afternoon. My party is continuing with the enlarged end of the stockade when one of the very little boys darts over.

—Hear it!

So he says with his hand up, he is quite a commander though he is all dust and without a shirt or shoes.

We stop, we hear it. The pounding of hoofs from across the fields. Some of the men go for their guns, but before they can load I see two riders, more behind, all kicking up dirt and crushing down the grasses. They are riding very hard, some holding down their hats.

Wait, I say. It is Kenton at the front, his big frame curled over his spotted horse as it runs its heart out. Along the edge of the corn he gallops and pulls up hard just before us with the horse sucking in air through its teeth. He rips off his hat and says very happy:

—How do! We have ten men, sir. Five each from Harrodsburg and Logan's.

London comes up next with his great cloud of black hair, the rest slower at his back. A few are blacks like him, some are faces I do not know. But one I do know, it is Irish Hugh McGary with his boiled-looking skin. He came out with us to Kentucky, but soon left for somewhere better, as he was quick to announce.

—How do, McGary.

He tilts back his hat and his red hair springs out in damp coils. He looks about and says:

—When do you expect the bastards who killed my boy?

His big liver-coloured hound yelps. McGary shouts at it, his voice cracks like a very young man's. The dog finds me and gives me a sniff and a low growl. A big black man dismounts to grab it by the collar but McGary waves him back. With a nod to the hound he says:

—I brought him to feed them to. Boone, you will want to do the same, of course, for your own son's sake.

My breath catches at his talk as though I am listening to some angry-all-over red version of myself. McGary's stepson was killed and scalped in the bloodiest way last year near Harrodsburg. I see him gone mad, riding out to find a Shawnee wearing a shirt like his boy's one. He hacked him to death and fed him to this dog, we all heard of it.

He is watching the hound circle me. I say:

—How is your wife?

His Mary has not spoken or moved from her bed since and McGary has got himself another wife instead. Everyone knows it. I know it. I ought not to say anything of wives. *Go on*: I shove the dog away with my knee. McGary sets to lighting his pipe, never taking his red eyes off me. I do not like to think of being anything like him. The dog barks again, Kenton's horse drips foam and gasps. In relief at having something else to look at I slap its spotted flank and I say:

48

—Well done, Kenton. Water these horses, then we will get you new men into homes and be sure each of you is armed. When this wall is up, all of us will be given porthole stations for when the time comes. All right?

Kenton leans over the horse's trembling neck and says very satisfied:

—We are all right.

McGary says:

—I am armed. You need not ask me. So is my man.

His sore-looking eyes are running over the fields now, his great hound drooling beside him. At the edge of my sight Dick Callaway appears from within the fort. He stands sleeking his hand over his head before he puts his hat back on.

—Here to survey our new recruits, Colonel?

So I say to him. I see his irritation but over it is a coat of cold smugness. He says only:

—Let us hope it is enough.

Before he can say any more to the men, I swing my axe:

—Dick, I have no time for your hopes. We will carry on now.

⌣

Squire tells me private that he has near no lead or iron left in the shop, and not much powder. Jemima hears. She goes about asking the women for lead from anything they have, locks or shoe buckles or box hinges. Pewter from some of their plates and mugs. *For your own good*, she says. Most give her something. She melts it all down at her kitchen fire and turns it into small shot and bullets with the girls she recruits.

Well if she can magic this up, I can get us more gunpowder. I go to Uncle Monk, James Estill's old black man, in his cabin, to tell him that there is less than everyone believes we have. He shrugs and says:

—Enough shit about for barrels of it. Takes time to make, you know.

—I know. But can you get some started, as much as you can?

He has a stooped back and two deep furrows ploughed either side of his nose, but his movement is careful like Squire's. And like Squire he is clever with his hands.

He rides out to a cave he knows to fetch batshit. And before it is quite dark I have the little black boys help shovel up the chicken and cow dung from the pile where it has been rotting, and everything from the heap where the women leave the night-pot mess. Into leach tubs it all goes. We fill these with water to drip through the shit overnight and all the next day and overnight again. Monk says it is not quite long enough, but it will have to do.

Then we slow-boil the remains with charcoal and brimstone in our three fattest kettles on good fires outside Monk's door. We keep them going all day. The heat strikes our faces in blasts, the devilish smell does also.

In the evening, Elizabeth Callaway comes out with a few women to milk the cows we have left fenced outside the walls for the time, and to fill all the remaining buckets and pots at the spring again. They trot faster once they smell what Monk and I are cooking. I say:

—Like a taste? Good for anything that ails you.

Elizabeth ignores me, but her girl Kezia fires one of her worst faces my way and runs off bumping her bucket along the ground. I call:

—Good! Run faster, that is right. Six days now.

Six days. Monk keeps the pots stirred and the fires going. His little boy Jerry comes over, tottering along before his slight young ma. He drops a handful of chicken seed, the few fowl left come poking over and he gives a great laugh. He reaches his fist out towards the stick Monk is using to stir. Monk smiles and says:

—First child born here, ought to be first to test the powder.

I think of my own boys. I think of my living boy Jesse, my youngest one, so far from here. I grasp this little fellow's seedy fingers to feel the life in them and I say:

—Well Jerry. We will have Squire make a baby gun for you. We need all the men we can get.

Monk lifts his boy to show him the contents of the kettle, at which he struggles and lets out a yell. I go to the well for more water. I find it somewhat broader, but it is still a bad well, narrow, with only dirty water in it. To Tice Prock, the thick-bodied old Dutchman sitting on his arse beside it, I say:

—Is this all you have done? A grave would be deeper.

The brimstone smell drifts over to us. Prock raises his brows under his yellow hair and he says:

—We use the spring.

—You think the Shawnee and their friends will allow that? Let us go about our business just as we please? You think they will not poison the spring, given a chance?

I take up the shovel he has thrown down beside him. Holding it out to him I say:

—We all have our work here. All of us. This is not difficult, Prock. It is digging a hole.

—This place was meant an easier life.

He says it in his odd country-Dutch fashion but I understand him well enough. An easier life. It is not what it was meant to be, it is nothing like. I hurl the shovel so its blade just misses his shoulder and sticks in the well bottom. He looks up at me with his great dirty face and pale eyes. I say:

—It is not an easier life. Try another place if this one is not to your liking. See if you can find one. Meantime, get to work.

6

THE AUGUST SUN is a brute, it bares itself at us all day. The wind comes only in weak breaths now and then. Three days left, by Hancock's count. Three is an ugly humpbacked number, as it seems to me.

The fort is better, though not as strong as it ought to be. The corner bastions are still without roofs, the Shawnee will shoot any guard who shows himself in them. But the stockade is near closed at last, the gates are fixed. We have powder and shot. Though when I sleep I see the whole fort spilling apart like a game of jackstraws. And the talk does not stop. McGary stalks about very angry in his waiting, Old Dick is quite calm by comparison as though he is certain of something. My demise, very likely.

When are they coming?

No sign, nothing.

They blame me for the waiting. The little boys keeping watch grow loose and lazy. They play in the river or the canebrakes rather than walk up and down the bank on the lookout. More of the men set down their tools for longer rests, as though the heat has made them stupid as cows. I go about shouting and sick in my heart. And I see how very happy this makes Colonel Dick in his.

Day is just rising when Kenton comes to my cabin. He sits himself on the table, stretching out his big legs, and says all quizzical:

—The Indians are coming, are they?

I am yet without my shirt and my head itches where the stubble of hair is coming in like hay. Putting on my moccasins I sigh:

—Your fellows sent you for a talk with me?

He rolls his big feet about.

—Kenton, do you really have to ask me this? Go and ask Hancock yourself. They said they are coming, they do not lie. I know you know them, it is clear enough.

I point at the dented purple scar on the side of his head where no hair grows after its meeting with a tomahawk. Another two thick marks are on his forearm, lined up neat. He grins and says:

—I do know. Only so many are saying it is false, even the new men from Harrodsburg and Logan's. They are not cowards, they want fights. They love fights! I love fights! They are tired of waiting and of not knowing, that is all.

He points to my ribs and the scars left on me when I took my knocks in the Shawnee gauntlet. He says:

—I know what fights you have been through too. I know all the stories. Everyone does.

—Well Kenton, I am glad to hear it. Some of them are even true.

He smirks and at once I am glad of his noisy breath and his smelly warmth beside me. I hold up my leg by my scarred ankle and I say:

—Look here. You carried me in through the gates the day I got that bullet last year. We have shared at least one real fight. But fights are not always the way out.

He puffs through his nose and folds his lower lip up over the top one. Then he says:

—I do not know what that firehead McGary will get up to before then.

—Send him out with a bucket over that head. See if he draws anyone here.

What the firehead does is kick in a blockhouse door and roar that he has had enough of pulling his prick here. Old Dick's black woman Doll has taken to praying loud whenever she sees him. Now McGary sends a kick in her direction also but she veers off praying the louder when she sees me. I turn away. It makes me sick to think of God waiting to see what we will do here. And is it all we can do, to wait? Is it?

Some of the little boys on watch say they see Indians every-where, every minute, it is impossible to know what to believe from them. By afternoon McGary says he is going out to find the Shawnee and kill them all himself, as we are such useless bastards here. Seeing me looking, he calls me an Indian-lover and lets his slobbery hound lunge at me. Then he gets his big black man and their horses, and they ride west at a canter. I watch until they are gone. They do not come back.

Well he may go then. Though he leaves us less two guns. As Colonel Dick points out to me, then goes to march some of the boys up and down along the riverbank, talking under his breath of Indian-lovers.

I cannot tear off like McGary, though I would like to do so. I am so uneasy in my skin that I go to Hancock's cabin for a look at him. Molly lets me in, saying nothing. The shutters are closed against the heat of the day, it is quite dark.

A girl rushes at me and squeezes my hand in her dirty small one. Ned and Martha's daughter Sarah.

—Oh! I love you!

—Well well. I have not heard so from anyone for some time. Thank you, Sarah.

She drapes herself over my arm. She is a fair-haired girl and full of love, the sort of love that will settle itself anywhere. Perhaps it comes from her daddy, who found himself loving my wife when I was gone. *Do not think.*

Neddy sits in the gloom beside Hancock, with Martha standing beside him. She pulls her loving girl back, and with his old easy smile Ned says:

—How do, Dan. Glad to see you. Only just getting on my feet again.

He is very thin, his eyes have the gloss of fever, but his skin has its old clear health. He looks as I might look if I still had my hair to plait up. Twins, our old ma said. Only twins have one mind and we do not.

—Ned.

I hardly know what to say to him. A flash ignites in me, a rough scent is deep in my nose. For a moment I look to Martha. Seeing my mouth set, she gives her head the smallest shake and purses up her mouth in a silent no. Ned does not know what I know about him. He can smile and smile this way and be glad to see me, just as though he had never had my wife in secret at my house when I was gone.

Well. This is not the time. There is no time, and this is no place to talk of wives, in spite of Martha moving about very nervous with all her knowing. Ned is still smiling, half up off the stool beside the bed where Hancock lies with his feet stuck out from the sheets. I say loud:

—Hancock, you look very well. Your feet look better than mine. Time you got up and set to work with the rest of us. Three days left, by your count. Did you have that right?

Hancock bounces himself up onto his elbows. His face is plumper already, though scowling. Before he can open his mouth I go on:

—And no need to keep telling everyone what a villain I am. We have all heard it. You can do that after the Shawnee have come. Your talk is doing no good at such a time.

He knows just what I am telling him, but he snorts:

—Your concern for morale touches me, *Daniel*, but forgive me if I have trouble believing in it.

I fight down the anger stirring in my gut. I say quiet:

—I thought you had my soul in mind. Ought we to believe all you say, Hancock? William? Are you quite well?

Hancock lies back and flaps a hand:

—We have believed you too often. The men left behind in that dirty Indian town believed you would get them out. What will your Indian friends do with them now? Kill them certainly, if they have not done it already, before they come here to kill us. My belief is only in the Lord to keep His people safe and take us straight to the Promised Land when our time comes.

—The time may come soon, it may come today, and you lying here in bed.

He begins to pray loud. Ned and Martha bend their heads, and I say:

—Well Ned, I did not know the two of you for such believing Baptists. Forgot your Quaker boyhood, brother? Got yourself baptized down at the creek?

Ned looks up, his face innocent. Darling Neddy, always Ma's pet and everyone else's. Hancock takes up his Bible as if he would beat me with it:

—You know all about false baptisms. Look what the filthy Indians tried to do to us in that cold river. They tried to change our names—

Molly comes to hush him, to me she says he needs more medicine but there are no roots to be had, and none of the women wishes to go beyond the fields looking. As she turns to me, my throat dries out. I cough, I say:

—I will tell you all again, I will speak with them, I am the right one to do it. We will make some sort of peace if we can.

Hancock belts out:

—The Lord wanted me to come back, to tell you what you have done.

I grip Molly's round shoulder, and Hancock halts. I tell her:

—Your husband ought to think on whether a godly man needs medicine at all. Pray on it, maybe. See what answer he gets.

Molly gives a little *oh*. Martha's big eyes shine like the cat's in the dim of the room. I stalk out, I bang the door and the soft talk behind me goes on and on, world without end as God would say, if God were here.

⌣

The twelfth day. And they do not come.

The thirteenth. The fourteenth. More.

Twenty days drag by. And no sign. I try to listen to the air, but it tells me nothing, or I do not understand it.

But Hancock says no more bad of me, not that I hear of. Busy hobbling down to the river to pray his heart out. Perhaps giving himself a good wash while he is at it, as he is so concerned with dirt.

I nail the small side postern door shut to make his trips outside harder, and to keep us safer. I keep my eye on him and on everything round us. August near finished now. A fat moon at night. The ripening moon, the corn moon, the Delaware called it. My dead brother Israel's wife was a Delaware. She once drew a circle on my slate, with hills below it. I do not remember her word for moon now. I was a boy, I did not know what I was saying when she taught me words.

We keep everyone occupied though no one is happy. Major Billy orders the young boys to quit playing and keep better watch along the banks. Four of the older men are set to watch all the time up in the new corner bastions. They are soon fatigued with watching, as we all are. The rest of us go to the fields to get the corn in.

The ears are very fat in their pale green husks now. The women pull them from their stalks and throw them into baskets, and the men carry these to the cabins. Doing this I can keep myself to myself. Soon enough we have the cabin lofts near full with the ears. It is a good crop, I will say that. It will feed us all. So I tell myself at this time.

In the dark of my loft the hairy corn silk floats about on the air with the dust and settles on me. I kneel and I wipe my face on my sleeve and look up at the cracks of daylight coming through some of the shingles, I will have to split a few new ones. I am climbing down into my house when I hear low cries like birds, like water birds, the odd beautiful sounds these birds make in Kentucky. Outside, the guards are opening the gates, the boys are swarming up from the river, some are wet, and the women are running in from the fields with corn heaped in their arms and skirts. The men without their guns are running into their houses for them. I see Ned standing outside his cabin fumbling to load his shot. I do not see Squire. Jemima comes in a rush, spilling cobs and treading on them—*Daddy Daddy*—and with my gun I run out to her:

—What is it?

She is breathless, she locks her eyes on mine:

—They are here. One of the boys saw them.

—How many of them? Which boy?

—Jacky. Black London's boy.

I run against the current of fear and praying and crying. I cry *Jacky, Jacky* with all my power. *Here*, someone yells, and I find him in a corner near the gate with Neddy's Sarah. A few other boys remain huddled round while others whoop and run about with wild excitement or tear off for their houses. Jacky looks up at me all fear, his round brown eyes wet with it. I say:

—Jacky. You are a good boy. Now you must tell me what you have seen.

He shakes his head, his hair alight with trapped drops from the river. Sarah kisses his cheek and stretches out his name in a little song: *Jaaacky!* He sobs now. He is a very little black boy Nat Henderson bought somewhere for his man London to bring up. I say:

—Do you know the story of Gulliver? The brave man who went travelling everywhere? Will you be like him and show me?

He looks up with wet running from his nose. He sucks it into his mouth. My little son Jamesie listening to my stories at our house, all I used to tell him. *Do not think.*

Jacky shudders:

—They will get me.

London comes at a run with his gun over his shoulder and sweat running down his neck. He says:

—There you are.

To Jacky I say:

—London and I will go with you. They will not get near you, and if they try it, we will shoot them. All right?

He nods and lets London take him up into the crook of his arm. The guards have shut the gates now but I order them opened just enough for us to get out. I tell Sarah she cannot follow and she looks quite cast down, but she trots off to find another child to lavish herself on.

Two men have their guns aimed outward in each corner bastion now. Jacky points upriver along the bank. We walk very silent, with only a small hiccup now and then from Jacky jogging in London's arm.

I look hard, I look for what is invisible. I believe I see faces in everything, but there is nothing but branches and leaves across the river, the smallest breeze shifting them. When we walk round the side of the fort, there is nothing in the thin peach orchard or the apples. Jacky points us into the corn and we walk straight between tall rows, the stalks feathery over my head. London is taller but sees nothing, as I can judge from his watching face.

I have my gun ready. The earth is black and so soft beneath our feet, it would welcome us in. Jacky is holding tight to London's gun barrel with one hand and looking ahead. We are near the far edge of the field now, and when we come out into the sun Jacky begins to cry very fierce. London hushes him, I watch the woods. We crouch and wait as Jacky smothers his bawling in London's shoulder and grabs at London's puff of hair. I say:

—Jacky, you have been very good to show us where you were. Now you must show us what you saw.

He gulps and clutches London who struggles to lift him higher. London points and he says:

—Here, sir.

He is pointing at the ground some ten feet off. I walk up and see a footprint, a long moccasin print, set very firm into the earth. Only a single print with no other near. My skin pricks. I say:

—Jacky, did you see this man? Was it a Shawnee man with hair like mine was? Or a Cherokee with spiked quills standing up—so? Was he alone?

Jacky nods his head, then drops it heavy as a fat bud. I follow the direction of the footprint, I see more, they travel in great broad steps through the good soil at the edge of the field and then into the harder dirt going on into the woods. I run into the trees to follow, but there are no blazes, no other prints, no path, no scent of fire, no sign.

It is as if the man flew off into the air. For a moment I want it to be so. I want it to be the footprint of my son's murderer, a giant leaving prints only every seven leagues upon the earth, disappearing when he likes, but always having to come back down. A giant will always be found. Cherokee Jim is a giant man, he killed my Jamesie for nothing, only as a sign for me to be gone, then he vanished.

I want to make a murderer of myself, a true one, to kill him with my own hands round his throat. My want snarls through me. I look and look but there is no other mark on the ground.

When I come back, London is crouched, looking close at the first print. He says:

—A scout most likely. A bold one. See how close he came with all of us in the field hard by him.

—Yes. Jacky was not wrong. They are here. But not all of them, not yet.

—When will they be coming, sir? They should have been here some days ago by now?

He wishes to trust me as I know, though he is not sure he can. This is the face on everyone in the fort, everyone who does not hate me straight out. I sigh deep just as little Jacky is doing, I say:

—London, I wish I knew.

⌣

We walk back with Jacky sniffling. London hushes him in low word-less fashion that puts me in mind of Methoataske speaking to her girl Eliza in Shawnee in the dark. Perhaps it is your footprint in the field, perhaps you have come to speak to me, but what you would have to say I do not know.

Once we pass through the front gates, I tell the guards to keep them shut. Old Dick who is brushing his bay gelding calls out to them:

—You are not to shut them yet. My Virginia messenger is back. So is yours, Captain Boone.

I look behind and Colonel Dick is right, it is Alexander Montgomery riding up with Dick's man some yards behind. Before they can ride in Old Dick is mounted without a saddle and bounc-ing along the flat towards them, yelling:

—How many troops are they sending? When do they arrive?

Montgomery rides straight past him and Dick wheels to follow at his heels. Once inside the gates, young copper-headed Montgomery catches my eye. He is breathing so hard he cannot speak. He only

pulls up his horse and shakes his head. Behind Dick's man cries out
all breathless: *Not yet.*

Dick slides off his horse and stands with the look of one who
sees the world has turned the way he has predicted. His nephew was
much like him. James Callaway hanging at Detroit, his red rooster-
lock of hair and his bruised ruined face with eyes open. *I knew this
was coming.*

Montgomery's breath still comes raw, he is bent over. Now
Colonel Dick turns to his man and says:

—Did you tell them about Captain Boone? It is urgent they
know of him. I will write again to the lieutenant in Virginia today.
Major Smith said I may do so.

The young man bows from where he sits on his horse and
begins to speak. My chest bursts. I say:

—You may fuck yourself, Colonel Callaway. You may do so all
day long, and then you may fuck your horse if she will have you.

A small shot of laughter from a few of the men. Flanders up in
the corner bastion nearest me turns to see Jemima, who has come
out of their cabin with her shins and feet showing bare below her
ragged hem. He stares, I see him staring. If he gets my daughter with
child now I will string him up myself and let the Shawnee burn him.
I would leave all these people if she were not here.

I go out the rear gate. I yell to the two older boys set to watch
at the riverbank:

—Anything?

They cup their mouths and shout back *No, no.* A hawk drifts
in a figure of eight over the shrubs and stumps outside the wall,
over the river and the trees on the other side. It sees nothing at all.
There is nothing to see.

I stalk back into the fort. The faces swivel. Montgomery stands
beside his horse now, still breathing hard, his shirt with all the
fringe soaked with sweat. He gives me a helpless look and says:

—They said they would try to come when they can. Only not yet. Old Dick turns to me:

—Nothing to see, and no help coming. Why do you not go to your Indians, Boone, and have a word with them? Afraid they will not speak to you any longer?

His grey eyes brighten. *Afraid.* He loves the word, he loves to tell me what I am. My head heats, it feels as red inside as McGary's is. I will be a McGary then:

—Is that what you want? Then we will go, we will go, we will find them first.

7

YOUNG ALEXANDER MONTGOMERY comes out before the rest. He is in a shirt covered with the fringe he likes, as well as dozens of trade beads, it is very fine. He must have kept it put away specially.

He asks me to paint him up Indian. He is abashed to ask, but his excitement makes him do it. I say all right. I do not have the right berries for red and so I use only black. I get some of the charcoal in his hair. Recklessness is all I can feel, like a rush of hornets through my blood.

There are hornets in Kentucky, as I know. They will sting whites, as Captain Will told me once. A long time ago, before he was Hancock's father, before Chillicothe. When he called me Wide Mouth and told me to go home and stay there. Cherokee Jim told me the same thing.

The Indian town I see in my mind is defenceless. I saw it when Black Fish and I returned from our visit to Detroit, one of the other Shawnee towns, with a quiet ring of bark houses and stand of pines behind. It is north, up the Ohio River, on a creek where there are Indian paintings on the rocks and trees. Horses, pelts, ammunition, money. Perhaps prisoners we can coax news from. Perhaps other things—

It is an easy few days' trip, we can cut east and take the Warrior's Path. It will give us something to do, it will keep the young men happy. So I tell myself. When Old Dick sees I have thirty of the men game for it, his fury rips out of him. He stampedes about, groaning from his marrow. I hear him still as we set out. *You will hang for this stupidity, halving our defences, leaving women and children open to slaughter.* Well Dick, my women and children appear to think they can do better without me. See how you can do for the time. Major Billy remains in charge, at any rate. Squire and Ned have stayed back, I have told them to keep good order, they know the Virginia troops should be on the way to us sometime. I have told Jemima to keep watch but I did not have to tell her that, I know my girl's eyes.

We ride and I do not look back. Rebecca, for a half mile I think of you telling the children about Lot's wife running from the burning city and turning round. I do not wish to turn to salt in that fashion.

On our second evening, we stop to hunt at a salt flat on the Licking River, surrounded by buffalo roads. I know this place. I get a deer straight away. It has some fat beneath its summer coat, though the skin is not worth taking.

The men are cheerful and easy, checking their horses over, looking about. The younger ones lie with their feet to their fire, talking of women. Skinny young Jess Hodges talks very long about a girl he had in Virginia. In drawling fashion he says:

—She had a crooked inside, but she was hot as anything. And it did not stop me having her in the barn every time I wished.

—Did she like it?

This from round-headed Pem Rollins, one of the youngest. His voice comes shy but too curious to stop itself. Hodges squeezes the air with both hands as if he had a pair of breasts in them:

—Of course she liked it. They all do once they are used to it.

I call over:

—She told you so, Hodges, did she?

He turns to me with his mouth pursed up. He tosses a twig into the fire and says:

—She did not have to tell me, I knew it without her telling.

—You know women then.

—I do.

Big Kenton has appeared out of the trees, back from scouting. He spouts a great laugh and he says:

—My bet is they know you have no balls, Hodges.

The men laugh also now as Hodges hurls a few pebbles. Kenton says he has seen nothing. He settles to sort his powder and shot and begins singing under his breath in his rough voice. Hodges throws another stone and screeches very tuneless: *She reached for his balls, he had no balls at all.* Now some of the rest join in: *No balls at all, no balls at all.*

—That will have all the game running straight for us.

So I tell them, but they only laugh and I do also. A few of them take off their shirts and go to lie in the last of the sun by the spring where it bubbles out of the river, though it is getting low this time of year. They close their eyes and taste the salt in the water with their fingers. Hodges goes on with his song. I say:

—I will be cook tonight, you boys, if you can entertain us better than that.

I am setting the strips of venison to roast when Alexander Montgomery comes to crouch by me, his coppery hair all raked up. He has not taken off his fine beaded shirt, his face is still smudged with charcoal. He says:

—Is this the place where you and the others were taken? Where the Shawnee caught you?

—It is.

I have not wished to think of it but it is this place, the Blue Licks. All the Shawnee in their blankets, their silver ear hoops frozen, their faces frozen. The chiefs watching me, Pompey their black man telling me just what they thought of us all. And their vote on whether or not to kill us on the spot. *Fifty-nine say die, sixty-one say live.* I hear it in Pompey's slow pleased voice just as if he were here. I look about me, I look to the shadows of the trees at the edge of the bare ground. But Montgomery is talking:

—Then are they not likely to try here again?

—They might.

His eyes go very green in the evening light, giving him the look of a thin cat in hope of food. I say:

—Perhaps you would prefer to go on to Chillicothe and visit them at home? I know the way.

—Do you?

I laugh and I say:

—I do know, but we are not going that way.

—What is it like there?

For a moment I let myself think of it, the ice breaking on the river, the bark houses in the snowy cornfields. The black earth showing in the spring. I say only:

—It is not a bad place.

It is all I can say. Montgomery is tense all through now like a child waiting for a treat. He says:

—I would like to see it. But I would not have stayed as long as you did.

—Well. Do you want a haircut like mine? I know how it is done.

He laughs but I see his hand creep to his hair, the colour of a bright penny. Montgomery shifts on his heels and says:

—Do you miss it?

—I have enough to do here, Montgomery.

I hand him a strip of meat and shake my singed fingers. He blows hard on it. I think of little Eliza and Methoataske, their thinness. I hope you have enough to eat, more than enough. Perhaps you are not so far from here. Perhaps they have punished you for being mine. But I must shut you away in your drawers. It seems I am full of drawers, quite a chest of them.

At once I am full of ghosts also, they breathe between my ribs, though I do not know who they are now and I will not listen. I stand and I say:

—We will cross the Ohio tomorrow.

⌣

I am still lying on my bedroll when they come. For a moment I think they are ghosts themselves. Eleven of the men stand before me in the blue early morning. James Estill is in front, looking tired. He says he has dreamt of his children talking all night, telling him woeful things. Now the rest of the married men with him say so as well, as though the same dream were good enough for all of them. I say:

—All your children said so? Every one? Curious.

Estill raises his hand and says they are returning to the fort. I lie watching them ride off the way we came. Well Old Dick will be pleased. I had no dreams, myself.

The lone young men stay, Kenton and Montgomery the most eager. We move on. I put them in charge of the raft building once we reach the river. The current is still quick enough though the water is quite low. On the other side, we make a camp for the night, and in the morning, Montgomery paints up his own face this time, very careful about it, and careful not to mark up his fancy beads. Kenton blacks round his own eyes and grins:

—They will think they are looking in a mirror.

Montgomery laughs and claps Kenton's big hand. I send the two of them to scout out the Paint Creek town while the rest of us wait. We sit on our arses silent in a canebrake, or as silent as I can keep such young men. They twitch and mutter. They want to shoot, to yell, to go straight to the Indian town and burn it. They keep their clubs and guns out, they are restless all day and all night.

Very early the next morning Kenton returns with Montgomery at his back. The men stir and rustle. I sit up and I say:

—Well? Was the town all you had dreamed?

Kenton says:

—Looks just as you said it did. All the wigwams are standing. But all empty.

—Nobody there at all?

—Only two of them, and a pony. I got this. The other ran off.

What he holds up is a scalp, still wet at the roots of the long black lock. He keeps his gun raised in his other hand.

The Shawnee heads I know parade along inside my eyelids. The scalp dangling from his hand tells me nothing, as if it never belonged on anyone's skull.

Montgomery shuffles his moccasin in the dirt. The black paint has bled away round his eyes so he has the look of a backward raccoon. He says low:

—Thought I would get something. The houses were emptied out.

Kenton brandishes the scalp:

—You are not having this!

Young Hodges is standing now, shivering bare-legged in the dawn light. He says:

—Captain Boone, will we go back there and look for them?

The others begin to rouse themselves, already they are checking their powder and shot again. Kenton bellows:

—There was no one there, I told you. Would have seen them if there was.

Hodges swings up his gun:

—I would rather see for myself.

All at once I see everything, as if a paper has been stuck before my eyes. My back teeth begin an old ache. I say:

—No.

Kenton pulls his back up. His great bruised kneecap shows through a hole in his leggings. He gives my shoulder a slap, it is not a light slap. I feel his wish to argue. The men are gathering, planning what they will take once we hunt down the Indians.

Well. There will be no arguing, there will be no planning. I stand and I say:

—All of you. I am sorry to have to give you bad news, unless you have seen it for yourselves already.

The faces are perplexed. Kenton's mind is turning inside his great head, but he does not see. No one does. I tell them:

—If the town is empty, they are already on their way to meet us.

Montgomery whoops:

—Get ready for them, boys! Get your scalp blades out!

At this they all tug their knives from their belts. I say:

—No. They are not on their way here. They are on their way to the fort. They have gone to meet the others who will be coming from the north. This is why they have left their town.

—How do you know?

Montgomery's eyes are pale and furious. I say:

—I know it. We must get back.

He flings out his arms:

—You take us all the way out here and now you want to go running back? With nothing? You will not let us even see them? I want to see them.

I can see it all, I can see how all will be. Kentucky stretched out like a great quilt, the goddamned fort a hole falling inward. Rebecca, I see your hand tugging your needle through the air, stitch upon stitch from all directions. The piece at the centre is the first to tear.

I feel the needle in my own brains. *I want to see them.* Is this what I have brought them here for, my own want?

What have I done—

Kenton is still looking at me sideways, Montgomery has turned on his heel in his sparkling shirt, the others are quiet and uncertain. I say:

—We must go back, for God's sake.

8

WE GO, we do not stop all day. We cannot take the Warrior's Path, we keep to the woods. I do not even try to make trail through the brush and roots and trees, I feel us back to the Ohio even if I go blind doing it. Leading their horses, the men crash and swear, and I turn and hiss. For a time there is quiet until someone stumbles and falls again. I shut my eyes to stop myself from murder. I have done enough of it as I believe at this time.

At noon I halt us and we sit, I pass some jerked meat down the line. Skinny Jess Hodges behind me wishes to go off and get a deer, but I tell him no, it is not safe to shoot, we will be heard. He grows louder, he says he will not go far, he saw one not long ago, he will get it with his knife, he is a good thrower. I tell him:

—Shut your goddamned mouth.

He snaps his jaw shut, his face curdles like a skin on a pan of milk left in the sun. These young men are full of fire and piss, indeed one of them is always stopping to piss on a tree. They do not hold themselves in, not in any fashion.

Kenton and Montgomery are not with us. They rode off back to the empty Paint Creek town, as though they could magic up some plunder and scalps, as though disappointment ought by rights to make these appear.

Among these men I feel my age in my joints. I walk faster.

~

72 In the evening I stop us and let Hodges go off and hunt something with his goddamned knife. For a moment he is grinning like a small boy, then he is off into the trees. The rest sit stretching out their legs, all weary with the day's walk. We will keep on towards the river and cross at a shallows I know in the morning.

I am bent over when I hear the bang and echo of the shot. Hodges, damn you. I stand straight and I say:

—If any of you shoots again, I will kill you myself.

Three of the men pick themselves up and follow me. The trace is easy to track, snapped twigs everywhere. God damn it, Hodges. When we find him, he is standing very proud over a buffalo. I have not seen one since I came back. Blood streams from its eye-hole. I say:

—Well. A nice shot. But you are a goddamned fool. Do that again and you will answer for it.

He kicks the buffalo's side with his skinny leg and laughs. I say:

—You will only hurt your foot, Hodges. Get butchering and we will eat some now in camp.

As I am still speaking, I hear it behind my own voice, the soft rush of a word I know. *Nishwapitaki.* Twenty.

It seems as though it has flown straight to my ear out of the sky. But as I turn, the dropping sun catches and flares some yards off. A silver earring, I see it.

Two faces burn from the trees. One's name comes into my mouth: Kaskee. My young guard in Chillicothe, tied to me half the time. I know his pimpled cheeks, his startling smile, I near smell him. He has his ears split and ringed with silver now, and his hair has been shaved. They have made him a warrior, his deepest wish.

And now he is gone, with the other whose face I did not know. But he was here and he saw me, his smile flashed out, I saw his teeth.

—Kaskee—

I stop myself speaking. Twenty. They have counted us then. They know where we are.

I shout the word back, *Nishwapitaki*, and my four young men stop their butchering to stare. I call:

—Take what you have cut and come on.

They are up to their elbows in the buffalo's rib cage, Hodges has the great liver in his two hands. I slip back through the trees, running all the way to the grassy opening where the rest have started a fire and laid out bedrolls. I say:

—No. Pack up. We must go, we are going.

Pem Rollins is squatted down at the weak fire trying to stir it up. He is not yet seventeen. He peers up from under his hat and he says:

—We are going? Where?

His face is like a moon, the wrong side of the moon, it is pure white and blank, it might as well be without eyes. Rollins, I am sorry for thinking it. I say low:

—To the river, farther down. Now. Pack up quick. They are coming.

—Sir, how do you know?

This question makes me wish to beat Rollins to porridge, him and his innocent eyes that have never seen a thing. Behind me Hodges and the rest crash out of the trees all bloody, carrying thick cuts of meat. I look past them, Kaskee's face is still in my mind, but he is not there now, or does not choose to show himself. Hodges throws down the heavy buffalo liver and says:

—Now what is it?

I am still looking about, but they are not here, I do not feel them. I tell him:

—They could have killed us just now but they did not.

—Why?

This from Rollins.

—We are nothing, we are small fish to them. They know where we are and they do not care, they are after more. Eat now, eat it raw, we have to go.

$\smile$

There is a thin slip of moon to see by. We ride along a wide old buffalo road, packed flat by years of herds coming through, it is easy going. Boonesborough is two days from us if we keep to this route. I hope you are asleep Jemima, safe with Flanders nowhere near you. Keep him off you, no babies, no more bad births.

The road begins to drag uphill, the stony slope catches the horses' feet and Rollins's mount stumbles. He is thrown:

—Shit. Sir.

He has not thought, and has spoken too loud. I crouch and bend his foot about between my hands. He gives a yelp, and I whisper:

—Hush. Not broken.

He sucks in air, again he says:

—How do you know?

My own ankle nags at me always. I am all irritation but I say only:

—Get up.

I get him back on his horse. At the top of the hill, the buffalo road is wider again, following a long flat with the slope dropping away beside us. I keep us to the path. I know this place from the first time I was in Kentucky, when I was alone. I wish I were alone now.

Rollins pants with his pain. Through his noise I hear the river's low hurry. Nothing else. I whistle low. The rest gather in a hoop about us, I see their dark outlines. I wait until Rollins halts his puffing and I say very soft to everyone:

—Just down the next hill we will be at the water. We stop at the edge for the rest of the night. There is an easy crossing place, and we will go over at the first sign of daylight. No talk. And no sleep if you can help yourselves.

They wait for me to move and I do. We go on, the river noise growing louder. Clouds have spread over the dark like great blots of ink, I can hardly see. When I bend and touch the ground, it is very flat. I taste the earth on my fingers. Salt.

Here I can feel it is treeless, open. My back pricks. Standing here we must appear helpless as the game I first saw in such places before Kentucky was spoilt and torn. All innocent, only standing here waiting to be shot.

A breeze comes as we reach the water. I strain my ears but I hear only insects winging above the mud and the water, a fish jumping with a clean splash that turns quick to silence. Kaskee, you are silent again too. Where are you?

The wind opens the cloud, the moon has risen higher and brightened. Some yards downriver two does and their fawns pick their way towards the water. They smell us but they carry on after they give us a good stare. Hodges has his gun up at once, his hair wild as though someone has swept out a chimney with him.

—No.

This I say too loud. I go to him and I shove the barrel down into the dirt. But Hodges is not looking at me. No one is looking at me. They are looking across the river.

A long barb of smoke rising. It is dark grey, like lead against the moon. More such barbs hooking into the air, a great circle of them.

I raise my palms. Stop. We smell it, we all smell it. Meat cooking.

My stomach roars, I cannot help it. The deer are very still in shadow. A fawn tugs at its mother's teat and she kicks it from her. She stands a moment and then springs off away into the trees, the rest follow and are gone. We know who it is, we all know it.

I walk into the river. On the bank I leave my gun, I leave my shirt, I leave the men, I leave everything. The water climbs up under my arms, my ribs shrink from the cold, but it is low enough at this ford to walk straight across. On the other side I run in a crouch into the trees, then I stand and run faster, far enough to see what I know I will see on the fort side of the Ohio. Some of them are standing and scratching themselves and pissing, most are on bedrolls round the fires. Bare skin in the firelight, buckskin hunting shirts, red jackets off in a tight knot of their own. Not so many British then. But of the rest, the Shawnee and others, there are hundreds. Perhaps four hundred. My eyes tick and tick as I count. Their camp sprawls for a mile back through the trees on this side. The Paint Creek town people have not gone north. The north has come here to meet them. And here they are.

Black Fish, my father, I look for you. And Methoataske, Eliza— my eyes try to find you also. I search and search. I want to go close. I want to fall, to make a great crash, I want you to see I am here, I want to be found.

I have to stop. I have to place my hands flat on the ground before me.

I watch. They are all so easy in their camp. They know we are about and they do not care, they are not troubling to hide. They are making their slow procession to the fort just as they please, just as though they had all the days left in the world. All round the trees are kindling orange and yellow, the leaves are on the turn. September already. Winter is not so very far off. And four hundred warriors coming to call on us at home.

I tear my eyes and my desire from the great camp. I go back through the woods and back over the river to where my men are still standing on the salt flat as though they are houses someone forgot. Young Rollins whispers from where he is sat holding his ankle:

—The Indian army?

—Yes.

—Very many of them?

—Yes.

Hodges is keeping his gun down as he eyes my face. He says: 77

—What will we do?

The smoke from their cooking fires blows at us in a gust. Full of bluster as Old Dick now, I say:

—We will go round them.

⌣

I hack us a way through the thickest brush, it is quite dark beneath the furry pines, their trunks are cool. We slip on needles, the horses slide also as we tug them along, we go fast as we can, Rollins limps and the skin peels again from the soles of my feet, they have healed up too soft after my last run. In my mind I follow a line away from the Shawnee camp, which I will turn sharp back to the fort. A great letter *V*. Victory.

A night and another day we go until we are at the walls. Squire lets us in and Dick is upon us before I can say a word to my brother. Dick says:

—Have you brought your Indians with you?

At once I am tired out, not least of Colonel Dick's existence in my life. I sit in the dirt and I lift my bloody feet at him:

—We have come fast enough to beat them. But they will be here in the morning.

The young men burst out with how we saw the Indians, the great army camped, how we were not caught and outwitted them. They have made a great tale of it already. Old Dick is almost pleased as I can see, he believes it now, the enemy of his dreams coming at last.

Major Billy has come down from the top wall with his gun. He says:

—We have been ready long enough.

I say:

—We will be more ready. Get water, get all the food and animals in from the fields. Clean all the guns tonight. Make more shot if there is anything to make it from.

And here is my girl Jemima, she is smiling, she is running back to the cabin for her buckets. The other women do the same. Martha looks at me as she passes, Squire keeps watch over them outside the front gates. The grass shivers, the corn shivers in the fields.

⌣

The morning comes clear. It is a warm day. No clouds.

9

VOICES BREAK the quiet first, blurred by splashing. In one of the back bastions, guns catch and lock, the men aim. Now comes more calling, clearer. And laughing.

When I get out the rear gate and across to the riverbank, I see Squire's boys with the four horses they have taken out to water. They have mounted two and are in the river up to the animals' shins. Little Isaiah is prodding his horse with his knob-knees, leaning over its neck and pointing to the ridge ahead. I shout:

—Moses! Isaiah!

I run towards them. One of my sore feet tears open, but I stagger up and run on. Moses hears me, I see him turn. He pulls up his horse and calls back in his grave fashion:

—The Virginia soldiers, Uncle Daniel. Red coats, see!

Red coats. He is not wrong. Red coats, bright as flags, moving out of the line of trees and behind the ridge. A stream of them. Then another stream, bare-skinned and paint-skinned, a long file of horses and Indians, making a great loop in our direction. Hundreds.

—Boys! Get back here now!

My voice rips from my throat, it tears my eyes away from the moving army downriver. Moses pulls up his horse and reaches for Isaiah's bridle, his face is quizzical.

—Now!

I run into the water as best I can, Squire overtakes me. He leaps up behind Isaiah and pounds the horse's sides with his heels. Moses follows quick. I snatch the bridles of the other two animals drinking at the river's edge and turn them back.

—Do not shoot! Do nothing!

This I shout to the guards in the bastions and on the walls. *Do nothing, nothing!* My eye lands on Old Dick still aiming. Dick, if you shoot now I will rip out your goddamned eyes that think they see all there is. Two of our scouts come riding hard, one on each side of the river, they see we know already what has come. What is here.

We smash the back gate shut behind us. Jemima freezes in her doorway. The fort seems a tiny world made of twigs, a bird's nest. My breath comes tight through my nose, the horses' breathing the same after their run. I tell the women to get the children inside the cabins, and they spin off at a run. I tell Moses to take Isaiah and go look after his ma and he runs also. Isaiah's small face turns for one look back at me before his brother hauls him away. Dick has not dropped his gun by an inch and his thick finger is jerking back and forth about the trigger. The others in the bastions are frozen with their weapons ready also. I shin up to the parapet between the two front bastions, keeping my head low. Near me young Johnny Gass's freckled hands shake as he looks out. He is fourteen years of age, I have near forgotten how close to being boys some of the men are.

Between the spikes of the logs I see the first of the long line of Indians reach the patchy meadow beyond the farthest of our corn. Shawnee paint and silver jewellery flare in the light. A lesser number are Cherokee. His name flies into my brains: Cherokee Jim, the murderer.

Murder.

The great tail of them coils into the meadow like a snake eating itself for lazy enjoyment. My guts clench. My girl is beside me, her tough small hand on my back. I tell her:

—Get down for God's sake, get indoors. They are here.

—I want to see them.

—Christ, Jemima.

Johnny Gass is hissing behind my head:

—Sir, they are cutting our trees.

I look. He is right. Some of the Indians have gone to the orchard of young peach trees at the edge of the field.

—What are they doing?

Jemima says it, her breath warms my shoulder, and we see them stack the feathery tops of the thin boughs they have cut and begin to cut more. These men are Shawnee, their eyes are painted up black and red, two are wearing hunting shirts with tiny bells sewn on. Four of them go back towards the woods, we hear their axes clang. Then they each return with a fair-sized pine, they limb these and drive them as posts into the ground some sixty yards from our front gate. The rest make a roof with the peach boughs. It is quite an arbour.

Old Dick is muttering: *Do nothing.* He turns my words to spit and poison. He is not the only one speaking, everyone is turning about asking what this is, what they mean to do. I call:

—They are beyond our range, you know it and they do. And we are beyond theirs. Do not waste your shot. Wait.

Jemima breathes:

—Daddy, are they coming in?

—No.

As I say it I see the four Shawnee retreat to the meadow where the great army has looped itself. Someone else is walking out slow and holding a great truce flag that flaps very white before his face. All our guards take aim. I hold up my hand. He has no gun, we cannot shoot a man asking for peace.

Is it peace?

My ribs go soft in me, I move my ankles about in their crouch. Peace. The thought of it washes all through my chest. Before I can pull her back, Jemima raises her head above the wall to get a clearer view. She says loud:

—It is a black. Do they have slaves?

I kneel, I lift my head also. I know it, the slow rolling walk, the princely indolence. The man carries on with the flag before his face, but I know his face without seeing it. He climbs the cornfield fence until he stands on the top of it some hundred yards from our wall. When his voice comes, I know it also, the cool singing tone of it. He says:

—I am here to speak with your man Boone.

I stand. I shout:

—I am here, Pompey.

In my ear Jemima says loud:

—You know him, Daddy?

He drops the flag. His skin shines dark in the noon, his teeth shine as he smiles. I want to grin back at him though my heart is banging at me like a set of fists. Yes I do know him, and he knows everything of me. The first Shawnee words he taught me rock about in my brains, waking themselves: *Neppa. Neppoa.* Sleeping. Dead.

He is with the Shawnee yet. He has never escaped, has he tried to do it without me? I could not help you get free, Pompey, and here you are with the knowing of it spread over your face. I can see the bright blue of your headscarf. A trade thing. You would have made a fine trader in another life, if you were magicked white. But no such magic here, or not for you. You wanted a new life and here I am in mine. Though it is all old in truth, all of it.

He stands on the fence-top staring in my direction, smiling and smiling. A sudden breeze runs over the corn before him, which ruffles like the back of an angry dog. He stands silent and looking all along the fort wall, with all the guns bristling from it. He stretches the fingers of one hand at his side, he rubs at his leggings. After a time he calls in his lazy fashion:

—Boone, your father Chief Black Fish has come to accept your surrender, as you promised it to us.

Your father. Us. I hear him weight these words as if he had a stone stored up in his cheek for each one.

Hancock has heard it where he is crouched at a gunslit below the ramparts. He cries out:

—You hear? Boone promised!

The men along the parapet keep their guns on Pompey but swivel their eyes to me. Johnny Gass goes tense as a cat beside us, Jemima's hand goes flat on my shoulder. *Surrender* is scratched hard on each eye and into my girl's palm. I shout:

—Is that so!

It is all I can think to say. Hancock is speaking very urgent to someone below but I cannot listen, I will not. Pompey reaches into his shirt. He pulls out a paper and opens it but does not look at it, he goes on looking at me. He could say anything at all, he has always been one for storing things up and then telling them. What is he going to tell them of me? My heart gallops harder. He calls:

—I have in my hand a letter from Governor Hamilton guaranteeing your people's safety if you will all go with us to Detroit. This is another promise you made.

In his bastion Dick yells big-throated with his cheek pressed tight to his gun:

—Give us the letter! Leave it on the ground and get back.

Some of the other men take up his shout. Billy Smith comes careful along the rampart to me:

—Captain, Colonel Callaway is right. We ought to read it, if it has come with them from Detroit.

Billy's pale eyes say nothing, but he does not call me Dan now. He stands with his back to the spiked wall and says only:

—They use a black as their interpreter?

Pompey calls:

—Governor Hamilton has sent his king's men all the way from Quebec to help you.

—I know this black well. He is bad trouble.

This from Hancock below, bobbing his head like a wise old man, his upturned face grinning at me. I think to tell him he does not know Pompey in the least, but this is no help here. Squire and Ned stand behind him looking up also, their puzzlement as clear as anyone else's. Billy begins to speak but as he does so Pompey's voice carries to us again:

—Boone, is this your famous daughter with you?

His voice is dark and amused. *Your daughter is a whore.* He does not say it but I know the line well enough. And then it comes through the air. All the Shawnee know it, for some it is their only English. *Whore whore whore.*

Jemima pushes round me and leans out with her hands on two log points. She is scarlet-faced and bawls from the bottoms of her lungs:

—Yes I am his daughter!

A short hooting comes from the Indian army, faint as a tired owl. The chiefs have sat themselves in the peach arbour, their thin laughing carries to us also. Jemima, I did not want you ever to know what they say of you, but how can you not know. Everyone here has said such things of you too. I pull her back, she is set to yell something more poisonous, but before she can do it I stop. We all stop.

A man is walking from the arbour towards Pompey. A Shawnee, with the warrior's lock and chief's paint and silver brooches over the bright red blanket wrapped round him. He takes his time to climb the fence, he stands at Pompey's side. He is not a tall man. He circles his mouth with his hands. His call is clearer than Pompey's, not so singsong. Urgent and sorrowful at once, like a horn in the earliest morning.

—Sheltowee. Sheltowee.

My father is calling me. Sheltowee is the name they gave me, it goes straight through me, it is my name.

⌣

I am down from the parapet and at the front gate before my heart can give another beat. I pull up the bar and am out before any of the guards has time to shut his wide-open mouth and stop me. The gate bangs closed at my back. There is talk from inside the walls but I walk out across the flat. I am all pain again.

No one on the fence now, I cannot see them. I carry on walking slow. When I am close to the corn I stop, I hear a rustling, I close my eyes a moment and I listen to the low hum in the air.

They are here. They are coming round the side of the cornfield. Pompey and Black Fish and another chief, an old and important one in a wine-coloured jacket with a fringe of lace round its collar. He is one I know from our long walk to Detroit with the Shawnee. I do not know the jacket, he must have taken it somewhere, perhaps at another of the settlements. But I know the bones of his face and his eyes, which do not change when he sees me. My own face has the feel of an anthill about to break open.

Smooth your expression you goddamned ape.

Pompey has a greyish blanket folded over the shoulder of his shirt and cinched in by his belt in Shawnee fashion. As he moves closer his smell strikes me, cloves and heat. Perhaps he means to wrap me up and take me to be reborn a Shawnee here in the Kentucky River.

They will wash the whiteness from me again, they will shave my hair that has grown in, they will take me back and it will be my home. The walls of my throat close and I cough up a sour taste. Pompey folds his arms and says:

—Sheltowee. Chief Black Fish and Chief Moluntha.

He talks as though we do not know each other at all. Well perhaps we do not.

I am afraid to look Black Fish full in the face. I am looking at where his hands are folded beneath the blanket when he speaks. He says:

—My son.

His voice catches and I look, I look in his eyes and they are black as ever, they are shining with tears. His face is tired but the same, he is hardly older than I am, this man who took me as his own son after we killed his. He is speaking in English, he is speaking straight to me. His hand comes out from the red blanket, its palm up and its fingers curled like a beggar's cup. He steps towards me and says in Shawnee:

—What made you run away from me, my son?

—Father.

The word cuts its way from my mouth as if it is a blade. His face is wet now with his silent weeping. I take his open hand, the skin is dry. I feel Pompey and Moluntha watching us, I feel the fort watching us. I pull in a hard breath before I am able to say:

—I wanted—I wanted to see my wife and children so badly that I could not stay any longer.

The Shawnee words are strange shapes in my mouth. In my mind Rebecca and the children are brittle as frost, they will melt away. I weep too, my father and I are weeping as the sun blazes on our heads. My father holds hard to my hand, he touches the side of my head where my hair has grown. Now he takes the other hand also and he says very gentle:

—You have a wife and a daughter. I gave you these, Sheltowee.

—I know it.

Where are they, are they here? Methoataske and Eliza, my girls. But I cannot ask it, I cannot or I will break. I drop my head and feel the long bones of my father's hands beneath his skin. In the same soft fashion he says:

—If you had asked me I would have let you come.

All I am able to do is shake my head. Pompey gives a great bow and says we ought to go to the arbour now to talk. I look to the fort, where hot sun flashes from all the guns. Again I shake my head and I say:

—I cannot go so far.

Pompey gives a short call, *Skillawethetha*, boys, and in a moment two come with some of the peach boughs and begin to fan us as Pompey pulls his blanket from his shoulder and belt and lays it on the ground with a great flourish and a smile. These boys do not look at me and I do not think I know them.

Black Fish takes his hands from mine and gestures to Chief Moluntha to sit first. The old man sits straight. His scalp lock is long and sleek with a streak of white in it, it slips halfway down the back of his velvet jacket. I wipe my face on my shirt and sit between him and Black Fish, I keep myself a distance from both of them. Pompey walks about along the edge of the corn, he looks over the fields as though he were a lord.

All at once Moluntha barks to him, and he ambles over with his hands behind his back and his face amiable. The chief holds out his hand, Pompey bows and gives him the paper he has kept tucked into his shirt. In Shawnee Moluntha says:

—Here is a letter from the white chief, he reminds you what you have promised.

He hands the letter back to Pompey, who holds it out to me on his palm as if it were a tray. He is swallowing a grin. I take the paper and I look. It is all looping hand and great inked capital letters.

Surrender. Promises. Your people. A long signature, *Henry Hamilton His Majesty The KING'S Governor at Fort Detroit and et cetera.*

Moluntha looks at me now with his heavy lined brow lifted. He says:

—You know already what it says. I will tell you what he told me with his own mouth. If your people insist on trying to stay in this place, he cannot protect you. He will not be responsible for what becomes of you, women and children and all. Will you be responsible for it?

Pompey begins to interpret in English but I put up my hand. I know what has been said. I am responsible for everything, I have always known it. My insides burn and the top of my head is burning through. The swish of the boughs above us has the feel of a lazy swarm.

Black Fish nods and again Pompey reaches into his shirt. He brings out a pouch of soft beaten leather, sewn all over with tiny patterns in thin white gut. I have seen my Shawnee mother doing such fancy work in firelight. The small breeze shifts the cornstalks one by one and I see women's hands moving, the same soft quick moving in air. My own old ma in Carolina, in your grave a year. I have not seen it, though I can picture your hands still, very easy. And if you were here, what would you think of it?

My Shawnee father takes the pouch and draws it open very careful. Out comes a thick long belt strung with tiny shells of different colours, red and white and black. It is fancier work yet, a subtle thing. Black Fish lifts it by both ends so it is strung between his hands, I can see its weight and its strength. He holds up his left hand first and he says:

—Detroit.

Now he raises the other end and he says:

—This place.

The tears have dried on his cheeks, his eyes have shrunk back to the black rock I know. It seems to me now that they can breach my

skin. I rub my shirt sleeve over my own damp face and in Shawnee
I say:

—These colours?

Pompey crouches beside Black Fish and points to the belt. He
says in loud English:

—Red is the road of war. White is the road we can walk
together. Black is death. You see?

He speaks as if I am an idiot child, as if I am little Andy Johnson
playing the fool at Chillicothe. Pompey is playing the servant with
Black Fish more than ever, and more than that, he is showing me his
closeness to my father. How truly he understands him. What a poor
rotten son I am in comparison.

Moluntha sits unmoving, I can see his pulse slow in his neck. In
Shawnee I speak direct to Black Fish:

—Which am I to choose?

My Shawnee father's eyes crack again for a single instant. A horse-
fly gets too close and is brained by the sweep of the fanning boughs.
His face turns to follow it over the ground.

—Father.

But he says nothing, and Moluntha says nothing, they could sit
there for all eternity saying nothing as I know. To the boys Pompey
says:

—Fan this good man a little faster, the day is warm.

I wish to say, No need to act the slave with me, Pompey, I do
not own you. But I do not say it. I see his eyes blaze up again, I see
the corners of his lips rise, I know he is turning over some private
knowledge in his mind. I do not yet wish to know what it is. Again
I look at the bright shells sewn into the belt, again I put my sleeve
to my face.

A metal clicking, a small enough sound, like the sound of
crickets rubbing their legs. I turn and I see two men standing outside the fort gates now, my brothers Squire and Ned come out to

watch. I know it is Squire telling me he has cocked the hammer of his gun and made it ready, or ready enough. Just who he has it ready for I am not quite certain. He sets his gun butt upon the ground and holds a palm up to the men in the bastions. *Wait.* Now I hold up both hands in their direction and to Black Fish I say:

—You have given me much to think on. I must speak with the other head men. I am not the only chief here, I was gone so long.

My father says very cool:

—Have they taken you back, Sheltowee?

And what I can say to this, I do not know.

10

WHEN I REACH the gate, the back of my shirt is soaked through with sweat. Ned says in his easy fashion:

—All right Dan?

I say:

—All right.

Squire lifts his head and shouts to the guards, and we are let back in. Jemima has climbed down from the parapet. Her face and neck are still all angry blotches. She says:

—What did they call you?

The women are in their doorways keeping the smaller children behind their frayed skirts. They are listening, the guards on the walls are listening though they watch the Indians setting up camp in the meadow. I say:

—My Indian name. Sheltowee. Big Turtle.

Jemima frowns:

—Daddy, what did they give you?

—They gave us time. They gave us a choice.

—What kind of a choice, Mr. Turtle?

This from Hancock, leaning against the wall with the look of a dog waiting at a rat-hole. *Dogs with another dog,* so the Shawnee said my men thought of me, always watching to see what I have got in case they ought to have it. I do not look at him any longer. I hold out the shell belt looped in my fist. The brilliance of the colours makes Jemima suck in a breath. I look at it again also. We have grown unused to such beautiful things. I say:

—Well. We can go with them now or we can fight it out.

—Is that all? Surrender and die later, or die sooner? Quite a choice, Captain.

I look to Hancock's shoes, I say:

—Those buckles of yours would make fine bullets. I hope you do not forget what the women here have given up to make ammunition.

The women nearby ruffle themselves but Hancock takes no notice, he only points to the bundle beneath my arm. He says:

—And they gave their favourite another gift, I see.

—Chief Black Fish has sent jerked buffalo tongues as a gift for the women.

From behind her ma Kezia Callaway shrieks:

—Poison! Poison!

She clamps her small bulldog jaw shut, she is quite satisfied with her pronouncement. The fort stirs, questions rise from everyone's skin. Elizabeth Callaway is the first to ask one aloud:

—What makes them think we would eat them? What makes you think we would, Captain Boone?

I set down the bundle and I take out one of the dried tongues, I cut off a piece from the narrower end with my knife. I say:

—Not hungry? We have gone without dainties for a long time.

The meat and salt have a fine smoky taste. I chew and I hold out the rest of the long tongue. If it is poison I will die with a good flavour in my mouth. Elizabeth and Kezia would slam their door at the sight if they were not so deadly curious by nature. They watch as Jemima takes a piece. Ned's young Sarah comes dragging London's little Jacky by the hand as if he were her pull toy. Bold as brass she says:

—Give us big bits.

—Yes miss, as you like.

I give them each a long strip. Martha is looking but she does not stop me. As I am cutting more the shots begin outside. They are only a few, they pepper the air and stop again as fast. The gun hammers knock back, the riflemen in the bastions are so quick—

—Stop. Stop!

My voice tears my ears. And now no sound. Christ, a miracle. Nobody wishes to be first to shoot, but they stand ready and twitching. I call:

—They are not shooting at us. They are shooting cattle.

Jemima's black eyes are huge. Hancock shapes his mouth to speak. Colonel Dick can no longer keep himself contained. Snapping at the others to keep a close watch, he climbs down from his place as fast as his thick legs will go. He wrenches the meat from my hand and hurls it across the fort, where it falls in the well, which is still a poor hole. The tongue will not have far to fall. His Kezia breaks from her ma and runs to him shrieking:

—Now the poison is in the water! You said they would poison it!

She is looking wild-eyed at me as she says it, she clutches her daddy's leg. Locking her in his arms he cries:

—You let them kill our stock. You are as good as murdering all of us on the spot, you goddamned madman!

—I told them they could have the rest of the crops also.

At this Miss Kezia sets up wailing, her daddy covers her ears with his hands, he says:

—That letter they brought from Detroit—it shows clear as day that Boone is a traitor. Major Smith, all of you, I ask you, can we not hang him now? Shoot him? I will do it myself.

His face is a plate of disgust. Someone on the ramparts curses under his breath. Ned's girl and little Jacky are chewing and watching hard. Billy Smith puts himself between us. With his eyes not quite on mine he says:

—Captain Boone, what is your answer to this?

—Major Smith and all of you, everything I have done has been to save you and this place. They would have taken some of the stock and crops regardless. They mean what they say, only you have to listen close to their words. Listen to mine. I am keeping peace.

Colonel Dick starts in:

—Major Smith, where are the men captured by the Indians through this man's Indian-loving insanity? We ought to ask them if they feel saved.

I say:

—They may be with the Shawnee army. I do not think so but I do not know. They will not have killed them all.

It is a weak point, I know it is. But I go on loud:

—The army outside our walls is no small one. They will not go back with nothing. The redcoats may have brought cannon, I do not know. I will tell you there is no certainty of beating them but we may have the chance for peace now, if you will listen.

—We ought to vote on it.

This from Hancock with one heel tipped up so his shoe buckle catches the light. He knows as well as I do how votes go. He was there when we all near lost our scalps to the Shawnee vote at the Blue Licks. But Major Billy nods. Here is something to catch hold of. He announces:

—We will vote, that is if we have your approval, Captain Boone.

—You have it. I will accept what the greater number wishes to do. Who votes to surrender now and go with the army to Fort Detroit and be British again?

—I will shoot the first one who does.

This from Colonel Dick, he has lifted his gun with one arm. Kezia bawls harder, a mess running from her nose. He hushes her again and keeps her close. No one speaks. I say:

—Major Smith—Billy, what do you think?

He shakes his head, his face is troubled as he thinks. He says:

—We ought to defend ourselves. And the Virginia troops ought to be on their way to us now.

—I would rather die here than move.

This from Squire, he speaks uncommonly loud. Ned at his side raises his chin. Keep-home Neddy, who has loved home since we were boys in Daddy's house in Pennsylvania. But Squire's passion is a surprise. Until I recall his wife Jane in childbed with no child, his baby's grave outside the walls, dug while I was gone and did not know of it.

The men's talk boils up, the women keep to their doorways and speak low, I see Hancock's wife Molly weeping and twisting her hands and Old Dick's pretty girl Fanny coming out to get Kezia. Jemima's Flanders is looking down at me from the wall just above, he opens his mouth as though waiting for a beakful, working himself up to ask what I will do.

What will you do now?

And so I say:

—Well well, I will tell them what you have decided. And die with the rest.

⌣

In his best hat with its ragged plume and his old red army coat, Billy stands in my door stiff and waiting. I say:

—The British lot will feel quite at home when they see you in that.

I have nothing so grand to wear. I keep to the shirt and breeches Jemima took from Flanders. She wraps one of his cloths round my neck. It has gone quite yellow and thin but I know it is the best Flanders has left. He passes behind Billy and gives us a tight nod. To my girl I say:

—Your husband wants his clothing back. Perhaps I ought to go out bare as the day I was born.

Jemima ties the cloth tight and says:

—You are fit to be looked at. Will Uncle Squire and Uncle Neddy go with you?

Uncle Neddy. Jemima's eyes are clear as a lake. Ought I to tell you here and now before all is finished, would you like to have all the answers?

I do not ask. I pinch her chin and I say:

—No, duck. Best to keep the party small. We would not wish to frighten them with our strength, would we Billy?

Major Billy holds himself stiff beneath his hat though its feather drifts like a sail in the smallest wind. Jemima laughs, which frightens the cat. It runs in a circle but finds no escape and so darts beneath the bed. The laugh frightens me also, it has a helplessness under it. Well Tibby, we will see if you live another day.

The sun is still hot though dropping now. A course of sweat douses these fresh clothes as I walk to the gate with Billy. One of the horses in the paddock coughs as we pass, and a cow sets to complaining. The air inside the walls feels as though it had been cut from a thick block and set there. Outside it is not much better. We stand a moment, we wait.

We do not wait long. The boys with their peach-bough fans lead. Behind them is Black Fish still in his scarlet blanket and silver brooches, old Moluntha and other chiefs in their finery filing slow after him with some twenty warriors at their backs. The warriors tread the ground in the same easy rhythm. The chiefs glide along footless with their blankets and robes trailing. Hamilton's men have kept to their separate camp and so Billy is the only red-coated one about after all.

They stop where we sat before. Billy and I walk to meet them. Two more boys come now, rolling a log which they set out. And

Pompey appears holding a skin in his arms. It is a panther skin, it shines as though he has brushed and brushed it. He lays it on the log with the animal's empty face drooping from one end. Now he holds out his arms and bows to show me we are to sit here, and so we do.

Seeing our hands are empty, the warriors set down their guns and clubs though they keep a sharp eye on us and the fort. A lump on the log digs into me, but I will not move now. Billy looks at me sidelong as the chiefs come past. Each in turn gives us his hand as Pompey goes on bowing and announcing their names. Black Hoof, a great Shawnee, the rims of his ears stretched thin with the largest loops I have seen. Black Beard, an older Shawnee man with a calm wide face and light gold eyes. A few Wyandot with only half their heads shaved, the hair running sleek as oil down their left sides. And Cherokee with bunches of brown and gold feathers spiked up like quills round their warrior locks.

Cherokee. As the first one shakes my hand, I grip it tight and my eyes rush over them. I do not see the face, the long bony face I know. At once I am shot through with my old recklessness, I could raise a hand and have lead spewed from the fort walls, bodies flung broken all over the ground. This ground is why we have come here, it is why they killed my boy, and why should I mind making it darker and bloodier? Perhaps it is what the place wants of me, perhaps it is what I have been meant to do all this time.

Do not think.

The chiefs sit now on blankets and skins. My hands have clenched after all the shaking. I loose them and it pains my wrists to do it. Pompey lays out another beautiful skin and Black Fish stands upon it. His eyes do not quite reach mine, they settle instead on the air before my face. In Shawnee he says:

—Now you have had time to consider the belt and the letter from Detroit. What are your thoughts?

Pompey repeats this in English, very pious and more booming than Black Fish, just as though he were a preacher. Major Billy leans forward and says:

—Thank you for bringing the offer, but we cannot take our families so far.

Before Pompey can begin booming again, Black Fish says:

—We have made everything easy. I have brought forty horses just for your wives and children and old women to ride.

Billy looks to me as Pompey speaks it in English. In Shawnee I say:

—You are good to us. We will need time to talk it over.

A flock of chickadees scatters overhead like tossed seeds. For a moment I think of throwing my club and seeing how many of the birds I can bring down. In English Black Fish says:

—One day.

His face is set and cool as pewter. Pompey holds up a finger and says:

—Chief Black Fish gives you one day to talk among your people.

—I know what he said.

This seems to amuse Pompey. His mouth curves and he folds his hands in front of him before he booms out my words in Shawnee. Before I can say more he is ordering the boys to get out the pipes so we can seal our one-day peace with a smoke. Then he is passing a pipe between Major Billy and Black Fish and interpreting as they stand together setting out rules for the day we have been given. No shooting, keep well back from each other, the women can go out for water. Again they shake hands.

The sun is low now, falling behind the trees. Chief Moluntha comes to sit beside me on my log as the others talk and smoke. It is just as though we were on a Philadelphia street idly looking at people walking about. After a time he says to me:

—You killed my son the other day.

98

He is not looking at me, he is watching the rest as easy as ever. I say:

—I killed no one.

—You and your men did, over the Ohio River.

I grip the panther skin between us and the fur rucks under my fingers. It has the feel of a scalp. I see Kenton holding out the fresh one near the empty town. I say:

—We were not there.

He runs his creased hand back and forth over the fur. As he does it he says:

—It was you. I know who you are—everyone knows. I tracked you to this place. Some of your men are still away there, ha?

Kenton and Montgomery. My blood is flying through me, I know Moluntha's blood is doing the same though he keeps himself still in his wine-coloured jacket. I watch his heavy brow as he takes his hand away from the panther skin and says it is time he took his pull on the pipe. I say:

—What did you do to them?

He says nothing. He only stands and walks back to the chiefs who are wrapped in a fog of smoke from the sweet leafy Indian tobacco. The smell pierces me through. It was my dead brother Israel's smell, he is now so many years dead. It was the evening smell of my Shawnee father's house. It blows into my eyes now but I keep them open.

—sss.

   —Nasty.

   —Dirty.

   —Dirty.

The women hiss into the morning. After the men and I have marched out to guard them as they do the milking in the fields, we give them our clothes, that is to say whatever spare clothes we have, and these are not many. Some put on the Sunday breeches and Sunday shirts, and some others put on our long coats with nothing but their ragged shifts and stockings beneath. It is the best we can do.

Martha comes out in Ned's coat, her feet bare. She takes a short turn back and forth before the door. I see the white arches of her feet and the rounds of her heels. Nat Hart's black women, Silva and Ratta, shake hats fierce out the windows as though to rid them of fleas. Old Dick's Doll refuses to put any such thing on her head, as she says loud enough for all outside to hear. They and the rest stew all the time they are dressing. *So we will go to our graves like this, filthy and stinking.*

Or to Detroit.

Jemima yells:

—You stop! My daddy knows what we have to do!

Here is my girl defending me when I know nothing. It strikes me how stupid loyalty is, like an old hound following someone about for the sake of their smell only.

We do not have enough working guns for all these false men and so Squire gives some of them old barrels and other things he digs up in his shop and the forge. Some of the smaller girls are equipped with broomsticks. Ned teaches them to walk like men before we send them up the ramparts and onto the cabin roofs. From the parapet I hear him telling them what to do:

—Spread your feet more. Put the gun against your shoulder, not across your bosom. Do not swing so much. There, there, you have it.

For Neddy they laugh soft and do their best. They pull up their backs and push their hips forward and march all about with their faces serious. Darling Neddy.

The children run about within the walls as though it were a holiday. The smaller girls go out with pails and bowls to the spring, and I send Uncle Monk and London to guard them. I say:

—Girls, any cow or pig you see, give it something to eat so it will follow you back, and we will shut it in here.

Monk nods. Ned's Sarah says:

—What will we give them?

—Take a corncob each. Tickle their noses with your hair, they will like that. They like yellow, did you know it?

She laughs and little Jacky laughs with her, I am glad to hear it though the sound is a strange one at this time. I climb up to a rampart and I watch them go.

Soon enough Pompey rides up from the camp on a pony. Sweet Apples, his shaggy little mount, she took him singing all the way to Detroit when Black Fish marched us there. I near laugh too when I see her swaying under his weight, still living, her sides puffing in and out. Pompey sits watching the little girls in his princely manner. He gives a long nod to Jacky who has stopped to stare at a black man in

Indian clothes. Monk and London look a long moment also, and turn their heads to keep looking as they walk behind the girls. When an old cow shows its face at the edge of the corn, Sarah shrieks.

Some of the women come marching along the rampart to see who made the noise. Pompey calls to Sarah:

—You may take that one.

From a bastion, narrow young John Holder shouts:

—It is our cow, you black shit.

Estill's wife Rachel gasps, then levels her false gun at Pompey. Stepping over to her I tell her to put it down, but she looks fit to strike me in the face with it. Hancock's round little wife Molly comes wobbling along too with the same look, and with an iron pan handle as long as she is. Pompey grins, and again he calls:

—What will you give me for this pony? She is a fine one. I will take a good gun for her. Have you any of those?

John Holder shouts again:

—You can fuck off on that lousy animal.

Old Dick looking out his own bastion permits himself a brief smirk at his son-in-law's tongue. The little girls scatter back towards the gate with Monk shooing them along, while London goes for the cow. Pompey smiles in the direction of the fort, he turns the pony and trots her back towards the camp. As he goes we all hear him singing *Over the hills and far away*. My old friend William Hill's favourite song. I taught it to some of the Shawnee though they did not understand the words. It strikes me harder than any slap.

The smell of cooking fires and meat floats up to us. Molly Hancock clutches her pan and says:

—Those Indians are fanning the smell this way to make us suffer.

I say:

—You have become very fierce, Molly. Perhaps we ought to give you a real gun.

Her eyes grow rounder watching the smoke threading the air from the camp. She will not look at me. She says:

—Oh I do not mind deprivation, not a bit. I take what the Lord sees fit to give me. But the children are hungry enough already.

I hear the acres of resentment in her. I say:

—If we asked them for some of what they are cooking, they would share it.

Now she turns and spits on my neck. It is the first time in her life she has spat at anyone as I can see, she is as shocked with herself as I am. She stands holding the pan with a string of wet stuck to her own chin and her mouth open. She takes a breath and spits at me again. I let her do it, what else can I do?

Pompey is back on Sweet Apples in the afternoon. He trots up closer to the fort and rides in a great loop. Someone yells:

—Fuck off with you!

Likely Holder again and his supremely ill tongue, he loves to shout *fuck* at anything. Most of the young men and many of the women join him in this sentiment. A shiver of hate goes along the fort wall, I feel it pass through me. It is an enlivening shiver, everyone seems to have woken with it.

Molly Hancock shifts her weight about on the slope of her cabin roof. Her expression says she would brain Pompey with her pan handle given the chance. Now she has spat upon me, she looks quite capable of murder. Pompey gives her a nod. Well. I say loud and even:

—What have you come to tell us?

He grins up at me:

—I come with a request.

—You are not having any more of our animals.

This very lofty from Madam Callaway in Old Dick's Sunday hat and shirt. I call:

—Take what you need, as we told you.

Pompey raises his voice to its announcing tones:

—The chiefs and men wish to see Boone's famous white women, having heard of their many charms.

He grins very wide. He looks at each of us lined up along the walls. Some he looks at longer, he looks quite up and down. The women begin to boil, the mothers especially. They make their voices deep like men's to go with their outfits, but they shout worse things than any man here has dared to. Johnny Gass is smirking behind his freckle-skinned hand, and I know others are doing the same. Calm as I can I call back:

—You Shawnee stole my daughter and other girls from here once. You will not get another look at any of them.

Old Dick stalks along the rampart towards me, but Jemima is at my side first in a great coat and hat, saying:

—Daddy you are not going out there again, are you?

Dick calls before he reaches me:

—By God, if you try to send my girls out I will roast you alive and that black can watch me do it.

Betsy and Fanny and little Kezia, who has charcoaled a beard round her mouth, are huddled with their ma. When the older two were taken with Jemima, we near killed Betsy when we found them at last. With her long black hair let down to her knees, she looked like an Indian. My jaw clamps to think of it, of what could have happened. And Black Fish's son lying shot, dead across their campfire. When I did not know Black Fish.

Old Dick's black woman Doll comes to stand in front of the girls, staring me down. My gun is heavy in my hands. We must slow down, we must make time heavy as melting iron. This is all I can see.

The rest carry on yelling at Pompey as he laughs and bows. He is still sitting on the pony, and he snaps its shaggy head up when it tries to bite a tuft of grass. I get up to go towards the ladder. Perhaps I ought to talk with him myself before he is shot.

But Jemima pushes past me, she darts down the ladder and into her cabin. Flanders comes over to me to ask what she is about, but she runs out again in only her white undershift with its frayed fingerlike hem, she runs to the front gate and speaks quick with Ned there. With a glance to me Ned shrugs and opens the gate a crack. She ducks out. I call:

—Jemima!

I run with Flanders behind me and more coming, we all run into the corner bastion from where we can see her standing just outside the gate. Ned is there with his gun ready, which makes me sore and queer. I train my gun square on Pompey's forehead. When he lifts his head and turns, I have to shift my sight. He gives a slow call. *Ichquewa.* Woman.

And from the side of the corn come some of the chiefs and warriors. They are unarmed, holding out their hands to show it. They keep well back, they move no closer. With another bow, Pompey says very sweet:

—Sheltowee's girl, the chiefs have asked if you will let down your hair as a gift to them. They have heard of its beauty. Will you?

Flanders is breathing hard, mumbling *God damn.* Bodies press at my back, all trying to see. Jemima in the woods, taken, they said they did not hurt her.

My girl is tugging the combs from her hair and unwinding the plaits tied up in back of her head. I cannot see her face, I see the long spill of black, black as her mother's and Ned's. And mine. It falls like a great splash of ink over her shift and down past her knees. She stands barefooted with her elbows turned out, she spins herself about to show them. Then she does so again. The chiefs speak low to each other, their faces go soft. I see even old Moluntha's go soft for a moment before he controls it. I know he is thinking of his child, his lost child, another child lost through my fault.

My heart kicks at my ribs. With my eye along my gun barrel I watch my girl, and I hear what they are saying. *Sheltowee ichquewa. Ah. Skihotie. Skihotie weeletha.* Sheltowee's woman. Yes. Beautiful. Beautiful hair.

Black Fish speaks to Pompey but is smiling at Jemima. Pompey calls:

—We have presents for your lovely famous daughter.

He takes a pouch from my Shawnee father and holds it high. To my girl Black Fish says:

—*Skihotie.*

It seems to me no one in the fort has swallowed for quite some time. I take a breath and I call to her:

—Jemima.

But she speaks to Black Fish:

—You are not changing my name.

Dust kicks up round her ankles as she stalks back into the fort. Ned shuts the gates behind her. I go down to her. I hold her arms and I say:

—Jemima, that was a true gift for you, that is their way. They said you were beautiful. They would not have done you any harm.

A few of her hairs crackle and rise from her head as she shoves them away from her face. The great black sheet of it over her makes her look small, a child wrapped in a blanket. Two hot tears rush from the corners of her eyes. Her eyes are Rebecca's, they are two black questions. I rub the tears away quick as they come. There are no more. She says:

—I did it but I will not do it again. Do not go out there Daddy.

—My duck—

—I know what they think about me and I do not care. I know they think you are theirs.

This last she says with her eyes hard on my face. I see what her loyalty is costing her. Callaway's Doll wraps Jemima's hair into a quick twist. Her hands say *Look at her half naked, her own mother gone because of you.* Flanders tears off his hunting shirt to put over her and takes her to their cabin.

With the rest watching I climb back up to the rampart. The chiefs and Pompey have already vanished behind the corn.

I am shaken, I remain so until evening, when Major Billy and I take Squire and two of the other older men out with us. I feel Isaac Crabtree keeping himself a few steps away from me. Whenever we see each other we can only think of my boy dead. Crabtree saw it happen, I cannot forget it. But we walk, we will not talk of it, we have no choice.

The air is cooling fast now. Our shadows have long peg legs. The insects keep up their usual noise.

The chiefs wait at the same place as yesterday, the same furs and blankets ready. Our one day is finished and what have we accomplished in it? No one has said anything new, it is only the same old feeling of being dogs or cocks caged up before a fight. I think we will all tear out the nearest throat, any throat, if we are let loose.

I speak in English before anyone can say a word:

—My people will not surrender as long as there is a man living. You have seen we have many men.

A look flares behind Pompey's eyes as he opens his lips to begin his interpreting. It says, *Many men, is that so?* But Black Fish cuts in with quick hard Shawnee:

—Your white chief in Detroit ordered me to avoid killing if at all possible, but how can I avoid it now?

Major Billy and the rest look to me without understanding. Pompey says nothing. A flat silence falls on us all. Black Fish stares at me. He tucks his hands behind his blanket and nothing of him moves. The warriors stir and stretch their necks, horses nicker in the Shawnee camp behind us. The other chiefs begin to speak to one another, but Black Fish halts them. He says:

—We must discuss how to live with each other now. Tomorrow I will bring all my chiefs, you will bring your head men, and we will parley.

Pompey repeats it in English. Squire brushes his sleeve against mine, a warning as I know well enough. There was a time he would not have felt the need to do it. When he trusted me entire.

Old Moluntha takes two steps forward and says:

—We will meet in your fort, make it easy for you.

Pompey interprets with his head high. Billy coughs, Squire takes his arm away and I feel the lack of it. I say:

—Our women are frightened, they keep indoors all the time. We cannot meet in the fort with them there, and they will not have us going to your camp.

Black Fish turns to his men and says in a lighter fashion:

—It is good to keep peace with your women. Though not easy.

The chiefs and warriors laugh, and the air eases somewhat. Black Fish dips his chin and sets his eyes on me. Father, I know you are trying to help me, I know it.

Squire beside me says to him quiet:

—You should know that an army from Virginia is coming to our aid.

Pompey turns this to Shawnee, and Black Fish goes still again. Major Billy says:

—We will meet you here with all our leaders tomorrow.

He turns on his heel and the others follow. With a last look back at my father I do the same. As we near the gate I say:

—This has given us time, Billy. Another day means there is a chance for a treaty. They will get the pipes out again.

Billy shakes his head, and the feather on his hat bobs and turns like a fighter:

—I have no heart for smoking and more talk just now, Dan. How long can this carry on?

He marches ahead. Squire tucks his thumbs into his belt and says in his dry fashion:

—One more day living.

I say:

—That is right.

Behind us the chiefs go on talking very soft, I catch no words at all.

When we are at the gate I let the others go in first. I stay outside as the dark sinks down. There is a humming above me, it passes back and forth. When I look up I see Martha walking in a lazy oblong on the rampart, swinging her gun barrel like a tail. She thinks she is giving me something.

A night bird rustles and twitters over the river. It is all blue shade round me now. I am struck by a thought that the sun is up on the other side of the earth. Ma and Daddy I think of you in England before you came to this country. Perhaps there you are children, still living, who can tell what possibilities there are?

There are possibilities still. I know there are.

And I know that someone is coming slow round the corner of the fort. I stay where I am. I know him by his walk. My Shawnee father, going very careful and silent and looking up at the walls and the bastions. He goes straight past me as though I am not here at all. Round the next corner he passes and I do not move, I do not follow, I do not see where he goes.

MY EYES BURN DRY when the sun creeps up above the wall. I am alone on watch inside the front gate, sitting to rest my feet, when I hear a great bawling outside it some way off. I get up stiff and I look through the wall slit. It is the remaining cows in a great mass. They need milking, and their bellowing grows more miserable every moment. But we need our women to keep up our false numbers, walking about on the ramparts. I cannot let them go out. Even if they would go out.

One girl up on the walls screeches like a jay when she sees the cattle heading for the gate. I go up, and I see that they are herded by Shawnee and Cherokee warriors. They call in high voices like ladies' at this women's work and laugh with each other. *This way pretty cow. Do you love me? I will milk you so you will, I will touch you so, so.*

The cows bawl to be admitted. I call down to Ned to let them in:

—This is no Troy, these cows are not made of wood and full of enemies!

The Shawnee herders look up at me but keep back, they only flick their soft switches when a cow tries to turn round again. I yell a thank-you down to them, and some nod and grin. One is Kaskee, my young guard. He claps and shouts, *Over the hills and far away.*

Over the *heels*, he says still, as they did in Chillicothe. A few of the others join in before they turn and walk back and I watch them go.

The cows mill at the centre of the fort, they groan as they look about for help. Their bags swing low. I tell the older girls to get down and milk, and leave their mas to march about on the roofs and walls. I climb down also and push my way through the flies and hills of warm milky flesh to find Major Billy and Ned and Squire near the gate:

—Another gift. We must return it in some way.

Squire pushes up his hat and says:

—Kind of them to give us our own cows.

—I know how this works, Squire. We must give them a good meal before the treaty making.

Billy laughs or coughs, I am unsure which it is. He says:

—I would like a good meal myself. I do not think any woman here has much to spare me.

—Billy, I must ask you to plead with the women to cook up all they have. They can take it in shifts, and the girls will help. We have to make a show of plenty.

—Dan. Have we not given them enough?

—If they think we have plenty to eat, they will not bother trying to starve us out.

Major Billy coughs or laughs again and smoothes the sides of his fluffy white hair. He says:

—I am trying my damndest to do as you say. People want to believe you but you are not making it easy.

I have no answer to this. In the silence a cow lets out a great bawl. Ned says:

—Let me speak to the women.

—Do that now, and Squire, you tell the men at the slits and the bastion closest to the meeting place to keep there. They will have to shoot in a heartbeat if there is any trouble.

As Ned goes off, Squire says:

—Some are talking of shooting that black man straight, peace or no peace. If it starts you know how it will go.

—Go and tell them. They will listen to you, they trust you. And I am afraid you will have to trust me, Squire.

Squire brushes a fly from his face and says:

—And you have nothing to trust but your own gut, is that right?

The cows go on moaning. My blood knocks in my ears, *I I I*, an empty noise.

⌣

The feast is near everything we have. Corn, greens, tiny hard apples from the small orchard Uncle Monk started. Sweating wheels of cheese pulled early from the dark of the dairy house, enough fresh milk for all of us to take a swim in, new butter, hot cornbread, jerked venison softened in water, the buffalo tongues Black Fish gave us, dressed up to look different. So unused are we all to this plenty that we sit staring as though it might fly off if we blink.

The chiefs sit across from us at the tables we have rigged up from boards and logs on the flat before the fort, each with two warriors standing behind. They are not painted up now. Some wear coloured headscarves and not feathers. I do not look at the food, I look at their shirts, all weighed down with silver pins and brooches and bells. The ones in blankets throw these back over their shoulders to free their arms. Seeing this I say:

—Might as well get out of our coats, boys, what do you say? Another warm day.

It is hot here in the open. Major Billy stands and salutes as though I have given him an order, he takes off his red coat and folds it and salutes again. Squire takes off his jacket and the rest follow, Flanders and Crabtree and others. Our calmest men, but

112 appears in margin.

for Colonel Dick, who is far down the length of the tables, keeping very silent. I do not know how he is doing it, perhaps it is because he has taken a hank of bread and is already chewing it as if to say, *Try to take this from me!* But he does not remove his red coat and this seems to satisfy him, though I feel his hard eye follow me as though it is sewn to me with gut.

We eat, stiff as puppets. I see Black Fish take a lump of cheese and set it down again. He takes instead a piece of tongue. He looks at me as he does so but he says nothing. I think of thanking him for his kind gift but I do not, I chew a cob of corn, though I have never been one for corn. We eat on and on to keep from talking.

Well. The talk must come eventually. When we have made a wreck of the meal, I stand and I say:

—Will you follow us to the big elm, where there is more shade?

Pompey tells them what I have said. He has eaten nothing, as though eating were beneath him. The chiefs look to one another. The elm is within shot of the fort, but within shot of their camp back in the meadow also. When they nod and stand, we all begin the walk. Pompey rushes to be first and spread his blanket for Black Fish on the grass beneath the huge tree. Old Dick keeps behind, walking very leisurely in his red coat. I look back to him, and I see the quick shine of a gun nose stuck out a wall slit and pulled back in. I watch the little boys and girls dart out the gate to clear the food from the table, they are filling their mouths and cheeks as they do it. In the group of sycamores down the slope I see quick shiftings, like small birds in autumn leaves. My arms go to gooseflesh in the sun. I say nothing.

At the tree we sit on the ground. Only Dick refuses to sit. He says:

—Too many of you.

He says it to Pompey, who does not trouble himself to turn it to Shawnee. Dick is counting off all the chiefs and warriors:

—Twice as many as us. What will you do about it, Captain Boone?

I hold up my hand to ease him. I say:

—We are here for peace, I think.

Black Fish looks at the warriors and lifts his own palm to them. They retreat a way. He says:

—You see we are willing to make a long peace.

In Shawnee I say:

—I am willing.

—Speak English.

This from Colonel Dick. I say no more, but wait as Pompey speaks my words again for the chiefs. Without looking at his men, Black Fish says:

—Here is our proposal. We will use the Ohio River as a wall between us. When we both have kept peace for some time and your Detroit chief agrees to our treaty, we will cross for trade and hunting, and be two parts of one family.

My hope rises, my men's faces lift slightly as Pompey tells them what is proposed. The other chiefs are very still, I cannot read them. Dick barks:

—And what must we do to get this peace out of you?

Black Fish looks at me:

—Your people must all promise to keep to it and swear loyalty to the white king again. Detroit asks this.

Pompey near sings this in English. *Loyalty to the white king, to King George in Britain, whom you have thrown away, you whites with all your kings and your fights.* So he is thinking. Major Billy and the rest begin talking at once to each other. Colonel Dick comes straight to me and says hot in my ear:

—I will never do it, Boone, and neither will anyone else in Kentucky, except perhaps for your wife's family. But most of them have run off back to Carolina. Closer to the king at any rate.

His breathing smells of meat. Slow. Slow. I turn to Squire and Billy and I say low:

—It is only saying words. Only words, the same as any others. They do not have to mean anything.

Major Billy says:

—We have always taken you at your word, Captain.

—Billy—

Here Black Fish speaks again:

—You have no right to be on this ground. I have promised my warriors many scalps and much treasure here. They will be angry with me now. So you must trust what I say. I have put myself in danger to say it.

The warriors indeed have a sulky look though the chiefs keep their faces still, even Moluntha. Before Pompey can say it, I lean closer to my Shawnee father and I speak soft:

—My father. You are good to me, you have already lost much in your life.

I see the smallest ripple in the depths of his eye. He says:

—Your wife is waiting for you. She is your wife still. Where is your white wife?

I shake my head, I cannot say her name, I cannot say anything of her. Out of my mouth comes my other wife's name all in a breath, I say:

—Methoataske.

Here Colonel Dick calls:

—We cannot hear.

Pompey leans in with his face all officious, as though he were nothing but a page for writing on. Black Fish pays him no heed. He says to me:

—Your mother weeps, your wife is sick at heart. Your child and your little sisters miss you. Bring your girl, my granddaughter. I have seen her. I will love her as you do.

I see it costs Black Fish to say this, to talk of his wife and daughters this way. My Shawnee mother, always full of tears, her real son lost and me a poor replacement. My little sisters turning their backs to me. Eliza, waiting for me to come. My wife, Methoataske. And my father here, looking me in my face. I cannot say anything. I feel Pompey's happy breath on my head.

Black Fish is holding his mouth still. In English Pompey says low:

—You may answer now. It is only saying words. The same as any others. Just a play you are performing, Sheltowee.

Pompey smiles very bright with his strong white teeth. I look again to my father but he has retreated as if behind a wall and gives no sign of understanding what Pompey says, though I know he does.

Smooth your expression. Slow, slow. So I say to myself in my mind.

I stand and fold my arms, I say very loud:

—Get your pipes. We will smoke after we sign the treaty.

Colonel Dick seethes and tries to get Billy's ear without me hearing. The others keep where they are. I do not listen, I do not care. I call for a table to be fetched, and I have Flanders sit and write it all out, the agreement. He has a fine slanting hand, he makes only two blots on the paper's edge. Words. Some of the warriors watch him do it, their faces are curious. Two of them are smiling at it.

The elm leaves judder in the breeze. Their shadows pass over our faces and hands as we stand. Once Flanders has done with writing he holds up the paper to dry it. Black Fish speaks in a great voice to all his warriors and chiefs, then Pompey repeats for my men:

—We have made a long peace and now we will shake hands and let our hearts beat close as brothers' hearts should.

The smell of the tobacco spreads like a sheet over us. A warrior begins to pass the pipe among the chiefs. Black Fish locks his arm through mine, he takes my other hand also, and the left sides of our chests are pressed together. His silver brooches dig into me through my shirt, his hair is against my cheek and my eye. I am so happy, I am too happy.

I watch the other chiefs do the same, very slow, to my men. Old Moluntha steps up to Old Dick and sizes him up before grasping his arm. Dick will not let himself be embraced, he is yelling and sputtering *Goddamned son of a bitch*, he is dragging Moluntha who does not let go. He goes on fighting and yelling louder *You will not have me—*

I see it all coming. I say:

—My father.

His arm presses mine hard, his fingers are like roots searching out water in the dry. And before I can say a word more the bullets are crying through the air and no one can hear anyone.

13

BLACK FISH is on the ground, I have thrown him from me as if he were nothing, an empty bag. Then my head bursts at the back, I am struck hard there and again lower down, and I am on the ground also, crawling over my father's arm. I cannot see right and my arms do not work right. My head is hot and sodden, my back is the same between my shoulders. I am everywhere wet. My father—

Father—

—Get up. Get up, Dan!

Squire is yanking me to my feet, he rips something out of my back and I see it in his hand, the peace pipe with its little bowl and hard edge. He roars:

—Run! Now!

He has just the sound of our old daddy with his roaring. I get to my feet with his arm tight about my body, I look back and I see a chief lying shot through the face. A silver half-moon brooch at his throat catches the sun and flares. The gate is open, some of the men are rushing out, young Pem Rollins with his round face limps at the back of them and stops to look round as though he had just arrived on the moon. He is blasted through the arm, he falls sideways and goes down.

—They are in the sycamores. More coming. Shut the gate!

Squire calls it, Major Billy is with us, Crabtree is coming behind, we are all running for the fort. Again Squire yells:

—Shut the gate! Shut it now, Ned!

The men who have come out run back in, I see Ned's face halved through the opening as it shrinks and he shuts us out. Bullets pierce the air and the grass and the earth. My blood slides down my back into my breeches, which are wet in front from my piss. Squire has my gun, he shoves it into my arms and pants in my ear:

—The postern door, west side—

We run round the fort corner, under the bastion, where they are shooting and yelling. A bullet sings over my head, and another just past my shoulder. I am staggering, I am nowhere near quick enough.

Squire disappears from my side. My legs carry on towards the small hidden door cut into the stockade, my eye fixes on its edges. It is nailed shut as I know, but I breathe in as if I am about to dive and hurl my shoulder at it. It cracks open and I am gasping on my stomach inside the walls. I kick the door to and roll my body against it. My gun is under my side, my blood is running out of me, my breath is loud as anything, in and out.

Where the rest are I do not know. How long I am down I do not know.

Get up, you fool. You ape. You arse. The shooting is ongoing. The dogs and horses have gone mad with the noise, the cows are bawling. I crawl forward into the great haze of dirt they have all kicked up. My backside is warm with the seep of blood. One of the horses pulls itself out of its hobble rope and kicks the wall. The children are running and screaming, a little one standing still is near trampled by cows. The dust and powder are so thick I am half choked.

Two shots fly down into the fort centre from the direction of the river. One goes straight through Old Dick's starry flag. Some of the Shawnee must have set up on the higher ground over the water, they can see into the fort very fine from there. I am reminded of our poor position and our poor building work here. My back stabs me with each breath. I cannot get up.

Some of the women are down from the ramparts and trying to catch the smallest children. A boy runs screaming from his ma, he does not know her in his daddy's clothes. I see her lose him among the animals.

Squire—

I do not see him anywhere, I cannot see.

—Captain Boone!

Elizabeth Callaway is gripping my arm, wrenching me to my knees. Her Kezia is screeching, her face hidden in her ma's hip. Elizabeth says straight into my ear:

—Get these children safe before they are all killed.

My tongue is stupid, my brains are stupid, I have been cut right through and am two stupid people. Elizabeth's face is a smear in my vision. I stand, I say:

—Squire.

—Fine. We will put them in your brother's shop, if you think that a safe place.

—It is a safe place—away from the walls—

Kezia turns her face up and screams all the louder until her ma drags her off towards Squire's gunshop. Snatching at the sleeves of children running past, Elizabeth gets a small clutch of them and herds them inside. A bullet falls hot onto my shoulder and singes my shirt. I tuck my gun under one arm and seize London's little Jacky who is standing alone beneath the rampart with tears threading the dust on his cheeks. He sets up howling as I carry him through the animals' mad noise and stink.

—Jacky, Jacky—

He does not hear. I hardly hear myself. I cannot hear Elizabeth though I can see her yelling from Squire's doorway. Old Dick runs past me with a shove, trying to catch the loose horse. There is hammering, someone has brains enough to nail a plank across the postern door I broke. Jacky struggles and kicks. I near drop him as he twists himself about and hits the wound in my back. I gasp and cover his eyes with my shirt as though he were a pony, and I push on.

At the gunshop, Elizabeth is beating a man with a broomstick, it is Tice Prock with soot all over his big face and yellow hair, who has refused all along to soldier with the rest. Old Dick now chases big Tice into the sea of animals, Elizabeth blocks the door with her body and thrusts the broom after him like a spear. I push past her with Jacky. The other children are tucked in behind the bellows and boxes, some are crying loud for their mas, and this starts Jacky up again. I set him free and he stands bewildered and blinking and set to howl his loudest, only Kezia screams first:

—Tice Prock was hiding under the bellows, my ma got him out!

—Did you, Elizabeth. Well done.

Blocking the door again, she cries:

—My husband will see that he fights like the rest of us.

She is telling me that I have not managed it. I have not managed anything. I am still stupid and slow, I say:

—He will get that well dug.

She throws up her chin and says:

—Perhaps he will meet his end in it.

I wipe my forehead, my hand comes away all blood. My heart beats in my hurt back, my brains swim. Black Fish, my father, I see your face rushing up at me from the ground as I fall. And now it vanishes, I do not see at all.

Elizabeth snatches up another child in the doorway, a slice of her thin arse shows through a split in the breeches. Jemima elbows in past her, panting, her hair coming down under Flanders's hat:

—Daddy.

She has an odd look, her edges are blurred, as if she is a ghost. The ghost of a boy, in boy's clothes. Jamesie, Jamesie. I say:

—Jemima, you are not dead, are you?

She frowns and then her hand is on my face. She tears off a strip of the great shirt she is wearing, it comes away easy. She holds the cloth to the back of my head. Jemima, your poor ribs show, you are so lean, there is nothing to you. She says:

—I was shot.

A loud crash outside as though the gate has come down, the children bawl, all fear and misery, someone runs past the door saying *Jesus, Jesus*, I am spinning, I am gone, I am gone.

The dust is caught in my lids and I can see almost nothing, as though I have walked through thick spiderwebs. I rub at my face and my head. I am on hard ground. The world is still this one, it is shrunk, the noise of it has not changed, it is all firing and howling.

—Daddy, do not pull at the bandage. You are still bleeding.

I am slow to know my girl's voice though her earlier words bang and bang in my ear. *I was shot.* I say:

—I am all right, but you, are you hurt?

I pull the cloth from my eye, I push Jemima's hand away. She says:

—Only a bruised backside. The bullet stuck in my breeches. I thought someone had pinched me. Look.

Close to my face she holds up a half-flattened lead ball between her fingers. I say:

—Go put your skirts on.

I do not like looking at her as a boy. I try to heave myself up, but my head and my back burn. Hidden in their various places, the children stare out at us, I see Jacky still all tears. A blast of quick shots fires high outside, close to the roof. My girl ducks:

—I poulticed up your head and your back where they axed you.
The wounds are not deep, you were lucky, like me. Your eye is still
swelling up from when you fell.

—Well.

She grasps my shoulder, she says:

—You ought to stay here. Flanders got his finger shot off and I
have sent him to our house. I have to help him now.

I get to my feet. The room totters like a boat. My breeches
are still wet in front, they are cold and heavy now. I can smell my
piss over the rusted-out smell of my blood and all the other
stench. I say:

—Have they got in? The gate—

Jemima says:

—None of them got in. They are only shooting all the time. We
are shooting back. Stay here Daddy.

Spikes of energy crack from her. She flies off out the door.
Elizabeth tells me:

—Not much good you will do in your state.

She is eyeing the wet front of my breeches. I say:

—You keep the children here. I am going.

And I go back into the sound of the world falling in.

The firing is heavy. Above me young Hodges is sitting barefooted,
ramming his rifle and swearing at the top of his lungs and enjoying
himself mightily. The other young men near him are the same.

—Captain.

It is Billy Smith beside me, his face grey. I say:

—Billy. Major. Were you hurt outside?

His fine hat is gone, his white hair a thin point above his forehead. He says:

—No. It is very bad though.

—Did everyone get in? I cannot—I did not see.

—Most of the men are in, so far as I know. It is madness.

—Squire?

He shakes his head. I say:

—Christ. Callaway should not have fought them.

—We are fighting them now. We have corralled the animals in here as best we can. What would you have us do, Captain Boone?

124

I stiffen my spine though it hurts me. The bandage on my back is wet. I say:

—Tell the men to carry on firing.

It is a stupid order as I know, but it is all I can say and all we can do. I drag myself over to the front gates as if my body is not mine, as if it is a stupid log I found. Ned has his eye to a gunslit at the side of the gate.

—What can you see?

He does not take his eye away, and only says:

—The same. They are shooting from everywhere.

I do not want to ask it but I do:

—Any bodies?

—No.

—Pem Rollins? I saw him fall.

—We got him in. Not dead, last I heard.

I do not want to ask Ned about Squire. I do not want to ask him anything more. I drag myself off, my gut beginning to hurt me more than my wounds, it is saying *Squire, Squire.* Another great crashing outside. From one of the rear bastions someone yells:

—Bastards have brought down another tree across the river to hide behind. Watch the north, they can see us.

I ought to climb up onto the ramparts but I cannot, my body is heavy and ruined and my heart is worse so. I see Squire when he was a boy, he is walking away, he turns his small serious face back to see me.

It is not Squire, it is his boy Moses, carrying a bowl of water from the poor well where perhaps Colonel Dick has sat on big Tice

Prock to drown him. I go as best I can to catch up with the boy, I put my arm about his shoulders and I say into his ear:

—Keep to the walls. You are a good boy to your ma.

He nods, his eyes flinch and flinch at the sounds of firing but he keeps the bowl very straight and does not spill a drop. I walk with him along the wall to his cabin next to Squire's shop. My heart beats slow.

A low groan comes as I open the door. I say:

—Jane. It is only Dan with your boy.

Jane is next to the bed in her shift. On the bed is Squire, his eyes shut and his mouth open. He looks as though he had been whittled of bone but for the soaked red cloth over his shoulder. He is still, still.

Moses sets the bowl down at his ma's side, she kisses his head without taking her eyes from Squire. She says something low to her smaller boy Isaiah, she wets a cloth, her hands wring it over the bowl.

Another groan, it is a hard raw one this time. Squire, not dead. I go to kneel next to Jane, I put my face near his. He turns his head back and forth on the mattress just as he did when he was small and laid up with summer fever and I climbed in the window to surprise him. I gave him the fever. Squire, I remember it.

—Dan.

He speaks through his teeth. I laugh again, I am so glad he is alive.

—Squire, they got you too, did they? You are still the better looking man here.

He takes a hard breath and his words come out as a sigh:

—Shot is still inside.

I pull my knife from my belt, my hand is glad for its weight. I say:

—Moses, you hold your daddy's hand now, hold it hard.

Moses comes and takes Squire's hand in both his small ones. Squire keeps his eyes shut, Jane covers Isaiah's, and with my one eye

I see my way into his wound. It is an ugly one, black with powder. The ball peers up unblinking as a fish eye out of the white bone. I cut a circle into the flesh and I wedge the blade under one side of the lead. I lift as gentle as I can, and with my finger and thumb I pull at the ball until with a creak and a suck it comes free. Squire's breath hisses. A gun cracks outside. I laugh, I cannot help laughing. I say:

—Jemima was shot also, you are in fair company. Only hers fell straight out of her breeches.

Squire's eyes waver as he opens them, he steadies them on my face and looks at me all quizzical. Jane holds the cloth to the wound, Moses's knuckles are shuddering as he keeps his hold on his daddy's hand. Isaiah is holding his nose against the smell of me. Squire wets his lips and he says:

—They are not using enough powder. Young South was shot four times outside, he has only grazes.

—Did you see Rollins?

—Shot between the bones above the elbow. All right.

—Well Squire, that is good. Good for young South and Rollins especially.

Squire gasps very sudden. Jane looks at him and at me with her white little face and tilted eyes. He rolls his head towards me:

—No. Not good. They are saving their powder. Planning a long stay.

He shuts his mouth tight. I have the ball from his shoulder in my hand. I want to ask him if he saw Black Fish outside, if he was still on the ground. But I only pinch the lead ball and I squint at it. I think of it being made in the Shawnee town, on a Shawnee fire.

14

NO ONE SLEEPS, though the night is quiet and the watch sees nothing. I see nothing though I stare myself blind. As soon as first light comes we creep out from the cabins into the centre of the fort. Shot cows and horses sprawl dead all round, we must get the meat off them before they bloat.

I am dizzy and stinking of stale piss yet, but not bleeding any longer. I work, I strip the skin from a milk cow. Well old cow, you made a long journey to this place to meet your end, not every cow can say the same. I peel the muscle away from her flank. No salt as ever. I tell the women to cook what they can. Squire stands propped in his doorway with an axe in his hand, though he looks half dead.

Hancock and his wife lead the Baptists in a prayer round the well as they are lacking a river to go to this morning. They lower their heads and put their hands together. Hancock asks God to preserve us from our enemies, he praises him for our victory yesterday and the halt to the fighting. He says:

—And we praise you O God that the enemy has not brought any cannon as we believed they might. We put our trust in you, our great Lord.

His wife Molly says:

—A miracle. Praise Him.

With my arms coated in blood and cow fat up to the pits, I say loud:

—Victory, was it? A miracle, is that what this is?

Molly cries out:

—You are free to accept God's grace and you throw it away. You cannot throw it away for all of us! We will not be thrown away with you!

As she says it a spatter of shots comes from across the river. The men in the rear bastions set to firing back. The living animals scream, the remaining corpses seem to scream too with their jaws lying open. The women snatch up the children and run again to the gunshop to hide them, the men swarm up to the ramparts with some of the women following, it is all yesterday again as though no time at all had gone by. And if God is here, He is a spy, a poker, a brainless ball of lead.

All day the shooting goes on without a stop, I am deaf with it, my tongue is dead with the taste of powder. My back and my head pain me still but I will not think of them. *Do not think.* When the sun is high, I get up to a front bastion to see if there is still an outside beyond this place. To see bodies, if there are bodies. My father, if your body is there I swear I will look at it, I will walk out of the fort into the bullets. I will crouch, I will look you in your face and tell you I am sorry, if my sorry is worth anything.

I crouch now next to David Bundrin at his gunslit. He is country Dutch like Tice Prock, the same faded hair and eyes and big bones, though of course old Tice is nowhere to be seen. Into Bundrin's ear I shout:

—Anyone dead?

He tips more powder into his gun's pan. He grins at me and points to my swelled eye. In his odd English he says:

—I hope for dead. I want that black. He is behind stumps and trees, he smiles, he smiles.

Pompey, keep yourself to yourself. I find your body is not one I wish to have to look at. I say:

—Save your powder, Bundrin. Save your shot. We do not have so very much of it, and they are not going away.

He grins again, he sets down his gun and takes off his hat. Now he props it on a stick and waves it just above the wall. Several bullets whip past it. He says:

—You see? They think more men.

—Well Bundrin. I will not contradict you.

He does not hear me, he is again taking up his gun and firing it with a great laugh.

Evening falls very quick, quicker because of the black haze hanging in the air. With it the Shawnee fire stops. I order ours to stop also. The quiet peals in my ears. The animals have gone dumb with their terror now, they huddle snuffing at each other in the big paddock we have knocked together, as if their reek is the only comfort left them in this world.

Old Dick finds me the minute I am down from the wall. Before he can start in I say:

—Colonel Callaway, we might have had peace. We had it.

—Peace will never come here until they are dead to the last man, the last infant.

—And so you thought you would bring that about, did you?

—Why do you not go over to them, Boone? All of us can see you are only waiting for a time to do it.

I keep my voice steady though I wish to pull out his eyes:

—You may call me Captain Boone. Would you like to start a mutiny as well? Now is certainly the ideal time. What do the rest of you say?

My insides twist and my wounds throb, but I hold myself still. Major Billy stands a ways off. Squire has come to his door with his axe. Little Jacky puts his head out the front of the gunshop, Ned's girl Sarah has her hands on his shoulders. At her back Martha says something to Elizabeth Callaway, who makes a sourer face than usual. Martha's eyes are on me, I know they are on me, just as everyone else's are. *What will you do now?* The old question shot at me all my life, the same arrow over and over again.

—God damn it all to Hell. Water!

Young Holder yells it from the far rear bastion. I see his narrow skull dipping below the wall then popping up again. Old Dick barks after his son-in-law:

—What is it?

Holder shouts again, I run to him as best I can, but he is already down, he is running for the front gate and screaming for water, *fucking water.* A woman comes out of her cabin with a bucket, he takes it and runs on slopping it as he goes.

—Open the gate! Get it open now!

So Holder yells, and Ned does so without asking why. I cry:

—Stop. Holder!

But Holder carries on outside, he is gone. I call down to Ned to shut the gate, keep everyone inside.

A whiff of smoke, the sharpness of scorched grass. Back to the front bastion I run, my nose has the smell in it. No one speaks, other men set to running along the ramparts to see, women get more buckets out of their houses. Once up the ladder I look down through the slit in the floor. Dirty smoke is puffing from a stack of drying flax, the flames are short ones but growing, they are too close to the wall. Who put it so close—

Below, Holder flings his bucket over the fire. It sizzles and coughs, the smoke rises in a fat grey tower, the flames fall. He turns to run back to the gate, and three shots fly from behind a felled tree some yards off. Holder dips and dances away:

—Fucking red-boys might be smart enough to set a fire, but they will never have me!

It has the sound of a child's song, he is so cheerful about it. The shots follow Holder as he flies back round the wall. The young men roar as though he were their horse in a race. Ned lets him in, and as the gate bangs the men roar louder. Below Hancock and his wife begin to thank God again, for my benefit as I know. Young Holder bellows:

—I have no time to pray, God damn it! Is the fire out?

I hear Elizabeth Callaway hiss at her son-in-law's language. On the walls someone yells it is out well enough, and some of the men begin firing into the falling dark. The smoke from the flax drifts away. Shouts fly from the Shawnee camp, I cannot make out the words. I keep myself up in the bastion and I listen. Old Dick comes to the top of the ladder and stays there. It strikes me that he would have liked the fire to catch the wall, just enough to cause a stir, just a measure more trouble, just for me.

Once night comes full, the moon is a thin blade, and we can see little from the ramparts. I tell the men to chop holes between the cabins so the women and children can pass between them and not have to hide in the gunshop all the time. I know Holder and his friends would rather set to drinking, though there is little enough to drink. Our water supply is low, the troughs are empty. Another worry to gnaw at my brains. *Do not think.*

The men get their hatchets and a few torches. Their chopping is loud and unsteady, it rings through the air as their talk does, all of it makes me uneasy. I look out a slit into the black. My neck pricks, I go stiff as the cat. I see nothing moving, but I feel movement in the soles of my feet.

Before morning has quite dawned I go to Squire. He is awake and his eyes are not so hooked with pain, though his shoulder still oozes. When I ask him about ammunition, he swings himself up from where he lies and insists we go to the shop. Holding his hurt arm close to his body, he looks into the boxes with a fat-lamp, and says the young men are too fond of shooting, we must ration our supply better. I say:

—I will tell them to choose their targets.

—Plenty of them would like to take a chief.

—Or Pompey.

—That their black man? You call him by name, Dan?

—I do. He was good to me in their town.

As I say it I know I am putting Pompey in a kindly light, too kindly. He was not always good to me, but I was not always good to him. I am struck at how easy it is to smooth out my past when I wish to. Squire says:

—Is that so. More of your Indian family. Perhaps he is the one who shot me, out of jealousy that I call myself your brother.

—He might have shot Ned also then.

Squire smiles small in the flicker of the torch and I smile also. Ned's name is still like a chip of bone caught at the top of my throat. The sky is lightening, and the goddamned firing starts up again sharp. I go out and yell to the men on the ramparts:

—Hold fire. Hold it!

They do so for a time, though they look at me like wolves disturbed over a deer they have brought down, and I am not fond of thinking about wolves. But it is not long before they are again shooting at anything that moves, anything at all, though there is nothing to see but the twitch of shadows on the edges of the trees. These might be true wolves for all I can say. The wolves that dug at my Jamesie's grave, come back again to see us sink.

Do not think. I walk the whole of the rampart. The Shawnee camp is quiet, there is hardly any firing from them at all. Perhaps they have run out of powder before we have, perhaps we are safe as long as the fort stands. I walk the walls, all sides, and still there are no shots. I go to a rear bastion to look over the river, and as I step to the gunslit I crouch. Before I can look out I feel it, the odd movement again. At this time I think it is my feet themselves reminding me of their many old pains. I am still, I spread my toes in my moccasins. I wait. Again it comes, a small quaking, very small. I shut my eyes to feel it better, I put my shoulder to the wall. The quaking rolls through my body, like my wife turning next to me on the pallet in sleep. Rebecca, I think of you even now, do not forget it.

Young Holder on the rear rampart shouts very sudden:

—Shit!

—What is it?

—Look.

I go to him, I do look. The river water is always clear, even when the level is low, and now it is mud just opposite the fort, a great brown fan of it.

—Shit, Captain, what is it?

Holder leans out over the wall to see better. I pull him down, expecting a shot at his narrow head, but there is none. He yells out:

—What are you doing, you Indian fuckers and your British fucking friends?

—Get down, Holder, before they kill you. You have used up at least two of your lives in the last day.

A call comes to us from the river:

—Come out and see.

It is Pompey's voice, it is his blue headscarf I see appearing just above the bank on this side. Before I can stop him Holder swings up his gun and fires, Pompey ducks, and we hear him laugh and begin one of his meandering Shawnee songs. As I push Holder down again, he cackles and yells:

—You are a fucker too, you black shit.

He sets to singing loud through the gunslit: *My bonny black hare.* Below us others join in, it is just as though they had been waiting to do it. I hear Neddy's sweet voice above the rest:

His gun he reloaded and fired once more
She cried, Draw your trigger and never give over
Your powder and balls are so sweet I declare
Keep shooting away at my bonny black hare.

His voice is always level and joyful, even singing such words, even here. The beauty of it scrapes at my ears in this terrible place. I give Holder's back a shove:

—Stop your noise. Save your own powder. Listen.

In a moment he stops and the rest trail off. In the little silence there is no firing, no singing of birds, no talk. The movement shudders beneath my feet again, the river swamped with mud. Neddy goes on humming soft at the gate. *Mm mm, mm mm, mm mm.*

⌣

As night nears again, the women take their buckets to the cattle penned at the fort centre, who have had no water today, and their milk has slowed. I watch Jemima, her face laid against the cow's side, she looks to be asleep. We are all so tired but sleep does not come here, how can it?

In the later dark I see torches dipping and swelling on the riverbank, though I feel no more shaking. The campfires ripple low in the Shawnee camp also. The wind is light, the narrow moon hangs plain. The watch calls now and then, *All clear.*

I go to look in on Jane, who has her children in the bed with her, she tries to keep them all in her arms. Little lights quiver in their eyes from the rushlight on the floor. Squire has gone out to take his place at his porthole though he cannot lift his arm.

—All right, Jane?

She nods and shifts herself, her face passing out of the light's circle. She says in her soft way:

—Quiet tonight. Have you finished?

I sink down inside. I manage to say:

—We have not finished. But it is quiet.

I touch the boys' hair, and I say low:

—All of you try to sleep, be good for your ma. Have you had something to eat?

Jane breathes in to speak, but she stops. A smell drifts in, sure as an animal finding its den. We all know what it is. Powder, the black scent of it igniting. Jane does not close her mouth, she does not breathe. I say:

—Stay inside.

Out the door, the smell is bitter and everywhere, the wind pushing it hard at us now. I run to the gate where Ned is at a gunslit, I ask:

—What is it? I have heard no firing.

—No, no firing Dan.

—What are they doing?

But as I say it I know what they are doing. Ned turns to me and before I can speak there is a great raw screaming like something being torn to pieces, and the night with it.

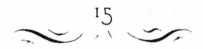

15

FROM THE RAMPARTS comes a wild babble, a wild cry. A cabin roof is on fire. Shrieks rear up outside the walls, growing louder.

The smell makes itself at home inside my skull, which is shrinking down to nothing. Burning pitch and powder. They have rubbed hickory branches with this mixture and are throwing them at the roofs. Flames catch the shingles of Jemima's cabin and jump at the dark. Another torch is flung, another roof sparks and blazes up.

Elizabeth Callaway comes out yelling and runs back in again, now she is out with Kezia hiding under her arm and the other women and children pouring after them. In the burning light I see Jemima with a broom, smacking the roof and sweeping the bright torch down from it. She steps back and lifts the sides of her breeches as if they were her skirts, watching the torch burn out on the ground. More girls run for brooms, they swing them all frantic as torches fly onto other roofs or straight into the walls.

I haul myself up to the rampart to see more warriors bolting straight for the walls. They run howling in twos as though trying to beat one another to a prize, their lit branches sparking and spitting above their heads. Firing blasts out of the Shawnee camp and from behind the felled trees, and begins to fly from over the river. I crouch, I yell *Get down*, but I do not know if anyone hears.

Holder crawls along and finds me. His face is like a candle, thin and bright with fire and joy, he salutes and bawls in my ear:

—Can we shoot these bastards now?

My gut gives a lurch but I say:

—Yes.

Before the word leaves my mouth he is taking aim and laughing. He fires, then he yells:

—Fuckers are making it easy. No sport at all.

I raise my gun. The Shawnee Holder has shot is flat on his face, his torch lies burning across his arm. More run past him and I shoot into the air. The rest along the ramparts fire straight at the runners. I see some stumbling and falling, I see more who do not get up again. I can hardly bear to watch. One goes down, his torch catches his lock of hair, and it flares up bright. Names scramble together in my mind: Captain Will, Moluntha, Black Fish, Father—

I do not let myself blink though my eyes are parched with the cloud of powder and smoke we are all of us caught in.

—Dan!

Squire is below with his unhurt arm full of gun barrels. The light round him is bright as day. Another roof is blazing, the torch jammed between shingles, the women are batting at it as if they are trying to kill a bird that got into the house. I go down and yell close to his head:

—What are you doing?

—Help me give these out to the children, quick now.

—What?

He drops all the barrels but for one which he tucks in to his body, with his good hand he pumps a rough rod like a piston at the end of it. Water shoots me in the neck, the cool wet is startling. Squire, calm enough to invent machinery while his house burns.

Without thinking I clap him on his hurt shoulder and he flinches, but he gives me the water shooters. I hand these to any children I see, I show them how to make rain on the burning roofs and the torches that lie fallen, and how to fill the guns up again at the well-hole. The last I have I give to Squire's littlest boy Isaiah, who I find shadowing me. He speaks, but the guns and howling are too loud. The burning light shows all his freckles. I kneel and I pull him straight to me:

—See what the others are doing. Shoot your water at the fires.

His breath is hot in my ear:

—I can see everything all over the ground. I found this.

He holds up a pin before my eye. Hancock rushes by, praying at the top of his voice, *God and all Heaven's angels be with us.*

Isaiah says:

—Is it Heaven now?

—You know better Isaiah, you are smarter than that!

I give his shoulders a shake, I am sorry for it. He does know better, he is a big enough boy, but his face is so bewildered and sleepless. I hug him to me and I say:

—It is not Heaven.

I do not scream out all the times I have believed myself to be in Heaven in this place, in Kentucky, all the times I have been cast out of it again into this.

⌣

They had more powder than we believed. They were only waiting to use it. The shooting keeps up, they howl their war cries on and on, the pairs of them keep coming with burning branches. We are running out of bullets now, the children screaming endlessly, we all have run out of words.

The sky is light as day still though day is far off, perhaps it will never come again. I hand what shot we have got up to the ramparts. Old Dick calls down from his bastion, but I do not know what he says and I do not care to know. Another great crackle of shots comes from over the river, and he turns back to his post, ramming his gun.

Isaiah has kept near me, he ducks in and out beneath the ladder. Now his brother Moses comes and jabs at my arm, pointing to the paddock where a torch has landed at the base of a post and is flaring high. The animals have herded themselves backward, they will crush themselves against the wall. I yell:

—Put it out!

Squire's boys run quick for the pen, they have been waiting to be told what to do. Everyone is waiting to be told. They pump water over the flames with their shooters, and I am up the ladder to look out, the blood from my wounds seeping down my back again.

Smoke is pouring up into the night outside, fire leaps all jagged beneath it. A small paddock fence outside our rear wall is blazing, the wind pushing the flames towards us. The warriors who set it on fire are fleeing, their voices spiking the dark. I jump down and run for the gunshop:

—Squire—shovels!

The cows are all bellowing now, which sets the dogs and littlest children crying louder. Squire has two shovels ready, we go to John South's cabin at the base of the corner bastion nearest the paddock fire and set to digging under its wall. South's old wife totters on her heels next to the bed with a lamp, she is weeping:

—Do not let them in, do not let them.

There is no answer to this, I do not answer. I yell hard as I can and more men come, London is the first, with Jacky riding his hip. London pushes the boy into the corner with Mrs. South and takes up a shovel. Quicker than Squire or me with our weaknesses, he opens a hole below the lowest log in the wall in a moment and pushes his great cloud of hair out through it. I lean down near him and I say:

—Get the fence put out, Squire will get another water gun.

Squire is partway out the door when London pulls himself back again. He sits up quick and says low through his teeth:

—Get me a real gun. One of the Indians is just outside this wall.

We are all silent now, even the shooting jolts to a stop for a moment. Mrs. South's lamp sputters. I pass London my gun:

—Steady.

His deep black skin and eyes shine in the quaver of the light, he whispers:

—They will never see me. Or you, will they Jacky?

A short smile for Jacky who has hidden himself against Mrs. South, and London is sliding his body out the hole. Crouched there, I hear the lock of my gun snap. No bang. I say:

—London, London, do you need more powder?

He reaches back through the hole to me, his hand is open, I put a measure of powder in it. There is a sudden crack just outside the wall and London's arm falls, his legs give a great backward jerk, his fingers curl and uncurl and stop.

⌣

I am out of the cabin, Jacky's high wail behind me like a kite. I cannot get away from it though I walk the whole inside of the fort. The air is darkening. All I see behind my eyelids is London's legs bending all contrary from his spine.

Martha is with Ned next to the animal pen, where the beasts have quieted, perhaps at his presence. She is in his old coat, giving him a cup of water. She says:

—Daniel? What is it?

To her I say very rough:

—Get back inside. Look after your children.

—What is it?

I do not answer, I only give Ned a shove and I say:

—Go back to your watch. The shooting may have stopped but they have not finished.

Ned looks at me half a moment, then takes his light back to the gate. Martha melts herself into the dark of the fort again with a flash of her great eyes. I go up to walk the ramparts. At a half crouch my wounded back hurts me more and I stand to stretch it. As I do so a shot sings past my head, and the stillness cracks open like an egg. Holder and the rest set to shouting straight away: *You cowards. You bastards. You goddamned spiders, you sons of bitches.*

Your sister is a whore. In the firing I hear it, I have heard it since I was a boy. And *Your daughter is a whore*, I hear this now also. They are not shooting at us now, only these words creep in on the wind in low Shawnee voices that do not know just what they say, though they understand it well enough.

—Your daughter is a whore.

Just below me I hear it now, I do hear it, I know the voice, the dark high amusement of it. I go down the ladder, and through a split in the logs I say:

—Pompey.

My mouth is pressed to the wall, splinters pierce my lips but I press harder:

—Pompey!

No answer, only a low whistle. Two of the dogs inside bark, though they have done so much of it they can hardly make a noise. I hear him whistle again, I know his whistling and his breath, in my mind is his face and his smile. Still there is no firing, only urgent talk in the cabins. I try again to call to him:

—Something to say to me?

—A few things, Sheltowee.

—Not the first time you people have told me I have a family of whores.

He laughs in his high fashion:

—We people? Your own people say the same, have you forgot your white brothers at Old Chillicothe? Have you forgot everything?

I see the men's faces, all of them in a line, all dismal and hating, waiting for me to do something. I say:

142

—Are they at Old Chillicothe still, or have you killed the rest?

—You are the one with the taste for killing. You have only to ask Chief Moluntha, or your father. Or look out here and you will see.

Pompey is in the roots of my teeth and the roots of my hair. I know all the deaths he is speaking of. Have I not seen bodies of every sort, white and Shawnee, flung about the ground, have I not seen them every minute of my life since Chillicothe? I say:

—Damn you, Pompey, Moluntha killed two of my men at the Paint Creek town, I know it! You have this minute murdered one of your own people, a good black man is dead—

—I am a Shawnee.

He says it in Shawnee, so calm it boils up my blood:

—You are nothing, I do not know what you are.

—And what are you?

I strike the wall with my palm and I cry:

—I ought to have bought you myself! Would that have served you better?

He pauses a moment before he answers in his cool fashion:

—With what money, Sheltowee? They did give you some at Detroit, did they not? Silver coins. Good British money.

He is right, I could have bought him, he could have been free, or at any rate mine.

—Is it that black of theirs?

Holder has appeared next to me. He yells:

—You can shut your mouth before I shoot you a new hole through your goddamned face.

With another laugh, Pompey says:

—Then I will be able to fill it with more of your food.

Holder gives a squawk, a shot cracks quick from a front bastion, where the big Dutchman David Bundrin is hollering. He stands upright and his fair hair glows in the smoke of his firing. Another bang, this one from outside, and he goes down.

Holder is before me, up the ladder and crawling along the rampart, we reach the bastion with our heads still on. I say:

—Bundrin.

Holder breathes out:

—Fuck.

Bundrin is slouched crooked into the corner with his hands to his face. I say:

—Get the light, get it close.

Holder goes for the small rushlight on the floor, he holds it to Bundrin who shrinks back. I say:

—Bundrin, let us see you.

His cupped hands fall only slightly as though he were afraid of dropping something. When I pull them down I see they are dark with powder stains and wet with blood. His eyes are near white in the bright of the flame, they look at me blinking and blinking. His forehead is a black bleeding hole, his whole head slumps forward and I catch it between my palms. I say:

—Get the light closer, Holder.

Holder's narrow face pokes in above the rushlight:

—Huh. Not dead.

—No.

I move Bundrin's head as gentle as I can so I can see the back of it, but there is no wound there. The ball is in his brains, there is no getting at it. His neck is like a poor broken stem, his hurt head wobbles on it. Very stupid I say:

—Bundrin. David. You are all right now.

I say it as if we had been at a tavern all evening and he had fallen in the gutter on our way home. Holder has his hand to his own forehead, as if this will help anything. Bundrin manages to lift his hands back to his face and he rocks and rocks on the base of his spine. Then he slumps forward onto his knees and elbows and goes on rocking. Holder caws all strangled:

—God damn.

He takes up his gun and runs off along the rampart towards his own position, and in a moment he is shooting and so are the rest. I yell:

—Hold your fire. No shots!

They do not hear me, I cannot make them hear. More firing comes from outside, the sky shines as if the whole fort were a torch we had lit to stare at ourselves with. I go down to find Jemima or some other woman to sit with Bundrin. When I see my girl, she is marching about with her broom, watching the cabin roofs for sparks. I think of telling her to take the broom up with her into Bundrin's bastion and strike him hard with it until he is dead.

She goes to find his wife and I keep away, I make myself watch the burning.

16

TWO TO BURY. We do it before the sun is visible, within the walls. The animals huff and bawl their hunger and the women all stand dry-eyed in the rushlights. The children are told to keep indoors though they peep out the windows, chewing on the corncobs they have been given to keep them quiet. My girl stands with Bundrin's wife as we dig the graves. The wife could be a sister to her lost husband, she is as fair all over and with as big a head.

We have no cloth to spare for wrapping Bundrin or for poor London. Instead we dig very hard to make big graves, they are over-big, I would go on digging all my life though my back pains me and weeps bloody water. London, if you had never come back from riding to get more men at Logan's. If you had ridden off somewhere else and tried to be free, though where could you have gone?

It is Pompey's dream I know, caught in my mind now as though he were camped out in it himself.

Looking into her husband's grave Bundrin's wife thanks God over and over that the bullet did not hit him in the eye. With her hand round the woman's shoulders, Jemima looks at me, her own black eyes as big as if she has taken a poison. The madness here is like a slow fever taking everyone.

Uncle Monk and the other black men swing London's big body into the grave. Jacky has come out with Ned's Sarah and stands watching. Seeing him I am slapped by a thought of Eliza's face, my Shawnee wife's girl in Chillicothe, she is my girl also. It is the same private face all orphans have when they think they are not seen. Eliza. Have they shunned you because of me, have they sent you away into the wilderness with your ma?

Do not think.

Jacky watches close as London goes into the ground. Monk's wife has put her kerchief round the dead man's neck to hide the bullet holes. Bundrin's big wife did the same with her husband's head. She sets to thanking God again now as we cover him with dirt.

⌣

The quiet is full of tension, though everyone but the watch has gone back to their cabins and it is early yet. I go indoors, and I feel her there in the shadow before I see her. Martha in my cabin in Ned's greatcoat, his shirt beneath it and her legs bare above the shredded stockings falling down to her calves. Ned's hat, her hair under it coming loose from its plait. She is quite aware that it is loose as I can see, she moves her head very unconcerned. She says:

—I brought you bread, Daniel. Captain.

There is only the smallest heel of it in her hand but she wants to give me something, she thinks this is the way to do it. *Captain.* She shifts her knees so the coat parts. Her face is very nervous, more nervous than her body is, it says *You have no wife here, you have no wife.*

—Martha.

She holds out the bread, which I take in a stupid fashion. She sees my arm does not move right with the pain in my back, and she says:

—You are tired.

—I am.

She takes off the hat and tugs a strand of hair free, which sits in a black loop on her shoulder. She does not take her eyes off me. Very soft, she says:

—I know you are.

The loop of her hair. I think of other black hair. Rebecca's and Methoataske's. I am tired to death, she is not wrong. She parts the coat farther and I cannot help looking at her knees and her thighs, and the rest of her. My want cannot help coming back to life, though I do not know just what it is I want.

Then she says:

—Please.

And here is something I can do. It is something. I will not take her on the bed where you have slept Rebecca, do you hear it? I keep her standing at the wall. I want to turn her round and put her back to me, but she will not turn. She closes her eyes but I do not. I am hard on her, I tear the shirt hem as I shove it up, I am rough on her hips and between her legs with my hands. Her thighs are about me, she locks her heels tight and I brace my spine to hold her up. Her hand catches the wound in the back of my head and flies off again. She has wanted and wanted this and it makes me sick to think of it. I press her thin breasts hard with one hand. But I cannot carry on.

For a moment my legs tremble, I wilt against her as if I will never get myself right, then I am straight again and I set her on her feet. I turn as I set my breechcloth back in place, I do not wish to see her open legs or her questioning face. After a moment she says low:

—Daniel.

I do not answer. Again she says my name:

—Daniel.

—What is it?

She plucks at my shoulders very gentle as if I were some musical thing she could play. She says:

—It is natural to want—even at such a time.

—Is it.

Touching my cheek and trying to stare me in the eye, she says:

—Perhaps this is not the best time.

I pull my head away, I am about to leave her when she speaks up louder:

—She loves you. Rebecca does.

A bomb bursts in my chest. I say:

—I will thank you not to speak of my wife to me.

—Daniel. She will not have stopped loving you.

—And you know everything your sister thinks, is that right? You always have? What is she thinking this minute, what is she doing in Carolina, has she found someone there to do what I just did to you?

—Danny.

Her voice is so like Rebecca's that I want to squeeze her throat. I take the hard bread from the table and cram it into my mouth as I go for the door. Her fingers catch at my arm, and she says:

—Neddy is sorry for what he did. He is sorry.

I spit the wad of bread onto the floor, I turn and seize her shoulders with their narrow bones:

—Is that right.

Her mouth shifts as if it is trying to fashion the right words:

—He is. You could ask him yourself.

—Is this your repayment to him for what he did with Rebecca? Is that what you are doing here, again? Are you going to tell her all about it someday?

I give her a shake, I cannot help myself, old anger like half-melted lead slugs its way through me. Her head bobs, her eyes stay hooked on mine, she says nothing. She will say nothing to Rebecca or to my brother, she has too much pleasure in keeping her knowledge secret and acting prim as a blossom. I squeeze her arms and I say close to her face:

—Well. Our darling Neddy has always had good luck, he is

lucky to have found God to forgive him. The two of you might pray on it together, pray for me. Chew on my bones and my daughter Jemima's too.

At this Jemima opens the door as though her name has summoned her. Her eyes are still over-big, and I see them swallow me and Martha locked together in anger, Martha's torn shirt and bare thighs. My girl spins and goes straight out again, we never speak of it in all my life. Jemima, another thing I am sorry for.

⌣

Outside the day comes white. I go to check the ammunition stores, and I take a handful of the scant shot for myself. Ned is over at the gate, and I do not speak to him. I go up one of the rear ramparts. Major Billy is here staring out towards the river. Holder is with him, though he will not go into the bastion where Bundrin's brains leaked out until he was dead. He paces about like an unhappy dog on a rope, saying:

—I need a woman. I need a woman.

Can he smell Martha on me? Can everyone? Holder tugs his hat from his unhappy narrow head. I say:

—Go and find your wife then.

—She will not have me while we are so goddamned unsafe here. Shit. Shit.

He pushes his gun out the slit, he will fire at anything as he thinks of being denied by Fanny, Colonel Dick's pretty girl. I say:

—She is right not to have you. We need no more children here.

My stomach jumps thinking of what sort of child I could have started in Martha if I had given her what she wanted. Something twisted and misshapen, all helpless and dreadful to look at. Holder turns with more to complain of, but before he can speak Major Billy says:

—Captain, here.

His voice is cold, he points over the river where the sweep of mud in the water has spread. The tremble is back now, in an instant I feel it, and my toes curl into my moccasins. It is stronger than before. Holder says:

—What in Hell is it? Is the Virginia army so heavy on its feet? Do they have that much to eat? I should have stayed.

It is not the Virginia reinforcements. I know just what it is. But Holder yells with all his power:

—What are you doing now, you snaky painted bastards?

A young man appears just above the bank. Kaskee. His shaved head and long lock startle me again as they did near the Paint Creek town. He roars in Shawnee, in his man's voice, before he vanishes again. Holder swivels:

—What did the fucker say?

Now Pompey's voice rises from the river:

—Did you understand? Kaskee informs you we are digging a long hole to blow you all to Hell before morning.

Holder sees now what they are about. He yells:

—Dig on, we will dig and meet you with a hole big enough to bury five hundred of you sons of bitches!

Major Billy says:

—It is the British who have put them up to digging a tunnel, they may have brought the parts to reinforce it, and the explosives. Listen.

Below the thumps and shaking are a few shouted words. A red jacket is set on a stump above the riverbank. I think of a cannon being shoved through a tunnel, its great black mouth finding its blind way into the fort. Holder cries out:

—You never burned us out and you will not blow us out of here either.

In slow English a Shawnee voice sings:

—Your wife came out last night.

Another says:

—I love your wife in her hole.

In an instant Holder is purple in the face. He fires but no one is to be seen, they only laugh. As he curses and loads again I say:

—Do not waste any more of your shot on them, Holder.   151

—Then what are you going to do to keep my wife's name out of their fucking mouths? What are you going to do?

Holder's eyes are wet gashes in his face, he is angrier than I have ever seen him. Does he think I do not know about my own wife being called a whore, my own daughters, my sister? Holder tips too much powder into his gun pan, I do not stop him, I go along the rampart and down the far ladder. On the ground I roar:

—Get your shovels and dig. Make a trench along the back wall here. Do it now.

Squire's boy Moses says:

—Who is dead now?

His face is all alarm, his voice carries. Old Dick in his bastion hears everything as he always does, and comes down to ask why I want them to dig. I tell him he is not to ask me. As I go for a shovel he barks:

—I have every right to know what you are having us do.

Everyone is still and silent, they are watching us. I keep walking. Dick calls:

—I will not dig.

At this I turn and I say:

—Then go up and defend your daughter Fanny's honour. That will be useful to her when she is blown to pieces with the rest of us.

⌣

I did not mean to say it, I meant to keep everyone from panic, but they have long been tight as traps. Two of the girls are at once in

tears, their mas hold them and begin to cry also. Jemima darts back
into her house before I can speak to her. Squire says loud:

—Dan is right. They are digging in from the riverbank. We can
dig to meet them and collapse their tunnel before they can blow up
anything.

Some of the people listen to him and go for shovels, and I am
glad for it. Hancock and his wife Molly find one another and set to
praying at the tops of their voices. Others go slow as sleepwalkers
to where they stand with faces turned up like bowls meant to catch
rain. Ned steps along from his place at the gate. Martha comes out
her door with the coat wrapped tight about her, very quick she
bows her head.

I go to the wall near the new graves where some shovels were
left, I take one and set to work digging hard. Squire follows and
does his best with his one good arm. With the others we soon
enough have a trench lined out along the rear wall. We all dig at it
very fierce. The shovels cut and scrape, they hide the noise of the
Shawnee digging outside. A fat blister bubbles on my palm but I dig
on and on. Squire beside me does his best, but when he slows, I say
low to him:

—You do not have to do this.

—You do not have to do it either, Dan.

—It is something to do.

—It is that.

Gently I touch his bad shoulder:

—Go up and tell the riflemen to be very careful with their
shot, Holder especially. We have so little. And you and I are not
much good in our state.

Squire nods. He turns to go, but as he does it he picks up a stone
we have dug up, and with his unhurt arm he hurls it in a long sweep
over the wall towards the river. A howl goes up outside. Squire
smiles very fleeting and limps to the ladder.

We have plenty of stones, we have more than enough! We send them flying from our side. I throw a few myself, I will say their weight is very satisfying to let loose. We hear the Indians and the British army swearing and shouting, and I go up the rampart again to look. Kaskee's strange grown voice yells in Shawnee that we ought to come out and fight like men, not children.

Holder is watching close. When I tell him what is said, he shouts back:

—Come out and I will shoot you like a goddamned man! Through your goddamned balls, if you have any!

Pompey's call comes now in English:

—We have plenty, are you in need of some?

Holder looks set to burst and shouts every threat he can think of. Some of the other young men along the walls begin shouting also though no one has fired yet, a relief. Then a dark face rises above the riverbank and very quick Holder shoots at it. But it does not go down, it waggles and bounces with a hole through its forehead. We both think at once of Bundrin, and Holder screams raw:

—You can die now, you black shit-licking pig!

It is no pig, it is a wooden face, a rough mask on a stick with punched-out eyes and mouth, and the Shawnee laugh as they puppet it up and down. False men everywhere. I grip Holder's arm hard:

—Do not shoot again. They will see just where you are and fire back.

—Then give me some of those goddamned rocks, I will bash out all their brains.

Pompey begins singing one of his loose Shawnee songs, I can hear his delight. More stones come flying past us on their way to the riverbank. The singing stops, the sounds of their digging come louder. Below in the fort, I hear a woman all tears:

—Do not throw any more stones, for God's sake. They will make the Indians angry.

It is old Mrs. South who says it, shaking as she was in her cabin when London was killed. A great hollering laugh bursts from the men digging, they throw more and more stones over and say in high womanish voices, *Do not throw stones!*

Mrs. South has her apron on over the breeches she wears. She throws it up over her face and walks about this way, she near falls into the trench and one of the men plucks her back. Now she trips over a rock and sits crying on the ground and will not let anyone pick her up again. All afternoon the yelling goes on. *Do not throw stones. Come out and let us look at you. Or is there nothing to look at, are you all women with no pricks?*

So they know we have put our women in men's clothes. They know everything. Their digging continues, the stones continue flying, a few shots crack from both sides, but not so very many. How much powder and shot have they got? I know so little now. Black Fish, my father, your face moves into my mind again but you have nothing to say to me, I have not once seen you since the treaty that fell into these dreadful pieces. Are you in a tent at the camp telling your warriors what to do, are you smoking in your calm fashion, are you telling them to find me?

I go back to digging. We have our trench long and deep by evening. It may be no help if they manage to tunnel in past the wall, but it has kept the men busy and made us richer still in stones. Squire sits handing them out, he sorts them by size first, he is precise as ever.

I am telling the men they can stop for tonight when a huge shout comes from a bastion. Colonel Dick is leaning out over the wall. I call:

—Colonel, get down, you will get yourself killed.

He shouts:

—One of them is showing his arse over by the trees, slapping it at us! By God, I will kill him!

Johnny Gass next to him is crouched below the wall trying to hide his chuckling. Calm as I can, I say:

—Colonel, get below the wall.

But Old Dick has all his powder measures out, he is tipping them all into his gun, he spills one over his feet. Major Billy is near me now, calling:

—Dick, Dick, he is out of range.

I say:

—You will waste all your powder when we have none to waste, he is only being a stupid child, do not shoot.

—Show him your own arse!

This from Holder across the way, and the call is taken up by the young men round the trench: *Show him your arse.* Some of them drop their breechcloths and get up the ladder half naked.

A yell comes from outside in Shawnee: *Weethennie. Kitochquelita.* Eat it. You love it. Kaskee's voice, I know it again. I say:

—Do not shoot, Dick.

But Old Dick has ruffled himself up like a great turkey cock, he has been waiting for this outrage every minute since the Shawnee came. An enormous bang tears up the twilight. Dick staggers back with the kick of all the powder but he keeps himself upright and looks very satisfied. So do his wife and his Kezia down outside their door, though they hold their ears covered for some time. My own ears ring. Holder is yelling:

—Did you get him?

—He is down.

This from Old Dick all calm, as if he has just finished a great dinner and has wiped his mouth. I do not believe him, I do not wish to believe him. Kaskee's young pimpled face, the sulking look of him dragging after me when I was prisoner. I say:

—Can you see him?

Dick does not answer, he only yells at the trees:

—That is what you deserve. For my nephew, you red bastards. James Callaway was his name!

Turning to me with wet shining in his eyes, he says:

—That should make you remember his name too.

James Callaway longed to see me dead, now his uncle stares me down, full of his own longing. Well. If enough people wish it so, perhaps it will come about.

~

There is no way for me to go out and look for the body. Their digging continues into the night, they have torches lit at the riverbank to see by, and they do not come to hurl them at us now. A few burning arrows fly at our roofs from the camp in the meadow, but these are nothing. The women sing to the children in the cabins to block the noise, a mess of different songs bubbles up in a stew. Ned joins in at his post, he picks out what Martha is singing to their girls: *Sleep sleep sleep.*

We are all stupid with tiredness and hunger and fear, so stupid some of the men drop and curl up like pups. Some are flat out on the ramparts. Going past the cabin windows I see women with their mouths open as if they cannot stop their alarm even in sleep.

I go to my cabin and I lay down also. I drop into a surprising blackness I have not known for days. I dream hard but I see nothing, I have only the sweet tobacco smell of Black Fish's house in my brains. And when I wake before it is light I find my own mouth dry and trying to make an *F* sound, for *Father*. But he is not there, no one is there, only the heavy silent waiting that has sat over us all like a cat in a tree since we arrived so long ago and I said *This will be the place, this—*

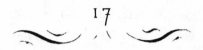

17

WE SET UP a watch at our trench in case they come through it, but they never do. They go on digging and taunting. I listen above their noise for bird calls, if there are still birds.

Two days more it goes on like this. The night following, I sleep a few hours, and I try to dream of my father in case there is some way he can speak to me in my sleep. But I only see others I do not wish to see now, and I wake with my hands balled up and my jaws tight. I think of surrender, or of trying again for a treaty. Perhaps it is not mad to think of it—the Shawnee have kept themselves to themselves but for the ongoing digging of their tunnel. Perhaps they have run out of food and shot, perhaps they are tired of the fighting also, after near a week of it.

I get up and go out into the dark, though it is not yet my turn on watch. I take no light, I go along feeling the walls, the moon is patched over with clouds. I catch the end of my gun on Ned's side as I go past the gate.

—All clear, Dan.

His voice is calm as always. I carry on with my round of the fort. As I go past the well a single burning arrow flies into the ground close by. It has a scrap of cloth wrapped round it and smells of pitch but not powder. At this time it seems to me a good sign. I watch it for a moment before I stamp out the flame.

A murmur comes from over by the river, where they have their diggings. I look out a slit in the rear wall, but I can see nothing there, no torches or campfire. Until a light strikes me in the face from the other side and makes me blind. I get my gun up and shield my eyes.

—Sheltowee.

For an instant I think it is my father come for me, and my heart flies up. Poor heart, it is only Pompey. He keeps the light straight in my face so I cannot see him, but it is his voice and his clove smell. He says quiet:

—I have come with a message.

—Ready for peace?

A brief chuckle. I look for his outlines, I see only the light. He says:

—Is that what you think?

—I do not know. Why do you not tell me what I think, as you always do?

—Who is it, sir?

Old Monk is at my shoulder, smelling of sulphur and cowshit. He has been trying to brew up more powder but it takes such a time, there will never be enough of it in all this world, though this world seems to have shrunk down considerably. I tell him it is all right. A child's wailing starts up, then another, and the old man turns. I say:

—Go to your little Jerry, Uncle Monk. Get some sleep.

Off Monk goes, the smell stays behind him on the air. Perhaps it will give Pompey an idea that we have more powder than we do. It is all a show here, we are all playing.

—You never called me Uncle. Not once, Sheltowee. You ought to start.

—I thought you wished us to be brothers, Uncle Pompey. You

be Abel, I will be Cain then. Do you still wish to run off with me?

His light dips lower and for a moment I can see the hard line of his forehead and nose and chin, black on the black of the night, we are just as we were in Old Chillicothe, him speaking to me through the wall of the prison house. We have gone nowhere at all, we are trapped as ever. He says very sharp:

—Your way and Black Fish's way is to say we are all brothers and must live together. It is not possible, do you not see it? I do not know how you cannot.

—It is possible.

I speak as sharp as he does, I hiss at the porthole:

—Tell Black Fish to come with a peace flag, I will make sure he is safe, we will talk again.

My throat is taut with want. So much do I wish for this, I can near see the shape of Black Fish walking from the camp under a white flag out of the dark towards me. But Pompey is furious now:

—My brother died of a whipping in Virginia. I buried my money in his grave to keep it safe. That is all the good brotherhood has ever done me.

—You told me that, Pompey. In Chillicothe.

—Then you know it.

He clicks his teeth. I say:

—Tell Black Fish I am willing. Please.

—And are the rest of your people willing? Or are you planning to leave them here again? *What will you do now?* Pompey does not say it, but he is thinking it. He gives another of his laughs and he calls very sudden and loud:

—Daniel Boone, your true wife expects you home to Chillicothe very soon.

—God damn you, that is not for here.

—Have they heard of it then?

—Pompey.

Again he lifts his voice:

—The Shawnee wife of Sheltowee awaits him at his home with their child.

It moves across the silence like river ice cracking, crazed and loud. I speak through my teeth:

—Pompey. Is she all right, my wife? And the girl?

—Why do you ask?

—Why do you think I ask? I think of her—

His voice goes smooth as a fur:

—What makes you think they have not married her to someone else?

I choke a laugh:

—What, to you?

—I do not need your leavings.

—Ha—you think my wife would have you?

But he is gone with the light, I am left spitting my empty words into the empty air. I pivot to walk back round the fort and I crack into a body. Ned. He has his little rushlight held up now, his face all shadows and hollows. He pushes back his hat, he says soft:

—Dan. Heard your voice. Who are you talking to?

—No one.

—Dan—

—Get back to your post.

I walk on quick, the horses startle as I pass their pen, they stamp and blow. I walk round and round all night until I see in the dark, I see the edges of the buildings and the animals, I see everything that is there and I wish for things that are not.

At first light I go up to the bastion facing the camp. All night my heart has chewed on its hope that my father will come, that we will have peace. And on my other hope, that no one here has understood Pompey. I stare out at the camp, the smoke of their fires curls up slow and vanishes against the cloudy dawn. Nothing comes, no one walks forward, only the smoke keeps up its curling path towards the fort. Below, the cattle set to moaning their misery again. I go down to see what we can spare them. I tell a pack of the young girls to get a few cobs from the cabin lofts to give to the animals, two apiece. Ned's happy girl Sarah trots off in the lead.

A shot comes shrieking past her yellow head. She freezes with one foot up as if about to tumble into icy water. I call:

—Sarah. Get inside, get the rest.

They all run for the gunshop, some of the mothers run out crying all tired and helpless, which sets the children crying also. Sarah screams:

—My Jacky!

—He is with Uncle Monk, he is safe. Now go.

But she screams for Jacky all the way to Squire's shop, and Martha stares at me with her eyes lightening from their usual black. I know she is thinking of me with a wife, another wife, an Indian wife waiting for me. I do not wish to be imagined.

I yell for the men to get to their positions, for some to stay at the trench we have dug ready to fire or bash the Shawnee heads in with shovels if they come through with their tunnel. Once they are in their places there is terrible silence for one minute, two. And now shots come from outside in a great stuttering volley. They have bullets and powder yet, so much the air burns black. I run along under the ramparts, I yell once more to the riflemen above to save their shot until they see someone to shoot. Holder calls out that the bastards are closer with their diggings, he fires towards the near side of the river.

I run towards his corner and I am falling, I am on my face in the dirt with a bullet hole in the back of my shoulder. My skin burns as though it has been stung, as though hornets are creeping into the wound. I lie and watch my blood puddle round my shoulder and neck, a small river of it trickles along the ground towards my chin. It smells of old metal, old tools.

—Get up.

Jemima tugs my arm and pain bellows all through me. I get up and run at a ducking limp behind her. In her cabin, she tears my shirt from my shoulder and looks at the shot above the axe wound I took when this began. She plucks the shot out of my flesh and bandages me up without a word.

As she stands to go, she says very stiff:

—It is not a bad wound. But you should lie down a while.

I sit myself up, giddy-headed, and I test my shoulder's movement. I look round at what my girl has in her house, her married house, and it is not so very much. Jemima, I have not done anything for you.

We killed Boone. We killed Boone.

This I hear in pieces at first, between the shots and the crying and yelling. It carries on. My whole side hurts me and I cannot raise my arm, but I rush outside and up the ladder. In Holder's bastion I stand for them to see me above the wall. Covered in blood and dirt I yell out at the camp and the riverbank diggers:

—Here, try it again! I am ready for you.

A great laugh from the river.

A gunful of shot flies at me but I am quick enough yet to get down. Pompey's voice, always his voice. He fills the young men with such rage that they shoot at him on and on, all thoughtless. I do not try to stop them now. Out the slit I see Pompey's head above the bank, he keeps his bright blue scarf on, it says *Look at me, shoot at me.* And they do go on shooting, but it does not stop him appearing and

162

laughing in different places along the bank, and it does not stop the tunnelling.

At noon, Major Billy comes to me and says very weary:

—They are all digging now, Captain. They will be at our walls by tonight.

—I know it.

—Is there any sign of the Virginia reinforcements?

—You tell me, Major.

Billy's shoulders give way. He says:

—It looks bad, you know. This talk of you having an Indian wife.

I hate her being talked of aloud, I hate all of it. Billy straightens and says only:

—Captain, what shall we do?

I cough. I say:

—Throw stones.

I feel Billy's eye on me a moment longer but then he goes. I feel myself coming to pieces inside my skin. I grip my gun, I keep to the bastion, I shout with the rest, but I do not fire my last powder. After a time the stones begin to fly again from our trench. It seems Pompey has taught the Shawnee more English, they all bellow as a chorus from the bank in return:

—Your mothers are whores. Your daughters are whores. Your wives are whores.

The hours crawl endlessly, they shout when they are not shooting and digging, and all they shout is *whores*. We can see the earth move where they are below it, coming towards us like a snake swallowing its slow way along a smaller animal. Our young men return the compliments. *I will have all your women. I will have them before we kill them. You can watch.*

—Fucking buggers.

Holder says it, scrambling in his pouch for shot as the sun is wearing away behind the cloud. He begs:

—Captain, give me a bullet. I will get that son-of-a-bitch black of theirs with it before we are gone.

He is near weeping as he says it. Do not go crying, Holder, or we will all start. The tunnelling thumps below us. From the bank comes Pompey's voice again, light and happy in Shawnee, a song of his own devising.

Rage billows me up, it does the same in the rest along the rampart. At once everyone is shooting with what they have left, and Holder is begging me for a bullet or even a buckshot ball, only one, anything I have. But I stand with my gun and I aim at the singing perched above all the other noise, like the smallest bird on a thick tree. I shoot. The singing stops.

Holder roars over the wall:

—Where is your black man now, you fucking sons of whores?

The rest take up his call: *Where is your black? Where is your Pompey?*

At last a Shawnee voice calls back:

—Pompey *neppa.*

To this I yell in Shawnee:

—Sleeping, is he? Let him sleep.

⌣

But there is no sleep. As dark begins to scratch through the cloud, they come at us over the ground. Running and howling with burning torches again, and fires burst up everywhere. The children are too frightened to put them out with Squire's water guns, they stand screaming wherever they are until they are shoved out of the way. I put the women back in men's coats and have them crawl the ramparts with the water pistols or brooms, putting out the flames when they can. I call some of the young men down from the bastions if they are out of bullets, and tell them to shin up the cabin roofs with buckets. Holder is near shot doing so, he dodges down again and screams at the night:

—You will have to kill us all if you want to come in through your goddamned tunnel, you little coward bitches!

Do not say it, Holder. This I think at him. But he has already said it, and some of the children have heard and are howling at the thought. Hancock stands with his wife at the well, praying loud. I hurl my gun at him two-handed, it strikes his chest and clatters down. I say:

—Take it, you are not injured, get up on the wall and fight.

Hancock opens his watery eyes and says:

—You would do well to pray too, Boone. This is the end of time, as He has promised us in His book.

—Praise Him.

This from Molly Hancock, she looks surprised as ever saying it. I shout at her:

—We do not live in His book!

I take up the gun again and shove it at Hancock's neck:

—I promise you I will kill you myself first. Fight.

—We are fighting for all the souls here, Boone. God may yet forgive you—

I cannot listen, I strike Hancock's chest with the gun butt as I rip it back from him. A fire torch flies at us and lands across the well, Hancock gives me a look that says, *You see His noble works?* Before I can take it up and set him ablaze, Squire is at my side:

—Dan, come.

His face is bright in the light of all the fires. I follow him to the gunshop, where many of the children have hidden themselves, weeping in gusts. But Squire has a small box out. He shows me, it is full of powder. He drags out another one full of buckshot.

—I have kept it back. I need it for my cannon. I can see enough to aim at their camp.

165

—What—a cannon? You made it? Can you blow up their tunnel with it? Can you?

He shakes his head, it is a slight shake but I see all he means by it, I see his sorriness for what he cannot do when there is not enough. I take a grainy black fistful of powder from the box, and I say:

—Take it. Use it all.

He nods and carries the box outside, while Moses helps me push Squire's little round cannon out from its hidden corner. We roll it to the ladder, and I have two of the young men haul it up to the rampart. A burning arrow lands near us, but Moses brushes it away, his young face so set it looks carved of wood.

Squire goes up and readies his machine with powder. He covers his boy's ears when he has it lit. The noise of it cracks the night, the flash is wide, the shot in it surges out everywhere, the cannon blows itself to pieces and my shin is cut by a flying shard of the barrel. Cries go up outside, even from as far as the camp. I wait for Pompey's high voice to call *Why do you not fire again?* But there are only groanings from low down, and bodies on the ground. And digging sounds, and the screaming of the fire runners who keep coming and coming, leaping over the bodies.

I go down to the trench, Squire following. We hear the dreary scrape and thump of shovels, they are not far from our wall now, but we cannot see just where under the ground. My wounded shoulder thumps in time with the digging. I yell:

—Throw the rest of the stones back into the trench, it will make harder going for them when they break through.

The men here set to do it though they are not happy. Another torch lands on a roof, Holder pulls himself up swearing hard, pebbles of shot bounce near him. He screams down:

—This is not the end. This is not the way we will fucking end!

The scream of a runner outside slashes through the night: *Whores.* His torch wheels quick and hard up into a bastion. A woman gasps into her lungs, and says *Look up, look*. It is Martha. And it is raining.

⌣

All night rain whips down in sheets. All the fires are out, all the lights are out, we are in a wet dark pit.

I sit at the trench in the rain. My bones ache, they feel nailed into place, as if I am a chair. I can hardly get myself to standing when dawn comes, I expected no dawn ever again. If it had not rained—

—Captain. Captain.

It is young Johnny Gass on his hands and knees on one of the wet cabin roofs. The air feels washed and squeezed out. I cough and say:

—Get down, Gass, they will shoot you.

He turns. His freckly face is all amazement and too wide for his boyish frame. He says:

—They are gone.

With Squire, I get my cold hurt body in its soaked clothes up the rampart. Rain is still coming down, though lighter now. Holder comes sleepy out of his bastion and kneels at a gunslit blinking. Again and again he says *God damn*.

The camp is empty, a clutter of tent poles and cold fire rings. The peach bower sits under a fur of black smoke, they have tried to burn it but it has not caught in the wet. They have tried to do the same with the great elm, but it has not caught at all.

The tunnel has fallen in on itself, a long trough of mud that stops some yards from our rear wall. Shallow smeared tracks drag from near the fort to the fields. The bodies. They have taken these with them. So many of these marks. See the burying ground at Chillicothe, the painted sticks sunk in the ground there so the dead can find their way and have air. My father, you and I were going there to see your son, the son killed through what I did trying to get my daughter back. *We make our trades.* So you said to me.

—Dan. Come down. Do not look.

This from Squire, but Holder bursts out with a yell:

—Shit! Look! Ha!

And I look where he is looking, towards the river. Up the bank a little distance is a blue thing, blue as the sky. It has come loose from a body, it trails from it. The body has been pulled along a way by the hogs that have come out of the woods and are rooting round it.

I know the body, it is Pompey's, left uncovered, the clothing pulled away from the skin. I see a foot bare, its sole is terrible, pale and naked. It pains me so I have to turn away before I am sick. My guts heave in waves. Why would they not take you to be buried, Pompey?

Neppa. Neppoa. Sleeping, dead. You taught me these words. They are too close. Holder is screaming with joy:

—We killed their bastard black! We killed him! We did it! Boone did it!

More howls of triumph come from all the fort corners, they are so happy to know of the death, they are all scrambling up the walls to see. *We killed him.* This death is enough for them to feel they have won everything.

A shot echoes, then another, but they come from some way north and over the river. Squire tilts his head that way and says:

—Hunting now for their trip back.

I can say nothing. What is this place now? Kaskee dead, Pompey left here dead by his brothers who were not his brothers. My father gone without another word to me. No ghosts, no one speaks to me.

Victory.

I will go out to Pompey and bury him somewhere. But a knot of firing sounds again, from slightly farther north. A vague angry singing comes with it: *Whores. Whores.* They sing as they are leaving me, and I am left alive, but with what?

Another pulsing of shots. Some of the children begin to cry in long fatigued sobs. Jemima comes at a run, she bursts up onto the rampart and pushes past me, she throws Flanders's hat from her head down off the wall so her hair tumbles out. She is throwing off his coat now, she is screaming in her shift, she is tugging that up over her shoulders with her feet apart and her legs in her torn stockings, holding her long black hair out with her hands. She screams half bare at the men on the walls and out at all the country:

—I am not a goddamned man! Look at me! Will it make you stop?

PART TWO

REBECCA

BROKE
ALL HE
CAME NEAR

18

Autumn 1778

—GET IT OUT OF ME—why will the damned thing not be born?

—Susy, fetch some fat.

My daughter nods and goes quickly. She has her own little girl and has seen a few childbeds with me, but not a side breech like this. I get my half sister Anna up off the stool and onto her hands and knees on the bed. The other women file quietly out, knowing how this can go. Polly drags her feet, with cake held in her cheek. I do not know why I let my uncle's girl come today.

—Polly, leave.

Off she flounces. Anna flings her arm over her face and says she does not want to see the baby, it is a devil, it is tearing her up.

—No, Anna. Soon we will have it out and you will see.

Who believes in devils now? Granddaddy's oldest black woman, Silvy, used to scare us with them long ago—tiny devils floating about like dandelion seeds for bad children to breathe in. When Susy hurries in with a pot of lard, I grease my right hand with it to the wrist. She watches. There will be a time she will need to know how—I will not live forever.

—Is she all right, Ma?

—She will be.

I fold my fingers together and slide my hand into Anna's body. A trickle of her water soaks my rolled sleeve. She gasps and tenses. She is a thin woman, but her hips are broad enough, like a bell. I catch the baby's foot. And now where is the other little foot? I inch my fingers higher, with my other hand on the outside of Anna's belly. When I find the sole bent up against the child's body, I push the first leg up to join it. Gently.

The small wet feet writhe together. Anna cries:

—Get it out, get it *out*!

I close my ears and eyes to her, there is nothing but my slippery hand to see with. It finds the baby's head pushed against Anna's right hipbone, under the broken bag of waters, which I slide back. Its blood beats under its hair. I feel for its face, tucked down with a small arm folded over it. With my longest finger, I hook the arm and pull it down along the child's side so it will not break. The neck is not twisted or bent back—I slide upward to reach for the cord, and my finger brushes the child's lips. It tries to suck.

I breathe in. And cannot help thinking of my last baby, William, the last I will have, dead at nine days.

And James, my first baby, before he was born, and was safe. Of the long birth, when I wanted him out, like Anna, but at the same time did not want him separated from me.

He was a grave little child. Great interested eyes.

—Rebecca, please—

Anna rolls her head. The baby is a big one, but I know just how it is lying in its little dark world. The cord is not knotted, no twists. It is only looped loosely round the baby's other arm. With my finger I catch it and slip it off. The plump arm twitches. I feel for the chin with my eyes shut again.

I never wish to think of Jamesie, but some nights I dream of him as a small boy, falling from a great tree near the creek where we lived then, crying for me on the ground but quietly, afraid I would be angry with him for climbing. I dream of him smiling in his bed, and dreaming I lift him and find his little arms and body scratched and bloodied, as though he had been crawling through nettles. I dream of him as an old man, walking along bent over—I dream of him born blue, the cord knotted round his neck. I feel him leaving my body in a great rush, again and again. I wake gasping.

Anna now weeps quietly. In her dark inside, the baby sucks again at my fingertip. I tighten my own mouth. Little one, I am not your mother. But I cannot see you lost—

—Susy, you might give us a song.

—What shall I sing?

Susy feels my difficulty and keeps her voice gentle. From through the door comes another voice:

Then the spider, she
Daily waits on me
Oh round about my bed
She weaves her tender web
When I am weary weary oh—

—Polly, that is no help. Enough.

I know the words that come further on. *When the child does cry, I must sing goodbye.* I could shake this girl my uncle left to me, with her great mouth and her loudness. I ought to have told her to keep home with the other young ones.

I open my fingers slightly, my arm halfway to the elbow inside Anna, my other hand on the hard round of her belly. A smell of damp, cider, fat. *Be soft now, soften your bones*, I tell the baby and Anna, as well as myself.

The baby twists its head, searching again for my finger. Susy in a crouch holds Anna's shoulders as she makes a deep distressed sound. Susy whispers *Hush, hush.* I want to pull my fingers back out—but I do not. With my outside hand I push on the lump of the child's head and shoulders. *Move. You cannot come out this way. Turn your head down. Turn.* But it will not turn. Anna is nearly silent now, her mouth gaping, her head hanging. From past her shoulders, Susy looks at me, asking. I nod to her. Watch—

—Come now, little sleepyhead. No more lying on your side.

Its small reaching lips follow my finger. And the baby begins to shift. It is difficult, a big child. I ease it along until it cannot go farther. Do not breathe, baby, not yet. And from the outside I turn the head, I shift the shoulders downward. Slowly, slowly—

—Susy, your hand now.

I put her palm where the child's rump lies curled. I tell her to push up under it as I push the head down. I feel for the inside curve of Anna's hipbone, and I move the head along it with care. And the head shifts down until I have it between Anna's bones. The baby's limbs roll in this new position. Anna howls *goddammit goddammit* over and over again. At least she is breathing. And the child is still moving—

When the next pain is done, we have it righted. I slip my fingers partly out, I can feel the wet hair on the head. It is coming down. I slide my hand out and wipe it clean. Anna shudders. *God damn him.* I nod to Susy. She asks:

—Aunt Anna, who is the father of this child?

Anna groans. The midwife's stupid question, always the same. A giggle bursts through the door. Polly again. I stroke Anna's thigh:

—I am sorry, Anna. You know we must ask. Tell us and you can be quiet.

—You know who. My husband, of course it is—damn him, Ben—

Another pain grips her and she cries and rounds her back. I see the top of the baby's head. *Of course it is.*

—You are sure, Anna?

She looks back at me over her shoulder. Susy looks at me. *Who is the father*—they asked me this when my Jemima came, and I said nothing. I said nothing at all that whole labouring.

Another laugh from Polly outside. But now Anna's baby is rushing down, a great head gasping before the shoulders and body are out. I have it—it sucks in another great breath and bellows. A smell of blood and wax. The thick cord ripples. Anna drops her head and shoulders and cries.

—Look, Anna. A boy.

—A big boy, Aunt Anna.

Susy's eyes shine with tears as she laughs softly. She is remembering her own little daughter's birth not long ago, as we all remember at such times—she helps Anna over onto her back, and says:

—Look at him! What will you call him?

I stand. My dress is soaked with Anna's waters, and there is a great tear where she knelt on it. I begin to tidy the baby. Anna tries to look at him, but is still caught with the last pains and unsure of this big backward child. She throws her head into the pillows and squeezes her eyes shut.

—Little imposter.

I laugh as I tell him so, smoothing and cleaning off his face and drying his hair, which has not grown in on the side that was against Anna's hip. He roots again for my finger. My wet dress clings to my legs. It tears again when I step on it going to the table for another cloth.

The child has not stopped yowling. Anna stares past Susy, who is taking the afterbirth away. Her face is pink now. Satisfaction at being alive, with a living baby, comes over it. She says:

—Let me see him. Give him to me.

I wrap him up. He fights me with his flailing fists and cries harder, trying all the while for my finger. Once he is well bundled I take him to where Anna sits against the bed. She holds out her arms.

—I will call him Daniel, for you, Rebecca.

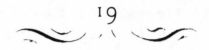

19

And Billy broke locks and Billy broke bolts
And Billy broke all he came near—

MY EARS RING with it as Susy and I walk home, leaving Anna and the baby with the other women, who brought in plates and drink as soon as we had the boy right. They were singing the old *Billy Broke Locks* to the woman made a mother again. Anna was smiling all the time. I did not care to stay. Her husband paid me on the way out. He was smiling as well, proud as can be.

Of course Daniel is the name she likes. She has no Daniel yet among her other children. I call my own son Daniel by his middle name, Morgan, now, for my grandfather.

There is no Daniel, he is dead.

I picked Jemima for my second daughter. Nobody's name.

She is in Kentucky, alive, I hope. She would not come back with us. She would never give up waiting for her daddy, as she calls him.

Susy and I go along in silence. The breeze is fresh and smells of rain. Polly trails behind us, smarting after the scolding I gave her for giggling and making a little spy of herself. She calls loudly:

—How would anyone know if that baby was not Uncle Ben's?

Susy looks back, about to laugh, then sees my face and stops. We walk on. Polly takes to singing *Oh weary weary oh—*

We pass along the back of Granddaddy's property, where my brothers have their houses now that he is gone. I feel more at home once I see the buildings in the broad sloping fields. My brothers and my older boys have cleared so much land here, we can see anyone coming. Once we are away from the creek I listen for the low current of the Yadkin. Autumn is settling. Smoke in the air, leaves damp beneath the trees. The smell makes me think of a spring cellar—there was one in my daddy's house when I was very little, I believe, before he married again and began having more children like Anna, before Martha and I were sent to live with Granddaddy. We do not have a cellar here.

I do not like to be reminded of things.

—I want to cut out my new skirt tonight.

Susy gives a little twirl on the path. She is always ready to be happy. With her arms up, she is very slender. She checks to see if Polly is in earshot, then says:

—I have started another baby, Ma.

I put my arm about her shoulder:

—Did you think I did not know?

She laughs, and I say:

—You will have an easier time with this one.

Her little Lizzy was born when Susy was fifteen years of age. I did not think she would come through. Her hipbones were close-set like a child's still. I could touch both with the fingers of one hand. The fort was so poor and unclean, such a place to begin a life. That poor baby opening its eyes for the first time there.

I have wondered at times about the first birth there ever was. Eve's, it would be, I suppose. When there was no one to help.

Susy hugs me. She does not like to be reminded of unhappy things. She says:

—Will is wishing for a boy.

—They usually are.

At home a pig is loose, scurrying along the kitchen-garden fence. The children are hooting and running after it, led by Israel, who taps its flanks with a stick to send it in different directions. It butts its head against a rail with a squeal, then swerves off to try to get into the corn, but Israel leaps in front of it. It runs straight into his leg. My daughters Becky and Levina scream with laughter and run after it with my uncle's younger girls. One of them falls flat and pulls herself up covered in dirt. She stands looking at me, tugging her plait loose. So many children, I could run a school.

—Israel, keep it out of the field.

—I am trying, Ma!

—You could be trying harder.

His cheeks are redder than usual from his running and the cool air. He has always loved animals, hugging or teasing them, making pets. He laughs and crouches with his arms wide to catch the crazed pig. Polly runs up from somewhere behind me, her cap down her back, dashing into him before the animal can, and Israel falls backward with her on top of him.

—You will wear those clothes until wash day, you know.

—We know, Ma. Do we not, Polly?

—We know, Ma.

Polly has called me Ma from the night my uncle turned up with his six after his wife died. *They are motherless.* Taking his hat off to me, showing his big square forehead. Polly clung to my legs. Not such a little girl, but crying like one. Her daddy had nothing else to say but *Well. Life is a rum thing.* Setting down his smallest, he said: *This one here, we named her for her ma.* He coughed and looked around at my house. *And for you.* Then he headed north again on his own.

Uncle James. He is not so much older than I am. When we were children at Granddaddy's, he and I used to play that we were riding horses, rearing up and down on branches next to the creek. I call

his youngest Reba, not Rebecca. I do not like hearing my name. Or
my uncle's. James. Jamesie. What is the sense of it?

Polly's dress has slipped up, her legs are in the air behind her.
A stocking coming down. Thirteen, fourteen years old.

—Polly, get up. Get off him.

My voice is harder than I mean it to be. But it gets her to her
feet, and dusting off her skirts.

—Get that pig back to its pen now, Israel. Girls, get it fed. Is all
the butter made?

My thin-limbed Becky says it is mostly made. Her eyes are
downcast but I see them slip towards my uncle's boy Henry, as big
as Israel, who is walking off whistling and tapping the pig's hocks
with his stick to drive it along.

These are not children, most of them, not anymore.

Susy and I have been awake all night, as the ache in my head
reminds me now. My skirt is still damp from the birth, and my legs
are chilled.

—Polly, go and get the eggs in.

—I do not want to, Ma.

Polly stands with her stocking fallen just as it is. The way she
says *Ma* has become snappish recently, like a dog barking. Nobody
but me to throw her anger at, for not being her own mother. She
would throw an egg at my back if she could. If she would help
gather them as she is supposed to, and not forget or hide them
somewhere for spite or some feeling of secret riches, perhaps. She
thinks I do not know her.

—No cake today then, Polly.

I go indoors. Behind me Polly asks Susy if she brought home any
of the cake from Anna's birthing, and what sort.

Susy goes home for the time. When I have the house put right and clean, and a stew cooking, and more bread baking in the back ashes after Becky's efforts from the morning show themselves to be hard as bricks, it is dark. The children cram in at the table or wherever else they can find in the room to eat. Their noise fills the house to the roof. Susy returns with her husband, Will Hays, and her fat little daughter. She fell straight to sleep when she got back, she says, and did not cook a thing.

—No more births tonight, I hope! Not even a cat. Not one kitten.

She yawns and stretches, burning with happiness. I am so glad of her. Will Hays rests his hand on her back. He is a good young man, with a serious set to his posture. He helped us get back here in safety, a careful shot, never one to waste his ammunition or anything else. He helped with the house building. He knows how to prosper, and has bought two black servants, one for outdoors and one to help Susy. I see his eyes brighten when my daughter turns her smile on him. I want her life to be this way. A good life.

We have a good life now. I do not have to tell myself this so as much as I did when we were first back. I poke the ashes and stir what remains in the stewpot, onion and pork. That pig might have tried harder to get away. It will not be long for this world. How much salt will we need this year.

Daniel had gone to make salt, and is now lost—

But we will get anything we need here, ourselves.

Polly sits with her younger sister Reba, whispering into her ear and glancing occasionally at me. She coughs loudly with her mouth open. A morsel of food tumbles out and she lets it sit on her plate. My Morgan laughs, which sets Jesse laughing.

—Would you prefer something else to eat, Polly? You might go and dig up a potato and eat it outside. A cold meal would suit you tonight.

She gets up and stamps out the door, dragging Reba along. Her skirt brushes Israel as she passes. The room is tight with everyone sitting round the table, but she passes too close to him. She is young. Too young. And I have said too much, perhaps. Let her go.

Once everything is cleared and put away again, and Susy and her little family have gone home, and the youngest have been sent to wash themselves before they go to bed, I sit at the hearth to mend my skirt. My ankles are cold still from the long damp walk. I stretch them towards the embers. The great toe on my left foot aches and complains.

183

The children gather gradually and grow quieter. The fat-lamps throw out a little light, which the youngest like to sit in. The girls have their sewing or knitting, though they do not pay much attention to it. Israel sits on the floor doing something with his gun all in pieces. The boys watch this with interest, especially my littlest boy Jesse, five years old now. His hair hangs in his eyes and he shakes it away like a pony now and then, but his body leans towards me, his ear in my direction.

—Jesse, are you waiting for a story?

—Yes.

He speaks without taking his eyes from Israel's oiling and measuring. I say:

—One of you girls tell us one then. My head is tired.

They all shout: *No Ma no, you tell it.*

I smile. They think they want excitement, but nothing must change too much.

—Which shall it be then?

—Gulliver!

One of Jesse's favourites. His father's favourite. Jamesie's as well.

—No, Jesse. Tonight we will have Madoc.

It is the first story that comes to my mind. And so I tell again about Madoc who left Wales, where his brothers never stopped fighting over their father's crown. He took one hundred people, men and women and children, west across the sea to a new land. Some have said this very land.

—Why would they come here?

184 Polly says it from the doorway where she is now leaning, with Reba behind her.

—Close the door, girls. The evenings are too cold now.

—I would not come here, if I could go anywhere.

You are welcome to go anywhere else—

But I do not say it. I do not mean it. I tell the girls to come in and get warm. Polly's restless heels bounce as she comes to stand in front of the fire. They nag at me, round and red. *Can you not be still.*

Jesse knocks the back of his head on my shin where he has moved to sit at my feet:

—Ma.

And so I go on with the story: Now, on Madoc's crossing, a young man was lost to a shipwreck. No one could save him.

No one could save—

And then a monster came with a poison that sent nearly all the grown men and women into a deep sleep. They could not wake up. And Madoc went mad in a quiet way, sitting staring at the sun on the ship's deck until they reached the new shore.

—How did they know he was mad?

—How do you think, Jesse?

Morgan shoves him, and Jesse knits his brows together, as he always does. He is a thinker, if not the quickest one. I rub his head with the edge of my knee. Polly says:

—Maybe he was not mad at all. Maybe he never was.

She bounces faster. Jesse turns to watch.

—Damn it!

Part of Israel's gun clatters to the floor and gouges a piece from the board there. Jesse jumps up to scramble for it with Morgan. I say:

—Israel, watch your mouth, and put that away now. Time we had some quiet.

He goes on working at the parts with a rag, rubbing them smoother. Watching me press the soles of my feet together, he sends me a smile and says:

185

—Feet cold, Ma?

—They are.

—I will get you the softest doeskin for new shoes. And a rabbit to line them with. Two young rabbits, with the whitest fur.

—Very queenly.

Jesse says:

—Like Madoc's mother, the queen. And his wife, the other queen.

Polly puffs out her cheeks and says:

—Nobody knows anything about her.

I tell her:

—Maybe she prefers that.

She plays with her lower lip:

—He ought to have married someone else. Someone pretty.

Someone like you, a know-nothing, an infant stumbling about in the dark—she was very likely pretty to begin with, we all are.

I do not say this. I stroke Jesse's hair, which is far too long, hanging over his forehead. He will never keep it tied back. Israel grins sideways at Polly. He says:

—Well Ma, I will go long-hunting soon, once I have this gun working right.

He looks down the barrel. His voice is so like his father's. I say:

—You are not long-hunting, Israel.

He stands. He is no child, he is nineteen years old. I know he will tell me so again. He sets his jaw:

—Why not? I could go as far as Kentucky, see how they are at the fort—

—No.

I want no part of whatever remains there. He raises his voice:

—Ma. I would come back.

—I said no.

—I would see Daddy.

—Your daddy is dead, as you well know.

He knows. I have told all of them. We have all done our weeping. The younger ones are silent, watching us. Polly's eyes are fixed on me. But Israel will not let up:

—I would check in on Jemima.

—She is all right.

Is she? I cannot believe she is anything other than all right. She would not come back here with me. She would not believe Daniel is dead.

Israel sees my face, and tries again:

—We need—

—We need nothing.

—Not true, Ma.

—We need nothing here. We have everything here.

—I will get pelts, get us some money.

—We have enough. We need no further food this year. We are well set for winter. We are safe. Leave it alone.

—It is not enough—

—You think it is not enough to be safe? It is enough! You think there will never be enough of anything. But there is more than enough here if you look, and stop thinking all the time of somewhere else.

I stop myself. Jesse is stirring by my knee, turning to stare up at me. The rest have gone quiet. Israel tries again:

—Ma, are we going to be here forever? I do not want to stay.

—You are not going anywhere now.

—Ma. I want—

—Enough.

—I want—

—I said enough.

Israel slams out of the house into the dark with the pieces of his gun in his fists. His shot-pouch drops behind him and sends pellets bouncing everywhere. We all hear him crossing the yard and garden and going off who knows where. Polly gives me a sweet smile. *See how agreeable I can be when I am right and you are wrong.* She sets to gathering up Israel's shot as though it were pearls.

⌣

I look out at the stars for a moment after I put out the lamp. The embers rustle in the hearth. No more talking from upstairs. Everyone in bed but Israel.

I know my son. He will make a camp or sleep in the stable rather than come in tonight. Polly had no more to say, one mercy.

Tiny sparks burst in the fire. With no one speaking, thoughts come to me, and I am too tired to send them off. Jamesie, very little, perhaps not yet two, in a yellow dress of my mother's, the skirt round his neck. He looked like a flower with a face at its centre. He stumbled and caught his foot, tearing that poor worn dress into strips. And he halted himself, always serious, looking up at me to see if I was cross. My heart ached to see the ruin of all I had left of my mother, but he was never a child who needed scolding—he scolded himself for any small wrong. A little beauty with the sunny yellow round his face.

I listen to the fire. I think of quiet. I think—

At first of nothing—

But then you walk into my mind of your own will. Your feet, your knees, your legs—

Long bones. Black hair. Like Daniel's. But softer under my hands. Your chin not shaved since early morning, but still soft. It was night then, nearly. The dark barn seemed somewhere outside the world. A smell of hay, animal warmth. And of you. Something leafy, something mossy. A happiness.

I never let myself think of it. I never let myself want. It is only the birth, or my tiredness, or the way Israel was looking at Polly. That look girls and women can feel, like a bird landing on them.

You looked at me that way that one day. You came to see how we were, my little ones and me, with Daniel gone on a long-hunt for more than a year, no one knowing where he was. You brought venison and I was sorry for your trouble. You said the deer had come right to your door, an easy shot. I told you that was how Daniel courted me, dragging a dead deer to my granddaddy's house. He also threw his knife at my apron. He did not know how I grieved and raged for that ruined thing. I tied it up in knots and threw it away into the yard, only Martha found it before the goats did. She used a strip of lace from it on a cap. I tore that cap up one night when she slept. There is the history of that poor apron. So I told you, finding myself full of words.

You smiled, and you stayed to eat with us, which you had not done before. Perhaps Martha had been bad to you that day, going silent or taking herself off on a long tearful walk. I did not ask.

Once the children were asleep, we sat talking of nothing. When you stood to go, I stood too. I went outside with you and we walked to the barn. Your horse was there but you did nothing to ready it. You said I was too much alone. And you did not go.

Your smell. Rocks in a shallow creek. Or wet ferns. I pressed a fern once under a heavy pot. The smell did not keep.

I wanted something of you. I had your daughter, my daughter, but she is gone now, in Kentucky with her own husband. And too young to be married. Jemima was never mine, always pulling away, walking off as soon as she was able to stand. She does not know about you being her father. Not from me.

You are there with her, if you are living. Look out for her. When I left, you waved us off with the rest, but you went no farther than the fort gates. Some nights here I have wondered if you would come. If there were any chance of it. But all I see clearly is your back turned to me at the gates.

After the first night in the barn, I wanted to tell you to stay. Not beg, not even ask. To tell you—to show you.

You wanted to look at every part of me. You said I was like honey—

I wanted you to see, do you know? All of me. And more, to see in my heart, how I was afraid—all the time. I wonder if you and I will have any more time, Neddy.

One of the children wakes and gets out of bed, and I am up the stairs, leaving you down in the dark.

20

ISRAEL DOES NOT come back. In the morning I am slow and foot-sore. I get up and have the bread started before it is light. A sour smell of dough and smoke. The embers do not want to catch.

The children come down. They are quieter without Israel at home, and no hope of pigs set loose to chase in the yard. Everyone eats dully, then sets to work and lessons. I send my uncle's older boys to see if my brothers need help in their fields.

At the table, Jesse is fitful, groaning and lying face down on his slate, as Morgan is doing. Polly is meant to be minding the younger ones, keeping them at their work, but she is restless too, strolling back and forth between the door and the window and plucking at her lip.

—Polly.

—What is it, Ma?

She has her sweet voice on. I say:

—Go and fetch the eggs if you do not want to help indoors today.

At once her voice shifts. She says:

—I do not *want* to do either.

I poke the broom into a corner where a cobweb hangs in thin rags. I cannot see a spider. Polly begins to sing:

Then the spider she
Daily waits on me.

She is reminding me, of course, how she listened to everything at Anna's birthing. I hold out the broom to her:

—What do you want then? The broom? Here you are.

She comes very close, with a flake of porridge on her chin. I hold myself back from brushing it away. Her eyes are flat. She says:

—I want to go. Like Israel.

—You will never catch him. He will be back soon enough.

Again, my voice has gone harder than I meant it to. Hers hardens further:

—He does not wish to be trapped here either.

—Go then.

Off Polly flounces, throwing her cap off and shaking down her hair. Jesse and Morgan sit up to watch. I send them outside. They are roaring the minute they are out in the air.

I look again at the ceiling for the spider. Polly's ways make me think of Martha when we were children, with something to fight about every day. I was happy enough as a girl—Martha, perhaps not. Every so often in our bed at Granddaddy's she would breathe it out. *You killed our ma when you were born—you should give me that dress of hers, I am the one who can remember her.* She knew our mother's name and would never tell me. So I said no. I called her a witch and she would cry, always ready to do so.

So far as I know she is still with Neddy at the fort. At her wedding she held on to Ned as tight as could be. It was my wedding too, when I married Daniel, and he could not take his eyes away from me. Ned and Martha were in the room across the way that night at Granddaddy's big house. I did not think then, I did not know—

I had not truly looked at Neddy until I thought Daniel was gone from this world, the first time. As he is now. And Neddy in Kentucky.

I sweep the broom over the ceiling planks. Dust showers down. Always dust, in every house. The beginning of a headache is in my eyes. Perhaps a thunderstorm is coming. I usually know it.

The weather does turn. The skies are heavy, and Israel is gone three more days. He is a good woodsman, as I know, and he will do well even without a gun, but the nights are cold and wet. The fourth morning, we have a frost. The children run about crunching down the stiff white stubble in the field, and puffing clouds into the air.

Israel can fish. He can make snares. Daniel showed all the children how to make them when they were very little.

My Jesse comes into the dairy shed blowing on his cold hands, and asks when Israel will return.

—I do not know.

—I wish he would come back. I wish I could go hunting.

—If wishes were horses, beggars would ride.

Jesse pokes at a ripening cheese and leaves a hole in it. I swat at him. He flops to the ground with a great sigh:

—There is nothing to do here but letters.

—Write me a letter *O* in the dust there outside the door. Write twenty of them.

This is one of the letters I know how to write, so I watch him. He crawls over and begins making marks with a stick, but he does not last long at it. I set him to churning instead. There will be time enough for him to learn letters. I have hopes. The future will be a flat, clean place, like a green lawn. I will plant a patch of grass this spring, not for growing anything else on. In some of the dreams I have, the children walk and play on it.

Jesse looks up, tired of churning already, and asks:

—What can I do now?

I smile at him:

—Keep yourself busy, Jesse. That is all there is.

⌣

The morning I go to look in on Anna, the clouds are low and grey but the air is dry. Susy sees me passing and runs out to say she and her little girl will come too, but I tell her to keep home and rest.

—You will be feeling your own new one quicken soon enough. Then you will have no sleep.

She laughs and runs her hands down her stays. She says:

—Then I will not need these. I remember, Ma.

I remember too. A baby in its dark world in me, only I felt as if it were somewhere very distant. And no sleep ever again, it seems. I kiss Susy's round little Lizzy, who lived through being born in the fort, and who is still here. She fills me with fierce love and hope. Her life will be healthy, a good life. I smile and pat her fat cheeks. I tell her:

—Be a good girl and look after your mother, now.

She laughs just as Susy does, the same bubbling sound. Susy waves and dances off with her behind the house into the garden. It is the way we all are when happy about another baby, happy to be opened and turned inside out again.

Lying in bed with her bawling boy, Anna is very happy. Her face still shines. Her milk has come in now but it is not quick enough for this one. He stops his sucking to scream with rage, then he bangs his small fist against her breast with all his power, until he exhausts himself and falls into a sleep. Anna cannot take her eyes from him.

—He is a big boy yet, Anna. He has lost no fat.

The baby's head rolls. His mouth works furiously in his sleep. Anna says:

—Danny is my biggest, I think. My poor parsley patch knows it.

She winces as she shifts her hips. I do not like her silly words. But I check between her legs, and I tell her:

—Your parsley patch will be all right. You are not torn.

194

Her bleeding is clean. She did not rip open, by some mercy, in spite of my hand and this great child in her. Her skin is cool, she has no fever. I send one of her girls out to the garden to fetch cabbage leaves for her swollen breasts. The milk will move faster soon, with that big child sucking.

Jemima used to swat at my breast like this one does to Anna. I wondered if I might be carrying a boy. But she came out a screaming girl, with none of Ned's gentleness. Granddaddy's old Silvy used to say that quiet men make girls. She said eating apples did the same thing, though.

Neddy brought apples, the second time. He came late in the wagon with food for me and my children, and he and I went without speaking to the barn. He saw my belly, and he knew. He kissed it, and me—and before he went, he shook himself and his clothes straight and told me Martha was with child again. He did not say *also*. He looked slightly sad. He did not come again.

Martha delivered me of a daughter, not long after her own was born. A girl also. I would rather have had any other midwife. I do not know what she thought, or what she knew. We never spoke of it. I never told her, even in a spiteful moment, though we have had plenty. *You killed our ma.* When she said it aloud outside in daylight instead of in bed, swinging her feet from the fence where we sat picking slivers, I hit her. My palm showed up scarlet on her cheek. She stared ahead with her big eyes full of tears. We stayed where we were.

Anna's baby wakes and at once searches for his mother's dark nipple, but the cabbage leaf I set on her impedes him. He is soon arching and bellowing. Full of pride, she takes the leaf away and pushes his face to her:

—There now.

Smiling at him, she tells me:

—You will have others, Rebecca. There is time.

—Other children? No.

She gives me a pitying look:

—There are other men.

I know what she is thinking. I know what has been said of me. I stand to clean my hands in the bowl, and before I can stop myself I say:

—I am near forty, Anna. I am all right. I have enough children. I do not need any more to lose.

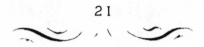

21

THE SUN BREAKS UP the cloud, but the air is not warm. A clear
night chills it further. Wash day again already. Before dawn I am out
getting the fires lit, but still Israel does not return. I dreamed of him
making a rough coat from a bearskin, leaving the head on to cover
his own. If he had the means to kill a bear. I dreamed too of Jemima
meeting him at whatever is left of the fort, her skirts more tattered
than my mother's old yellow dress. I'd kept one small piece of it, but
I must have left it in Kentucky. We left as quickly as we could.

You cannot help dreams. This one follows me all morning.

I am boiling up more water when I hear Polly's voice. She and
Reba and my Becky and Levina are meant to be beating some of
the sheets at the creek. A gale of shrieking comes. When I go down
to the water to look, there is Polly in just her shift, splashing about
in the shallows, displaying herself to the rest. A sheet drifts round
her legs and she squats down, screaming when her bottom touches
the cold creek. The shift is wet, her body shows through it. The
younger girls are laughing behind their hands. Becky pulls up her
own skirts and steps in. Levina stands staring on the bank, her long
feet planted apart.

Polly with hips, small pointed breasts, a small dark point
between her legs.

—Get your things on and do your work. You will catch cold.

—I do not care.

—You should care. Get dressed. You will be seen.

—You do not care who sees you, or who knows about you! Jemima is your bastard, everyone knows. You are not my mother and I am glad.

Levina sucks in a breath. Polly wades over the creek to the opposite bank and gets out. She is all gooseflesh, her limbs are trembling.

—Polly, take care. Some things should not be said.

—Some things *should* be said. They are already said! Why should I not say it?

She is terribly white, nearly blue. The shift clings to her. I know what she is doing, twirling about before the dark trees there, hoping Israel is somewhere quietly looking. Showing herself to be separate from me, not mine and not me.

—Polly. Your clothes are on this side, I remind you.

—Ha ha ha ha!

She dances on, but I know she can hear me:

—Stop now or you will have no more to eat today.

She laughs again and darts back and forth, trying to warm herself, laughing so I will hear. This rushing in the blood, why can one not stop it? Anger, love, they go wherever they wish. I turn and go back up to the house, leaving the girls behind to stare. The water in the great pot is boiling dry. When I bend to look into it, the steam is at the same heat as my face.

I bang the pot with the washing pole. I do not care if Israel was looking at Polly from the trees. I want to know where he is. He ought to be home. A tension adds to the heaviness in my belly. Perhaps my monthly time is coming on, though it is not the week for it. I stir the washing and splash my arms with hot water. Jesse dashes up. *Mama can I have some bread—*

—Soon, Jesse. Keep back from the fire.

Granddaddy's Silvy once told our fortunes. She said I would have many, many children. She said Martha would have sorrows and grow fat. Martha was thin as a post the last I saw her, half starved in the fort and watching me go. But not everything can be foreseen, no matter how you try.

With Jesse I fetch more wood. If it is for Polly that Israel comes back, so be it. They will not be allowed to marry yet. She is a child still, I remind myself, and my son is young too. They can live here and wait, and grow tired of each other, and realize it before they are bound for life. And perhaps find others more suited.

I pour in more water and set the big kettle boiling properly again. There is plenty of firewood, beautifully split. A lovely dry cidery smell from the exposed centres of the logs. Plenty of everything. I send Jesse indoors to wait for lunch, and I watch the bubbling in the pot.

When the girls come back up from the creek with a basket of wet sheets, Polly is not with them.

—Where did she go?

Levina says:

—She is at the creek, Ma. She says she is not coming up.

—There she may stay then.

The girls set the basket down and begin to pull out the wet twists of linen. They are quiet. They do not know what to say. I feel their expectations: *Ma ought to go and scold Polly, Ma ought to beat her. What will happen now?*

Children like to see rules put on other children. They need rules. But I am not going to Polly now. She has unsettled me more than I like. The girls put the sheets into the pot and I send them for more water. They look back at me as they go towards the creek again with their pails. *Are you coming, Ma?* But I do not go. I feel their other questions: *Jemima is what? What should not be spoken of? Ma. Ma. Ma.*

⌣

With all the *Ma*-ing at me, I might as well be a sheep—

A cow—

What woman has not felt herself a cow? The pit of my belly   199

aches again.

The girls keep away from me, doing their work quietly the rest of the morning. After lunch they help me lay out the last of the wash on the grass. After dinner, they help fold things and hang some still-damp stockings before the fire.

—Have you seen Polly since this morning?

Becky looks at her sisters and swings her foot. She says:

—I have not.

Levina says eagerly:

—I can go and look for her, Ma.

—No.

Levina sits back as if I have slapped her. She is easily hurt, and it shows all over her long face. I wonder sometimes whether it is my ma she looks like. Her hair is a great reddish tangle. I go to her and work a knot loose, and say more softly:

—She will come when she is ready. Go and brush your hair.

—No dinner for Polly.

Jesse comes up to say this, stern as a preacher. The girls have been telling him tales. Perhaps most boys are born with stern blood, preacher blood, soldier blood.

Once they are all quieter, knitting and talking, I take a lamp outside. It is close to dark, with the full moon coming up clear. I breathe the colder air. I walk the yard, looking behind the sheds. In the field, I walk the lines of dry cornstalks. Everything is all right here. The lamp makes odd shadows against the plants and the trees along the edge of the field.

I see nothing.

A smell of old smoke from the washing-pot fire, soap lingering in the cooled puddles. I lift the lamp higher and go down the path to the creek. The water is quiet, the creek is lower than last week. At the bank I stop to listen. A mockingbird rustles and cries in a tree upstream, but there is nothing else.

I shine the lamp high around me. Nothing. My arm shakes, holding it up, and I think of Polly, wet and shaking somewhere beneath a tree.

—Polly.

I say it softly. No answer comes, not even from the bird. I hope the girl has the sense to make herself a shelter of some kind.

I open my mouth to speak again but before I can say a word, my neck pricks, my thumbs prick. Someone is here.

I turn slowly, keeping the lamp high, and I look into the dark as best I can.

—Polly, where have you been?

A low short laugh. A man's laugh.

—And so you are back. Have you seen Polly? And where have you been, Israel? The pair of you have given me enough worry. Come on to the house.

He comes along the trees from up the creek. I cannot see him well. Only that he is leading an animal.

—Where did you get a horse? What have you been doing?

Israel laughs again. He is taking his time. The horse gives a puff. He stops to stroke its nose and murmur to it.

The voice.

The lines of the body.

The hair on my head lifts. I step forward, I hardly know I am walking, I nearly drop the lamp. It hisses. I step again, again. He is walking slowly. I am closer. I breathe out the name:

—Neddy.

I cannot step again. I stand without moving. I am sure I am asleep.

My whole back pricks now as though it is trying to wake me. I begin
to cry, I cannot help myself—I say:

—You are here.

He comes closer, close enough for me to see his face in the light.
He is not smiling. Not Neddy. He is Daniel—

22

HIS FACE HARDENS as I watch.

—No welcome, Rebecca? None?

I am hardly breathing. I cannot move. He says:

—No? Well.

He looks at the ground, then fixes his eye on me and says:

—I thought I might as well deliver this to you myself.

He pulls a folded page from his pouch. It looks softened and worn, like old leather. He says:

—Have you learned to read any better? No? What have you been doing?

I step back, but he steps with me, into the light of my lamp, and begins to read out very loudly. Some of his words—pierce me.

They all call you a whore
God damn you, the children are mine

It takes the breath from my body. When he is done I snatch the paper and tear it to pieces, I burn these with the lamp, but these words are still in my mind—they will never go. I stare at him—and he says, in his strange loud voice:

—Did you really think I was dead this time?

—Are you?

He gives one of his short laughs. His hair is strange, cut short and coming in grey. His beard is long and full of grey hairs also. An unwashed smell, old sweat and smoke. He is breathing too fast.

—Daniel—

He brushes his hand over his face and says:

—Well I hardly know. But here I am.

I shake my head:

—Where have you—what do you want?

—What do you think I want? Are you not at all happy to see me?

I step back. Do not touch me. Do not appear out of the air and kiss me again as though all these months have vanished, as though I can suddenly forget. Do not come back to life, do not do this to me again.

We continue to stare until I am able to speak:

—Why would you come for me now? You did not want us any longer. You liked your Indian life, we all heard it from Andy Johnson when he got back to the fort.

—So you did not think me dead, and you left anyway.

—I did not know what to think. I did not want to know. You were gone.

—And you were undone.

The whore undone. They all call you a whore. His letter is still in my ears. I never asked to be spoken of, to become a tale to amuse everyone, Polly or the people at that terrible fort. I tell him:

—You can call me whatever you like, but the children are not yours.

—This is no news to me, thank you. Though Jemima is mine now, did you not hear me? Did she not stay at the fort with me?

The lamp throws weird shadows over his face and under his eyes. I ask:

—How is she, Jemima?

—She is well enough without her mother. And do you care nothing about the fort? Have you missed it? Or have you missed nothing at all?

He is so angry, he has been saving it up. The old anger surges up in me also. I know it is stronger than his. I keep still, and I say:

—Where have you been all this time?

He turns on his heel, then back again. He looks fiercely at my face, trying to see through me. I keep still. His rage bursts out again, he is like one of the little boys when he says:

—I thought you would be glad enough to see me. I thought to make you happy.

—You have not made me happy.

His face falls. He looks very old suddenly, and very thin and hungry.

—Daniel—

He tries one of his smiles. Deep lines show in his cheeks and around his hollow eyes. He says:

—You may call me Danny again. I do not mind.

He gives a little bow. When he is upright again he winces and shifts his shoulders and neck. My own breathing pains me. I cannot live through this again. I clasp my hands tightly:

—What hurts you?

He touches his shoulder and he says:

—Well. You hurt me. I thought my wife would be welcoming to one six months a prisoner.

—Six months? You have been gone nearly ten. Where else have you been, other than with your Indians? Who else imprisoned you? Or is that something else you will not bother to tell me.

—Why should I tell you anything? You will believe whatever you like.

—You told me plenty in that letter just now, Daniel. How long did it take you to write?

I point to the ash scattered at my feet, the remains of his words. The wind shifts them along the ground. He says:

—You wrote to me as well. You left me that letter to find at the fort, full of loving things, saying you were going without another thought. *I do not care if you are dead, I will not wait for you*—so you said. Who wrote it for you? One of your brothers? Or Ned?

Neddy's face is in my eyes for a moment. Daniel's face, only soft and clean, full of tenderness. I never told—

—How did—

His face twists:

—I know. Everyone knows. I was one of the later ones to know it, in fact. Did he write that letter using your arse for a desk, in my cabin, in my bed?

I have bitten the inside of my cheek without knowing. A thin taste of blood. I say:

—Daniel. Daniel. Why are you back now?

—This is my home. My children need me, even if my wife does not.

—You do not believe in home, you never did. They do not need you. They are safe and well, they are happy.

—How can they be happy and safe and well without their father?

—They think you—

Are dead—

But before I can say it a white shape crashes through the dark, breaking twigs and crying.

Daniel's horse rears and dances back. He lunges for its bridle and puts his hand over its nearest eye, pulling its head round and murmuring into its ear. I swing the lamp out to see what is in the trees. A few gasps, and the figure is on the ground a few yards from us.

Daniel's knife sends the light back to me as he wrenches it from its sheath. He is standing stiff as a startled animal. I say:

—No.

—Help me, I am so cold.

The voice is pitiable in the darkness. Polly's good-girl voice, soft as Martha's can be when she likes. Daniel leaves the horse and strides towards her. His legs are shaking. I say:

—Put the knife away, Daniel, Daniel—it is only Polly.

—Daniel?

Polly's voice is louder. Daniel's legs have given way and he is kneeling. He speaks in his usual way though he looks likely to faint:

—Well. Miss Polly, is it? How do? And what are you doing out in only a shift? Damp too, you will catch cold.

He takes off his shirt to put over her. His ribs show like a rake all down his side. He is scarred.

I go over too and take off my apron. When I hold it out to Polly lying on the ground, I say:

—Where have you been?

But she is not looking at me. She is shivering, her eyes teary and squinting in my light. Her hair has dried loose every which way over her neck and shoulders. She reaches towards him unafraid, bold as can be:

—You are—Daniel? Then you are my daddy now.

Daniel's eyes light on me, swift and full of old accusation. But he says softly to Polly:

—Am I? If you say so.

—She is one of my uncle's children, Daniel. All mine now, living here. In my house.

—I am Rebecca's cousin.

What is this talk from Polly? She has never called me by my name. Always *Ma, Ma.*

Daniel reaches for her hand and says:

—Well we had best get her into the house then.

He does not say *your house.* He gets her to her feet though he is thin, so thin she nearly topples him. He loves to give pity. He loves to think himself a help.

He puts my apron round her shoulders, over his own shirt. The sash catches under her foot as he tries to tuck it round her, and tears in two strips. Another apron of mine he has ruined. And again he is in my house.

God damn you, the children are mine——

23

HOW DO I SAY—*Here is your daddy, he is not dead at all!*

I do not say it. They see him come in with an arm around Polly and they are all screaming with delight, mad with joy. They nearly knock him down, trying to touch him. Polly's brothers and sisters are as bad as my own children, though they do not know him. Even my quiet fretful Levina is running round him smiling, and he is holding her face and saying she has just the look of his ma now. I stand outside the door, the horse cropping my garden herbs over the fence behind me. My little Jesse has both arms tight round Daniel's waist.

How do they know him, half naked, his hair gone, his beard so long and grey? He is laughing. His own smell begins to warm and cut through the smoky scent. He says:

—Here I am again.

It is all he has to say. They believe it. They would believe anything he told them.

I turn back to look at the night. Israel—

As if he has heard me, Daniel calls:

—I do not see my son Israel.

And in half a moment he is here, walking out of the dark field with great strides, looking towards the light of the open door and his father standing in it.

He goes straight past me. He is dirty too, smelling of over-smoked jerk and bear grease, his dark hair slick with it. At least he has had something to eat while he has been gone.

—Daddy—

Israel's voice is full of tears. Daniel pulls him into his arms though Israel is far taller than he is now. They stand together, the younger ones circling like minnows. Israel says:

—I thought you were—

—I am not.

—I thought—

—Well here I am. Just look.

They stare at each other and begin to laugh. Daniel holds Israel's face in his hands. They are all laughing now, as though it were all some great joke. I have to walk out into the yard. My face is boiling with heat. The cold of the night is like a slap. My bowels will run away with me, I will be sick. I set out towards the privy, but I stop and pull the horse from where it is eating my garden. It grunts and tries to dance away. I yank the bridle and twist it round my fist so the horse cannot raise its head again. If I had a switch, I would whip its back to ribbons.

⌣

I stay outside the door far past the younger ones' bedtime, where I can hear the questionings and Daniel's proud talk. I cannot go in.

—Where were you, Daddy?

—With the Indians. They took us captive, but they liked the looks of me and adopted me. I have a Shawnee father and mother now.

—Why did they not come here with you?

—They did not like to leave their town.

—Can we go to their town?

—Perhaps one day. You would like it there. Live in a wigwam and be merry all day.

—What do they eat? I might not like it.

—You would like it. All of it delicious. Fish as big as your leg. Big as all your legs together.

They laugh, even when there is nothing to laugh at. He tells them that he was washed in the river before the Indian chief would have him as his son. They were all washed, he says, but he was the cleanest of all.

Here he stops for a moment, and I know he is thinking of that place and the people there. Polly says she is still cold and asks him to stoke up the fire, and he leaps to do it. He heaps too much wood on, but no one says anything, though they will be struck by burning drops of pitch. The floor will singe.

I step inside. Jesse is too close to the fire, sitting at Daniel's feet, the way Jamesie did when he wanted to hear a story. Jesse is half asleep but his eyes are fixed wide. He says:

—Did you fix the fort, Daddy?

How can he remember a thing about that fort, he is so young.

Daniel goes rigid. He says:

—We fixed the fort some.

Levina says very softly:

—Did the Indians come to the fort when you ran away from them?

She looks at him full of fear, my girl who is afraid of so much, remembering that place.

Daniel looks into the fire, his leg jogging up and down. He says yes.

Jesse pipes up:

—Did your mother and father come from that town to find you?

—My father did.

—Did he want you to go back there?

—He did.

I say:

—Why did you not go?

They are all startled. They have forgotten me. Daniel stands and says very heartily:

—Time we went to bed, my girl. Time we all did.

The younger children shout. Jesse cries as if Daniel will be conjured away from him again in the night. Perhaps he will be. Polly waves limply and says in a weak voice:

—Daddy, tell us another story first.

I say:

—Daniel, you can sleep here by the fire. You are very cold after your journey. Goodnight. The rest of us are going upstairs. Get up, Polly.

‿

I keep waking with a start, thinking myself out in an open camp with a great animal breathing nearby, and the children shivering in their sleep next to the dead fire, which I cannot start again, though I try until the flint cuts my hands. In the end I give up and sit awake. The children are restless too. I hear them turning and whispering for hours. I catch Jesse trying to stumble his way downstairs, but I stop him and rock him back to sleep in my arms. I keep him with me all night.

But when it is just light, I cannot stop him and the others from tramping down to find their daddy. I can hardly get the bread started for them all dancing in and out of my path. *Daddy talk Indian. Daddy do a dance. Daddy Daddy*—

I cannot help hearing it in James's voice, his baby voice.

Daniel is not thinking of Jamesie. He has gone out to bathe in the creek already, and coming in he looks less tired, almost happy. He shakes his short wet hair at the children and says:

—I am used to cold water now! My Shawnee family gave me the taste for river baths.

He comes to kiss my cheek. I stand very still. His beard is rough. A smell of the creek, a quick scent of Neddy. Only it is not Neddy.

Daniel looks me in the eyes. He thinks his place here was only waiting for him. He smiles, such a pure smile, and gives me another kiss. In my ear he whispers *Little girl*, then *Little witch*, his old names. He sets his hands at my waist. I do not know how he can do it without thinking I will strike him—I do not know how I do not do it.

I will not be made uncomfortable in my own house. I think only of the children and the baking. I move around him, getting out my pans and bowls. And soon he is sitting at the table, singing one of his old songs and clapping while the children leap about, overturning chairs and baskets and returning to touch him again and again. The Shawnee have not changed him. Nothing has. He is blind on purpose. Like a dog who will never lose its hopes no matter how you train it or beat it. Believing what it wants will come in the end, simply because of its wanting.

Then he stops singing, and says:

—But where is my Susy living? I must go and surprise her. I want to see my little granddaughter too. I am a granddaddy now, would you believe it of this youthful man?

He slaps his short grey hair. Polly says:

—I will take you.

She has quite recovered from all her foolishness yesterday. It is easy to see her youth and health. Daniel sees it too, smiling at her. His love plants itself quickly as a weed.

Jesse and Reba and Becky and Levina pipe up, they will go too. Daniel turns his smile on them and half stands, but I say:

—You are all going nowhere without breakfast. Sit.

They bolt the porridge down so fast that Daniel laughs. When he has finished his own bowl, he bangs it with the spoon and says:

—Very fine. Now my lady, we are off. Will you come with us?

I do not want to go. But I will not let Susy see him without me there. He piles three of the children onto the back of his horse, which I put in the stable myself last night, and sets off walking with the rest, Polly close at his side and Israel just behind, proud as can be with his polished gun against his shoulder. I trail them. Even Jesse is looking only at his daddy.

When we are close to Susy and Will's house up the creek, I say:

—Let me go first. Let me tell her.

But they are too far ahead, and not listening. I try to hurry. I see Susy in her garden at the side of her house, bending over a row of onions. Her little Lizzy sits in the dirt beside her. Before I can call, Susy stands to stretch her back and catches sight of us. She is running and screaming, running straight at Daniel. *Daddy Daddy*—

She bolts into his arms, and I hurry on towards them. My breath catches when I hear how she is crying:

—Susy, take care, think of your child.

Her hand goes to her belly a moment. Daniel steps back, holding her shoulders, with tears in his own eyes. He says:

—Susy. Are you making me a granddaddy twice over?

—Daddy, yes, we never thought to see you again—

—Never mind, never mind, here I am! Do not be so quick to have me buried! Where is my first grandchild?

In the garden Lizzy has begun crying softly. I turn, but Daniel strides to her quickly and picks her up. A dried beanpod hangs from her lips. She stares at him with her fat cheeks wet. He says:

—How do, little round face.

Israel has followed him. He grins and says:

—Is that a Shawnee name?

—Why not? They called me Wide Mouth sometimes. And Big Turtle.

Daniel's face drops for a moment and he looks more tired than ever. But he bobs Lizzy up and down and says:

—Do you like turtles? You would make a fine little Shawnee.

Susy is holding Daniel's arm now and wiping away Lizzy's tears, laughing. I say:

—We have heard enough of your stories for now.

Polly arrives at my elbow, saying:

—We have not! We want to hear all of it. Tell it again, Daddy.

Susy pulls at him:

—Come on, come and show yourself to Will.

They all go round to the barn, Israel leading the horse with the young ones on it kicking their legs. Lizzy bounces in Daniel's arms with his great steps. He has always walked as though he were a very tall man. She gapes back at me and I try to smile to show her it is all right.

In the barn, Will is bent over his grey mare's foot as he tries to help his black man pick out a stone. The smell of dung and seeds left to crumble away in boxes. When he looks up, he blinks and sneezes:

—What—

Susy tows her father along:

—Will, look! Did you ever think to see my daddy in your barn? Look!

Daniel grins and shifts Lizzy into one arm so he can clasp Will's hand. Poor Will looks unsure, but he gives half a smile to see his wife so happy. He leaves the horse to his man, takes Lizzy from Daniel, and says:

—Well Dan. Well. I do not know what to say to you.

Susy says:

—Will! Go and fetch a drink to celebrate. I will see what food I have for everyone.

Off she bustles. I go with her, taking bewildered little Lizzy and leaving the rest to jump round Daniel and Will in the yellow dust of the barn.

⌣

—Have I time to make an apple pie? You are staying the day?

Susy bustles about indoors, pulling out bread and butter, onions and apples and sugar, everything she has, sending her black girl Cotty outside for lettuce.

—No, Susy. We will not trouble you long.

She stops in the middle of a twirl, and says:

—Ma. What is it? Why are you not happy?

—I can see you are.

Her eyes narrow and try to read my face. Again she says:

—Are you not happy?

—I am happy enough.

She laughs:

—Ma, I know you are not one to wear your heart on your sleeve. Did Daddy bring you a present?

Lizzy sucks in her lips at the sound of the word. I touch her fine hair:

—You like presents, do you not, my little dolly?

—Ma—

—I said I am happy, Susy. Now give me some butter and I will start your pastry for you. They will eat you alive, you know.

Susy and Cotty fetch more things, and soon enough we have two pies baking in the embers and a soup cooking above. We hear the talk, talk, talk from outside as Will shows Daniel around the place. The children point out everything they see, as though they were all babies again. As though we have gone backward. *Look at the birds. Look at the clouds. Look at the sky. Look at Daddy.*

Susy calls them in to eat, delighted at hosting so many. Her stomach is small yet under her apron. She ought to have many children, if she is able. If her next birth goes well.

She has Daniel sit at the head of the table. Will readily gives up his place and whispers to Lizzy when she climbs up onto his knee. The rest go on pointing things out to Daniel: Jelly. Cream. Pie.

—Well well. Quite a feast. We could have used you as cook when the Shawnee came calling at the fort, Susy.

Daniel takes a sip of rum, raising his cup to my girl. Will raises his as well and drinks long. Then he says:

—They came calling?

Daniel swallows all the rest of his rum. Will says:

—How many of them?

When he looks up from his cup, Daniel's eyes are over-bright. He says only:

—Some.

From where she is poking at the fire, Susy calls:

—Daddy, what did they want?

Daniel's cup tumbles over. He starts at the noise, but he only says:

—Aha, this means it is time for more. Do you have any?

Israel leans across the table and says:

—Were they coming to fight?

Daniel breathes out strangely, as if his throat were very dry. He says:

—There was some fighting. All through with that now.

Israel's face sets hard. He says:

—I would have killed any of them. All of them.

Daniel stands quickly and flattens his hands on the table. His look is wild:

—There has been enough killing—

Susy stops in the middle of the floor with a platter and says:

—Who was killed?

Daniel shakes his head.

—Who?

—Only two at the fort.

—Who, Daddy?

—It does not matter now—

I say:

—It does matter, Daniel. Who was killed?

The children are all looking at me as I speak. He looks at me too before he says:

—London, Henderson's black. And David Bundrin, the Dutchman. But that is all.

Susy looks stricken and sets the plate before Will. She says:

—Big London, with his hair? He was killed?

She holds out her hands from her head to make a round shape like London's hair. Israel says louder:

—Did you kill many of the Indians?

—Some were killed, yes. The rest have gone now.

His face is deeply sad, though his eyes still flash. He sits and picks up his cup again as if it might have filled itself. Will tries to mend things in his gentle way:

—Well Dan. How did the fort receive you when you went back?

Daniel wipes his hand over his mouth, and says:

—Like you. Surprised to see me living.

He gives Will a half smile, but Susy says:

—Dick Callaway said he would arrest you if you ever came back. Or kill you himself!—Well. We all know Old Dick's mouth. We will talk of him no more.

Susy persists, standing behind Daniel now and gripping his shoulder. He pulls away as though it hurts. She says:

—Were they not all angry you had been gone so long? Did they let you leave again to come back here? Why did you not come sooner?

Daniel says nothing, but gets up again. Polly watches everything, her loose red lips open. He turns to the door and says:

—The fort—

Then he stops and asks where the damned rum has got to. He rummages on Susy's shelf. Polly leaps up to help. No one speaks, until Israel says:

—Well when are we going back to Kentucky to see it?

Before Daniel can answer, I am standing too. I snatch Lizzy from her father and I am out the door with her in my arms, her face tucked into my neck. She struggles to be put down, but I am walking hard, and why would I stop—

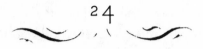

2 4

TWO WEEKS in my house and I hardly speak to him, though he makes his presence felt. He is restless in his old way, but worse, always moving. He keeps himself busy in the fields and the barn with the horses, the children following him everywhere. I do not know what he does or what he tells them. I do not care.

November. A clear night. Very cold.

Another wash day, and the linen freezes on the grass.

I go to see Anna, who is up and about and well. Late that night Jos, one of my brother's blacks, comes over the fields for me and stands outside spinning his hat in his hands. His wife's time is here, her second baby. She lost her first to a fever. The usual black midwife is at another birth and Jos is nervous asking me, but I say I will come. Daniel, taking something apart by the fire, hears me on the stairs and says he will ready me a horse, but I tell him no. I want nothing from him. I walk with Jos in the cold dark, a smell of ice in the air.

The labour is long, but it goes as it should. The baby comes out clean and quiet and opens its eyes to look at its ma. A girl, with plenty of curling dark hair. The black women in the small cabin take turns to hold her tight and sing to her. *Come in, come in.* One brings spiced tea for the mother, who smiles hugely though her eyes are shut. When I get them settled, Jos gives me a great jug of cider, then tries to put a coin in my hand. I tell him to put it away for his new daughter, and he shrugs and says:

—All right. For her wedding day maybe.

I leave the warm cabin and walk out into the dull afternoon. My eyes itch in the wind. I think of the new baby growing old enough to be a young married woman, and to have more babies.

A hawk with black tips to its wings makes a slow circle over the trees and flies off. I stop a moment and take a drink of the cider. It is very sharp. I should not have more, but I do.

⌣

I put the cider behind a box in a corner of the hayloft. I do not drink any more, and at any rate we have plenty of our own in the house. The girls and I made another several jugs with the softest of the fall apples. But I like having Jos's bottle put away. Something of my own, which I earned myself, and no one needs.

It is snowing when I think of it one evening as I am going back to the barn with a shovel one of the boys left out. The children are all indoors now with Daniel and his twitching restlessness. And so I think of the jug in the loft, which I might go and sit with for a short while.

But Daniel is inside the barn, brushing his horse. He looks thin yet, and cold, with drops of melted snow in his hair. I can see him thinking whether to try speaking to me. Then he says:

—Got two good-sized does this afternoon. Plenty for every-one.

—We have plenty already. Everyone has been fed.

I set down the shovel and brush snow from my shoulders. The horse swings its head. Dan makes kisses into its ear, then speaks to me, though he is still looking at the animal:

—My son Israel was born a good shot, like his daddy.

—*Your* son—do you have to say this again, Daniel? Is it all you have to say?

—Seems it needs saying.

He looks at me now. I breathe in:

—Here is what needs saying—did you find him? Your old Cherokee friend, who used to come visiting, then went and killed my first son?

He drops his face against the horse's nose and puts his arm round its neck.

—Rebecca—

—Did you?

—I did not find him.

—Why not? What else was left to do?

—There was some trouble at the fort. And afterwards—

His face goes dark, he cuts himself off from saying more, though I see there is far more to tell. I say:

—Trouble is an easy word.

He strokes the horse's cheek with a flat hand, and says quietly:

—Rebecca, I did look. I do not know where he is.

—Did you not ask your Indian friends? Your Indian father, who you love so much?

—My Shawnee wife knew of him.

I step back without meaning to. His eyes are like cold water now, set straight on me. He says:

—Yes, I have another wife.

—How pleasant for you.

My chest aches as I say it. The thought of him happy as can be with an Indian woman, in an Indian house.

—She was more wife to me than you have been.

—Go to her then.

—I do not know where she is. I do not know if she is—

—Still kindly favoured towards you? Since you left her, I would imagine she is not. I cannot see how she would want you back.

—You know nothing, nothing of her.

—I know *you.*

Daniel comes towards me, white spittle gathered in the corners of his lips. He says:

—Do you know me, Rebecca?

His voice is quieter than I expect. The pain goes through to my backbone. I say:

—Do you not think of him? Jamesie?

Daniel's shoulders sag. He says:

—All I do is think of him.

I go cold inside, I cannot help it. My feet and fingertips ache with it. I cannot help crying out the dreadful words again:

—It was your idea to send him back for food, it was your idea to go to that dreadful place at all. He was only a boy, a child—

—He was not a child.

Daniel's voice breaks and we both stand helpless to move. I cannot get enough air. I stumble backward, but Daniel catches my shoulder, his face twisting. He says:

—We do not have to talk of it. It will never happen again. I promise you. I promise.

He is kissing my wet cheeks and eyes. My lashes catch between his dry lips. His smell—

I push him from me, but he catches my arms, searching my face.

—We will have a happier life now, Rebecca. Better for us all. Forget everything else, we can forget it. Land for all the children, our own fresh land, not your brothers' charity.

I look at his eyes, where joy is rising. I twist away from his hands and I say:

—I do know you, and I know you are wrong. We are happy here already, we have a happy life, and you are wrong.

He begins slowly.

When winter is coming on, he says there is a place some eight miles up the river. We could have it. A *safe place all our own*. He plans a bigger cabin there. I hear him talking to the children about it. Plank floors. A great tall hearth, taller than Jesse. A chimney of smooth river stones. Several rooms upstairs, with chinked walls between. He has already begun it, just in case. *Room for all of us together*, he says, more than once. *All right, my girl?*

His heart beats fast all the time. I can see it through his shirt. He is desperate for plans and busyness, scratching out all he has done before, trying to make things new. His happiness is wild, like an animal that needs trapping.

The children are delighted. A bigger house, flat land, already cleared. *No more stones to pick out of the furrows, my big Jesse, though you are as strong as your daddy, you are pony-built like me*, says Daniel. And Jesse laughs and loves him.

Closer to the Blue Ridge. Closer to good pelts and good hunting. For Israel. Who laughs and loves him.

Nothing in me wishes to leave this place. Only the children love the idea of the future. They are so happy.

The flat green lawn in my dream. I try to see it. The children playing and sitting on it.

Daniel persuades Will to think of coming upriver and building a house close by, though Susy is bigger with child every day. When I go on a cold Monday to see how she is and help her and Cotty with the washing, I have her sit a moment at her table with her feet up on a chair. She has shadows beneath her eyes but is still lively. Her fingers skip over the tabletop, drumming out a tune.

—Are you never still, Susy?

—Why should I be?

She points and stretches her feet as I go to the window to check the fire is still high under the washpot. I ask her:

—Do you wish to move upriver?

—Why not? I like new houses.

—Do you not like this house?

—I do, but I might like it there better.

—You are your father's girl.

—I am.

She jumps up, her hand cradling her belly:

—We ought to get Lizzy's old baby things out and washed, Ma. This one is eager to see the world. Look how it kicks me! It must be a boy.

Another Daniel. Another Jamesie—

I ask:

—Do you really wish to go? Can you see us all there? I cannot.

—Ma, you are too afraid of everything.

She pokes me with her elbow and kisses my cheek. I take a breath and stroke my daughter's back:

—Well Susy.

—Well Ma. I am never wrong.

I laugh:

—Perhaps a new place is no bad thing for a new little life.

—And no bad thing for you, Ma. We could all use more room, at any rate.

So I carry their plump Lizzy warm and sleepy on my knee when we ride to the new house with all our things in the wagon. It is the day before Christmas. The sky is grey and low, the snow crusty. Daniel has gone ahead, and stands pleased in the doorway to meet us. He has built a big place. He has even scraped the logs clean of bark, so the house shines yellow. He helps the girls down from the wagon and horses. Polly says it is the best house she has ever seen in her life. She throws her arms about him and he dances her in a circle. She is like a cat that once had a home and is determined to get itself another, the same look as Martha always had. The same slipping in to make quiet trouble.

I have Jos's cider put away in a chest under my linen.

Daniel does not mention that this land is still my granddaddy's, only none of my brothers is using it and they have told him he can build on it. He is so easily able to make things seem true—and everyone listens.

—

Three more births for the women around us over December. I lose none of them. The babies are all fat healthy ones and come head down. The mothers heal quickly and have plenty of milk. No one is ill, not even a cold.

After Twelfth Night I have my birthday, and I am forty years old. Susy makes a fuss and an enormous currant cake. Slicing it, I cut my palm, and I stand watching it bleed a moment, then I bind it up. The cut throbs and I feel quite alive. I cannot stop my smile at the way the children are singing all over the big house. Their faces are red in the firelight when they run up to kiss me.

A draft spills snow from the roof outside the window. My limbs soften into the chair. Daniel sewed a birthday cushion for it with the girls. His big clumsy stitches made me laugh when he handed it to me. Lizzy curls in my lap and reaches up under my cap to feel my hair.

I feel my tiredness. But I feel we are quite safe again, or nearly so. I am not used to feeling this. Daniel keeps across the room, but he smiles at me and I smile also before I think. I tell him it is a good house, and he gives a little bow. He wants to give me things—I shut my eyes as Lizzy's small fingers rake my hair out of its knot.

In spring, we plant on all the clear acres. Everything grows tall. The cow has twin calves and makes more thick milk than they can drink. I cannot understand how well it all does, and how huge the children are growing too, as if Daniel has some fresh magic about him. What did he sell for it?

His happiness is still wild, but he controls it. He works and works when he is not off hunting with Israel in the mountains, showing him the grounds of his youth, as he says. He always says it. He kisses my cheek in the mornings. He takes care to do no more.

Perhaps this place will be a good one for us. A good home for many years. My heart wishes to believe it. Often I dream of this yellow house as I sleep in it.

A warm day, high thin clouds. I think of making a green where the house faces the creek. We are tending the garden between our houses, tying up the long bean vines, when Susy stops and stands, arching her back, and frowns.

—Ma, I think this baby is ready today.

I had thought it might be my girl's time. Over the last week, the baby has dropped low, and Susy's breasts have begun to leak in the night. Her face cramps now with her womb, which I can see from the shifting of her belly under her skirt. I say:

—I think you are right. Come indoors.

Polly has been weeding with Cotty and hears everything, as she always does. She pops her head up and says she will help midwife. She might be a help, we have no one else near, but her curiosity chafes at me. I say:

—No, Polly. You keep at your work here.

She thinks to argue, but seeing Israel and Daniel coming down-river from the mountain trail, she only turns and bends with her backside high in the air for their benefit. I tell my Becky to watch the little ones, and I take Susy in to her bedroom.

The pains grip Susy very fast this time. I tell her the baby is impatient to see its ma and its big sister, but there is almost no rest between the cramps, great waves that seize her and make her gasp. Daniel knocks and asks if he should send for some of my sisters and aunts to help, but there is no time. He hears my worry, and hovers outside. I hear him thinking he might help, he might deliver this one himself as he insisted on trying to do when my Jesse was born. Watching between my legs for his child—*his* child—to come into the world.

I tell him we are all right. He says, If you are sure, and I say Yes, we are all right, Daniel, do not worry yourself.

He goes. The pupils of Susy's eyes are large, her hair gummed to her forehead. She cannot keep from groaning with the pains. I can only hold her hands and stroke her face. But I will have no one else here. I want only us, and quiet. I tell her:

—All the births this year have been good. Your baby will be here soon to join the rest.

—Ma, I cannot—

—You can, sweet.

She is still very small. Her hips are narrow, a small forked branch.

I move her from the bed to the birth stool and have her open her thighs wide. I rub between them with grease, pressing with my thumbs to soften her. It has been so quick and she is already exhausted, with no rest at all from the pains.

—Ma—Ma—

—Not long now, Susy. It will not be much longer.

I am kneeling to see. The baby's head shows a moment, then is pulled back up inside into the dark. This happens again. Again.

—Ma, please—

She twists on the stool. Her knuckles are pale and shaking on the armrests. My hand inside her makes her howl, I cannot grip the baby. I am helpless. I cannot bear to watch.

We need no ghosts in this new-smelling house.

—*Please*—

I stretch Susy's opening down hard with my thumb. A great burst of a pain tears down her, and in a gush of warm red water the baby is born, slipping quietly out all at once.

It is blue.

It is perfect. And perfectly still—

I fetch a cloth, I rub at it with my hands, roll it onto its side and press on its chest and stomach. The smell is of damp, tired air.

—It is all right, Ma?

It has fair hair, fair little lashes. Soft skin. I bend over it and whisper:

—You must not go. You must stay. We will all stay here.

When I make it this promise, it shudders under my palm and moves its head. Its tiny mouth opens with a sputter and a mew. Good girl. She breathes in and out, in and out. I smooth her cheeks. Susy is laughing and crying on the stool, shuddering with the after-pains. I tell her she has a daughter, a little swan.

Not another Jamesie, not another Daniel. Her own fair little self.

Once the afterbirth has come, I help Susy back to the bed. I give her the baby once I have cleaned and wrapped the girl. My poor daughter looks at the small thing cradled in her arm. After a time she says with a thin smile:

—A girl. I am glad. Are you happy, Ma?

—I am.

And I am happy watching the two of them. I am thankful for the quiet and peace that have come into the house with the child. She has made it a new house, truly.

Until the door bangs open and Polly strides in without knocking.

—Polly, have you been indoors listening all this time?

—No. Let me see the baby. What is it?

She is saucier than ever, going to stroke the baby's head and coo in its small face. She wants to hold it but I tell her no. Susy tells her it is a girl, and she runs back out, tugging up her skirts and calling like a trumpet:

—Daddy Daddy, you have another granddaughter! Susy has a girl!

I hear Daniel's voice, his proud laughter. *Well well. Another little miss for the new country.*

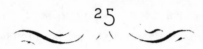

25

ONE NIGHT soon afterwards in the dark new house, I realize I did not ask my Susy in her labour who the father was.

I have never forgotten the midwife's question before. Maybe I am getting old. But of course the father is Will. I see him in the tiny girl's cautious look. My new granddaughter keeps her feathery white hair and lashes, and watches about her all the time. She is light as a bird, with a long slender neck. Her ma has named her for Jemima, but I call her Swan. Perhaps I saw one once in a book, when I was very young. I have a dream that she flies off, her tiny feet kicking at the air behind her. When I go to see Susy, I hold the little one and keep her feet in my hands.

Perhaps my daughter Jemima has a child now too in Kentucky. I wonder if I will ever know it. I do not ask Daniel if his Shawnee wife has children.

I do not ask him about her at all. I do not wish to know any more. I will forget what he said and look at my little granddaughter and have my own thoughts.

He lets me be private. He is always courteous with me, and is often off hunting. When he is here, he plays with the children and talks with Will about making money. And he visits my brothers downriver, getting the news, he says. He has never been a great friend of theirs, but he must always be busy now, and he is happy in that. He does not talk often of Kentucky, though Israel and the other boys are forever asking him about it, the fort, the fighting and killing. He tells Jesse once that he set the children there to gather bullets after the fight. They picked up a woman's body-weight of lead from the fort and fields. Another hundredweight dug out of the walls.

He lowers his arms and curls them to mime the heaviness, and staggers about in a circle, grinning. When he sees me watching, he stands straight and talks instead of how well the corn is coming on here, what a fine crop it will be.

I know he is trying to keep me happy. I tidy the yellow house. The grass is growing. We are staying here.

He is happy still, though I see him twitch when the horses make any noise in the barn and his eyes are always moving. He kisses me one morning and goes off without a word. He is gone five nights, then six, then eleven. The longest he has left us since he returned. Jesse and Morgan go about frowning and pretending to shoot each other with long sticks. Israel goes off to hunt on his own, impatient and irritated. Polly hardly speaks to me, as though it were all my doing.

The days grow longer. July is dry and hot. We scythe the hay twice, and the flax is already cut and soaking. The river goes down a few inches but is still high. Daniel is still gone, and I find myself worrying after him in the old way, when I do not wish to.

It is twilight and I am cleaning pots when Susy's Will comes to the door. His face is cold and strained. My chest goes tight.

—Will?

—Lizzy. Have you seen her?

Her little round face leaps before my eyes:

—She is not here. Is she, Becky? Levina? Polly? Have you seen her today?

The girls all shake their heads. I tell Becky to look upstairs, and she runs up with Levina, but is down again in a minute, saying no, not there.

—Will, where did you see her last?

—Susy had her in the garden and went in to feed the baby. We have seen nothing of her since.

—Oh God—

This bursts from me before I can stop it. My heart is racing. I walk outside though my feet feel cold and unsteady, and my heart pounds faster in the outdoor warmth. The girls follow at my heels, but I tell them to look round the garden and the fields.

—Do it now.

Following me, Will says:

—Where are you going?

I do not answer. I begin to run now, down past the barn to the river. The spot Lizzy likes to stand throwing pebbles in. The shallow clear place where we wash when it is warm. Before the bend, where it slides off into a deep pool.

As I run stumbling over the rough hay stubble I can *see* her, my round little girl standing with her apron full of stones, scattering them all at once into the water with her eyes screwed shut. I see bears, wolves, water, the face of that Cherokee they called Jim—

—Lizzy!

In the birches along the river I keep calling. Will is behind me now, crashing, calling too, as loud as he can. His hoarse voice is terrible. I turn and tell him to hush. The hoofbeats I could feel through the ground without knowing it catch up to our hearing.

—Will—

At my side now he nods, he hears them too, some distance away down the river. He yells:

—Who is there?

He fires a shot high. The flash brightens his wild cold face. At the bang a bird flies into the air. I think of my dream, my little bird flying off—only not this bird, not Lizzy.

The noise does not stop the rider. Will is loading again but his hands are shaking, he is cursing into his powder. I stand where I am, watching the horse come towards us, trying to see. The rider calls:

—I have her.

All I can think of is the Cherokee who killed my boy, and those who took my girl Jemima.

I have her. Daniel called this across the fort to me when they came back with her and the Callaway girls. My eyes ache, looking. And again it is Daniel's voice, Daniel on the horse, now beside us with his beard grown in again and his eyes pale in the dusk. Lizzy is astride in front of him, her fat little legs bumping the saddle. She turns her face to me and reaches down—*Gramama*—and I take her in my arms and breathe her in, her own sweet coppery scent.

Daniel dismounts too and bends over, hands on knees. Will says:

—Where did you find her?

—I ran into her walking downriver. Going to Grandmama's house on her own, without that baby, she said.

—Oh Lizzy, you must not do such things without telling your ma.

She pulls her cheek away from mine and begins to cry, a tired sound.

Daniel stands to pat her hand and says:

—She was right as a little soldier marching along. You are Granddaddy's own flesh and blood, are you not, my wandering Eliza?

He reaches to take her, but I hold on:

—She is not a soldier. And that is not her name.

—Well. I did find her.

—You were gone again.

—But here I am, and with her.

—You do not know a thing about her.

Lizzy tips her head back and cries harder, and I am crying with her. I feel how tired I am as well, tired of the old fear that is always with me, even when I think it has gone. Daniel squats again and coughs dryly. Will goes to him. I spin and walk back towards the hayfield with my granddaughter heavy in my arms.

234

⌣

I cannot sleep after Will comes to take Lizzy home to her poor mother. I sit up rocking by the empty hearth late in the night. My back aches, and the room is hot and stale, but I do not move. When the door creaks open, I stay in the chair. Daniel steps over the threshold slowly and lifts the light. He is pale and shaking, and smells of rum. At once he says:

—I knew—another child. By that name. Eliza. I knew her. She had reddish hair, lighter than the others in the town. I do not know where she is now. I do not know if they sent her away because of me, I do not know if she is alive—

Words tumble from him. I do not wish to hear of his other life, any of his stories. I say:

—Your granddaughter's name is Elizabeth.

—I know it. I know it. I found her, did I not? She is all right.

He walks in a tight circle. I say:

—You did not tell us where *you* were this time.

He stops and looks at me a moment, then he says:

—Oh, I checked my old trapline. I saw your brothers.

—What do you want with them? You have never liked any of them.

He shrugs. He is as restless as an ant, pacing the room.

—Set down the light. What is troubling you, Daniel? You have been like this since you came back. You are white as a ghost now.

He bursts out:

—Do not talk of ghosts! They have left me, they do not come when I want them.

—What do you mean?

He swings round to look at me, breathing rum into my face and holding the lamp to it:

—I have to go back. I cannot let them murder me.

—What—murder you? Ghosts? Indians, more likely.

—No. No. Never the Shawnee.

—Who, then? Dick Callaway at the fort? Your friend William Hill will always speak for you, even if no one else will.

Daniel moans as if sick:

—No, no, no. Hill is gone.

—Gone where?

—I do not know. Detroit. Dead, most likely. Gone. I do not feel him about me anymore, he is gone.

—Detroit. Daniel, I cannot understand you.

He sinks onto his heels before my chair, setting down the light and hanging onto my hand:

—The Shawnee took me there to bargain. The British tried to buy me. My Shawnee father would not sell me. He loved me, I loved him. We tried to stop what was coming, the terrible fighting, I did not tell you how bad.

—Daniel, why—

—There was meant to be help, the Virginia militia was meant to come sooner. And then, then, the people at the fort wanted to imprison me. After all I did to help. I cannot be there, but I cannot be here.

—I do not know what you mean.

—I killed a man. I am afraid I did. A man I knew, Pompey, a black man the Shawnee had. It could have been my shot that killed

235

him. He was right, I ought to have bought him, if they would have let me. I keep waiting for him.

He begins to shake harder and gives a dry coughing sob before he steadies himself with his hands on my knee. I do not know what more to say to him. His backbone almost rattles with his shaking. It hurts me to watch. As if he were as little as Jesse, I reach for his shoulders and I tell him:

—We are safe here. The house is new. No ghosts. It was a fair place to build, you were right about that.

He laughs, looking down at the floorboard and rapping on it three times. He says:

—It is all right here, but not enough.

—It is enough. You have made a good home.

—Do you like it? Have I made you happy? It is not enough.

—It is enough.

His fingers grip my knee. I look at his hand, a white scar across its back, and I touch it and say:

—Your poor old ma told me once that you were born hands-first. Reaching for some other place already.

He looks up at me. His eyes are wet, and one has a small spot of blood in the white. He kisses my knee, my palm. His beard pricks at my skin. When he looks up his face is sweetened, softened, like Neddy's.

I loved his body once. When we were married and very young. His boyish thinness, the narrow patch of black hair on his chest, the slope of his backbone. His thicker legs.

He touches me, his hands asking. I do not stop them. It is a strange relief not to do so, as though we have fallen back in time and we are the way we were when young. No children, Jamesie never even born. Perhaps that would have been better.

Daniel calls me his witch, in his old way. *If we could go back*, he says.

On the floor before the dry bare hearth we lie. He is thin still, the skin slightly loose round his waist, the hair down his stomach black still. He is scarred everywhere, one quite fresh on his shoulder, another a swollen lump on his back. It pains me to feel his skin come to this. The rum on his breath, the same old taste of his mouth beneath that. Daniel. I pull my head back. He does not try to kiss me again. He only strokes my arms. Above me his face is sweet still, with its deep sad channels. I line them out with my finger. Then I keep my eyes shut.

⌣

Over the next weeks he comes and goes from the house again several times. He does as he pleases, restless but quieter in himself, decided somehow. I am easier watching him. The air stays calm, hardly a breeze through August.

I am tired down to my bones. Not even harvest yet, and the girls have to help me more and more. In September I know it, I know it for certain, what I have been unable to let myself believe, what cannot be possible. He has what he wants. A fresh life. I am pregnant.

My other life flies off easily as a bird——

LIVE-FOREVER

2 6

Autumn 1779

The Author gives some account of himself and family. His first inducements to travel. He is shipwrecked, and swims for his life. Gets safe on shore in the country of Lilliput, is made a prisoner, and carried up the country.

THE WORDS from Gulliver's book roll about in my head when I lead the packed horse through one of the narrower passes. We are going up the country too but I am no prisoner now. I never will be again. I am some yards out in front of the rest. We are not quick, with so many of us. But I am easy, I know the way. I tell the story of Gulliver to myself as I used to tell it to the children.

The Clinch River is low, and we get all the animals and children across easy. Into Powell's Valley with its bristling forest. Not far from where you died, Jamesie. Leaves are spinning down from the maples and birches into the creeks now, as they were when you were killed.

We will not pass close to your grave this time. I will not say so to Rebecca. She is all right, riding at the back with her brothers, who are game to scout out claims farther over the Kentucky River from the fort, on better land I know, and make money to add to their heaps of it. I talked and talked with them in Carolina until they agreed to come. I told them they could turn round again if they didn't like it. *You can always go back.*

I have promised my wife a new thick-walled house, with as big a fence as she likes. There are more of us, fresh people, a hundred. It will be better.

My horse stumbles and brays at a rockfall. It stiffens its legs as if it wishes to go no farther back towards Kentucky. See Colonel Dick's prize bay gelding gaping up twist-necked out of the terrible well after the siege, where it fell or chose to hide itself during the last Hell of shots and fire before the rain set in. The big Dutch well-digger Tice Prock laughing like a crow. Dick muttering about how he should never have had the horse's balls off, it had been too meek for this place.

Old Dick ought to have had his own balls off. But once the quiet settled and we knew the Shawnee were truly gone, his swelled up instead. He stalked about counting all that had gone wrong, making a tally. Well by my count and the look of the drag-marks on the ground, they had more than thirty dead. We had only Bundrin and London. Nat Henderson muttered about suing someone for the loss of his good black man. But Hancock and his glowing Baptists said it was all a miracle, having changed their minds about the end of the world. Neddy prayed with them. My head seemed set on too tight, with too much stuffed in it.

The animals never ceased moaning, even when we were able to scrape up some meadow grass and stalks for them. The children kept hearing things, Dick's Kezia bawled day and night about the sound of shots that were not there but were just going to start, she knew it. London's little Jacky saw me once as I passed Uncle Monk's door, and flew back into the dark.

Big Simon Kenton and Alexander Montgomery in his fine beaded shirt came riding in two days after the siege, not scalped at all. The pair of them had kept to the forest after their trip back to the empty Paint Creek town, knowing the Shawnee were about. When they decided it was safe to journey back to the fort, they heard our screaming and saw the smoke from miles away over the river. They made instead for Harrodsburg to tell them we were all lost. They had come back to bury us.

Seeing me outside the gate, big-boned Kenton rubbed his face with his hat and said, I never heard such awful hollering in my life. We were sure you were all dead. I said, And how do you know we are not ghosts? To which Old Dick said, And how do *you* know it, Captain Boone?

I ought to have seen what he had in his mind by the composed way he said it, by the way his girls never looked at me when I passed.

I sent the children to gather bullets, to get them used to being outside the walls again. Ned's young Sarah showed me her fingers with the dull metal shine on them. She said it would not wash off, she thought it might never do so. She pressed them onto my forearm to try to mark me, but I did not mark.

A small Virginia militia turned up much too late. All we had for them to do was help rebuild the wrecked parts of the fort. Until Dick came out with his plan to have me court-martialled for giving us up to the Indians, for putting us all in danger of murder over and over again. For playing double all my life here.

He wrote to Logan's Fort and got silent black-headed Lieutenant Ben Logan on his side, and they decided to try me there before him and the other officers. Coming to announce this to me, Dick said he took no pleasure in doing his duty, but I saw his grimness was cut through with joy. He had been waiting very long to see me a prisoner of the right sort.

They took my gun and tied my hands to my saddle horn, I laughed when they did it. A group of us rode the twenty miles to Logan's Station, southwest along the Kentucky River. Jemima and Flanders kept to the rear, they did not talk to me. I pulled up my horse for a minute when I saw the crab orchard I found my first time in Kentucky. In blossom then, in paradise. Now grey and unbreathing. Well.

Colonel Dick gave my horse a kick and on we went. Logan's Fort had a defiant squat look, set in its pickets. Lieutenant Logan told us the Shawnee had been about doing mischief but could not do much of it. He showed us very proud how he had built a long covered ditch from the spring to the fort. For a time we all stood about listening to the slow glugging of the water and acting as though my wrists were not bound. I thought to tell Logan how easy his ditch would be to blow up or poison with a rotten carcass, but I did not.

The court sat outside though the air was cold. Ben Logan has a nephew who was one of the salt boilers taken prisoner with me, I remembered it when I saw Logan's face shift beneath his black brow as Dick announced me formally. The witnesses were marched up: Kenton was told to tell the jury about our Paint Creek trip. Was it a stupid time to leave the fort? Yes it was. Was anything of value taken at the town? Only a scalp, Kenton mumbled round his big teeth. Then Hancock stood and talked long and preacherly of my ways at Old Chillicothe, my loving friendship with my Indian father and others. He said he had prayed and prayed for me, but now was the time for truth. And Ned had to say he overheard me during the siege talking to someone outside the walls about a wife. A Shawnee wife? Yes. And perhaps a child. Neddy looked out with his mild face, innocent as a pat of soap.

He did everything backward, everything wrong, he ought to be broken of his commission! So Colonel Dick could not stop himself from yelling. Then I got up. I said I had all along been using a strategem to fool the enemy and keep us safe. That is all I had ever done. I sat myself down on the ground, the chill of it came up through my backside. I was tired of saying so, they were tired of hearing it.

White-headed Major Billy stared me up and down as if he were ciphering. Dick then strode forward and asked that Jemima tell of anything I had said to her in private, but I got back up and said very quiet they would have to kill me first. Old Dick's face was a fiery triumph. But Logan said he would not call up Jemima. My daughter stood at the rear with Flanders, she watched and held herself with her arms crossed about her. I know she was still seeing me too close to Martha in my cabin at the fort.

There is an easy trail to the falls of the Ohio from Logan's, as I know. I could have ridden off on it once Logan and his jury decided there was no proof of my having done any wilful wrong, in spite of Old Dick and Hancock and others. No *proof* of it. They made sure to put plenty of weight on that word. Logan is a careful man. Privately to me he said he was giving me this chance, but he wondered where his nephew was now.

Logan, I know I am in your debt. You and the jury watched me go back to my horse. I have never seen Old Dick in such a cold rage but he believes in order, he listened to your rules.

I could have ridden straight for Old Chillicothe. But I did not. I turned for Carolina.

And now I am here walking back again, past my son's hidden grave to the east. I do not stop to say so to Rebecca or the others. I do not say I have seen inside the grave. I do not tell them anything. I am so sore thinking of all that has happened since that day, Jamesie, my tongue dries up and takes on a grim taste. I know I will never talk of it again. It will go well this time, I know it with all my guts, which I trust as they are mine.

⌣

And here it is, all you have to do: plant a crop of corn. Build any sort of pigsty. Call it a cabin and have acres, all yours. Cheap! Cheap! Sound like a chicken saying so.

I did just that on a flat northwest of the fort some time ago, over the Kentucky River where a few buffalo roads meet. So it is mine. Far enough from the fort, which is no place at all. We will start fresh there. It is what we will do.

Rebecca's half brothers and their families and blacks, a couple of her Bryan uncles, some cousins of mine are all with us. The Bryans make noise about loyalty to the old king, and think they will be safe to say so in the new territory, which might go back to English rule yet if the fight goes that way. I do not care what they believe, so long as they are here.

Early snow begins before we are out of the mountains and on the flat of the Warrior's Path. But it is light drifting stuff only, and does not sit thick on the ground. There is plenty of grass for the livestock, the children are all right. When we camp each night they toast corncobs at the fires and spin the turkeys on the spits the women hang up over the flames. My son Israel gets plenty of those, he hardly has to go off the trail to find one perched in a tree. I tell him they like the red in his hair. This makes our young Miss Polly laugh and make gobbling noises and say that animals love Israel, and Israel grins and says he loves them too, well-cooked in his belly. His grin is so much like my dead brother's, who was Israel also. Well the two of you would have liked to know each other.

We keep moving each day, though we are very slow. No one is about, I feel it. Too late in the year for war parties. Still my eyes seem to jump out of my skull if I see any movement, or even before I see it. Without quite wanting to I am looking out for you, my father. What my eyes wish for is your soft footprint, your sign, a thin sharp blaze raked into bark where only I will see. Your knife dropped in the snow to point me the way you have gone. Your face waiting. And some way behind you in the trees, more faces, Methoataske's and young Eliza's.

We see no one, no sign, the rest of the way down into Kentucky. It is December and cool when we reach the edge of the meadow beyond the fields outside the fort, close enough to see the walls we put up, gone wet grey now. I stop us at the tree line, I will not go any closer. I look over towards the great elm on the flat, it is still standing, no leaves on it now. Bile burns a quick trail up into my mouth. This was where my father stood watching the fort and hoping we might make peace.

247

I send my son Israel out across the empty fields towards the walls. He makes a white flag of a shirt for a joke, and though I tell him there is no need for it, I am glad he goes waving it. He leaves dark prints in the thin skin of snow. Now he is inside and we sit waiting.

I do not go to Rebecca. She has ridden much of the way with Lizzy before her in the saddle, keeping close to the Bryans. They have told her it will be good to get fresh land, that there is more we can all have. When I do look at her I see tiredness on her face, the tiny channels in the corners of her eyes. Her belly is swollen now. She does not look much at me, she acts again as though I am dead or might be so any minute. She does not like to touch me, perhaps in case her hand goes straight through me. But Rebecca, it will be all right.

My legs wish to get me across the Kentucky River and onto my own land away from this dreadful place. I do not look at where the peach orchard was, at where we had our talks. It is burnt now and covered in snow at any rate. I do not look at the place where Pompey's body lay half bare and wrestled over by pigs. If I saw a pig I would shoot it.

One of the children howls back in the trees, his ma hushes him quick, but the noise makes me think of the children during the battle. I find I am watching the ramparts as if my own self will appear, waiting for the next attack all unknowing what to do. This makes me feel sick all through. And no one is on the ramparts now.

Israel comes back out, followed by Squire's thin shape, and Ned's. They stand in a knot close to the fort wall and so I get up, I go forward with my gun on my shoulder. Over the field I yell:

—Tell Dick he has no need to come out! Tell all the rest. We will be across the river, away from here. Tell them.

They have started towards me when someone bursts round the corner of the walls at a run. Jemima. She bolts across the white field with her head down and her arms tight to her chest. I go to meet her, but seeing me, she halts some feet away. She is thin, her face too pointed, she holds a bundle against her body. The memory of old anger falls over her eyes as she stares. She says nothing. I do not know what I can say. I try a laugh, I say:

—Well Jemima. Who is this?

The bundle moves and squalls, it is a very small baby wrapped in a bad beaver pelt. Jemima says flat:

—My daughter.

My girl looks so young and so lean, my heart falls to my feet. Jemima's mouth slants. From the trees Rebecca calls soft:

—Jemima.

This is all she says. Jemima looks past me:

—Oh.

She does not move but she watches as Rebecca walks out to us, moving as though her hips pain her. When she reaches us she looks only at the tiny child wrapped up. Again she says:

—Jemima—

All in a rush my girl cries:

—Ma!

—But—this is your baby?

Jemima pauses, then she holds the little one up so Rebecca can see:

—Her name is Sallie.

My oldest sister's name, another one they called a whore. Jemima's face blazes up fresh now, it fights itself until it twists and she begins to cry. She is not one for crying, and tries to cover her face with one arm. To her ma she says:

—You did not have to go.

Rebecca holds her by the elbows and hushes her. If she tells her mother about me I will say the truth, it is true, though the fort and Martha in it all have the feel of some ancient story. But Jemima is pulling something from the waist of her skirt, a little scrap of yellow cloth bright against the dirt and snow. Rebecca takes it very careful with her fingers. As if of its own accord, Jemima's hand has gone to her ma's round belly. She says:

—I kept that for you.

Rebecca breathes out. She says:

—It was my mother's.

—I know.

—You ought to have it. But thank you.

They both stand weeping and staring until Jemima's tiny child howls like one raising the devil. Rebecca bites her lip, she smiles and touches the baby's face:

—This is certainly your daughter.

They hold one another then, laughing and rocking slow with the little one squeaking and yelping between them.

—How do, Dan.

Squire and Neddy reach us with Israel. We are all how-doing and talking when movement back at the fort catches me. People on the walls now, watching. The blocky shape in the centre is Old Dick. He has his gun set on the wall in our direction. Near the front corner bastion is someone smaller. A woman, in women's clothes. She turns her head and shakes her cap down to her neck so her dark hair shows against the pale sky. It is Martha, and though I cannot see her eyes I know they are looking, looking, looking for me.

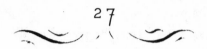

27

CHRISTMAS DAY and we set up our station camp in the new place over the river, the Bryans a few miles off on their own claim. A good place, Rebecca will see how good once the snow goes. I get us a buffalo cow for our dinner, it is a good sign. I ask her a few times to sing *Now the joyful bells a-ringing* for us, and at last she does so, and the children dance and make her smile. My Jesse bounces up afterwards to ask me what we will call our new town, I tell him I do not know. He says we can call it Madoc Town after the man in the story, the madman, and I say, All right, if you like.

Squire comes riding out over the snow to bring us a festive bottle, the last he has, as he tells me. We take a drink together and watch the children running about. He tells me:

—At the fort they are calling this place Boone's Folly. Among other things.

—Well. So it is.

—So.

—Will you come and live here, Squire?

He taps the side of the shelter with his elbow, and he says:

—Not yet. Jane is all nerves since the siege.

—I will save you a claim.

—Well.

He says he will stay the night at least, and I fetch him a drink of my own, and a slice of the buffalo hump. Once the rest are sleeping we sit at the fire in quiet for some time. I ask him:

—Any sign of our Shawnee friends?

Squire eyes me sideways, puffing on his pipe. He says:

—No sign of your Shawnee friends lately.

He looks away, and says:

—That young Alexander Montgomery went out on a raid a while ago, trying for horses, and they killed him.

—Montgomery killed?

—Yes. We found him.

—Was Kenton with him?

—Captured.

Squire says no more and I ask no more. Montgomery was always wanting in his secret heart to go Indian, I saw it under that beaded shirt that was the pride of his life. I will not let his green eyes open in my brains, I will not see big Simon Kenton tied to a stake and burning slow. I say:

—We won, Squire, you know it. There will be peace. There will be.

Squire keeps his eyes on the dark tree line, and says:

—I hope you are not wrong.

—I am not wrong. I know them.

I keep careful watch late into each night but I see nothing, and Israel sees nothing when he goes off looking for game and for a good claim of his own. When my boy is preparing to go to Virginia to get the papers for his land and mine, and for the claim I have made for Squire, Neddy rides up on his big pretty grey. I leave my wood splitting to meet him, my back pains me at any rate. Israel calls to him:

—I built my cabin, did you happen to see it? Two feet square and full of cobs, ha! I will make your claim for you too if you like, Uncle Ned.

Ned gives us one of his sweet sleepy smiles. His cheeks are redder with the wind, he is more a doll than ever, always somehow clean and young looking. His hair is still all black down at the roots. Looking at the heavy sky he says:

—Not just now, Israel. You go ahead.

To Ned I say:

—You wish to stay on in the remains of that goddamned hell-hole then?

Neddy shrugs:

—For now.

—That is fine, you do as you like. In the spring you will see our apple trees, you will smell the blossom from the fort. And the cherries. Is that not right, Rebecca? My wife is a lover of cherries, I know.

Rebecca is at the back of the shelter. I cannot see if she is looking at Ned, and he is watching the sky again as if he is embarrassed to look at our camp. Lean-tos built of boughs and boards and sticks, open to the fires in front of them. Fresh-cut stumps all round. We have a stockade up round us, though it is too cold to build cabin foundations yet. But it is a fine place to build, it will be very fine.

My wife keeps herself still in her old fashion, as though her bones were glass. She is all waiting. I have promised her a flat lawn in spring, she asked for that very sudden one morning.

She keeps the children huddled in the shelter much of the time until Israel comes back safe. She has Jemima too. My girl said she would not live in the fort another second. And so she and Flanders and their Sallie have a lean-to next to us. Jemima is still not easy with me, she cannot let herself love me as she wants to, I have done too much wrong. I pile their shelter with furs and kindling and whatever I hunt goes to them first. Though there is not so much to hunt. Israel says the same now every night when he comes back from looking with his friend, young Joseph Scholl. Too cold to load their guns even if they saw anything to shoot at.

The cold is bone-deep as January crawls forward. I brought
plenty of corn and I share it round, but we lose half the cattle and
five horses when a blizzard buries us early one morning. The rest of
the cows and pigs and two more horses go in the freeze that starts
a week later. When I go to inspect the carcasses I am struck with a
sudden thought of myself as a boy with another horse, Jezebel, riding
her in the night towards her death. She fell and broke her neck and
I had to help her die, I cut her throat. Neddy was there, he saw it, we
were drunk then and young. I have not named a horse since, I call
them all different things on different days, Spot or Paint or Nelly.

253

Jezebel followed me at times with my other dead when I was
younger, her hay-scented breath on me.

But no, I will not think of Jezebel in the ground or anyone else
as I look over the bodies. The meat is only meat, we jerk what we
can but there is not enough salt, never enough goddamned salt in
my life.

Well. I chop firewood until my arms are like to fly off. The fires
roar all day and night, I do not care if they burn down the lean-tos
as long as they keep burning. My thoughts creep upriver and over to
the Ohio, to Old Chillicothe town and my Shawnee family. Perhaps
I am no orphan. Perhaps I still have my father Black Fish, perhaps he
will come looking for me again and we will find our own peace.

I tell myself this story. At once I am torn up with pains for my
Indian house, as though I had left my legs there. I have not thought
of the black pot hanging from the smoke-hole in the roof, or the
stars showing there. Is it gone? This thought snaps on me like a trap.
It is an awful pain, it is like dying. In the night beside Rebecca I
dream of my other wife as a deer again, a woman caught in a deer's
body but knowing she is human.

All night I keep waking and wishing to prowl about, to give
my legs something to do and somewhere to go. But there is
nowhere to go.

⌣

We are all alive in the middle of February when the worst cold lifts off us like the skirts of some witch from one of Rebecca's old tales. The children are so happy to be allowed out of the lean-tos, they run about in a frenzy spinning wedges of crusty snow at one another and jumping on frozen puddles. Susy's black girl Cotty keeps her eyes on them. Rebecca sits in the entrance to our shelter rocking Jemima's baby, which has put on some fat but not much. Sallie has an elderly look, her eyes are the same as Rebecca's as she watches the children crashing through the snow. I say:

—Are you hungry? Shall I get you a turkey? Israel took a pair this morning, they have some meat on them.

Her free hand makes a net beneath her great belly. She says:

—I do not want anything.

—Nothing?

—No.

—Our baby likes turkey, I know.

I touch the top of her hard round stomach and receive a kick from the child square in my palm. I bend to speak low to it but Rebecca sits herself up high and says:

—I do not want to birth a big baby alone here. No more meat now, Daniel.

—Do you want the Harrodsburg midwife? We can send for her today, she might still be there, and Martha is at the fort.

—I do not want Martha.

—Well. All right.

I do not like to think of Martha and Rebecca talking together at any rate. I do not like to think of Ned near Rebecca either. Sallie gives one of her sudden howls and Rebecca blinks and smiles down at her. I pat the tufty little head and I say:

—You will have an aunty or an uncle to play with very soon, miss.

Rebecca bobs the baby up and down and looks full at me with her black eyes, crow-black, no pupils. She says:

—I dreamed it was a boy.

I take her hand:

—I know what your dreams are like, little girl. You are always telling me about them, and they always come true, is that right?

—Not always.

I pay no heed to the underside of her words. I touch her chin now and I say:

—Then it might well be a girl, another pretty Kentucky girl to make the boys wink.

She smiles, but soon looks away to the children running. Rebecca, I know your ways, or perhaps I do not. You were never only mine. You were Ned's twice, you said it was twice.

⌣

And Ned comes again, when the snow lessens and we set to building cabins and a good stockade round them. We make it tighter than Boonesborough ever was. A real place, not just a fort, everyone sees it now. I know Neddy sees it when he rides up to the wall I am raising with Hart's sulking black man Moe. Ned's fair-haired Sarah is with him on the great placid grey, she is happy to slide off and run about with the children here after giving me a good stare. Ned comes over to help Moe and me hoist a great sharpened log onto its end, and he says:

—We can hear your sawing back at the fort.

—Well enjoy it! If the weather holds I am going tomorrow to Virginia myself to make claims for Will and Susy and some of the rest. Some more of my own too. I can do yours while I am there, as you are so fond of home. Keep-home Neddy.

This last I say in our old ma's voice. It aches in my mouth, it makes me feel hollowed out in some fashion. Ned gives his head a shake and says:

—Not yet, Dan.

—You are always one to wait and see.

Rebecca is getting water with Jemima at the creek. Hearing our talk she looks back but does not come. She crouches very stiff and heavy with her bucket but I know she is softening in herself, her eyes on Ned. I follow Ned's own eyes to her and to Jemima. My chest goes hard, and harder when Jemima sets her back to me. I say:

—Well you will miss your chance at any good land. Do not blame me for it.

—Do not blame me either.

This from Moe, he slumps off with his axe for another log.

Neddy looks to the ground as though he is considering whether it is any good. He says:

—Old Dick Callaway plans to start his own place upriver some.

—Is that so? Have things all his own way in his own kingdom? March about all day in formation? Measure each loaf of bread just so? Is that where you wish to be, our Ned?

Ned smiles and holds up both hands:

—I am a peaceable man, Dan.

—Well. Do not say I did not give you the chance to be something other.

I go to help Moe with the next log for raising. When I look up again Ned has gone towards the river and the women who have gathered where Rebecca and Jemima are. The daylight is bright round them, it cuts straight through some of their skirts. But he stops himself before he gets there and only stands looking about my place and humming.

The ride to Virginia is quick. I go alone while Israel stays to clear
trees on his claim and hunt for the family. The snow is light even in
the higher passes, I have a stack of money for claims in my pouch,
as though a flock of birds has at last decided to settle on me. Well
I have been whistling for it long enough. I sit my arse on the mossy
ground under a big buckeye tree near a little stream. I pull the
money pouch and my powder up away from the damp. The air is
going blue with night falling but I get up and ride a little longer
before I camp and lie singing a tune in the dark with my feet bare
before the fire. *Lay lee lay lee la.* I sing until my own wordless song
has an eerie sound and I fall asleep silent.

I am only a few days getting across towards James City, flying on
the horse with dry snow kicking up into the air. I am all over alive
again. My limbs are stronger, the scar on my shoulder hurts me less, I
am getting a fresh skin. I grin to think of myself in so snakish a fashion. The pale watery sun shines all day and has not quite set when I
reach the town and find an inn. Even my horse steps high still when
I give it up to the stables, its legs tremble and sweat but still move as
though they wish to run. Well horse, I do know this feeling.

The inn is old and not a clean one, but I do not mind it. Once
I am indoors out of the fresh cold, my blood begins to slow. I have
not been in an inn for as long as I can think of. There is plenty of
company here and a good fire. The innkeeper is a rough jolly sort
and sees fit to give me my first ale for nothing when I pay for my
room and sit myself near the bar. He says:

—Boone, I have heard that name. I have read of you in the papers.
Kentucky, is it? All adventure?

—All adventure!

I raise the cup to him and he nods back. Two brothers and a
cousin sitting near are listening and ask me to join their table for
cards, they are all fat men with big necks. Two of them are called
James. I look at them to stop from thinking of my son, and I say:

—Then perhaps James City is no place for a Dan?

They laugh and bang the table. They know my name too, they have heard of Boonesborough and all the rest, there is no rubbing that out of anyone's brains.

Well. I am jolly enough myself, I win a few hands and lose a few more and win again. My head hisses and hums with this town-brewed drink. Cider and beer and why not rum, why not?

We drink plenty, we talk of Kentucky and land and horse breeding. They are horse breeders themselves. They say they will come out and see the place, and I say they ought to do so as soon as they can. The land is going quick, I tell them. Do not wait.

And more rum, and more gaming. I win some dollars and some pounds and some shilling coins. These clink and slip under the money in my pouch. The brothers stand to stretch themselves, they say they are going out to get whores and do I wish to go? Do I wish to? I do not know. I can only laugh. The bigger one winks at me and says:

—You had best go to bed alone, the state you are in. A drunk cock crows for no woman.

For a small moment it flies back at me, the Shawnee women washing us naked in the icy river and calling us limp, calling us white, *wochkonnickee*.

My legs and belly prickle with want, but I say:

—I leave you gents to see what the whores can do for yours. The whores of James City and their no-doubt dainty charms!

—And their no-doubt poxy cunts!

This last from the cousin or from me, I cannot tell, my tongue is thick as a slug. We laugh like fools for some time regardless and clasp hands, we are great friends. I tell them:

—Do your best for me, boys.

When they go I creep up the tight staircase to the room the innkeeper has given me, I keep my eye on the little circle of light from my wobbling candle following me along the wall all the way.

A step, a step, a step. When I find my door with the cold iron number three on it, I lock myself in. I am in a black sleep with one quick flash before my eyes, it is the skin of a whore I once knew in Philadelphia, the first I knew, her soft thighs and where they meet. Then the warm skin of a cheek, I do not know whose. Methoataske's, perhaps. I try to chase after her in my sleep and see her in the dark but she is gone.

In the morning it is all gone. My knife and powder and the money pouch gone from round my waist, and my breechcloth pulled down and loose from my belt. All the dollars and pounds. Will's money and Flanders's, my own money, others' money. Gone. Before I am up out of the sagging bed tearing up the pillows and upending the drawers and water jug, the name that blazes up in my brains is Cherokee Jim's. I do not know why it is here now but here it is. Perhaps it is the answer to the way things have all gone in my life. *Murder.* Why did you not murder me?

Feathers rain down on me from the ripped bedding. I run down the hall banging on all the doors, calling everyone out, crying for the bastard innkeeper to show his bastard face, but there is nothing, nothing.

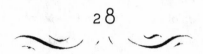

28

I LOOK ALL OVER the city and other towns for the horse-trading thieves. I am all right in the woods where I can see everything, but here I see nothing but blurred faces, wrong faces and dirty windows.

I will pay it all back.

I will earn it all back. I will make salt and sell it to the other new settlements. I will raise an extra crop of corn, an extra crop of anything. I will get furs. I will breed goddamned horses, for God's sake.

Do not think, you ape, you ass. You are alive yet.

I ride west again under the high cold clouds. I watch them but no answer comes. My body is still full of trembly hot life, my skin keeps up its uneasy feeling.

The horse balks at icy creeks, and I let it stand chewing needles and whatever grass it finds. I see no one, no Indian sign at all, though I wish for it. The quiet is very heavy with the mountains all round. This is peace, so I say to myself at this time. Be a peaceable man, be a Neddy, make your face his, it is like enough. This is the feeling of peace on the back of your neck, you goddamned ass. Take it back to the settlement. It is all you have.

But Will's face, and Susy's, when I tell them about the stolen money. Flanders's and Jemima's. Jemima fleeing off through the snowy station.

The rest level themselves out, they plant their feet and they say it is all right, all the men who had sent me to make their claims say so, but some of them look as though their hearts have fallen out through their arses. Miss Polly throws her arms about me and cries for my sake until I tell her to stop. Ned is here, watching with no change in his expression, but Martha is behind looking at me all holy, as if she saved me from taking Ned's money for a claim, as if she were some thin sort of angel.

I work and work through the last of February and into March, I plough and haul out stumps and hunt. And Ned comes to live here. I find I am glad of him, I am easier with him, as Rebecca is easier because of him. She is bigger now and more tired, her time is close. I plant blue grass for her square lawn, I stamp about flattening the earth. I send Israel off hunting and trapping though I would rather be going also.

Jemima makes maple sugar and has plans to sell it. We have not had anything like it for as long as I can think of. The trees drip out their sweetness, my girl gives some to her tiny daughter to suck from her fingertip and Sallie's eyes go wide at the taste. Jemima cannot help a short smile at me when I laugh to see it.

We store it up, we find some of last season's nuts and some wild leeks and chickweed. I set Polly to take the younger children picking in good places I have seen. Their mas are very wary of them going far, but there is peace, goddamned peace all the time, and no sign of Black Fish or anyone else. I try to think of the Shawnee words for maple or for oak but it seems to me I do not know them, perhaps I never did.

Martha forgets nothing. I am skinning three deer with Israel when she is at once at my back, so close my spine feels her. I am not a door she will open, not now. She says my name soft, it crawls all up me. *Daniel.*

—What is it?

I hold up my bloody fat-smeared palms. Israel pulls his head up from his butchering. Martha says:

—It is your wife's time.

Hear the way she says *your wife,* hear all the powder she has packed into it. I say:

—Does she want me? Is she all right?

—She is well, it has begun well. She does not want you. I only thought you ought to know.

—Does she want me in with her?

—No, not you, Susy and the others are there, I will midwife her.

—Does she want *you* with her, Martha?

She startles and covers her mouth in her old fashion. She says:

—I am going.

She turns and stalks off. Israel is watching, perplexed. I follow Martha some little distance away from where he sits cutting the venison from the bones, and I say to her back:

—What do you want?

She tugs at her skirts so they rise and fall, rise and fall over her feet. She says:

—I am not asking you for anything now.

—Martha.

—I am not.

Her skirt goes an inch higher, her ankles are thin and curving. She makes a half turn to see me. The blood is drying in rusted streaks up my arms. I say:

—Martha, it is done, all those bad old times. We have Ned and Rebecca now, we are here. It is all different.

Her eyes are wet now, she is fishing for something more. She says soft:

—What is done, what is different? How can you not think of things you have lost—we have lost?

—I do not think any longer. That is all. Is Rebecca all right?

She drops her head. When she raises it, she twists her hands together and says:

263

—I will tell you when your child is born and how my sister is.

And she goes, and in a moment I am following, calling back to Israel to carry on, we need the hides to sell. I walk towards the cabin and I think of the baby who is coming right now. I will not think of anything else at this time.

⌣

—I will build you a palace here hanging out over the river. With a tower. A glass one.

So I say to my wife as my new son snuffs and waves his fists with his eyes not yet opened, even for a moment.

—With what money?

—Do not think of the money, I am making it back. You will have your palace.

—What am I queen of then, the air?

Rebecca's face is very white at the centre of her loose hair, but there is a cautious happiness floating about her. She has that tiny scrap of yellow silky stuff in one hand, she slips it back and forth between her fingers. I give the baby my thumb to grip and I say:

—Look at the new little prince.

—We do not need any princes here, Daniel.

—But he would make a very fine king. Strong—look how he has my finger! And not so very big. He obliged you.

—Not so very. Like you.

She says this last very quick, though her voice is weak. She smiles at me, then back at the sleeping boy and I say:

—Were you all right in here?

The cabin smells of fresh sap and shavings, and the floor is dirt yet, but we brought the bedsteads and a featherbed from Carolina, at least she had those. And plenty of firewood. I stir up the embers and she shifts the baby to her other arm. Her expression is pained as she moves. She says:

—I did manage to keep Polly out.

—Why? She ought to learn. Our Israel will show her a thing or two if he has his way, or if she has hers.

I laugh but her face shrinks as if she had been pinched. The old word *whores* slips into my ears again. I shake my head, and she says:

—No. She is not ready for any of this.

—You cannot keep them children always. Curiosity is natural.

Her eyes snap:

—Curiosity—

But she looks away out the window, the sky is a fair windy blue today, she jigs the baby very gentle and says only:

—I had Jemima and Susy with me, and Martha delivered me.

I think to say *And did she ask for the father's name, did you tell her it was me?* But I do not say it, I do not say anything like. I know this boy is my boy. I stare him in the face until my sight blurs. He does not open his eyes for me in spite of all my looking. I like this boy and his ways. I will make sure he has land, money. I will do it in some way.

We do not talk yet of names and indeed for weeks he has no name, he is only Baby, until Rebecca begins to call him Nathan one day out of nowhere and so he is Nathan, my boy, my last-born, a new name in our new house.

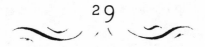

29

—HE IS BUILDING a ferry boat up there, at the mouth of the creek he named for himself. Near done. A great flat thing. You ought to see it. He could break river ice with it.

So says my son Israel to Squire and Ned and me one evening after he has come back from a few days' hunt upriver towards Ohio with his friend Joseph Scholl. The two of them squat down with us just outside the gate. He is talking of Old Dick and his new boat, set to take people farther up his way and get their claims in. Well.

Squire draws on his pipe and asks:

—How is his new place coming?

Israel says:

—He has it measured out and one blockhouse near up. It will be big. Has some signed on to go with him, that round-headed Pem Rollins for one, and a few of the other lone men. And his girls and their husbands. As though they had any choice.

I say:

—And did you delight him with a personal visit?

—No. I stayed in the trees. Might have thrown him a lump of bearshit over his wall. Or my shit! A gift!

Joseph roars, Israel grins and I give his shoulder a smack. I pass him my tobacco. He leans back all comfortable in his joints. He hides nothing of himself. Squire blows out smoke and asks:

—Did you see anyone else?

—Indians? No. Nowhere. And no one saw me, I go very quiet.

—He does that.

This from Joseph, giving Israel a cuff on the back. Israel swats him in return and they are rolling about on the ground like pups and laughing. I laugh too until I see Squire holding his pipe still in his hand and the smoke breathing itself off into the dusk. I know his way of thinking. I say:

—Squire, we would have seen sign when we have been in the fields. Unless they were the Lilliput sort of Indians, hiding in the corn shoots.

He does not laugh, though I feel Ned smiling as he begins to hum. Israel makes up words for the song in a squeaking voice: *Colonel Corn Kernel was the littlest man—the yellowest man—the—*. Unable to think of anything else he says:

—We would need squirrel shot for Lilliput Indians.

—And here I thought you grown.

Israel smiles round his pipe and says:

—I am taller than you, Daddy. Taller than Joe here also.

Joseph rubs his head where he hit the ground, and I say:

—Well! We must have Squire make a pile of tiny shot for us then in his new shop. That and a ferry boat, eh Squire?

Squire says nothing, only the muscles of his jaw work in and out. I say:

—Listen to me, the day for a treaty will come, it will be all right.

As I say it my chest floods with heat. We will make a treaty, I have been at treaty makings, we will do it ourselves here to secure peace. I know the words used. We will get Kenton back, and anyone else who is still living, perhaps even Hill or Callaway's nephew, or Logan's. It is not impossible. Black Fish wanted peace, we all do now.

I have to slow my heart, it is so full of wanting. At last Squire takes a puff on his pipe and says:

—Perhaps we ought to build ourselves a ferry boat. In case we ever have need to leave in a hurry.

Ned says:

—Not a bad thought. Ferrying would make us some money with new claimers.

Squire nods. I do not like thinking of money, but I am always thinking of it, always now it squats in the lowest part of my brains. We could charge Bryans to get across, or Baptists who want to come and go from the fort where Hancock and his like remain so far as I know, praying their days away.

One of the babies inside sets to yelling. Israel blows out smoke and a laugh:

—That my little pisser of a brother again?

—Your niece more likely. Jemima's Sallie. The lungs that little one has.

I do not like to say Jemima's name when Ned is near me. But darling Neddy keeps his peace as always, he takes up humming again and the baby stops its bawls straight away.

—

I take Israel to check our traplines for any beaver and otter with the last of the winter's good fur still on them. I am glad to be away from the fields for two days. I was not made for farming, my fingers have no care for dirt and seeds. And the station is safe and coming to life as if on its own. The others do not look to me so much, they keep themselves in their own houses, and it is more like a real town in this way than Boonesborough ever was. We all of us have our lives.

My boy and I take twelve good otter pelts, it is more than I thought we would find, we ought to get a fair price for them. I do not like my son to help me raise money for my own stupidity, but Israel is quick and nimble with the traps and with skinning. I say:

—You must do as you like, do you know it?

He looks up startled from an otter's weary-looking remains:

—I like to hunt. And trap.

—So do I.

—I know it.

—Then do it.

—Well all right, I will.

He grins at me and carries on with the otter until he has the pelt off in one smooth tug. Very sudden he says:

—Do you like Aunt Martha?

His voice is too light now. I wipe my knife across my leggings a few times and I say as light as he did:

—Well. Do you like her? You ought to like your aunt I suppose. It is good to like aunts. What makes you ask?

He smoothes the pelt and shrugs:

—The way she is always watching you.

I take the pelt from him and give him another animal, and I say:

—I have seen someone always watching you, Israel. Our Miss Polly. What do you think there?

—I halfway like her, maybe.

He looks up at me with his dark eyes. They crease up in a smile but it is a queer one, an asking one. I say:

—It is good to have someone to like. I liked a girl a bit like her once when I was very young.

Little Molly Black, dead of a fever after I kissed her, her boot hanging out of her coffin, I do not know how it is I see it still. I do not see her face anymore though I once did, it once followed me through my life with the heat of her sickened skin. But all of that is gone. To Israel I say:

—Polly seems a loving girl.

—Yes.

—Make sure it is the sort of love that will stay put on you.

He is quiet a moment, then says:

—I will start a real house of my own on my claim soon, after you make some sort of treaty, so Ma will leave off nagging me about going. Joe has got the land just past it.

He cuts into another pelt but it tears and he curses. A breeze ruffles the heap of furs. It is not so great a heap. I say:

—Perhaps a wife with money would be a better thing.

He groans and kicks the torn pelt away and says:

—Or a wife covered in fur.

My boy and I get some beaver and a few more otter in the higher trapline, we make a bushel of salt too at a good spring with just our cooking pot before we turn back for the station. We talk of how to make more salt and faster. We do not have many ideas but we enjoy talking of possibility. Squire might have better thoughts hidden in his clever mind. Well I will ask him.

Israel gets a small buck with two-pointed antlers when we have gone a few miles downriver. When he has the head off, I tell him:

—You ought to keep those horns to show off in your great new house.

With one of his sidelong grins he says:

—I will have the skin too, no bride could resist it.

The hide is ratty enough, fly-bitten and moulting, but once we have the hair all off it will do all right for shoe leather. Israel ties the body over his saddle and we ride the open flats to the east of the Kentucky with dragonflies mumbling all round. The horses flick their tails. The grass is everywhere growing now, it is gold and green and moving as if someone were blowing over it very soft.

Israel says:

—Like to see Dick Callaway's place? We could go round that way.

—Do you know, I would like to see it. Though not so much Old Dick. All right, we will have a look.

We ride closer to the river again, though we keep to the birches so no one will see us coming. No noise but the flies and the horses and the river, and the quick creek we are approaching. I say:

—Well well. No cannon to welcome us.

Israel keeps his voice low:

—Leave the horses here and come with me into the cane.

We hobble the horses. The dragonflies and a cloud of midges stay with them and Israel's scraggy deer. I follow my boy as he springs off into the thick canebrake where the creek meets the river. I push my way through the stiff stalks and I say:

—This is where Dick is building his famous ferry?

—It is—

Israel stops so sudden that I crash into his back and knock him forward onto his knees. When he turns to look up at me his forehead is scratched open from the cane. I say:

—I am sorry, it near got your eye, are you all right?

—Daddy, do not—

—What is it? Let me see you.

I bend and try to wipe the blood from his head, but he covers his face before he rises onto his knees and looks up again away from me.

Through the cane it stands out scarlet, red as a heart. Red as a coat.

Colonel Dick still in his red army jacket but without his scalp or his eyes or his balls, his hands and arms burnt black and all of him rolled onto his side in the mud on the riverbank. Israel behind me is gagging and spitting. Someone else is lying face-up, arms out straight and legs together, making a letter *T*. My brother Israel's wife teaching me my letters once at the table in your house, I do not know your name any longer though I wish to God I did, it would be a hook to hold onto here in this place that has rotted out again like old cloth. The face is young Pem Rollins's moon face, the scalp gone too, a dark red slash between the legs of the breeches, the great pale eyes still there and reflecting the sky just as though they were nothing but water, nothing at all.

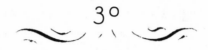

30

SQUIRE IS THE FIRST we see at the station, his narrow outlines at the gate. We get everyone out of the fields and inside the walls, saying only that we have seen bears about. Squire rides for Boonesborough to tell them the truth, I cannot do it.

I leave Israel with Will and Susy and I go to Rebecca. It is warm in the cabin, the sap in the walls smells clean at least, you might imagine you are in a forest if you shut your eyes. The baby is sound asleep in the cradle and Rebecca is in the bed in clean sheets and a poultice on her sore left breast. She looks to be asleep also. I lie beside her and I kiss the yellow weed-smelling poultice, my poor girl. She stirs, she says:

—Ouch.

When she sees my face her brows stitch themselves together:

—What is it?

—Only kissing your heart.

—I know what you were kissing. I do not need another baby on top of a milk fever, the age I am.

She gives me one of her curled smiles, and my throat closes. *Smooth your expression*: so I say to myself again. Do not think, show nothing, you are not a book. You have seen nothing today, nothing at all.

Before Rebecca can speak again I touch her forehead, she is not unduly hot, her eyes are black as ever and not shining in a sick fashion. I kiss her cheek, I close my own eyes.

—Danny, what has happened?

I keep my face at her shoulder, do not read it, Rebecca. I only kiss her cheek again. The baby sets to murmuring and so she sits up, holding the poultice in place. Her plait slips off her shoulder and down her back. I take it in my hand, I twist it about. I am no use for anything. I say:

—I will fetch the little man for you.

When I pick up my young Nathan, he twists like a fish and smacks his small mouth like one. I am glad to have him to look at, I am quite sorry to have to give him up to Rebecca. I ask:

—Can you manage him, the state you are in?

—I am all right.

She is still looking at me, but Nathan has begun to wail and so she pulls off the poultice and sets him to nurse. She shuts her eyes tight as he begins to suck the sore breast, he turns himself about in his bundle as he gulps. With her eyes still closed and her face pained Rebecca says:

—This one is a dancer.

—Or a criminal. But no prison will ever hold him, he will wriggle out of anywhere.

She smiles:

—He does look like you. See his long nose.

—Poor fellow.

—Yes.

The baby pulls hard at his poor ma and she rocks back and forth very gentle. As I am stroking her shoulder, the door opens. Martha comes in, her face startles in its usual manner when she sees me. She has a handful of stiff little pink flowers, and says all breathless:

—Oh, then you know what has happened at Callaway's—

—None of that in here, Martha. You go on, we are all right.

I say it very loud but she does not move. Martha, loving to hold private things and bad things inside herself to turn about there. Now she blinks a few times:

—I was going to find you next, Daniel.

—You can go now, I said we are all right.

—I came to check Rebecca for fever.

—She has no fever.

She puts her hand to her mouth and steps towards the bed. *No closer, Martha.* This I think at her and she feels it, she stops where she is. Realizing fresh that she has a fistful of flowers, she holds them up now:

—I have some live-forever for you, Rebecca. My Sarah found it earlier near the nettles up the woods. It might do you more good than the dandelion.

Rebecca says:

—I am all right, Martha, I am well enough. Leave it and I will try it later.

She looks to Rebecca and then back to me, their faces are so similar, their voices are the same. It strikes me that they are like two ways a thing can go, two sides of an apple or a coin. Heads or tails, one flip, flip again and see what comes. Well. Martha does go now, and Rebecca sends a look like an arrow in my direction:

—Do you have something to tell me, since Martha would not?

—No. Everything is fine here.

Smooth your expression and keep it smooth. Rebecca raises an eyebrow and nods towards the flowers left lying on the table, she says:

—Perhaps she brought that for you. You ought to eat some. Live-forever, live again and again, is that not what you want?

I feel her eyes going through me.

—It is not what I want.

—Is it not?

—No.

—Then you ought to stop asking for it.

The baby smacks his mouth and rolls in his ma's arms and she shuts her eyes once more.

⌣

She finds out soon enough about Dick Callaway and young Rollins, everyone knows it, everyone is poisoned again with fear. Squire says Old Dick's family went to get him. The girls insisted on going too. We heard thin wailing from upriver. His wetted-down hair torn from his head. His young Kezia's doggish face opening in a cry. How many times have I wished him dead? *Do not think.*

They bury the two men in one grave dug quick inside the Boonesborough walls near Dick's favourite blockhouse. I do not go to see it done, but Ned goes to pray over it. Well Dick, your own fort was not ready for you, my old one will have to do. Do not come haunting me Dick. Nor you either poor Rollins. They left you your eyes, do not turn them on me.

Ned and Squire and Israel go to Harrodsburg to tell them of the killings. I give my boy a bag of extra shot when he has mounted:

—Keep this on you. Do you hear me?

—I will, Daddy. I will get as many skins as I see.

—It is not only for skins.

He nods and gives me a tilted grin, he has beautiful teeth. He comes back with all of them still beautiful three days later, and again I can stop my mad ploughing and planting and patrolling the fields with the other men. Ned and Squire come back all right also, they saw nothing, no sign of Cherokee or Shawnee or anyone other. Harrodsburg sent parties out scouting, far up the Ohio even, but saw nothing of note, so Ned said. We help Israel with a pack of deerskins he got. When I am unrolling one, Squire says to me quiet:

—John Bowman was visiting at Harrodsburg from his place on the Cane Run. Says he and his men went up into Ohio a couple of months since with Logan and some of his militia. Surprised them before spring. Burned an Indian town, killed plenty, lost eight of their own.

276

—Which town?

He shakes his head:

—They did not give a name, nobody knows any of those town names but you.

My brains squeak and babble in my head. I say:

—Was it a Shawnee town? Was it Old Chillicothe?

Squire looks me in my face. He says:

—From the way you described it, I would say so. On the Little Miami River not far from where it leaves the Ohio. They believed that is where they were when they found it. Big cornfields all round the Indian houses. Plenty of those.

—Were they all killed? All the Shawnee? All burned?

Very careful, Squire says:

—I did not ask. They did say there were some whites there, they have a couple of the men at Logan's now, they call themselves by Indian names. Logan only said they got a chief in the leg and wished they had shot higher. They were driven back before they could do any more but set fires.

My father, my house, my wife and child burning. My eyes stream. I smear the wetness away but not before Squire sees me do it. He says in the same careful fashion:

—They did not say they killed him, they did not say any chief was dead. They said nothing about women, Dan.

Squire's face looks too soft, I wish to shove it out of my sight. I hold my forehead, I say:

—Did they find Cherokee Jim? Did they?

He folds his arms, he is all uncomfortable angles. It is a stupid question, I know it as I say it, it is all my stupid hope pouring out of me looking for a thing to land on. Ned is at Squire's back now, he comes round to touch my arm:

—Bowman said they did it for the fort, after they heard all about the siege. For you, Dan.

—Did he say my name?

—Yes.

—God damn him. God damn—

Israel steps out from the other side of his horse now all unhearing, his face is young and bright. He carries a big raw-ended pair of buffalo horns he got on the journey. He holds them out to show me:

—Look Daddy, for my house. I have some of the meat too.

He sits himself on the ground and leans back on his elbows. Then he rubs his head and turns to me, he says:

—What will we do now?

⌣

What will you do now?

What will you?

Everybody knows now about the Indian town being burned. Everybody is quite satisfied with this sum adding up. The men patrol in shifts, they are very alert, much more so than anyone was at Boonesborough. They do not question me much, though I hear muttering now and then about my court martial. I never talk of it.

At night in bed Rebecca is quieter in her body, her old stillness is about her, though it has not quite settled. She does not ask me about my Shawnee wife, but this question flies about me too like a bat. *Is she dead? Did she burn? Did she disappear, did the rest?*

I go outside and smoke the last of the Indian tobacco I bought from a trader near the Virginia border. Black Fish's smell. *We make our trades.* It is all I can think.

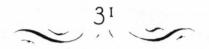

31

ALL SUMMER I am always listening for what I never hear.

Sell land, sell yourself as a surveyor. Take your chain and sticks and pace out the yards, with bees following you. Mark the acres in great squares on your map. Write the new owners' names in them. Collect your pay.

Go north and west with Israel, shoot as many deer as you can get, bundle and sell the skins to traders quick. Make salt too at the springs. Carry it to the new settlements. More money for paying your debts. Keep looking for the thieves, never find them.

Only there are others selling skins and making salt and surveying. There are other maps. Go to Virginia to make more claims and find there are questions about yours, others arguing they paced out the acres first. The clerk shows you a map like a shake roof, all squares overlapping one another.

Go back to the station and work the fields and keep up the patrols. Watch for someone coming with a white flag out of the wilderness. Only there is no one to see, even in the dawn or the last daylight, just the high grass and the corn shifting in the wind and the birds swooping in stretched circles. And never enough money though it is always just in sight, flying just ahead, flying so low you keep following and looking at nothing else though you know Fate uses you as a coin also.

⌣

But the children are happy, they run about free. I watch them and I am easier while doing it. My Morgan and Jesse are fine young patrollers now. I have had Squire make them their first guns, they will be as good at shooting as Israel is. I make a straw target for them and the other station boys to shoot at, I show them how to make bows and arrows in case they are ever out in the woods alone and have to get food.

—Or fight!

This from Jesse, waving his bow over his head. I say:

—You are right. When we go long-hunting later this autumn you will come and be our lookout. We will get so many skins and pelts, you will never believe it.

I know Rebecca hears this and I look at her sidelong, but she is smiling at our boy as he marches about and turns quick on his heels to march the other way in the hot sun. Our young Nathan crows in her arms. Now she does look at me and her face says, *Not too long a hunt you great oaf, there will be no more disappearing.* I give her the widest grin I can summon and her lips curl into a bigger smile. Then Jesse takes a mad shot at a hawk high overhead, and the bang makes the baby bawl.

Ned comes in from patrolling. He only gives us a nod before he goes on through the gates. I see Rebecca look at him and not look at him. I put my arm round her shoulders and say she ought to go in to bed. Go on and rest, I tell her. Bouncing the squalling little one, she says:

—When have I ever slept in an afternoon? There is plenty to do.

She touches the back of her neck where her hair has curled with sweat. I say:

—The girls will do it. Polly, Becky, come here and sort dinner out for your ma. Levina, take the baby. Your mother needs sleep.

The girls come up quick and I say:

—You see? They are eager to play at being women. They are women, near enough. Give them a turn, madam.

Polly says:

—I can do it. Give me the baby.

After a moment Rebecca passes Nathan to Levina and stands and goes back inside the walls with the girls jumping round her. She touches my hand with two fingers before she does it, and my skin is surprised.

I tell the boys to leave off shooting now. Jesse fires one last time at a crow dipping over the field, a great cackle rises from the others when it sails off unperturbed. I stay and watch the boys chasing the birds off the squash and corn until the sun is right down, then I fetch them all in. I walk the field edges in the twilight, but there is nothing as always. Back inside I pull the gate to, it is warmer here where the sun has struck the walls all afternoon. The horses and foals in the corral smell of heated flesh. I give them a pat and a nod as I make a count. All here, all in.

From the cabins some of the women's voices slip across the growing dark. Rebecca, as I listen the place on my hand pricks where you touched it, it is not like you to touch me for no reason anymore.

When I turn, you are there. Only it is not you, it is Martha. No apron on and no cap, her plait knotted up. Holding up a bucket, she says:

—I am going for water. Have you barred the gate already?

I know she has stitched out these words and this bucket in her mind ahead of time. I say:

—Looking for your freedom, are you? Well water not good enough?

—*You* are free.

I pull myself in:

—Dark enough now, do you have to go out?

She does not move, she only holds the pail, I know she will keep it there until I open the gate, and so I do it. She says:

—Will you walk with me?

—What, afraid of the dark now? Where is your husband?

The whites of her eyes show as she turns them on me. She says:

—Everyone is afraid of something here, Daniel.

—You do not seem so afraid.

Still she does not move and so I say:

—Well now, come on, we will get you some water.

We go out past the kitchen garden and along the biggest corn-field towards the little spring. She still has her quick way of walking, her feet step along very light. She says:

—You have seen no Indians? None? Today or another day?

I do not answer straight away. What are you thinking of me, Martha, what pictures are you seeing? The grasses sigh in the dark. I sigh also:

—I would have told you if I had. Do you not believe it?

—I hardly know what to believe.

Very light she says it, light as her quick feet. An animal rushes out of the corn, a young skunk with its tail up. Martha gasps and stops, I laugh:

—Well well, here I am caught without my gun.

The skunk backs up and vanishes in the stalks:

—No need to be afraid of you, at any rate. Goodnight, neighbour!

—You ought to have your gun with you out here, Daniel.

Her *Daniel* sounds so like Rebecca's. I will admit my body is listening. I say:

—We will not be long. Give me the bucket.

I stride ahead and I crouch at the spring to fill it for her. I listen properly, there is nothing about, all the skunks and everything else have gone quiet. The wind lifts slightly. Martha at my side now, her hands clasping and unclasping. She says:

—It is very warm.

—It is. Good for the corn.

She breathes out, and a light scent of maple sugar comes with it. She is close enough for me to catch it. I stand and she says very sudden:

—Ned told me about the Indian town being burnt down.

—Did he. Well.

She touches my hand just where Rebecca did. She says:

—Should you go and see it? Should you go—and make sure? Or make peace with whoever is still there? There ought to be a lasting peace, Daniel, so we can all—stay here. You could hunt on the way. You would be able to do it.

The soft drop of her voice says, *The others do not know it, only I know it, only I know you truly.*

—I promised my wife I would not leave. Not to go to Shawnee towns at any rate.

It is more than I ought to say, she knows this also, but she goes on standing before me as though I will do something. Perhaps I ought to throw the water over her, wake her up from her dreaming. Her wet dress clinging to her body, her cold skin, her cold breasts pressing through. No Martha, I cannot do it, I cannot now. I say:

—You ought to tell your Neddy to go. He is a peaceable man.

She takes half a step back, her face is very sad. Why such sadness, Martha? For whatever it is Ned does not give you that you think I can give you? For anything that has ever gone wrong in the world?

I shake water from my hands, and say:

—Well. Perhaps it would be no bad thing for someone to go. But we must get inside now.

She turns, and we begin the walk back. The bucket drips against my leg. The wet is quite refreshing and I cannot help a thought again of Martha in a wet dress. I feel her settle beside me, she is easier again in some fashion. We walk. I do not think at all and it is pleasant not to do so for a moment.

We listen to owls calling one another across the trees. They make quite a song of it. A few lightning bugs go spinning about in the air. When we get back to the gate we stand watching them a moment, and I say very stupid:

—Those flowers you put by your door, the yellow ones. What do you call them?

—Oh. I do not know what they are.

We stand looking at one another's edges in the dim. At once it seems she has grown very young again, she seems the girl I saw with Rebecca in the cherry orchard. She is soft still, and I am soft-hearted as I know. I am struck by a wish to be tender with her, I wish for tenderness myself. A lick of pleasure, a small drop of it to swim in. But I only say:

—You have your water then.

—I wanted water.

Her hand comes out towards mine, I feel it near touch me again and then stop. I open the gate and all I can think to say is yes.

Martha goes in but turns back to look in my direction, she says with a smile:

—Yes.

Rebecca, I did promise you not to go, I know it. But Martha's thought is my own thought risen to the surface of my brains, it will not leave me. Chillicothe. Is it still there? They move their towns as I know. If they are alive they will do it.

I am restless. I watch Israel go off to see to his claim and keep his field cleared. Many people are wandering about Kentucky now, they might decide to have it. I tell him he must take good care of his property, and he says he knows it.

Once September is out and the harvest done, Squire and I think to go on a hunt, a few days only, to get some quick money with the last autumn pelts. When I tell Rebecca we are going she says:

—All right.

—I will take Ned along too, there are enough men here to keep up the patrol.

—Do as you like.

—I will. And I will be back by Sunday with plenty of pelts and skins. A fine one to wrap our young fellow in. Right then, little girl?

—I said all right, Daniel.

—Then all right.

I kiss her mouth and she smiles under my lips as I do it. My young Nathan in his cradle gives a raccoon shriek and I kiss him too, he swats at my cheeks with his happy fists.

The morning we go is still and quite warm. Ned and I have our horses loaded early while the children scurry about helping, and Rebecca is still indoors with the baby, Susy and Jemima come out with their own, and make them wave their little hands. Jemima even gives me a wave herself when Susy runs to kiss me. Martha stands near her doorway in shadow. She has her hands flat against her stomach near her waist, they make a letter *V. V* is for victory. A sign, Martha, perhaps a small one, so I think at this time.

—Well Keep-home Neddy, will you be all right without your bed for a few days?

Ned is tightening the saddle round the belly of his big gentle grey, he says:

—Do I have much choice, Dan?

—Come on, we will have a fine time away. And some quiet.

The children are yelling now, chasing after a ball they have bundled together of vine leaves. It flies apart every few minutes and they tie it up again with more yelling. Ned strokes his horse's flank and says:

—That is true enough. Where is Squire?

As he says it, Squire comes out of his cabin looking yellow and green. I say:

—You are sick.

He shakes his head. When I go close, I see his eyes are shot with red. I say:

—You are. Does Jane's cooking not agree with you? Come out with us and have some fresh meat. You will get none fresher. Make a man of you!

Squire tries to smile:

—Ague seems to be back again. It is nothing. I will be all right.

Ned looks him over:

—You had best stay here.

—Keep-home Neddy would say so!

So I say but Jane comes out now with her narrow worried face and a hand at her neck. She says:

—You cannot go like this, Squire, get back to bed.

His thin arms are trembling, though he tries to hold them still. Jane pulls at him. I say:

—Well Jane, you can keep him. Ned, we will have to do our best on our own.

And so we wave and set off. Once we are beyond the fields and onto the grass flat, I dig my heels into the horse and off we fly, the thump of the hoofs shuddering up through my spine to the top of my skull and into all my joints. Very quick Neddy is beside me running his grey as well. I hear him laugh, and I cannot help doing the same, and yelling. It is as though we have won something or stolen it, it is that sort of relief. We ride whooping now and then through the gold grass and along the river and into the woods, and it seems to me we are quite young again.

We get a few deer and make camp the first night near a small creek upriver. Once we have eaten and done some skinning, we sit with our rum and our feet to the fire. We are silent now, in our older bones again. My old hurt ribs and shoulder ache on the cold ground, though Neddy looks young as ever and sounds young. He sings low:

> They have thrown the lady in,
> And the fire took fast on her fair body,
> She burned like holly green,
> She burned like holly green.

It makes my throat ache. The burning. I sit up and throw a left-over chunk of fat into the fire, where it hisses back at me. I say:

—A nice love song, Ned.

He gives a chuckle:

I do not mind the words, I only sing.

—Do you remember our Sallie singing that to scare us when we were young in Exeter, hiding in the spring cellar?

—I do, yes.

Our sister singing into a milk can in the deep rain-smelling cellar to make her voice hollow and dreadful. Sallie before she was called whore in front of the Quaker Meeting and was cast out. It seems very long ago now.

Neddy sings on and I drift in my mind upriver and through the woods towards Old Chillicothe, the Shawnee town, my home some six months and now far too. I will not believe everyone in it has gone, they cannot all be dead, there are so many. We would have smelled such a fire surely. I have smelled nothing. No such burning.

But why not go and see for myself, truly? The wish swells in my head. It would not take us long if we rode quick all the way, quick as we did earlier, we can do it still. I roll onto my side and I say:

—Neddy, what do you think of a ride over to the falls of the Ohio? Good hunting there, plenty of ducks too.

Ned eyes me. He says:

—You would know that. Shelty was it they called you?

My Shawnee name all wrong in his mouth makes me bristle. I say:

—Come on Ned, leave your cowardice home for once instead of yourself.

He puts his hands behind his head and lies back:

—I told Martha I would not be gone long. She is nervous when I go. And I like to be home.

—I know she is, I know you do! But the station is well built, we built it!

—You have made a good place of it, Dan.

—You have helped. Though we could do without your Baptist chatter there on Sundays. And your songs.

Now I give Ned an elbow to the side and he laughs and shuts his eyes. Very soon he is breathing deep and innocent. Well in the morning I will ask him, perhaps he will have forgotten I asked at all, and I will start again.

When the sun is up, we ride some way along the creek towards the Blue Licks. About midday Ned says he is tired, and so we stop at a grassy place where the stream is lined with flat stones. We sit very quiet and get a few more deer coming to drink and lick at the earth, which has some salt even here. The leaves on the thin birches and aspens along the water flash yellow in the breeze. Later Ned shoots a bear across the creek, we hop over and have its skin off and the

liver out while it still steams. We find a few chokeberries and walnuts to go with it. I sit on my heels watching Neddy with the pan:

—You always were a fine cook, Neddy. Good at cooking up
treaties too, I would bet, though you do not even know it.

He chuckles and hands me a slice of liver on his knife. He says:

—I know what you are thinking of.

—Am I so easy to see through? Can you see my liver too?

—Dan. I know of your Indian family. I know you are thinking
of them.

I am silent a moment. A deer cracks a branch where the grassy
flat meets the woods. I say:

—Well. Everyone knows me, that is what they are always telling me. But you are a cipher.

—Ha. I never learned to write as well as you. Or do figures.

—Why would you? You go where life takes you.

Ned bends over the pan and shakes it. Looking up at me, he
says:

—I will go up to the falls with you if you want to see your
Shawnee town.

I clap him on the shoulder, and I tell him:

—Almost straight west from here. It will not take us long. Your
wife will be all right another few days.

—Your wife too.

As we sit chewing in the smoke I am easy in my gut, though my
skin pricks. My wife's name in his mouth. I watch him cutting more
of the liver, and at once I think to ask him what I have never yet
asked him. We are alone here.

When he hands me another slice, I say quick:

—Why did you have my wife? Why did you do it?

He is silent for some time. Then he says slow:

—I thought to help. To comfort her. We thought you were
dead.

—Well well. So many times everyone has thought me dead, perhaps I am and do not know it.

Ned gives a short smile:

—It was a long time ago.

—Would you do it again, if you could go back?

—Dan.

He will not look at me, again I say:

—Would you?

—I would.

He is so simple in his answer. I feel myself a schoolteacher trying to dig something from a pupil who is cleverer than I am by appearing to be dull. Ned takes a piece of meat and chews again, comfortable where he is. At this time it strikes me that he is another Dan, an easier one and a better one than I am. Rebecca, your words click in my ears like a set of beads: *He looks so much like you.*

I get up. *I have had your wife, she looks so much like mine*: this I think at him though I will not say it. Ned is up too though he does not follow me to the horses, he walks over to a great buckeye tree and sits against it taking walnuts from his pouch. He cracks them against a stone and eats. Crack crack crack.

Now a great crack. The horses rear and mine bolts, too quick-footed for me to get its bridle. Ned's grey horse twists and follows. I run after it for a moment, but I cannot catch it either. When I look back, Ned is spilled over onto his side, his hunting shirt a great flower of blood below the neck, a black hole opened in his chest. I get myself to the trees and flatten myself behind a fallen one. My own blood pounds in my ears, it is a hideous sound. My hands are clutching the ground, the edge of a stone juts up under my thumb-nail. I have dropped my gun somewhere, where, goddammit, I look up again and I see what I have never wished to see. I did not ask for this, you must know it.

Ned on his side, entirely still and without breath, he is gone.

And now I feel you, you are very near and you see me, you still have breath and words. You are no ghosts.

—*Nientha.*

—We killed Boone.

—We killed Daniel.

The singing hisses from the trees over the flat at me, they do not see me go, they do not know who I am, I am running over the salty ground, my lungs are wretched and empty but I am running again as though my life were worth something.

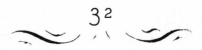

3²

ALL THE MILES to the station I run on my old legs, my old feet, God damn them for being mine, God damn my face and my name. It is dark when I get back. I pass the patrol unseen and go gasping straight to Squire's bedside. He does not weep, though the fever is shaking him down to his bones, and this terrible story makes him shake worse. I sleep on the floor next to him and listen to the bed quivering. The next morning very early he has to take two slugs of whiskey, but he insists on coming with me back towards the Licks, though Jane cannot understand it and throws up her hands at him. His boys Moses and Isaiah stand in their nightshirts watching us go in the dawn. We do not tell them where we are going. I have not yet seen Martha or Rebecca.

We find no one. We see nothing. We bury our Neddy, our poor boy, his chest stabbed through, his scalp taken, his fingers taken, his coat taken, though his face is still sweet somehow and unhurt, as if they did not dare harm that sweet expression. I look at him for a time, I make myself look, then we put him under the tree between two great roots. I heap rocks on his grave as I did for my boy Jamesie. It seems to me that my Fate has done another murder on my behalf, another one I did not want, I never wanted this, Neddy.

⌣

Murderer.

Murderer.

All the time I think of Neddy's old song at our last camp, the lady burning in the fire. *She burned like holly green.* The music bounces about in Ned's voice in my brains. *They have thrown the lady in. She burned like holly green.* I hear it in my sleep, I wake in a great sweat. I want to see you Ned, I want to see you again but you do not come.

And Martha. Squire is with me when I tell her, I am that much a coward. He says low to her:

—Ought to have been me. I am sorry.

He shakes still with his ague. Martha watches him, her face is startled in its usual fashion, it stays that way when she turns to stare at me and covers her mouth. Her children burst into crying and clutch at her. She says only *Oh.* It is a tired sound and a disappointed one, what else is there to say I suppose.

Martha keeps away from me for some weeks but I keep myself away also, I go on watch all the time, I go into the woods as far from the station as I can get in one day, but I see no signs anywhere, no foot marks or blazes or broken twigs, no one has walked or ridden anywhere near. The Shawnee have flown straight up into the air.

Rebecca will not look at me. And so I stay out longer.

One day I find Neddy's big grey horse, looking out at me all gentle from the trees. I take it back to the station and leave it at the gate, someone else can take it in to Martha.

Ought to have been me. I near struck sick Squire across his lean face for saying it.

It ought to have been you, you goddamned son of a bitch—so I say to myself again and again.

When I come back, Rebecca is very silent. She sits rocking the baby for long spells, though he keeps trying to get out of her arms now. She answers when I speak to her, but her mouth hardly moves. Polly busies herself taking charge of the wash, making a great show of it before Israel and the other young men. Rebecca only thanks her very quiet and rocks.

One night I sit up with her. The cold is growing, I bank up the fire so air rushes up the chimney and gives a great roar. She is nursing Nathan and does not move. I poke the wood about so it calms itself, and I say:

—You ought to put him into bed now, little girl. And get some rest yourself.

—I am all right here.

She stares at the flames. The sturdy baby rolls over in her arms and away from her breast, his sleepy head flops to one side. I get up, I say low:

—I will take you upstairs, young master.

She speaks sharp and sudden:

—No.

—Let me put him to bed, he is asleep.

—No.

She tightens her arms about him. Now she looks at me, the fire gutters on the surfaces of her black eyes, and she says:

—He is mine. He is yours—you can see he looks like you. But he is mine.

I crouch next to her, I touch her arm and the side of her heavy veined breast but my hand hardly wishes to do it, I am all knots and burrs. I say low as I can:

—I know he is mine, Rebecca.

Still sharp she says:

—Do not tell Jemima. Never tell her about—Neddy—

She speaks as if the name hurts her throat. I go still inside, still as she is, I take my hand back. I say:

—I will not tell her he is her father. That is for you to tell her, it is your concern now.

—It is mine, it is only mine. It always has been. He *was* her father.

Tears slip in wet ribbons from her eyes, but she does not move. My guts are knotted and hurting. I stroke the baby's curls, they are damp from where he was pressed against his ma. I say:

—Maybe we ought to have called this one Neddy. If I had known.

—Do you think that would have helped? There is no help.

With that she stands and is gone up the stairs without a light and with the baby's head lolling.

⌣

Will she ever run out of anger at me? I do not know.

I go outside. There is a frost coming, and the stars are piercing. I walk along to Will and Jemima's cabin, but it is dark there, and what would I say at any rate? There is nothing I can say.

I nod to Israel at the gate. Usually one of the Harts' blacks takes the night watch, but Israel says he likes it, he likes to be out on his own. I check the horses and I go back along the row of houses. A sliver of light shows round the curtain at Martha's. I knock and press the latch and the door swings in. Martha is at the table stitching and moving her lips, praying, I suppose. She looks up. I say:

—All right?

As soon as it is out of my mouth I see how stupid my question is:

—Do you want anything, water, wood? Meat? Anything the children need?

She shakes her head. Then she stands. She stands only, she does not move. She sets down her sewing. It catches her pot of pins, which rolls from the table and falls to the floor. It is something I can do. I pick up scattered pins all round her, the ones shining in the rushlight and some that roll off into the dark. She goes on standing. I feel myself pricked all over, Martha, you have left a path of pinpricks on me. I feel the depth of your want threading me and tying me as Gulliver found himself, I do not know what I can do about it.

Your feet are bare, I think of them as they were once before, up round my back. I feel my own want bend and sniff about in a black fashion of its own choosing. My brother's wife, my dead brother's wife. Ned, you thought to help my wife, you said so yourself.

I put my hands on her. Neddy had my wife twice. I will have his more. My want thumps its triumph in my blood, whatever it is I am triumphing over.

I know the bones of Martha's shoulders. She reaches her mouth to me but I turn my face into her neck and the dark. When she is beneath me and we are moving silent with the pins round us, my head swims, but I keep my eyes open to look. Look anywhere but her eyes, see her mouth open and close with every thrust I make in her, see the curve of her ear inside her loose black hair, see her breasts shake above her stays, her nipples stiff in the air. I open her dress to see better, I raise myself up straight on my arms. Her thin body on the ground. I have known other bodies. Rebecca's, soft and warm in the dark, Methoataske's low flat voice in my ear—*Sheltowee*—

I groan. Martha's insides are hot round me. *She burned like holly green.*

She grips, she is all want, she does not know what she wants, she is a pit of wanting. She is staring me in the face with her hands palms-up, she reaches up for my back now, all tears and no sound. I near say, *It was your thinking to send us on a hunt, to send us to the Shawnee town to see—*

But I do not say it. I only go on with what I am doing, trying to make something right though it is all wrong. She arches and gasps again and again. It exhausts me to hear. But I finish, and when I finish I get up quick, I say nothing, I pull a shining pin out of her sleeve where the tip has just pierced.

I am out the door, where everything is dark now but for Israel's lantern at the gate. He holds it up to see what made the noise. I stand where I am outside Martha's. I hear him talking low, then comes a light laugh. Polly is with him. All has run backward in my life and I am a boy again listening to my older brother Israel and his girl and their private talking in the cellar before they were both dead.

I go and bang a wall with the edge of my fist, they are tall walls and strong ones, and the bark cuts me. This could have been a good place, it can still be good. I stride on towards my house but as I go Martha's door cracks open and she says soft:

—I will pray for you, Daniel. God help you.

Well. Her voice has a strange smiling quality in it, her knowing of God, her sort of God. I hate her for it. Does God tell you what is what, Martha? Ask him then what is to be done with the great desire you were born with, when he seems to have only small poor things left for you.

I walk on, I say nothing. Rebecca at this time it seems to me you are right, you are right clean through—there is no help.

33

WE GO NOWHERE, I see to it. I will root this place a mile deep if we have to, we will make a fortress of it, we need no more plain poor goddamned forts! So many people are coming out with old and fresh claims that the Virginia governor makes a county here and me sheriff of it, and a colonel as well, knowing my name. I am sure the Boonesborough types do not care much for my name, or for my having the job, but it is mine at any rate. And I do not go to Boonesborough, I never speak that goddamned word.

Israel goes on day hunts with Joseph Scholl and gets some skins and furs, which he insists on sharing with me. It makes me sore inside myself. I tell him he ought to be saving up for doing as he likes, and he says he is doing it. He goes to his claim to work on his house when he can, with Joseph's help. I have seen it, it will be sound when it is done, with good foundations and a good thick chimney.

He rubs his arms, ropy with muscle, and he says:

—I am all right here yet.

My boy is another chance for me. I like to have him about. At any rate, he is right to stay here with us. There are small fights at other settlements, we hear of them, though no Indians come to us and I never see any.

Israel meets with a Cherokee group on a spring hunt upriver, they are friendly and have a smoke and a talk together. None of them is Jim. Israel knows his face from old times when he used to come to our Carolina place visiting, when my boys were young and sat eating candy with him. Before he killed Jamesie. Perhaps he killed Old Dick and Rollins and Neddy too. Perhaps he has turned to air and is all round me. I find myself thinking more and more of him. But I feel nothing.

But Israel thinks of him also. Smoking with me outside the house one night, he says:

—That Cherokee Jim was very tall, was he not? Not so difficult to spot. We will find him.

He looks to me as though I have an answer. I say only:

—It would be a good thing, to find him.

Two of the young men near the gate make a screaming racket, their lanterns swing about and cast wild moving light. They have set two roosters to fight. The bigger bird leaps on the smaller and rakes it open with its spurs, the men roar all the louder over the roosters' howls. Young Hart begins to sing all drunken:

By chance a fine Kentucky girl
I happened for to see
And promised I would marry her
If she would lie with me!

Well. It is no *God Save the King*. Hart is fumbling with his breeches:

—Which of the girls in this fort will lie with me now? Come on and get it!

If Martha comes out she will look to me, I will have to speak with her and I cannot do it. At once I think of her with a silky purse between her legs and me tipping coins into it. Hart roars away, his breeches down round his ankles. I go over with my gun out and I say:

—There is goddamned peace here, God damn the both of you, I will crack your heads together if you forget it.

Israel stands holding in a grin. Some of the girls are behind him, trying to hide their grins too.

Yes Sheriff. Yessir. Small voices say this falsely high.

I am not such an old fool as not to know they are laughing at me.

⌣

Months. We hold steady where we are, and no attacks. Peace. Ned, you were a peaceable man, I do not forget it when I go to look at your burying place the summer after you are dead. Some walnut shells still lie dry and cracked near it, I leave them where they are.

More months. More peace. A whole year, and it is summer again.

I keep out of Martha's way. I keep myself to myself, I listen to no talk. I work and work. But I do not sleep much, I never do. My eyes fly open before each day starts, before Rebecca stirs beside me. I am full of burning though I do not know what for.

A hot August morning I am up with the sun on watch when someone rides out of the woods. No white flag, no flag at all. A man on a chestnut horse, it is a beauty. I watch its light steps through the high grass. The rider keeps his head down, riding very easy with a dog lolloping behind. He looks to be white, though I cannot see his face under his hat. To the rest I call:

—Do not shoot.

But no one else is up on the walls, and he is already coming past the fields. I have my gun up, I yell with all my power:

—Who is it?

Close to the gate now he looks up, fierce light eyes in a face all sunburnt. Springing red hair over his ears. His great dog yelps and I know the sound:

—McGary is it? This is not Boonesborough, did you forget? What do you want here?

—Why, I want to come in, Boone. No hospitality in this place of yours?

His Irish voice. See him riding off from the fort before the siege to start everything himself. Hear him: *Call this man an officer? Call this man a man?* So he said when I was court-martialled, he spat out *man* as though it were grit in his teeth.

I go down and open the gate. I say:

—My hospitality is all yours, McGary, if you insist on coming in here. I cannot speak for your safety.

He is off his horse now, his cracked lips tightening across his face. I suppose this is what he would call a smile. With a short nod he comes past, followed by his slavering dog. Israel has come out of the house, and says:

—Who is that?

—Only Hugh McGary come visiting from Harrodsburg. Perhaps he wishes to see how a tight ship is run. Will you ask your ma to fetch us some refreshment? Cakes for you, McGary? Sugar lumps for you or your horse or your dog?

McGary has his hat off, he wipes the sweat from his brow, which is dead white above the line of his burn. He says:

—Ah, the famous hospitality of the Boone women, by God.

Smooth your expression. Israel is uneasy beside me, to him I say:

—Go and tell your ma to send out something particularly nice for our guest. What else can we do for you, McGary?

—I am not staying, no. Only came to tell you we saw your man.

—What man?

—Your Simon Kenton, big fellow. Goddamned red-boys had him. Could not catch them up. But it was him.

—Where was this?

So I say but Israel bursts in:

—Was it the Cherokee? One of them a big man too, very tall? 301

He holds his hand high to show just how tall. The dog gives a sudden yelp. McGary strikes it on the head and chews his dry freckly lip. He says:

—I do not care to try and tell them apart. Ask your daddy there, he knows better.

I say:

—Never mind that. Where was Kenton?

—Downriver some, to the west. You will not find him.

—I will if I set to. He was alive?

—He was. I cannot say if he still is. But you ought to worry about yourself, Boone. Begging your pardon. Sheriff, I ought to say.

His voice wavers again in its strangely youthful fashion. He gives a hunched bow just like mad little Andy Johnson. The two of them talking me over at Harrodsburg, telling tales out of their hairy faces, Boone this and Boone that. Boone the traitor, Boone the liar, Boone the coward, Boone the weak.

My knucklebones pain me, I force my fingers open. *Do not think.* I say:

—What is it you want to say, McGary?

He squints up his red eyes so they hardly show:

—They are coming, do you know it? The Indians are. We ought to get to them first, as I told you the last time.

—What do you mean?

—Are you losing your wits in your age? I mean just what I tell you. We have seen them about, they never go this long without an attack.

—Is this Irish knowledge, McGary? Fairy talk?

He laughs, it is a harsh laugh, his way of talking makes me think of Findley. The Irishman who showed me Kentucky first, who brought me here and showed me possibilities, too many of them for my poor heart to manage, it wanted all of them. He is another one vanished into this country.

302

McGary steps away and grips his horse's reins tighter. He says:

—I have warned you now, you are off my conscience.

—Do you have one?

So Israel barks, crossing his arms. I hear my own voice coming from his mouth. McGary hears it too, and smirks again:

—I do of course. It would like to save your women and children from God knows what sort of horror. But perhaps your daddy would rather take them to live with the Indians.

—We are not going raiding, McGary. I advise you to keep your head as well. They have come to accept that we are here, they are leaving us be. No stirring up hornets.

I believe it, I believe my words. McGary swings up onto his horse. He is wearing Sunday shoes, their buckles are dull, it is not Sunday. The great dog lopes in a circle. I say:

—Given up on moccasins at Harrodsburg? Gone back to all the Irish ways?

He peels a strip of dried skin from his forehead, it drifts like a feather to the ground and the dog stops to sniff at it. He says:

—Tell your wife I thank her for the offer of refreshment, but I will take none of it. You will need all you have to try to bargain with your red brothers. See how it goes for you this time. We hardly killed any of them at your last fort, my man.

He pulls off another piece of skin, he digs in his shoe heels and the horse swerves off through the gate with the dog bolting ahead. Israel mutters:

—Bastard.

I put my arm about him:

—You are not wrong, my boy.

When we go to the house the door is open a hair, Rebecca is stirring a pot at the fire, her whole back tells me she heard the talk. She does not turn round, she goes on stirring, stirring, stirring.

303

⌣

We go on. It is almost the end of summer before we catch the smell. A whiff of smoke, a dark lick of it on the air. Not enough to notice all day, not enough to taste.

The wind shifts now and then, and it comes again, but never for long. We carry on as usual in the fields. And then in the night come the riders tearing out of the dark with children on their backs and before them in their saddles, women and older girls and boys running breathless straight into the corn, the torches snapping to life inside our station, the tide of voices. Everyone awake and coming out of doors to see.

I am very still in the blockhouse. I keep where I am. When the gate opens and the lights are on the faces I see them, they are Bryans, they all pour in and one woman begs, *Shut the gate, shut the gate.* I go out onto the wall and Martha looks straight up, she is blind in the bright torchlight but still her eyes find me. *What will you do now?*

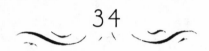

34

BRYANS' STATION in ruins.

Their corn burnt, all the crops burnt. Stock knifed and shot, some burnt. Some of the horses burnt alive, some taken. The dreadful counting of children here, women counting them out again and again. Their coughing all night from the smoke caught in their chests. They do not cry, they are quiet apart from the coughing. The smell of burning hangs on them all like a set of clothes.

I shut my eyes as I walk the walls, what could I wish to see here? My feet know the boards well enough, too well. I wish they did not. I near tip off the edge once, I wish I were falling and feeling my head shatter. I ought to go down to Rebecca but I cannot look her in the face.

Near morning, Israel rides hard out the gates. He goes for the river and does not come back. I stand watching until he is out of my sight. And Jemima comes up the ladder farther along the wall facing the water:

—What are you doing here, duck? What is Israel doing?

I am not sure she will answer me, but she says:

—He said he had to get somewhere quick, I do not know.

—Well. Where is your little Sallie?

—She slept through everything. Flanders is inside with her, he still has fever.

—Be sure you do not catch it.

—He is all right. He will be up by tomorrow.

She is in her nightdress and without shoes. I see her mind spinning as she shifts from foot to foot. Without turning to me, she says:

—Daddy, are we going to leave?

She has not called me Daddy in months. It is strange in my ears. I say:

—I do not know. Will you go with me if I do?

—I like it here.

It was always her gift to forget bad things and start up fresh. I feel her looking at me, wanting to forget what she knows of me with Martha, me with another family also. She leans over the wall and looks at the east where the sky is whitening. She pushes a strand of hair back from her face and says:

—We ought not to be here.

She says it in a musing fashion, as if she were puzzling out figures. I say:

—Well we are here.

—Will they come here too?

Only the tiniest wavering in her voice. I see her running for me out of the trees when we found her after they took her, skirts all torn up, *That is Daddy*, her certainty hanging on me like a chain. I feel it hanging again now. I say:

—They might.

—Then what—

—Do not ask me what I am going to do, Jemima.

My chest starts its stupid banging again. The sun is up now, the air already soupy with warmth. She stands considering me. I must look poor in her eyes. She is at once pitying, her pity surges up in her like strength. Taking my arm, she says:

—I know how to fight after the last time. I will not let any Indians near you.

The Bryans are ready to go after the Indians, though they do not all have guns now and some have only nightshirts to wear. They have gathered everyone to talk at the centre of the station. I stay up on the walls looking to the fields instead. But I cannot help hearing, though I ought to stop up my ears. Or cut them off.

—We can get rid of them all. Surprise them. They will not be expecting us to come so quick.

This from one of Rebecca's brothers with his thick legs bare. Black hair cut short, black beard, a sheen on him all over in spite of the soot, the sort of shine that comes from money. A Bryan through and through. The others nod like a set of ninepins. Do not tumble over, you Bryans.

Rebecca is at the edge of the group, away from the other women, and Martha stands not far off. They cannot pull themselves away from this talk, though their faces are stricken. Squire raises his arm, he is thinner still since his sickness and quieter than ever, but now he speaks loud:

—Is this the right time? How do you know just who to attack, for one?

Hearing Squire's voice, I am easier. I call down:

—We ought to wait. Send to Logan's for more men.

—How do you know what we ought to do, Boone? Did not your old place almost go Indian?

This from the shining black-haired brother. I lean down and I say:

—Did you not want to come out here with me?

—You promised us we would be safe.

—So you will be, if you listen.

Squire says:

—I sent Dan's son Israel to Harrodsburg to see if they are all
right.

—My boy rides fast. He will have more men here within a day.

So I say though I feel thick and stupid. I did not know it was where Israel was going, I do not know when he will come back and whether it will be with anyone else. Squire does not look up. The Bryan Station people talk soft. Their anger is not at a full boil, not yet. But there will be no stopping it, any of what has come back for me again.

⌣

Nothing but talk and restlessness all day. When night comes, I do not think I will sleep, but I do for a time. I dream I am a giant as I once dreamt Cherokee Jim was. I am stepping over great trees, I cannot stop walking, I go so far there is nothing but air to step on.

Next day at noon a great party comes riding, McGary leading on his bright horse. I look for Israel among the rest, I do not see him. At last he comes over the grass, trailing by a quarter-mile. I go down to meet him, I do not speak to McGary or anyone else:

—Israel, are you all right?

He leans over the horse, twisting up its mane. He says:

—Daddy, I got the men.

—I see that. You do not look right yourself.

He is holding his neck wry, his eyes pinched. He says:

—Only my neck and my head, I am too hot.

—It is too hot for anyone to be riding about like this.

I have him lean down so I can touch his forehead, and he is burning with fever, likely the same one Flanders has. The heat of his head seems to me a sign. All of it is wrong. I feel it building, this wrongness.

I walk beside Israel on his dripping horse. Once we are inside the station, it is all noise and horseshit and bellowing. McGary has got up on a corral rail and is bellowing the loudest:

—We will go to Bryans' and follow the red halfwits' trail from there. They will never see us coming.

His skin has the look of red leather now. His words screech high as he finishes, he falls into a fit of coughing. Squire is standing near with his arms crossed. He says:

—How many men have we got?

I get myself up onto another of the fence rails, my knees crack as I do it. I yell:

—The question is how many men have they got? And who are they? Do they have the British with them?

McGary yells hoarse back at me:

—We know who they are, by God! Fucking Indians is who!

I hold up my hands, they feel very empty, I say:

—If they are Shawnee, I know the way they will be thinking. Listen—

—Your Indian-loving is known, Sheriff. You ought to sit at home and sheriff your own self.

Now a laugh from some of the bare-legged Bryans and a slyer cough from McGary all covered in sweat. Rebecca's face tight at the door of the cabin as though waiting for a slap. I say:

—We should send to Logan's. At least see if they are all right there, if they can spare us any more men.

Israel says:

—I can go to Logan's.

His horse is puffing still, its soaked legs tremble. His face is red as an apple, his lips are colourless. To him I say:

—Well all right, go. I will go with you.

Now a great shout from behind:

—He says go! Boone says we are going now!

It is one of Rebecca's Bryan nephews just at Israel's back. He has a leaking scarlet burn on his forearm and soot still streaked on his glad face. My words swoop back on me like swallows after flies. The wounded Bryan arm is held up high as the roaring begins, the swinging up onto horses, the women bringing bags and shirts and powder.

—Wait. Wait!

I cry it with all my power but there is no waiting, there is only Martha running out to say *Take Neddy's horse, take it*. I turn away, I pay her no heed, so she forces the reins on Israel and says *Take it, it is Neddy's, it is fresh*. Polly is running up waving and calling, wrapping her arms round Israel as he leans over her. Squire's mouth is tight, his head dipping under his hat.

—Wait—

I say it again. But no one hears, they carry on. Beside Susy and her new baby boy, Will Hays stands shaking with ague. Another good rifleman they will not have with them. Jemima's long-necked Flanders has his gun in spite of having had the slow fever also. He bends to kiss her and touch her belly low. I know what his hand says, with its shot-off finger. Another child, always another child coming, a tide of them, a swamp of them, all full of need. And all of us riding away into the burning sun. My goddamned words have flown wrong and given us no choice.

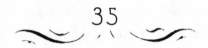

35

KEEP TO the rear, I count the backs before me as we ride out towards the remains of Bryans' Station. Some two hundred of us in a monstrous bulge. Let McGary lead if he so wishes, let him see what it is like.

Once we reach the scorched fields and the one blackened stockade wall left standing, McGary races all round it on his beautiful horse and yells:

—The tracks are here, they have gone northeast. Come on now, come on!

His great hound howls. No one stops, we all swing round and bang the Indian tracks flat with our own horses' hoofs the thudding shudders up into my neck.

We follow all day in the heat. Israel and I ride last, he on Neddy's big grey. I pour my canteen over his head and he gives one of his grins, but it is a tired one. His friend Joseph Scholl rides up with more water.

When we reach the Blue Licks in the evening, we make camp. It is a very poor one, we are scattered all about on the flat. Our fires everywhere are very obvious, but I say nothing. I only watch as McGary strides about in his buckle shoes. When he passes, I make myself say:

—No one about to catch.

He walks on. I am too tired and sore to argue further with him. I do not wish to be in this place, it has swallowed too much of me.

Sparks fly up into the night from all the campfires. I listen beside Israel where he sleeps. I do not sleep. Ned, I think of you close by in the salty ground, perhaps it will preserve you, perhaps you are waiting all unchanged there but for your poor lost fingers.

At dawn all my joints hurt me, my head aches, I have become very old overnight as it seems to me. I get to my feet and stand a moment with pain draining down in my old hurt ankle.

The river is slothful here, the salt spring is very low. The bank on the other side is greener and sloping and more heavily treed. McGary is up scouting along our side without his hat, the rising sun catches in his kinked red hair. He gives a raw shout:

—Devils! You killed my son, you skin-bags of shite!

The cry comes straight from the bottom of his guts. I feel it in mine. His dog sets to barking just as hard. McGary, you have already killed the Shawnee who had your dead son's shirt. I get to my knees so I can see who he is yelling at. Over the water and back some way near where a hill rises, two men are walking about. Indians. Shawnee? They look in our direction, they do not trouble to hide themselves. I near crawl down to the water to see them better. But McGary has more to say:

—We see you, you bastards. We see you very well.

He has calmed himself somewhat, now he has the Indians to address. A thin laughing from the other side. Some of the Harrodsburg men are at McGary's back with their guns ready. They yell as loud as he does from the river's edge. *Red fuckers. Think you can hide.*

Little Andy Johnson is there too yelling the loudest, I know his merry voice: *There is no hiding here, boys!*

One of the Bryans is barefooted and scratching at his beard. He says:

—Not the time for shooting yet.

—Why not? Indian friends of your beloved King George, Bryan? God save him and them?

This from McGary, who now sets to shouting *God Save the King* in his sawing Irish tone while Johnson prances about like the fool he pretended to be at Old Chillicothe. He catches me looking and stops. Stiff as a board, he salutes me. The Harrodsburg men roar and punch each other's arms. I salute Johnson back, I say loud:

—Well for once I will agree with my brother-in-law. No shooting.

—Have you turned British again too, Boone? Has love returned after your little quarrels? Will you have one of your loving talks together in the moonlight?

So Johnson says, he will not drop his mad smiling. I say:

—There are plenty of things I would turn back if I could. Listen to me now, do not shoot, do not act the madman here, Johnson.

—It was all acting *there*, it was all of it false, did you not see it, Dan? Did you think it a real place? Do you think it would be there if you went back again?

He is smiling on and on. I call to McGary:

—We ought to go round to their rear if we must.

McGary's gun is pointed over the river, his finger is ready, if I take another breath to speak he will fire and it will all begin and all be finished. Across the river the Indians are standing still and talking, as if they were only out for fresh air. They are not Shawnee as I can see now, no glint of big silver earbobs, none of the right paint. They turn and begin to walk up the hill. McGary roars again.

Beneath his shouting I strain to listen to their voices. Cherokee then? I do not know, I cannot see enough, I cannot hear. I do not know who they are. I cannot talk to them, I do not know enough of any tongue. I get up and go to McGary, who is standing in the water now. Into his ear I say:

—They have led us here.

McGary yells:

—We followed them!

—They are too quick to show themselves, they want us to see. Their trace was very obvious, McGary. They do not leave such clear marks generally. Why would they?

He turns to face me, his eyes a furious light blue. I count the beats of his heart in his neck. He says:

—That man of yours, Black Fish, he is dead, do you know it?

I do not breathe. I say:

—Dead?

—Yes, you goddamned fool.

I stare at his burnt face, I say:

—How do you know? How?

—A trader at Logan's told me a time ago. Your chief was shot when Bowman and Logan raided their town. Died later. Took him some time, thank Christ.

—How much later?

McGary bursts into wild laughing. His mouth is a black door. I think of the door to your house, my father, and you lying inside. How many days did you lie dying?

McGary stops his laugh, watching me hard, pricking at me. Johnson is watching me too, he is full of knowing. I only ask:

—Why did you not tell me?

—Why would I have done so? You believe what you wish to. But it is true, he is dead, buried or whatever they do with their corpses. You ought to be glad for it.

My knee bones grind as I step at him, I will stuff his words back into his head. Father, what were the last words you said? Why did I not hear? Before I can stop myself I yell:

—He made me his son!

McGary flips his gun to point at my heart. He cries:

—I had a son!

—I had one also!

I am inches from him, my breath is full of his iron sweat and his dirty-smelling shirt. The gun nose trembles. All at once McGary's eyes go redder than his face and run with tears. He lifts his gaze over my head, he will not look at me any longer, he only points the gun at my eye and yells out:

—My son John is not here to do it. So anyone who is no god-damned coward should follow me now and I will show you the Indians!

His crackling voice echoes round the flat. He whips his gun away from my face and is running to his horse, swinging into the saddle and storming into the low brown river. The Harrodsburg men are fast to mount and ride close behind him. The Bryans get to their horses too and follow. Water sprays up from the hoofs into a great screen.

Goddamned coward.

I will not be called a coward again, Jamesie, I will not hear it. And so we are all slaughtered men.

⌣

My son. My son. I go to Israel. I am half numb but I get to my horse near our fire on the flat. Israel is sleeping still on his belly with his long limbs spread wide. I say:

—Get up, we are going across.

He cracks an eye open, he says:

—To fight?

—Yes. Come on, I have your horse unhobbled, I have your gun. We are going.

There is no way not to go, I know it as I say it. I will make it right, it will be right this time. Israel turns over and half sits, then rolls to his knees with his head at a crazed angle. He says:

—I am sick still. My neck—

—You are no Andy Johnson, put your head on right my boy. We are going. You are no coward either.

I get him to his feet, I rub his neck under his clubbed-up plait, his skin is dry as paper and very hot. I hand him up onto his horse and tug his reins along with mine towards the water. When we have gone a few paces he says in a dreamy fashion:

—Aunt Martha's horse is a good one.

He is looking at me crooked, his eyes are over-bright with fever, but they are not mad. I do not answer my boy though I fear he sees you, Martha, walking through my mind barefoot, bare-legged, all bare. I do not know why this has come to you now, Israel, perhaps it comes from your uncle Neddy in his poor hidden grave behind us.

But we are in the river. We are going, we are already gone.

On the other side, the Indians have vanished, perhaps they have gone over the top of the hill. McGary has the men dismounting at the foot of the slope. It has a steeper look here, it is rocky in places amidst the bright green of the grass. McGary yells:

—Get yourselves into lines.

They are quick to do it. They like his swift marching about, his fast orders, no thinking to be done. The snapping of gun locks has the sound of small jaws all round.

To Israel I say low:

—Come on, come this way.

I straighten his gun where it is slipping from his back, and we ride round to the far left where some of the Bryans are getting themselves in order. I see his friend Joseph and I call for him to come to us. I get off my horse and I tell my boy to keep to the back behind his uncles. I give him all my shot and keep only a few bullets in my pouch. Israel is redder than ever in the face but he has his gun ready in his hand. He gives me a nod and rides back to the rear while I call to the rest:

—Get into line now, you heard McGary.

The Bryans shuffle themselves straight. McGary is leading a group up the hill already, they are digging their toes into the grass of the slope.

Now shots. Dozens of them, hundreds shattering the morning all to pieces. The men at the crest of the hill are hit and go straight down. The line just behind them turns back to look, I see their faces all confusion.

—Get the sons of bitches!

McGary's rough voice carries from the height of the hill, and others take up his yell. *Sons of bitches.*

I keep my men to the left and hold them back. It is all shots and horses braying, the smoke is already thick as a whole forest on fire. Powder burns in my lungs, it has woken my brains, it is the smell of the fort again.

And now in my mind I see Black Fish waiting outside at the fort, his hands folded beneath his blanket. Only he is not there, he will never be there, he is dead, though perhaps McGary lied to spite me. Perhaps he is at the top of the hill. My heart wants to see him in any form.

I will find him and the rest, if they are to be found. I call to my men to follow, I start up the hill now and climb hard. I know the deep ravine that splits the other side of the slope. It is choked up with waiting Indians in the thin trees, with some redcoats too. Near four hundred again, I know the number, it is the same number, it is all the same and I know how it will go. My eyes flick through the smoke, red everywhere, they are everywhere coming up out of the ravine, shooting and running at us, and we have been here only a minute, have we not? And so many down.

Our horses are mad with terror at the endless firing. I let mine go, and it careens off down a side of the ravine into the trees. A redcoat lunges for it. I crouch, I motion to my men to do the same:

—Get down! Get down.

They are pouring from the ravine now, spreading themselves across the hillside and coming for us. I turn and start back down the slope. The Bryans who were behind me see what I am about and begin to step backward, craning to see my face. I keep us to the far left of the slope as best I can. It is stony here and my knees weep blood onto my leggings, the arch of my foot cramps up tight. The men from my line follow. I see Joseph down near the bottom of the hill, I see Israel, he is crouching but not crawling.

—Down! Now!

So I call to my son. I hold up my arm to tell them all wait, wait. One of the Bryans cries something to me and I stretch to hear. Clouds of smoke hump up into the air like ghosts leaving this earth. But there is only human noise, there is nothing else here. And no path for leaving on. I keep my arm up, I yell something but I do not know what I am yelling.

The scrape and bang of hoofs comes so close they near knock me down. McGary on his horse hard at my side, his scarlet eyes above:

—Boone. They are coming round the hill on both sides, get gone. It is done here.

He speaks very cold but he wants to be sure I hear, I will give him that. I nod up at him, there is nothing to say. Once he sees I understand he pivots and gallops for the river. His shining horse brays and halts at a heap of bodies and near throws him. My men stand and begin to run also, they run like children in any direction. The redcoats and Indians are all through our lines, which are not lines any longer. The sound of rib cages bursting, arms cracking, men being torn out of this life. A knife flares bright in my eyes.

My son is not here to do it.

—Israel!

I turn, I yell for him, all the faces melt before me but his, I catch at it. I run to where he crouches near a big stone, shaking gently with his fever. When a grey horse bolts past, I have its reins, I pull it with all my weight towards my boy, it stumbles and near falls onto me. I grab at my boy's hot hand:

—Get up. Get on, run. Run.

—I will not leave you, Daddy.

His breathless voice, the sick trembling in it. I tug him to his feet. You are not fever-dreaming Israel, you are here in this terrible place, it is my doing. I say:

—Get on now.

The grey horse jerks out of my hand, Israel lets go of me. The flashing knife has caught up, it is close at my shoulder in the smoke and in the hand of an Indian I do not know. A Cherokee perhaps with enormous quills spiking sideways out of his scalp lock. But the eyes are wrong, the face is wrong, it is not Cherokee Jim. And it is not my father. Not my wife. Not you, not any of you I want. I have wished too hard to see you, and I have brought this on by it. *Do not think anymore, do not think again in your life, look what your thinking has made you.*

I shove the quilled man back with my gun. He plunges backward upslope, but he keeps his knife up and ready and does not run. He speaks as if he knows me. I swivel the gun at him and I fire. The bang is lost in the other shooting. I do not look to see if he is killed. He does not know me—

There must be another horse, they are running and tumbling all over the green hill and in the river among the men and bodies. My throat is in rags with the smoke. I cannot stop coughing and spitting. I bend and turn, I am too long in turning.

I do not see Israel. I do not see Neddy's grey. Has my boy gone? I stumble coughing back to the rock where he was. The smoke is less here but still I step on a man as I go, my foot crushes the breath out of someone. I keep running.

I see him. Down in the grass on his back, his head pointed down the slope, the grey's reins snarled round his fist and its head yanked downward near his. He is shot. Just below the neck, your poor sore neck, my boy. Your arms are thrown out, your mouth is slackened and bloodied, your blood runs in threads from it. Your eyes have the smallest life in their black pupils, it is trying to surface.

—Israel, Israel. Get up.

But he cannot get up. The horse tries to rear as I bend, the heat of my boy's hand is still in my palm. I take his hand again, I untangle the reins from it, I pull at his arm, his neck snaps back and pours a creek of blood down his shirt. I cannot hurt you this way, Israel, how can I move you?

I crouch, breathing close to your face, I think to roll you to the river, to float you someplace where I can fix you. The horse blows warm. There is still breath here. But a shower of powder comes at me on the wind. Again the smell of the fort, all that has burned.

We make our trades.

Your words, Black Fish. Were they your last ones? Were you thinking of me when you died? Were you thinking of this?

The powder strikes my eyes. And into them comes another face, another knife, blurred black and running down the hill towards me with a howl. It cannot be how things will go, it cannot be that all has turned into this knife and this howling coming for me forever.

My boy bleeds round us both. Israel, I cannot see you dead. I take the grey horse.

INDIAN
BOOK

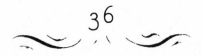

36

August 1782

SOMETHING I HAVE HEARD from one of the old Welshmen who turned up here seeking land—they are full of stories, they never stop talking.

He said that the Indians near the Ohio falls are Madoc's people. This is why some of them are fair, and their language is like Welsh. They call themselves Shawnee, which has a Welsh sound. Madoc left them hundreds of years ago, and one can say what became of him. When I asked why he would have come here, the old man shrugged and pushed his pipe into the hole in his teeth.

Daniel once talked of a little girl he knew among them—Eliza, he said, with fairer hair than the rest. He told me nothing more about her, and I did not ask. I did not want to know anything about that life.

But perhaps not knowing is worse. No one tells me my second son is dead. Daniel does not tell me. But Israel does not come back with him, and I know. How could I not know it.

When Daniel rides up alone on Neddy's grey horse.

And the horse looks perfectly well. It is not tired in the least. It stands grazing and looking round at the evening as if it has never witnessed any dreadful thing. There is another old story of a boy who turns into a beautiful horse and gallops off free. Sweet horse, my child on its back, and Neddy too, once. Neddy alone in the earth. Where is my son's body?

The day after their battle is dry and hot even very early. Before the sun is fully up, I set out to ride to the crossing at the Blue Licks. I have not said a word to Daniel, who has been outside somewhere all night. I take the grey horse, with a shovel and sheets bundled on the saddle behind me. I am the first there.

It is hotter already, even in the trees, and very hot once I am finally there. I slide down from Neddy's horse and walk across the river to wet my skirts.

The first bodies lie on the banks, some partly in the water. More are on the grass below the hillside, and more still on the hill. Dozens of them. They do not look like Indians. They do not look like anyone.

I walk everywhere, beginning on the flat beside the water and going up on the grassy slope. It is a beautiful place, green as the lawn I have often thought of. My legs dry quickly as the day heats further. I take off my damp shoes. I keep looking.

The men come later. They have shovels as well. I see Polly running through the river with her arms crossed over her chest, crying. I know Daniel has brought her. He comes over the water slowly. He keeps near me, but not too near. I see him turning over some of the bodies to see their faces. They are swollen—dark.

Most of the scalps are taken, and flies are everywhere. The smell is of hair and dry grass, with rot beginning already. I hold my cap over my nose and mouth, and I look at each one. But I do not see my son. Or I do not know him. There is no way of knowing. The heat has changed them.

All day the men work at digging graves, which ends up as one great grave. Polly sits wailing over it. In the evening, dark clouds heap up towards the east, and there is a thunderstorm far away. We do not hear the thunder, but I see the heat lightning. Daniel sits at the riverside as though waiting for someone else, and I walk the flat and the hill again.

Israel, I am not ready to tell—

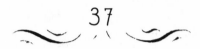

37

NEVER TALK to me of it again, Daniel—it is the only way I can go on. When I tell him so, he rides off without a word.

He often goes back to that place. He does not say, but I know it is where he goes nearly every day. He comes back in the night covered in dirt, his shirt blackened, with tears pouring from his eyes. Polly and Jemima sit up with him outside. I hear Martha's voice more than once. She has always been the sort to flock to sadness. Widowhood suits her, as though she has been waiting all her life for it. They talk on and on. I do not care to know what they talk of.

Daniel stays alive somehow, though he grows thinner and thinner. He lives on their love of him, perhaps.

I do not know how I am alive. But the children—the others—go on growing, needing more and more. My Morgan is bursting out of his shirts, leaving none to hand down to Jesse, ten years old already, and Nathan looks set to be an even bigger child than his brothers. The girls need hems let down. I make shirts and underclothes. I make bread, pies, barrels of butter and cream, wheels of cheese, salt pork and buffalo jerk, and cider, though we have only wild crabapples, nothing sweeter. When food is eaten, I make more.

I cannot sleep—I am afraid I will see Israel as a baby or a little boy, reaching up from his bed with one eye stuck shut from sleep, smiling at me, calling himself Dis as he was only able to say at first.

I walk into the woods before sunrise, where I fill my apron with so many nuts that my back hurts when I carry them back to the cabin. I pull honeycombs out of bee trees, even when my arms and face are stung. I catch fish in the dark with a net, and once between my hands.

327

I cannot bear spaces on the shelves or in the loft. I count jars, crocks, barrels, cobs.

I lose no mothers and no babies. There are several births at the station, and more coming. My daughter Jemima's, for one. When it comes, it is a long boy with a broad forehead. She is badly torn and frightened, and can hardly stand or pass her water for weeks. I hope she will be spared any others after this, but she tells me too soon that she is beginning another. I have to stop myself from weeping—I am so angry. I do not know how I can be so full of anger without it choking me to death. But I do not die.

A few of the cows are birthing calves still, though the season is wrong. The autumn is hot, even into November. Nothing is right, although Squire says the war is over. The war with the British, that is. They will not fight us anymore with their Indian friends, they have abandoned the country to us.

One morning Daniel gets up from bed even before I do. He goes outside calling for Flanders, Squire, and others, and they ride off upriver. When they return days later, Daniel is filthy and shivering, filled with a queer strength. He says they burned all the Indian towns and fields they found. This was the only thing to be done, this is the end of all, he roars before he has dismounted. He leads the rest in cheering. Late that night I ask him if he found what he wanted to. What I wanted him to. The Cherokee Jim. He does not answer. He has drunk too much and cannot wake up.

Not long afterwards, when the snow has settled in, the watch yells early in the morning. Riders are coming from the east. We are all up at once. White men, black horses, cries Squire's son Moses on the wall. The children ask if they may look, and I tell them to go. Jesse comes running back to me:

—Come and look, Ma. They have ropes and chains.

I do look. A long surveying chain swings from a tall man's belt. Little Nathan crows to see it catching the cold light. Pulling up his heavy horse, the man smiles and waves to the baby. They have come from Virginia, he tells us, holding up a sheaf of papers with a great red seal. Daniel keeps them at the gate, and does not invite them in.

The land is not ours after all, it turns out. The claims were all done wrongly. They tell us they are sorry. The tall man holds out the papers, which Daniel snatches. Looking at them, turning pages over, his face cracks open. He says: But—

Then he sinks onto his heels with his head in his hands. He tries again to speak:

—What, not a single acre?

His old injured ankle rolls, and he tips to one side.

I cannot watch. I go to the cabin with Nathan heavy on my hip. Before I am inside, I hear Daniel's voice, loud again. He is telling the officers we will move west, towards the Ohio. Towards the Shawnee land, which he knows. I know all of it, he says. We will move this whole place. His voice is louder and louder, desperation holding it up.

When he comes indoors, his face has hardened, as if it has turned to marble—as if it will not change again.

⌣

We stay the winter. Daniel vanishes on a long-hunt, refusing to take anyone with him. I smoke the meat the boys bring in, and pack some with snow in barrels so there is always plenty. I think all the time of leaving. Perhaps the yellow house in Carolina is empty and quiet, waiting for us to come back, as though none of this happened. I can fill it with food, plant the fields and garden. The soil is good there.

Polly crashes into the cabin, bringing snow and damp, and demanding with her noise that everyone look.

—Polly, if you are unable to contain yourself, go and pick nettles.

—I cannot do anything, I cannot do anything.

She is always weeping, wiping her eyes and mouth on her apron and sleeves. She has taken the weeping over from Daniel. I cannot bear it.

—Go and rock the baby for Jemima then. Peel onions. Do something with yourself. There is plenty to do if you open your eyes.

—My eyes do not work anymore, Ma, they are too unhappy.

Before I can stop myself, I am shaking her:

—You have no right. You have no—

I nearly say *children*.

She knows it. She bursts into loud tears without taking her gaze from mine, weeping for what she has imagined for herself and lost: a real mother and father, my beautiful son for a husband, children. And she is young still. I try to remember it. When I was the age she is—but I do not wish to remember.

I let her go, and say:

—Polly, I am sorry. There is no help for some things. Work will ease you.

She runs outside before I have to think of anything else to say, before she can shout my son's name, or Daniel's, or anyone else's. I send Reba after her. My anxious Levina gets up from her thread winding and says:

—Ma, what if the Virginia officers come back while Daddy is gone? Will they make us leave?

She takes my arm. Holding in a sigh, I tell her:

—I cannot see the future, sweet.

Becky, brushing the table, squints at her crumb-covered palm and says:

—I wish you could read hands. Daddy said his daddy could, but he never looked at mine.

—If I could—

But I do not finish this thought. I do not know how to finish it.

⌣

Daniel returns with a grey beard and a heap of furs, salt and meat, as wild as though he has a chest full of treasure. He lays it all at the door, full of his peculiar force. No tears now. His skin is dried out, as if his tears have tanned it.

When he sits a moment to let the children see him, he sets his hands on his knees and says he has found us our new home, and we are going. Very quickly he has the children packing up, taking apart the beds and penning in whatever hogs they can catch. He does not ask me—I do not say anything.

I bend my thoughts into the shape of a lawn. There may be one somewhere. Though the greenness brings to mind the battlefield, the grass growing over the bodies.

With Susy and Jemima and their families, we leave the station on a spring morning. The last I remember of it is Polly without shoes in the empty cabin. She has decided to stay behind with Martha, near to the resting places of the bodies they loved.

How can you leave them alone?

How can you leave us—How can you leave—

I will not leave my children and grandchildren, and I will not stay here. Polly has found her kind. She and Martha stand in their doorways watching us go. Squire will look out for them. He will not move Jane again. Daniel waves his arm high, then rides on ahead. When I look back, Polly and Martha remain where they were. Daniel is beyond sight. He left Neddy's grey horse.

He takes us upriver into the woods. We have to pass close to the Blue Licks, though he does not take us across the water there, but farther upstream. Then we go along a wide buffalo road beaten through miles of meadows. He will not say where we are going, though he keeps asking us to see how beautiful it is. See! The grass is coming up a pale green, nearly blue, rippling like a stream. The older boys ride at the front with him, and he tells them about the first time he saw buffalo in Kentucky, how fat they were from the good grass here, how they fairly begged to be shot. He sits easily in the saddle, his voice warming. I pull my shawl down to get the sun on my head, but I am not warm.

After days of riding and running with no buffalo to look at or shoot, the youngest children begin to complain, but Daniel says:

—Do not be tired yet! Look, here we are.

He turns his horse to face us. The road has ended at the Ohio River, at a narrows, where the banks are chalky. There is a tumble-down wharf and a blockhouse with a great hole in it. I say:

—And where is here?

—Home.

The water is foamy grey, rising with the melt. It sends a bilious taste up into my throat.

—There is nothing—

—There will be. One day a beautiful town, a city, you will see. The most beautiful.

—Will I?

—Will I, Daddy?

Jesse asks him, brushing his hair from his face to look around, and Daniel says of course he will. *You will be your daddy's eyes when he is gone.*

For now home is an old boat on the white bank at this place he calls Limestone. Will and Flanders set to putting up cabins along a rail fence, and Daniel and the older boys make a square stone foundation facing the river. For a trading post, a tavern, he says, with sweat dampening his head. For you, little girl.

I do not believe it. But he does, and his belief makes a truth of it. His happiness is so convincing, like a gift in a shining box. I can see how others see him. I can see how I once saw him, when I was young.

We can sell to people going west. There are enough of them coming through.

We can buy skins and whiskey from the backwoods sorts. Ship them up to Pittsburgh. Look, it is a perfect landing place.

I am afraid he is wrong. But he is right, more than right. People do come along to buy flour and salt, traps and shot, and to sell their corn whiskey and apple cider. Ginseng is the next thing, one of the rough old back-country men says, handing over a curly root. Make a man of you, he says, thrusting it up and down between his thighs with a grin. Daniel adds this to his belief. I hear him telling some of the other travellers that ginseng is the way to make good money.

But nobody has money. It is all trade. Venison for powder, a few pelts for a barrel of meal. A bundle of that hairy ginseng for a few nights' lodging. Will tries to help Daniel with his accounts, keep a correct record in straight lines, but Daniel only laughs and says he knows himself and Will is better at business than he will ever be. And he goes on trading and writing crooked columns in his book, and forgetting.

By summer, the tavern is busy every day. He buys a black woman, Easter, from a traveller. He beams when he tells me he has done it for me, as if he has settled one of his accounts for good. Easter has many opinions and is fond of telling them, but she is a hard worker and Nathan loves her ringing voice.

All the settlers coming through know Boone's, and Boone. They come to hear him talk of Kentucky, to ask him the best ways to go, the best land to claim. If I am not brewing ale, I am serving or cleaning the bedrooms with Easter. My body is glad for the work. It lets me fall asleep for a few hours unbroken, with no sight of my lost boy in my dreams. This is an open place. We can see everyone who comes.

333

A pink-skinned boy without a hat walks up out of the grassland on his own one afternoon. Where is his family? Lost, dead. This is all he is able to say for himself. He has a round baby's face. I give him a plate of soup, and Daniel says well well, he can stay here. He will be our boy now. He is happy to announce his loving generosity to the tavern, and the boy, Isaac, is eager to attach himself. He follows Daniel everywhere, doing all he is told.

Will gives us another young black girl, Luce, as part of a payment for some land to build a warehouse on. She is very young but she has a little child, Sammy, who trails around after her. She is a good worker too, and calm with the children. In the mornings I send her out with my young Nathan to help Jemima with her little ones. They are always in and out of the cool river like their mother, who is soon to have another baby, but cannot stop wading with her skirts hiked up under her growing belly. I do not bother trying to tell her to keep out of the heat.

I want my Susy to stay home, as she is very close to her own time again now, but she does not like to. I go to look in on her in the evening where she sits sewing at her table. I say:

—Come and rest in one of the tavern beds where I can keep my eye on you.

She laughs and hauls herself up from the stump-chair:

—Plenty of me to keep your eye on. You would do better to watch Becky, Ma.

—Why—what has she done?

Susy strokes her belly, and my mind goes at once to Isaac, the sweet-faced lonely boy seeking to tie himself to Daniel—but Susy sets down her needle and says quietly:

—I saw her walking up the road with one of that big group who is staying. The one with the nice hair and the broken nose.

I know just who she means. The nose has been broken more than once. The man drinks on and on quietly, always wanting the same table and tankard, his face going to mush under his wavy sand-coloured hair. He has shown no sign of leaving, though some of his company has gone already. Susy is looking at me with tired eyes. She has lines in her forehead now.

—How many times, Susy?

—A few. She cannot help herself, Ma. I never could.

I will help things. I go up the buffalo road myself in the warm pink evening air. Has Becky made a Polly of herself, now that Polly is not here? She laughed and splashed in the creek in Carolina when Polly danced there half naked, not quite bold enough to do the same. Now she is fourteen, fifteen.

It was Israel Polly was dancing for—

I look at the road, full of white chips of rock. The dust covers me and makes me cough. I will have to change my apron before dinner. I walk quickly before the children see me from the river, and take it into their heads to follow. I go half a mile in my dusty cloud, faster and faster. I do not wish to be afraid. I am angry at the thought of fear. My heart goes into a flap under my stays. If I find them together—if I find him on her.

Daniel is in the meadow he has fenced to the right of the road. He is breaking a horse someone traded him, a long-legged young chestnut, which keeps trying to crop the thick grasses, nearly throwing Daniel when he hauls its head up with the bridle. His face is set on winning, it is all he is thinking about. Isaac stands watching. His skin is pinker in the sunset, making him look even more a baby.

—This one will be a runner, Isaac! Look at the pretty white stockings on those hind legs! Though she seems to think I have put a burr under her saddle.

Daniel whips the horse's head up. It rears beneath him, and he laughs and calls it a good girl. We will breed her, he says, stroking its ears to the tips.

This talk of breeding—I cannot listen. I say to Isaac:

—Have you seen Becky with any of the guests from the tavern walking out here?

—No ma'am.

Isaac always calls me ma'am, and reaches to tug at the hat he does not have. I touch his arm and look him in his light eyes. Their pink lids look tender:

—Not anyone?

Daniel rides close now:

—What is it?

—I was asking Isaac if he had seen Becky with one of the men from the tavern. The one who drinks too much.

—More than enough of those! I have seen no one about, have you?

—Susy says Becky has been with that broken-nosed man.

Daniel's mouth tightens, but he turns it into a small smile. The chestnut skates to the side and bends its forelegs. Daniel laughs and slaps its back:

—Lively girls cannot be stopped. Can you, pretty?

—For God's sake, Daniel. Would you have your daughter run off with one of those travellers? You have seen how they live—she is fifteen—we can save her suffering.

Daniel's wild happiness snaps into rage. He says:

—You cannot stop things, God cannot stop things! She will do as she likes, goddammit, or I will throw this horse and myself off a cliff.

—There are no cliffs near here.

—Oh you are very cool now, my lady, knowing all about this country as you do. You have all the answers, you know what is in store for everyone.

—You have seen our other daughters with child too many times, and too young, and without homes—would you like never to see this one again?

The horse bucks. Daniel stays on, his neck and hands turning to purple knots. He says:

—She ought to be happy while she lives. I do not know what more I can do for her or any of them. I am getting them some good land.

—While she *lives*? Daniel!

—She is living! She is old enough to know what she wants!

I will not say Israel's name, or Jamesie's. I look round again for Becky, but there is only Isaac swatting at flies, trying to look as if he is not listening. I say:

—Do you think she wants land? Will that truly help her?

Daniel is still tight with fury:

—Yes, truly. I will get land for my children, dammit all.

—That is all you want.

—I do not want any more sadness, Rebecca. Why do you?

He has halted something in himself, he has made it stop working. I see this as he digs his heels into the horse's sides. This is how he is able to live. My throat aches with the kicked-up dust. I turn and go back towards the little settlement, swatting flies away from me and calling for Becky. I hear Isaac shuffling some way behind me. I know Daniel has sent him. I have not walked any distance alone for so long, perhaps it would not be possible for me to do it any longer. Perhaps I would fold up and vanish if I tried.

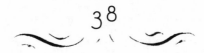

38

I DO HAVE happinesses. My girls' babies born safely into my hands. That scrap of my mother's dress, though I never look at it. My daughter Jemima with me again too. I remember these things. I do remember, he cannot say I do not.

At the tavern, I change my apron and clean my hands and face, and I give Isaac a cup of cool ale. He thanks me, but his thoughts are back at the pasture, and he keeps looking to the door. Daniel is like daylight to him and others, warming them and making them wish to live in it all the time. But it is not always daytime.

—Isaac, will you go and see if Easter needs any more flour ground?

He nods and trudges off. The children want their dinner, the guests want rum and whiskey—I look, but that broken-nosed man is not among them.

When I am in the tavern cellar later, Becky comes down quietly, brushing her hands on her skirts. Her face is half guilty, half shut, as it used to look when she had broken the eggs or let the milk go rotten but could not admit it even to herself. I have to turn away, but I say:

—You have made up your mind then, Becky.

—Ma—

—You do not have to explain yourself to me. Only be sure, as sure as you can be. This is not the only life for you.

I look at her, and her face closes fully. She does not understand me. Perhaps I do not understand myself. Is there another life? I upend a barrel and say:

—Help me get this upstairs.

At this she is relieved and comes over to carry the cask herself. And soon Daniel presides over her marriage to that handsome broken-nosed man Philip in the tavern, blessing them and saying:

—Philip was a friend to horses in the Bible, do I remember right? Good man, you can help us get the best of the horseflesh breeding here!

He does not remember right, but Becky hugs her daddy, crushing the garland of daisies Levina made her, the last of the year. Philip shakes Daniel's hand, looking as though he does not know quite where he is.

They are all talking of horses' gaits and shoulders, dancing and staggering and passing a jug, when there is a shot outside.

Some of them do not hear or do not mind it, and carry on spinning. Daniel grips my arm. He says:

—Over the river.

—What?

—That is where it came from.

He pushes through the dancers and out the door, strange and tense as an animal, the way he was when he came to find us again in Carolina. He is more than drunken. I follow him. Becky sees us going but does not leave her Philip's arms. The air from the river chills my face and neck. Daniel is in his good linen shirt from the wedding. It shines white in the water, where he is wading out and across before the next shot comes. He stands frozen. He does not have his gun.

—Daniel, what are you doing?

The music inside does not stop. I call louder:

—Who is there?

—Do you not know me?

The voice is booming. Another shot flies. A horse whinnies, and
our horses in the pasture behind begin to answer across the dark.
Daniel crouches. Then he is running deeper into the river, sending
up great splashes, crying out:

—Kenton?

The man riding in from the other side—I know him. Simon
Kenton, a big young man from the fort.

Daniel gasps:

—Not dead! Not dead!

—Not at all! Back again from an Indian holiday!

Daniel is up to his thighs in the water. Kenton slides down from
his horse, and they are laughing and grasping each other's arms.
Easter and Luce come out behind me, and Easter says in her
resounding way:

—That big man, is he a madman?

Luce murmurs:

—No more mad than the master.

I do not scold her. Daniel is laughing so hard he cannot breathe.

—⌣—

These men, back from the dead, showing just how alive they are.

Simon Kenton joins the dancing and tramps the bride around
the room in his arms, so high her feet do not touch the floor. He
takes a turn with Daniel, the two of them wet-legged and barefoot,
leaping and scrabbling like cubs. Kenton has a great bald scar on
one side of his head and a sore eye. All Daniel's scars, most faded
white now.

Kenton yells:

—We will be neighbours again! I am starting a station a few miles over. When I heard of Boone's tavern, I had to see it! And here you are! The man himself!

340

Kenton tugs at a thick hank of his hair and gives a clumsy bow. Daniel grabs him by his great jaw and says:

—Well well, we are all starting again! How was your time with the Indians—Shawnee?

Daniel's eyes are careful. But Kenton only laughs and says:

—Got me a Shawnee mother now! I do! Called me Cuttahotha!

Daniel's mouth slackens:

—Cuttahotha, condemned?

—That is right, ha! You see how much their names mean. Wait now, I have a gift.

He goes out to his horse. Daniel's eyes follow him, full of some sort of wish. Kenton comes back with a thin book under his arm, which he hands to Daniel with a broad grin:

—You will have to spell it out for us all, sir.

Daniel touches the cover. He reads aloud in a long breath:

—*The Discovery, Settlement and Present State of Kentucky. To which is added an appendix containing the adventures of Colonel Daniel Boone, comprehending every important occurrence.*

Now he looks round, a queer shine in his eyes. He has lost his smile. Kenton rubs at his swollen eye and sets to clapping, and Isaac soon follows, and so do the rest. The little ones still awake cover their ears and screech. I pick up Susy's Swan and hold her tight. Already her legs are long and without their baby fat.

Daniel sits down, silent. Kenton says:

—This book is everywhere, did you not know? I am sorry I cannot read.

—Then you did not write it.

Kenton booms out a laugh:

—Not me! Though I know the story already. Look, it is a real book, printed up nice.

—Well well. Every important occurrence.

Daniel is nearly trembling, as though he is held between happiness and terror. He holds the book too tight. He decides to believe it, I see him. He grins around the room and nods. His back loosens. Kenton cuffs his shoulder and says:

—I am only sorry I have nothing for the new pair. I did not know it was a wedding day.

He raises his tankard to Becky and Philip. Daniel says loudly now:

—Well. I have other daughters yet. What do you say, Levina?

Isaac, always near to Daniel, laughs. My poor shy girl rushes off down to the cellar. Daniel, do not tease, do not make things happen.

But he has risen on his current of happiness, and has begun to sing. *By chance a fine Kentucky girl, I happened for to see—*

⌣

Susy has a boy this time, quickly and easily. She calls him Boone. Soon Jemima has her own next boy, and she is torn again, but she comes through. She calls him James Israel. I call both of them Baby.

This book—does it talk of my girls? And my lost boys? I am glad I do not read enough to know.

More and more travellers are coming, some with families, although it is late in the year. I deliver a poor country-Dutch woman before her time one night. The child lives, though she is as spindly and tiny as Jemima's Sallie was when we first saw her at Boonesborough. I keep her by the fire and feed her some of Susy's milk soaked into a cloth. The woman is poorly and has to stay at the tavern for weeks. She says they cannot pay, and frets herself about it. I tell her it is no matter, but when her husband insists they go on to get Kentucky land before it is all gone, she pushes a set of silver spoons into my hands and will not take them back. You have, she says, and puts her hands behind her back. I can see they are her own by the way she stares at them. They are curious old things, prettier than I have ever seen, with tiny oak leaves patterned into the handles. I wonder if the woman ever thinks of them again and wishes she had them back.

Many of the people have copies of the book with them. Some of them cannot read a word, but they have it, calling it the Boone Book, or the Book of Daniel Boone. Some ask if he knows it, and he begins to enjoy telling them he is the very man it talks of. He widens his eyes when he does, he loves to see their surprise.

He goes back and forth with Simon Kenton, talking of horses and land, settling again into his skin, though I do not think he knows what his skin is truly like now. His back and ankle are often stiff, but he still walks with strides too long, as though he were always trying to step over something.

In October he is fifty. Living.

Well well, do you believe it? I do not, he says, patting one of the babies' cheeks, then his own. At the tavern Levina bakes him a cake of her own recipe, with some of the ginseng in it. He pronounces it the best cake he ever had. It will make me quite a lively man again, he says with a wink at me. Levina blushes fiercely, and Daniel passes slices around, saying it will make all of us lively, why not?

Afterwards, Jesse and Nathan have him read some of the book aloud. He laughs, but he does so. And tells them it is a true book. Truer than Gulliver!

I do not listen. I go to the boat cabin where we sleep still. There has been no time to build a proper house. When we have a house again I will make a bigger featherbed and new pillows. New sheets as well, when I can weave them.

It is a dark cabin with small windows, and I bump into the little table Daniel built to fold up into the wall. He has left it open, and now his ink has spilled onto the floor. I bend to scoop up the horn, but I knock a book from the table as well. I throw a cloth over the ink puddle, and I take the book to the door to see what damage I have done it. But there is no ink spattered on the red cover. Only words. In the fading daylight I peer at it: *Indan. Indian. Indian Book.*

343

No letters I know beyond the *O*. No *X* or *S*. I do not know the others well enough to be certain. The words are in his hand, but I will not ask him if this is what it says, and I will not have Jesse or Morgan read it to me. But inside is nothing, empty pages. The paper smells of nutshells, and is very smooth.

Daniel—if you write your own life, will this be all you have to say about it? Your Indian life—

I let the ink stain settle into the boards. I leave the book on the table. When I go outside, I hear someone strike up the fiddle in the tavern. He is a poor player, whoever he is. Someone else is banging a rhythm on a table. Not dark yet, and all this noise beginning. The evening will be busy. My leg throbs where I struck the table, and my right hand is covered in small ink spots.

And I hear it, a rustling in the grass over the water, a voice. Not English, not country Dutch. Another voice replying quietly. It is a soft voice, perhaps even a woman's. I stop and look hard and listen for a long time, but there is only the fiddling and banging, the river and the wind in the grass. Who are you? Did you take away my sons? Do you know my husband?

39

I KEEP WATCH whenever I am outside. I see no one in the grass or on the banks. Until a cold bright day, when the travellers' dogs tied at the tavern begin a loud barking, straining at their tugs. A flatboat is coming down the river with men sitting on its deck, their hands tied before them. Kenton rides along the bank just behind it. Daniel is out waiting, his own hands held together in front of him. I can see he has expected this.

The men are Indians. Some of them are very young, some in middle life. Some have their hair shaved except at the top. All look chilled and tired. Daniel pulls the boat in to the landing place upstream from where Easter and Luce and I are filling the wash kettles with my girls. The dogs go mad.

—Here you are. How do.

He says so to the officers on the boat. They pull the Indians to their feet and prod them off board. They are tied to one another by the waist. Daniel looks each one closely in the face as they come: How do, how do. I see his disappointment that he does not know any of them. Jemima beside me says in her sudden way:

—What are they doing?

Her young Sallie picks up a rock and hurls it. It splashes short of the boat. I take her little fists:

—Hush.

Susy says:

—Ma, who are they?

—Hush.

I watch the men standing on the bank in complete stillness.
Daniel has his red book with him, and sets to counting and writing
in it. *Indian Book.*

Waving towards the meadows, Kenton says to one of the officers:

—You see this is a pretty place for prisoners. Dan here will keep
them safe for you.

The officer nods and says:

—Colonel Boone. Captain Kenton.

Daniel and Kenton nod back in a very military fashion. The girls
and I watch them walk the Indians along the path to Will's warehouse, where Will is waiting. Susy says:

—He did not tell me.

Sallie picks up a handful of pebbles and eyes the boat. Jemima
shakes the stones loose from her girl's hand, and says:

—Did Daddy tell you, Ma?

—He tells me very little.

—Well then, you ought to ask him. What are they doing?

Jemima throws her plait over her shoulder, set to follow them,
but I stop her:

—Stay with the children. Get the wash water boiling, Easter
and Luce.

I go myself, picking through the frozen puddles. Through the
tavern window, I see Becky leaning across the bar to hold her Philip's
face and kiss him. He is hanging onto his tankard. Will's warehouse
smells of ginseng. Daniel and Kenton have the Indian men inside
now among the boxes and barrels, and are looping their ties to rings
in the wall at the back. A smell of wood smoke and sweet tobacco.
Looking up from his papers, Will sees me. He says:

—Susy all right?

—Yes. But are you? What are you doing with these men?

His shoulders rise, and his eyes shift towards Daniel. He says:

—We are keeping them here. The pay is good.

—Real pay? Not more ginseng?

He gives a short laugh and shakes his head:

—Government money. They sent them down from Fort Pitt. We can keep them cheaper than they can. Look.

He shows me all his lines of tidy figures. He knows I cannot read them, but I stare at them as though I have learned. His shoulders rise higher. I say:

—Then we are running a prison.

—I suppose so.

I hear Daniel speaking in a different tongue to one of the Indians, a short stocky man. He is very earnest, speaking gently and slowly. I catch my breath:

—Will, what is he saying?

Will shakes his head and takes his papers back. The man Daniel is speaking to is frowning and opening his tied hands as best he can. He does not understand either. I say:

—Do you know him, Daniel?

He turns to me in surprise:

—No. No.

—Then what are you talking of?

He gives me a hard look for a moment, then says:

—You know who I am looking for.

Your other wife, your child—

It hurts me to think. The short Indian man holds himself very still, watching my face. I hold myself more still, and I ask Daniel:

—Is this what you are doing?

—Yes. I told you I would find him, and I will.

—Him.

—You know who I mean.

—You think you will find—him—this way?

—Yes.

He cannot stand still. I cannot bear the thought of Cherokee Jim coming here, prisoner or not. And I cannot stand the underground smell of the ginseng any longer. I go outside and get to the washing.

❧

Indians steal horses in the night at Kenton's Station. He comes to the tavern in a rage to tell Daniel:

—Bold as can be, moccasin prints all over the snow in my paddock. I saw more near your fields on the way here. Cannot have been many of them, but they got three of my mares.

He bangs on the bar. Daniel frowns and gets up:

—Well. Our guests are locked up tight in the warehouse.

The girls and I have more cooking to do for these guests, on top of the tavern ones who keep coming. Bread baking from morning till night, flour drying out my hands and eyes. I hardly look up from the stoves and the taps. But now I brush my forehead and I say:

—Was it your Shawnee mother come for you, Simon?

Kenton gives me a gruff laugh, but Daniel stares at me sharply:

—It was not the prisoners, I know that.

Will says he will fashion another lock for the warehouse doors if Daniel will help. Keep everything safe on both sides. Daniel says he will of course, but I wonder how good his locks can be. *Billy Broke Locks*—the old song for new mothers. Susy began singing it the other night when Becky told us she is with child, her face red. My sadness surprised me. I will not be a mother again in my life. My Nathan is already nearly six years old, his face a copy of his father's, but a child's still, and sweeter.

When I go out for water I wonder how it would be to see an Indian standing at the river looking at us, unmoving. An Indian woman, perhaps. I wonder what I would do.

⌣

The Virginia people make Daniel a government representative. More prisoners come and go, and Daniel goes back and forth into Virginia on this business. He takes to wearing a cloth around his neck always, and a good shirt. With Morgan and Jesse he goes on longer trips to make claims he can sell to settlers, and to trade and sell his racing horses. They are faster and prettier all the time, fed on the good grass here, he says. He kisses me with a wink and says I am his prettiest.

—As though I am one of your horses, Daniel.

—Finest I ever had.

He kisses me again and swings away with the boys. It is hard not to catch his hope, even now. It is a warmth in my body as I stand in the snow.

Just before Christmas, he comes back prouder than ever and tells us he has been asked to make a treaty with the Shawnee at the mouth of the Great Miami, down the Ohio from here. We will have a lasting peace, we will be all right, he says. In the tavern there is much talk. The room is hot with agreement. Kenton yells:

—My horses will be safe, goddammit!

Daniel cheers and stands a round of rum for everyone. *Merry Christmas, Merry Christmas, peace on earth!*

Philip breaks a cask in the drunken dancing, and a patch of floor is soaked. The smell will never come out.

In the boat cabin that night I am alone. Morgan, Jesse and Isaac have taken Nathan to try trapping on one of the creeks. Not far and a shallow creek, they have promised me. I cannot stop thinking of my boy, my youngest, but he was so pleased to go, and they said they would have him home in the morning. I keep his little face in my mind. I do not think any further back, to how he was, to how any of them were.

The fire cracks and I jump—and Daniel is beside me now in the bed, moving about in his restless fashion, as though his limbs itch.

—What is it—what are you thinking of?

—The treaty, I suppose, little girl.

His voice is slow with drink. I say:

—You ought to sleep. Will you leave soon?

—In the morning.

—At Christmas?

—Best time for it. All arranged. We will meet them in a few days.

—You are certain.

—I am.

He throws his arm over me and presses closer, breathing on my neck and stroking my ear.

—What do you hope to get from this, Daniel?

—Some of your best love, your pretty—

I laugh and swat at his hand, which has crept up under my nightdress. I am so tired, but he is warm, and his drunkenness catches me:

—I meant from the meeting. Will it be a true peace this time?

—Yes.

He is stroking me, his fingers soft as mice. I say:

—Well. I hope you are right.

He tugs my arm backward and smacks a kiss on my palm:

—You are not a hopeful lady, but I will give you something, as it is Christmas.

—Daniel, I do not trust you—

I am laughing under his kisses now as he covers my face with them. He laughs also, his mouth over my lips:

—Trust me, trust me, I will show you how!

He slows, his mouth softens. We are hesitant with one another. Then I let my body know his again, and it is easier. He says into my ear:

—Can you not see? How things could be?

The fire is so low now I can see nothing at all, not even his face above mine. But I tell him I see, yes. I kiss his eyelids.

The winter sets in hard as he and Kenton and Flanders take some of the boys with them to the treaty making. I watch them disappear into a snowfall. I am called one night to a birth at Kenton's Station. Simon's young wife is deep in her labour by the time I get there through the drifts. It is long but goes well, and the baby comes out plump and pink, with a lovely round head. As I am cleaning the new little girl, I say:

—This will be a surprise for your husband when he is back.

She is slack-faced in her exhaustion, and can hardly speak:

—I have had enough of surprises.

I put the baby to her breast and she gives a sudden yell. I say:

—That is one surprise, I know. Here, hold her closer to you. Soon it will not hurt so much. We do get through it.

She glares down at the baby and sniffs, wiping her eyes. Her name is Martha. Perhaps all Marthas have this way about them, thinking they have been wronged by life.

It is evening again by the time I am near home, and my fingertips and ears are icy from the slow ride. As I pass Will's warehouse, I hear the prisoners talking in their soft language. I wonder what they are thinking of in the dark. I wonder if they are cold also. It is not good to be so cold.

Will keeps us in fresh meat through January, with no help from Philip. Susy is proud of her husband's abilities with a gun. Becky cannot keep her hopeful gaze from her own man, though he does so little.

When Daniel and the rest return, they ride in easily, talking and talking, as though they have not even realized they are home. Nathan is outside in the white sunlight with a stick he has sharpened and takes everywhere. He bellows to his daddy and brothers over the ice and water:

—Can we go trapping now?

At this, Daniel takes notice and waves with a whoop. Once across the river, he dismounts to pick up our boy:

—Well well, are you ready to take over for us all?

Nathan hurls the stick, which bounces off the frozen ground. Daniel laughs and sets him down, tucking his own hands under his armpits, stamping his feet:

—And where is your ma?

I watch him look for me. His eyes have the same hope as Becky's. I go just outside the tavern door and hold myself there until he sees me:

—Ah. What have you been doing with yourself, Mrs. Boone?

—Sewing fine seams and the like, of course. As always.

He comes to me and kisses my hand, then my cheek. His beard has grown in and scratches me. His skin is icy, his lashes frosted together. He says:

—One day that is all you shall do.

—Is that so.

—That is so!

Jemima wraps her arms around him from behind, and he spins to embrace her properly, rocking her side to side. She says:

—Did you bring more prisoners, Daddy?

—No no. Soon there will be no more prisoners. We signed the treaty. They have given us more of the Ohio valley. They will not come here.

He is smiling and dancing her about now. Flanders comes up as well, slapping his cold hands together, and he says:

—They were not so happy about it.

Daniel looks to him and says:

—I know Moluntha. He will keep the rest peaceful.

The name catches in my ears. The low way Daniel says it, as though his tongue has become someone else's. Jemima stops the little jig with a cry:

—Moluntha—that was one of them at the fort, I heard you talking of him when they came. He saw my hair—

What does she mean?

Jemima pulls her plait now and touches her belly, rounding again already. She stares at her daddy, then looks at me and closes her face up. She never does this. The silence cools. Daniel holds her until Flanders moves to embrace her himself. I wrap myself tighter in my shawl, and I say:

—Who is it?

Daniel says softly:

—Moluntha is a chief, a good chief, a sincere one. An old man. I know him.

—How do you know he is good? Did he tell you himself, in his own tongue?

Fury stirs through Daniel's body. It is always ready. But he says only:

—You will have to believe it. We signed the treaty, at any rate, and there will be safe land for all of us soon. Now we ought to get inside before we all turn to ice. Becky! What have you got to warm us?

Following Daniel, Flanders leads Jemima inside. She does not look at me again. At the bar, Becky is setting out cups and tankards. When Daniel turns, he is smiling, the ice in his eyelashes melting down his face.

He goes again. Longer and longer. Hunting, surveying, government work.

Still we do not have a real home, though we are busier than ever at the tavern and trade house, morning to night. Will keeps more prisoners. The children like to peer through the cracks in the warehouse walls and make the men speak. They learn a few words of Shawnee, or perhaps it is only nonsense they are all talking to each other.

It is autumn when Daniel announces he is going on a raid. Up the river to the Miami, where the Shawnee still have some towns. The people there did not agree with the treaty and are making noises about attacking settlements. Daniel's face is bright though he tries to control it:

—Who is with us? Any of you boys ready for a trip?

Some of the travellers roar and raise their tankards. Isaac get on a chair with his cup held high. Flanders is nodding, and does not see Jemima spin and leave the room. I leave as well, but I know my daughter. She does not wish to talk with me.

I go to the boat cabin to be alone. Nathan comes trotting in and I send him straight to bed. When the others arrive—*Ma, Ma*—I do the same.

I sit at Daniel's table. The hum of talk from the tavern is loud. I stare at the fat-lamp as its flame shudders. I do not open the Indian Book. I do not touch it.

—One last raid, Rebecca. It may not even be a fight. Likely not.

The boys are asleep by the time Daniel appears and tells me this. He is careful with his words. I lift the lamp to see his face better:

—Then why go?

—I am a colonel now, do you forget? And I told Ben Logan we would back him.

—Can Logan not do it himself?

I am careful with my words as well. Our carefulness is painful, a tightness around my ribs. He gets up and looks out the little window. He says:

—I owe Logan. He helped me once.

He says no more. I tell him:

—Go then. But you will not take my boys. None of them.

Nathan murmurs and rolls over with a smack of his lips. Jesse gives him a shove.

—All right.

—You will not.

The boys are still again. Daniel comes to where I sit at the little table, but he does not touch me:

—I said all right.

He gives me this. It is one thing he gives me.

40

THE DOGS HOWL at once, all at the same dreadful pitch. Flanders is the first back—he sinks from his horse on the path and does not get up.

Jemima flies up the street, past the open tavern door, her children trailing after her, the baby wailing back in her house:

—Flan!

She kneels and grips his neck, shaking him:

—Where is he?

The first question. She shakes him harder:

—You are all right, you are! Look at me! Where is Daddy?

Her cry is wild. I see Flanders shape his mouth into a word: *No*. My joints freeze. Levina and Becky, Easter, Luce and her little Sammy follow me outside carrying dirty sheets from the tavern beds, as if they cannot let go of them. Jemima screams:

—Where?

—I do not know. I did not see—afterwards.

Flanders tries to look at her, but his forehead and temple are cut, his thick brows clotted with blood. Jemima touches his head, then slaps his cheek:

—After what? What happened?

—He was all right—when I saw—

The dogs howl on. The children are crying and clutching at their ma. I say:

—Jemima, get him inside. Help him, girls.

Luce and Easter wrap the sheets around him, and Jemima gets him to his feet. Becky's Philip watches through the window. She goes to him and tucks herself under his arm. The rest of us help Flanders into the tavern and sit him near the fire. Luce takes the little ones away while I check his head. The cuts are not deep, but they are long and wide, and need cleaning and poulticing. I look into the openings in his skin, the blood dried in smears and trickles on his face.

Daniel—

When he has had water, Flanders tells us what he can.

They wanted a fight, we gave them one. We won.

A lot of them at the first town, not so many we could not give them a licking. Plenty on our side. Logan's men too. Ready.

Daniel was fighting someone, shouting. Then something struck me. A tomahawk or a club maybe—

—Flanders, what was Daniel shouting?

I cannot help asking as I wipe at his forehead, and he tries to speak further, but his words come slow and muddied. He rolls his eyes towards me, but he cannot lift his wounded head, though Jemima pulls it upward between her hands.

—Jemima, he is exhausted. Go and find Susy.

My oldest girl has lint bandages and dried oak bark for the bleeding, left over from her last birth. And I want her near me. With a sigh, Jemima gets up. But when she is at the door, she cries:

—Simon!

It is Kenton, riding hard at the front of a straggling line of other travellers. He pulls up outside and comes straight past her to me, tugging off his hat, his scar a deep sickly purple with cold. Unhurt, but changed. Taking a great breath, he works his mouth. No—you will not speak first:

—Simon. Where is he?

—I do not know. Not yet.

He takes my hand, wet from the cloth. His own are enormous,   357
dry and dented with the marks of the reins. He says:

—It was that firehead, that McGary, you know. It was not Dan's fault, none of it.

Hugh McGary, whose son was murdered like mine, like two of mine—I pull my hand away:

—I do not want to know. Only where is he?

The others have come in now and are standing in a shuffling row, some of them bruised, one holding a broken wrist against his chest. I say:

—Becky, Levina, get them hot drinks, something to eat. Tell Jemima and Susy to bring more bandages, and fetch my bag. Isaac, see to their horses, get the boys now.

They all run to help. Kenton catches at me again:

—Rebecca—ma'am—

I turn to stare at him:

—Simon, do not say a word to me if you cannot tell me where he is.

—I will go back and find him.

He looks fit to cry, like a great child who has ruined something precious, something that cannot be repaired. He says:

—We won. They agreed to a peace. It was McGary—

—Do not tell me! Will you never stop, any of you?

I brush past him and go outside and up the path to the boat cabin. Lint, oak bark, oak ooze, water. These are the only words I will allow in my head.

Kenton has left by the time I am back, and we settle everyone remaining. I brew a tea to make the men sleep. I tell the girls to keep the fires high, and the boys to see to all the animals. When it is done, I send them to bed as well.

The moon comes up very white and clear, shining on the river. When all is deeply quiet in the tavern, I go out to look at it. My head aches and my left eye shimmers, as though the weather were changing. But it does not change. No rain, no wind. Only the same frost we have had all this month.

I am thankful for the frost, all the silver lines and patches on the white riverbank. It gives me something to stare at. I cannot shut my eyes. I do not wish to see Daniel's face behind my lids, misshapen there. The drawings of him in the newspapers, they have never been true—always too big, shoulders too wide, the mouth a thick line without lips.

Hoofs ring on the cold earth. I look upriver. Kenton back again, with more words, unable to stop them. Thinking they will help. My toes curl. I hardly feel them.

I turn to go back indoors. The horse brays, and two of the dogs wake.

—Hush. Hush!

I throw a stick at them, harder than I mean to.

—I came back—to tell you—

My back freezes. He dismounts before he reaches me, and lets the horse loose. It goes straight for the river to drink. He staggers forward and the moon catches him. Daniel, white as a sheet, his eyes rolling upward. I force my cold feet to move, and my tongue to work:

—Are you hurt?

—No.

—You are, let me see—

—No, do not look at me.

I hold him by the arms. He stares upward, I cannot see his

expression. He smells only of cold and grease, no blood, no rum. When one of the dogs starts up again, he reaches for a stone and hurls it without looking. The dog whines.

—Come inside, you are frozen.

—I came to tell you—

He sinks to his knees. He does it on purpose, and slowly. One knee cracks as he bends.

—Daniel.

—No! You will listen, it is for you.

And he holds out his arms towards me while he tells me, as if it is a great gift he has been carrying all the way back from the Shawnee towns:

—He is dead. I saw him dead. First I saw him alive, I knew it was him, I saw his long face and his eyes, they knew me!

—What—

—No, no, listen to me! I shouted his name—I said, that is the man who killed my son in Powell's Valley, Cherokee Jim, the over-tall one, that giant—

My elbows are so tight to my sides they are bruising me. Daniel's head is still tilted back. He shakes it and says:

—Logan heard me. He came with some of his men. Big Jim tried to talk with us, then he tried to cut us, he swung his knife—

Daniel stops and shakes his head again. I have to shut my eyes. His knife, my son Jamesie stabbed and hurt—but Daniel keeps on, he will not be stopped:

—His voice was not what I remembered. He was trying to speak—but they shot him, they all stabbed him. He fought, but they got him down. When he was dead they took his scalp and cut him up. I watched.

—Oh God—

Now he does look at me. His face is bleached by the moon. He says:

—He is quite dead. All dead. I told Israel I would kill him one day, I told you also, and now I have done it.

He drops his arms. He has given me what he has wanted to since Jamesie died in the woods. *Have I done well, are you happy?* His thoughts are so plain. The pain moves into my eye. The light flickers on the water where the horse is moving, sharpening the ache. There is no relief. There is none. I hold myself tight and weep.

—Little girl. Rebecca.

I catch my breath:

—You did not bring the scalp—not for me, I do not want it.

He gets to his feet. His voice is surprised, but more his own again:

—No, I did not.

—Thank God you did not take the boys. The others—how many killed? You said there would be peace now—

—There will be.

—Are you certain?

—Yes. Yes.

—But Simon Kenton said McGary had done something, I thought he had killed you—

Daniel roars, he will wake the dogs and the children:

—That bastard, God damn him to hell! He ought to have killed me!

—Hush—

He staggers back along the bank to where the horse is browsing now. No one comes outside. In a moment I dry my face and follow him:

—What did he do?

He spins on his heel and nearly slips on the frost:

—Do you want me to tell you, truly?

—No, I do not. But you had best do it.

He lays his head and arm on the horse's side. His voice is dull:

—Moluntha was there. Afterwards. He said the peace would
hold now those who did not want it were beaten, he would see to
it. He had his pipe, I could smell his good tobacco, we were to have
a smoke together.

—The chief?

—One of them, a great one. The oldest of them. Eighty years,
must be, I do not know.

Daniel rubs his cheek on the horse. He says:

—Moluntha was taking his pull. He was in his fine old jacket, a
wine-coloured thing, he always wore it. And then McGary, that
fucking monster, came from behind him and cut his throat. And got
on his horse before I could cut his—

I gasp and my hands fly to my own neck:

—Oh—

Daniel is weeping. He slides down at the horse's front leg:

—Blood all over his jacket, all down the front of it, like Israel.

—Oh, do not—

He turns and cries to me:

—We killed his son, Moluntha's son, at Paint Creek. They killed
our sons, Jamesie and Israel, but we killed his, without even knowing it. And I killed my own father's son myself, without knowing.
They knew it, and they did not kill us.

—Your father—your Indian father?

He turns away, then back again, his face soaked and shining, his
breath hitching. He says:

—I wanted to see him. Black Fish. McGary told me once that
he was dead too. But I wanted to see for myself. I wanted to see my
family, that family. I did not see him, he was not there. I did not
see—

My eye pounds. I kneel beside him. His whole body shudders
with sobs, as Nathan's does when he wakes in the night. I cover my
eye with my arm, and put my other hand on his back:

—I know they were good to you. You have told me.

He quiets himself. He breathes through his teeth. The horse shifts its legs and blows, but does not walk on. Leaning towards me now, Daniel says:

—I wanted to see if there could be peace. My father believed it, Moluntha did also. *Wewossakie*—

He goes into his other tongue with a few more of those subtle strange words, followed by a silence. He wipes his nose roughly. I shake my head, which makes it ache the more. He feels my movement and looks up:

—It was supposed to be finished after Cherokee Jim was dead. That should have been the end. I thought I could see everything. I thought I knew every way things could go. I have won enough times.

He coughs. He straightens his back and says:

—I will find McGary.

He picks up another stone. I pull his arm back:

—No.

—I will kill him. I have had dreams, terrible dreams I *am* him, walking about with that son-of-a-bitch evil slavering dog, and those red eyes in my own head, I do not want it—

—Do you want to be killed? Is that what you want?

—I do.

—No.

He drops the stone. He puts his cheek on mine. His tears are cool on my face when he turns to see me:

—All of this, I did it for you. I would do that also, little girl.

His smile is crooked, half hopeful, willing me to love him and say so. I say:

—You will not.

His smile falls, and his expression is just like Nathan's when he was very little. A boy's disappointment and insistence. Innocent of what he has really done. Was he always this way, even before I knew him, when he was a child in Pennsylvania doing as he liked? The moon has made his hair silver and his face too smooth.

—You cannot go back, Daniel. You are here now, look. You cannot go backward.

He stands, then gets on the horse. The dogs bark and whine as he rides off. I cannot hear if he speaks again.

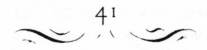

41

HE COMES and goes. Alive. Unhappy, cracked inside. When he is up and walking about again, Flanders comes to sit by the tavern fire, and tells me that Cherokee Jim was not what he had imagined. He would hardly have noticed the man if it had not been for his height, the particular way he carried himself. He likes to talk of it now that he is healing, making a story of that fight. I wish to say: *I thought you did not see him at all, I thought you were already knocked down and senseless—*

When Daniel is here, we do not speak of that man or of Hugh McGary or of Shawnee towns. It is done.

And in another year, it is all done here. None of the newer Kentucky claims belong to us, the new government has decided. Most of the surveying Daniel did has been cancelled by other claims as well. Daniel is taken to the law by some he has sold land to, and is called a liar and a fraud in the court. Will tells me so very low one evening when he returns, pulling on his ears as if he wishes he had not heard it. I think we will never see Daniel again, but he comes home one evening weeks later, stiff as a lamed horse.

He kicks a shaggy root of ginseng up and down the path without bending his knees. No one wants ginseng, as it turns out. This variety does not make men men enough. The cows and horses will not touch it.

The trade at Limestone has slowed as the news of too many claims spreads in the east. We sell most of the racing horses. We have to sell Luce also. It is bitter to see her going on a boat with her little boy and the last of the Indian prisoners. She keeps her back to me while Easter calls out a long goodbye. Daniel says there is no other way—*I am always owing, always! I do not know what they expect to get out of me.*

Easter is coldly polite with me after this, taking away her love of the girls' babies. I send her off to help with the packing of Will's warehouse when Becky's Philip buys the tavern for almost nothing, with whatever family money he has managed to keep back, or with whatever his father sends him. When we go, Easter walks at the back, alone behind the last wagon.

Watching us, Becky holds her baby Danny high in the air. She would not leave that man and his broken nose, though I pleaded with her on the last night.

A turn south. This is the direction Daniel plans for, though his eyes look worn to blankness, a paler blue than they ever were. Back into the heart of Kentucky, as though he has hidden this idea from everyone. Isaac speaks up in blushing agreement straight away. But Will and Flanders argue, and so do Morgan and Jesse. My boys are men now. They still wrestle and tease, but with loud sure voices and great long limbs. Both of them put me in mind of my grand-daddy, the certainty he was born with. He had lilies in his big house, and I thought their pollen was fairy's gold. He told me once that his own great-grandfather had been a duke, and lived in castles. Morgan and Jesse look quite princely to me. Like Madoc and his brothers, arguing all the time:

—It is finished there. Why not the Spanish territory? Plenty of land. All you have to do is swear you love their king.

—I swear it!

—Why leave it all to the fat Spanish?

—Why not go there?

—Why not, Daddy?

Why not. The idea sticks to Daniel. He sends the boys with Will and Flanders to scout out the Spanish Mississippi Valley, but he takes the rest of us south as he intended, back along the buffalo road, past the empty racing horse pastures. We go along slowly. Daniel seems to be peering at every leaf, every branch, every bird, stopping all the time to look, letting Isaac lead. When we reach a broad creek after some days, we turn off the buffalo road. Here, he says. All right.

The little ones are happy with camping and sleeping outdoors for the time, though it is difficult to settle them at night. I sit with Susy and Jemima's babies while Levina helps them bathe the older ones in the creek. They sound like ducks and owls having a quarrel.

I do not sleep much any night now. My body seems to have tired of it. Late one night I get up to move my legs, and find Daniel awake also, lying very still at the fireside, not singing or humming to himself. His silence wakes me further. I say:

—Not to Boone's Station. Not to Boonesborough.

He looks up:

—Why would I go there? Those are not mine either.

—Do not forget it.

He rolls his ankles about before the flames, clenching his jaw. His bones pain him. He says:

—I could build you a house here, just as you like.

—This is not the right place.

—Well. How do you know where that is?

—I know it is not here.

A small sadness comes over us both. I know he wishes to give me something more, something that is not real, and I wish I had some easy thing to tell him in return. I sit beside him for a time until he is asleep, talking with himself in murmurs and snores.

We stay a little time at this creek, but I find myself restless, thinking of houses. Perhaps a house I have never had and have only imagined all my life. A big house, a chimney that draws properly without any noise. A clock like my granddaddy's. I used to sit with my ear to the side of it, listening to the tock of the pendulum.

Daniel insists on going for a few days' hunt. We need to eat, he says when he sees me watching him lay out powder measures. I say:

—All right, but you are taking Isaac with you.

—Then I will take Nathan also. Time he came along.

He looks always as if he were trying to read something held too far away for him to see properly. When he tips out the powder, his right hand slips, and he curses horribly.

—The little ones will hear you.

I try to help him, but he elbows me off:

—I am not quite ready for soft eggs and skirts yet, madam. Neither are they.

He is hardening himself again, trying to keep to the shape he always has fit himself into. His eyes blaze at everyone: *Do not tell me what you think of me.* Well I will not.

Isaac is happy to go, and Nathan even happier, singing at the top of his lungs as he packs a little bag with the shot his daddy has given him. Nine years old and sturdy, but a boy still. I cannot stop myself from grabbing him before they ride off—*Be careful, be careful*—but he grins and shrugs me away. I cannot let him go without saying the words, as though they are magic ones.

For the rest of the day, I have the children picking berries, so many we do not have enough baskets to contain them, so many the flies and midges bury themselves in the heaps, and Susy's boy Boone is bitten everywhere and cries that he wishes he had gone hunting.

368   In a week they do come back, all of them, and more. Nathan is first to the camp, with a skin bundled behind him, and shouting for joy:

—I got a deer all by myself! A big one! And look who we found, Ma!

—Or who found us!

Daniel cries it as they ride up. Beside Isaac is Israel's friend Joseph Scholl. He has a ruddy skin and a new-looking hunting shirt. He was not killed that day at the battle, he is here alive. He nods and looks away when he sees me. And a little distance behind is Squire, smiling with his chin tucked in. His hair is almost as grey as Daniel's, his bones lean as ever. I call:

—Well. Who found who?

Squire pulls up and dismounts, tapping the horse's flank. He embraces me lightly, hardly touching me. He smells of the fort somehow, as it was. I pull myself back, and ask:

—How is Jane, Squire? The children?

—All well.

Daniel drops a pack of meat. Joseph Scholl leaps off to help. Bent over it and breathing hard, Daniel says:

—We asked them to come visiting, as my wife does not wish to visit them at home, did we not, boys?

Nathan shows me his gun, the lock, the empty pan. *Look, Ma—Ma—*

Daniel keeps his back to me, busying himself with the tugs. I say:

—Nathan, Isaac, help your daddy now.

The girls come flocking, the children rush to see what has

been brought. No buffalo tongue this time, a shame. Another day! So Daniel says.

Squire looks over the camp as he stretches his back, then sinks back into his hunch. He says to me quietly:

—Show me the creek?

I laugh, it is such an odd request:

—It is just there.

—Will you show me, Rebecca?

He looks at me with a frankness I do not understand. He was a boy when I first knew him, keeping himself in the stables, never having much to say for himself. I asked him if he liked horses, and he considered for a long time before saying yes.

I walk through the grass to the water, and he follows. We stand looking at the flies and the water bugs that creep over the surface. I will cut some of the reeds later.

—Here it is.

He tips his hat to the back of his head, and says:

—Martha has died. I am sorry.

I am stung by how little feeling I have. As if I had just seen one of the insects go under and vanish. Perhaps I have run out of feeling. I touch my chest.

—How?

He shakes his head:

—Some sickness, I do not know. She was living with her children north of us. Two of them came to tell Jane afterwards. That Polly and Reba you were raising in Carolina.

—Polly. I see.

—They wanted to tell us how good God is to those who really believe. Believe and be chosen, all you have to do. Those were her words, close to the last.

He watches a bobwhite giving itself a dust bath across the creek:

—They said she went very peaceful. Blessed Daniel's family. She wanted you to know it.

Martha, believing most in her own powers, summoning her own death, making sure it is known.

I think a moment before I ask:

—Did you bury her with Neddy?

—We hid Ned pretty well. I am sure her children put her somewhere close to where they are living.

I watch the bobwhite flicking its wings. I say:

—Thank you. For coming to tell me.

Squire nods, and says:

—I told Dan. You do not have to.

With this he sets out for the camp. Partway there, he comes back again, and says:

—Do not let him stay here. He will fight those people suing him until he is dead too.

The bobwhite gives itself a shake and flies off clean. I say:

—I know it.

—Well. All right.

He turns again, but I say:

—Squire, will you and Jane go with us? He has talked of the Spanish territory, did he tell you?

—Not us. We are all right.

He stays only a night, and when he leaves, I watch until I cannot see him anymore.

⌣

We stay some weeks. Joseph Scholl stays too. He says the Spanish territory is not for him, he likes Kentucky. I grow used to his presence, though I can never see him without thinking how Israel would have looked at this age. I am glad Joseph is so ruddy-skinned, big and fair. My son was dark.

No one talks of going. This place is not a special one that I can see. But the weather is gentle, high clouds softening the last heat of the summer.

Daniel is somewhat more settled in his bones. He goes miles up and down the creek during the day, showing things to Joseph and Isaac and the children, talking and talking as though he must get all his knowledge out. *Here is how you make a fish trap, here is how you make a spear, here is how you follow a trace. Look. No, look here.*

The children are hungrier and dirtier than ever after their tramping walks with Daniel. Levina is a help to me, always knowing what needs doing before I ask, darting about in her quiet anxious way. But even she falls behind on the washing. At dinner one evening, Jemima appears in a pair of her husband's breeches when the baby has soiled her skirts and all the cloths she has for him. Holding the little one out before her, she says:

—Look at me, ha! These might be the ones I wore at the fort, when all the girls wore breeches! Fanny and Betsy Callaway and I made very good men. Aunt Martha in Uncle Neddy's coat.

The children spit out crumbs of bread laughing, and Joseph Scholl gives a guffaw, but Daniel says nothing. He holds his face flat. Jemima flattens hers as well, with a sideways look at me, and goes off in silence, patting a rhythm on the baby's bare bottom. I miss her then, my one sister. My heart feels squeezed by her fist somehow. She was at the fort with my daughter when I was not. She knew my boys. She knew Neddy's body. She knew our mother, and now she is gone.

Daniel sets to building a cabin on his own, waving Joseph Scholl and Isaac away when they try to help. We will not be here forever, he says, slapping one plank down on another, sweating and red-faced. But might as well have a real roof while we are.

There is no telling him anything. I have all the older children help with rolling his felled trees across the grass from the woods' edge, making a game of it so he will stop and watch. I call:

—Who can go fastest? Show me!

And Daniel does stop, with a thin smile. But the children keep falling over, Lizzy and Swan staying hidden in the long grass when they do, one of Jemima's boys cracking his chin on a trunk and howling. He is such a howler that he sets the smallest ones off, and we do not hear the riders coming along the creek. Morgan and Jesse, sunburnt brown and trotting the horses easily, as if they own all they see.

—Boys!

They wave and canter towards us, bracing themselves over the horses' necks. Morgan is first, Jesse close, throwing back his untidy hair and complaining:

—Would have beat you if she had not lost a shoe before.

Morgan raises his arms in victory, and most of the little ones stop their crying to watch him dance the horse in a circle. Susy says:

—You are back! And Will?

Jemima joins her:

—What did you do with our husbands?

Morgan leaps down to embrace me and rolls his eyes at his sister:

—They are a day or two behind. Sorting out claims.

—In the Spanish territory?

—Yes. They have the money for it. But it is not so expensive.

Jemima bounces her baby up and down. He has a clean cloth again, now that Easter and Levina and I have got the washing dry. Daniel sits down on the sloping log he was hacking at, rubbing his shoulder. Susy says:

—Did you hear, Daddy?

—I heard.

He hears what he likes. He stands now and says:

—And did they swear their allegiance to that Spanish king?

His eyes are fiery. Morgan shrugs:

—It is not hard to do. Only words.

Jesse bursts forth with a long string of muddle ending in *lalala*. It might be Spanish for all I know. Lizzy and Swan giggle, and Joseph grins. Daniel says:

—Well.

He sits down again, and I say:

—We had best feed these travellers.

The boys have brought some Spanish drink with them, but even this does not soften Daniel. He is sunk in himself for the rest of the night, and shows no happiness at seeing Will and Flanders when they arrive two days later with all kinds of talk of the murky Mississippi River, the valley soil, the Spanish horses. He goes up and down the creek in his usual way, looking hard at the trees, until he announces he is going west on a hunt, on his own. It is the time for it, no one else is coming, we can all stay here.

～

Perhaps he will not come back. Perhaps this is the time he never does.

There is enough to do here. Susy is heavy with another child, more tired than usual. She rests in the shelter when I tell her to, and I take her dandelion-root tea, which she says smells too bad to drink. I tell her she will drink it, and she holds her nose and does so. She asks what is happening outside in the world, and I tell her it is still warm. The boys have found a great patch of that ginseng, which they have set to digging and plotting over. The children are nut-collecting with Easter, and bring me pretty red and orange leaves. I give Susy one from a maple, which she lays on her belly. She says:

—This one will be another Kentucky girl, if we stay much longer.

—Or boy. You are carrying high.

I pat her stomach, and the leaf slides off. She says:

—Are we staying, Ma? Will would like to go before the snow.

—I do not know, sweet.

Jemima puts her head in and says fiercely:

—We are not going without Daddy. How can you think of it?

Her anger stops me:

—We will see, Jemima.

She whirls off. When I come out, I see Jesse and Nathan trying to lift a log onto the cabin, which is hardly a cabin at all. Only the one corner shows it is not a heap of wood. I tell the boys to leave it, their daddy will not like to see it done without him.

When the weather turns and we begin to lose daylight, I cannot stop my thoughts. I worry he will be cold—he is alone—or perhaps not alone. *White Indian*. They all said so of him when he did not return from the Shawnee, when he did not even try—

⌣

It is winter, too late to go. I cannot leave him lost this time, coming back here to find us gone. When I try for a few hours' sleep, I see his grey hair in the snow—it troubles me all day.

He comes back in a great blizzard. We do not see him until he is upon us, stumbling outside the door of the cabin Will built for his family. He does not call out. The horse is walking head down, without direction. He is huddled on its back, wrapped in a hide against the blowing. Jemima is the first to reach him, crying that

Daddy is back, Daddy is back. Come down and get inside, Daddy!

Will and Isaac go out with lights, calling and reaching for the reins, but he does not speak to them. He does not move as they walk the horse to us. Is he frozen? Is he breathing?

Over the wind, I call:

—Daniel, you are home. Come in and get warm, now. Fetch him some rum, Jemima.

She does not listen. She pulls at him, whatever she can reach through the frozen hide:

—Daddy!

Now he turns his head. His beard is white with ice, his nose and cheeks chapped purple. Joseph Scholl behind me says:

—Can I help you down, sir?

At this Daniel speaks:

—Well all right. But take care.

His voice is thin. He turns his body stiffly and holds out one arm, which shifts the hide.

A child, curled sideways into a ball on the saddle before him, wrapped in a bearskin. Wide eyes. A shining face, a wet-looking head. Daniel says:

—Keep her warm.

—Daniel—

He blinks stiffly at me, as though his eyelids are freezing shut. He says:

—Get her inside.

I reach for his arm:

—Take her, Joseph. Jemima, did I not tell you to get some rum?

Joseph takes the girl into his arms. Jemima pulls again at Daniel, and he shifts himself to dismount, but can hardly swing his hip to do it. She helps him to stand, and calls for Flanders and everyone else:

—Here is Daddy!

They press into the cabin, where Levina is piling more wood on the fire and Easter is gently pulling the heavy bearskin from around the girl, who sits staring at everyone, her skin gleaming. She is not wet, she is covered in grease. With this and the way she keeps her legs curled up, she looks like a newborn, though she must be five years old, or six. A smell of bear fat begins to spread as she warms. Jemima pushes Daniel down onto a stool. His backside strikes it hard, and he winces. He sits breathing roughly, and waves off questions:

—Enough fuss.

I fetch a blanket for the child, though she is not shaking. She scratches her head and looks alertly at me when I put it over her shoulders. Her hair is a dark snarl at the ends. Daniel says:

—She is quite warm. I greased her up well before we set out.

—Where did you find her?

—At a camp with a few Shawnee hunters, sitting on that very bearskin, happy as could be. Traded some meat and a bottle for her. I made the better bargain, would you not say?

He winks at the girl, who gives him a hesitant grin. Her grown-up teeth are halfway in. Her eyes are a light brown.

—Where is her family?

—She does not know. No matter.

—Is she—

He warns me off with a look and raises his palms to the fire. Then he bends to take her on his knee. He bounces her and says:

—She is mine now. Ours! How do, miss?

Levina gives the girl a cup and says softly:

—What is your name?

The girl tucks her head into her shoulders. Daniel laughs and says:

—She looks like an Eliza to me. What do you say, missy? A pretty name.

She does not answer. She does not say much when Daniel insists on carrying her back to our shelter, only frowning when I wipe the grease from her face and neck and put her into one of the children's shirts to sleep. I ask him now if she is a Shawnee, but he shakes his head as if I am a moth, and goes straight to sleep. The girl shuffles for a while, her fingernails scratching at the sheets, before she is asleep also. Eliza. That child he said he knew and lost.

In the morning, Daniel is happier than he has been in years. One of Susy's small daughters cries out of rage and jealousy when he trots the new girl about on his back in the snow, as if he were a young man, as if this were his only child. Even the bigger girls cry a little, hiding their faces behind the shelter, picking off icicles and throwing them at the ground.

In the spring we hear of a family missing her up the Ohio. She was taken in an attack on a farm, her mother killed when she was putting out the sheets to dry. Her true name is Chloe. She smiles when I say it to her. That is your name, I tell her, squeezing her hand so she will not forget it again.

He will not take her back himself. He sends her home on a flat-boat passing. He will not watch it go.

Only now does he say we are going. *Get me away from here—*

He takes a torch and limps over to the small cabin he has nearly finished all on his own. He sets fire to it, and stands watching in the smoke until there is nothing left.

377

1800s

MY SUSY'S last baby comes too soon. He slips into the world well enough, though small, and she names him Jesse. She has three days with him before her fever sets in, and nothing she says makes sense any longer. I cannot save her. We have to bury her in the middle of an empty meadow in Kentucky.

Will is drunk for a month. I keep Susy's children near me. I tell him we are taking them with us. I tell him to pack.

The day before we are at last set to leave, Levina asks Daniel to marry her and Joseph Scholl. I see her grasping for any sort of certainty, standing with him before everyone. She is more like me than I had known. Late that night, she comes to find me, and says they are remaining here, as Joseph wants. She will name the child already in her belly after me. I tell her she will not.

Then we go. Daniel and I live with Jemima and Flanders on a broad creek called Charrette, in the Spanish territory. They have many acres, and build a big double house. Will has another large claim nearby. He takes too much to the Spanish rum, but he keeps alive. In a year Isaac asks Lizzy, my Susy's Lizzy, to be his wife, to make himself part of the family for good, and I say if they must be married, they cannot go far. Lizzy says, in her grave way, that she will stay close to her daddy, of course. I embrace her and shut my eyes at thoughts of what is to come for her.

Her new husband and my boys raise oxen and horses and make enough money to make good claims also. It is a beautiful place here, flatter, different. I am glad of its difference. None of it belongs to Daniel and me.

Daniel goes off all the time. He hunts and traps, and says it will be easy to sell enough pelts to make a good living, get us some land east of here. When he is gone, I can hardly think. I have no young children left to think of, and so he occupies my mind. He limps everywhere now, and goes about with his jaw set hard. I ask Morgan and Nathan to help, and they buy him a young black man with big eyes, Derry. Daniel does not like him tagging along, but Derry is gentle and watchful, a good woodsman, and takes care to stay a way behind on hunts. I say to him:

—Do not let him go too far.

Derry nods and says he will not. But one winter it is very cold, and Daniel has insisted on a long-hunt, and they are gone weeks longer than Derry promised me. I spin more thread than I ever have to keep myself from watching out the window all day. My fingertips are left without any feeling.

Derry has to hold him up when they come back—Daniel has sprung a trap on his hand and broken all its bones. He is very cheerful about it, saying they had to hide in a cave from some Indians they saw, Osage, after these had told them to keep away and go home. Could not see the damned trap in the dark, he says, holding up his crippled hand, which he has wrapped in a bloodstained skin.

Later, Derry tells me in his careful way that Daniel was very bad at first with the pain, fevered and raging and full of confusion. He said Derry ought to kill him, smash the rest of him and finish it. When Derry said he would not, he would fetch oak ooze to help, Daniel asked: Are you my son? What happened to you?

Derry told him no and calmed him as best he could, but when he returned with the oak, Daniel reached for him and said, gasping: You will be my son now, will you? Are you my boy?

I soak the hand in salt. Then I straighten and splint the long bones as best I can, and poultice them. He has no fever now, but I give him teas he refuses to drink, saying:

—I am not such a shipwreck. All my own hair, my own teeth, and they are good teeth—

I say:

—No long-hunting.

—Next year.

—We will see then.

—Next year.

He sits and reads to Jemima's little ones. Gulliver, his old favourite. I have heard quite enough of it in my life. But again and again he reads out a part when Gulliver meets a man who can summon any ghosts he chooses. Famous men, emperors and kings and the like. *Now I am ready to tell about Gulliver and the ghosts! He met Alexander the Great though he was dead, did you know it? A king called Julius Caesar, a general called Pompey.*

Here he breaks off and says:

—I knew a man named Pompey once. I would like to talk to him again.

The children begin to whine for something else, but he only laughs, holding up his hand muffled in bandages:

—No no, the trouble is in your ears, listen better!

At last they win by climbing onto his knees all at once until he cries for mercy, and he reads the Lilliputians, which they love. Larkin, one of the youngest, asks if they can tie Granddaddy up that way, and Daniel says he will consider it.

It does something—that old book, and his reading it again and again.

It brings a woman. She is an Indian woman, walking from the river path straight for the house. The children hear the ringing of the tiny bells on her skirts. Jemima calls for Flanders, who goes out with his gun. But Daniel gets up from the chair in the window and yells:

384

—She has nothing with her, you can see that. Leave her be.

He limps outside to look. I stay in the doorway, watching her walk slowly up the slope. She is in middle life, with some white in the plaits that hang below her headscarf, and heavy lines beneath her eyes. Her forehead is set in an arrow-shaped frown, like the mark some babies have when they are born. When she sees all of us looking, she gives a short nod, and says:

—How do.

Daniel has stopped dead, staring. She stares back, her skirts jingling slightly in the breeze. She covers her mouth, and her severe face shifts. She points at his bandaged hand and says:

—Sheltowee. Always hurt.

Her English is quiet. He says very low:

—I know you. Pimmepessy.

—Ah!

They clutch at one another, weeping and smiling, babbling non-sense and soft words.

I go indoors. I slice a cake and bread and butter, and fetch cups for coffee and rum. I do not know what to offer. But I take all of it outside and leave it on the porch. They are still holding each other in the yard, even with Daniel's poor hand, talking and pointing and laughing at how old they are.

⌣

When it is night, and Daniel has not yet come back inside, Jemima comes to me where I am knitting in bed. The woman would not stay, she says.

—Well then.

She sits on the bed and tells me it was Daniel's Shawnee sister, who lived with him in the Indian town years ago when he was taken. She was only a little girl then, but she remembered him, and had heard of him over the years, like everyone else. He had played games with her and another sister in their bark house, he had taught them some English.

I drop a stitch, and I say:

—Well.

Jemima jabs me with her elbow:

—I know you want to ask him things, Ma.

—No, I do not.

—Well I will tell you anyhow. His Indian father and mother are dead, and the younger sister lives somewhere else up the Ohio and has dozens of children. And his wife—

—Jemima, do not—

—His wife is somewhere else too, the woman did not know where. Gone in a raid with her little girl when everything was going to pieces. She could not think of her name, but she remembered the girl. Said she was good with an arrow, got turkeys every time she tried. Clever, like Daddy.

—He was not her daddy.

Jemima takes a pull on the pipe she has taken up using. I quiet myself. I do not know how much she knows. I say:

—Why you must smoke that thing, sweet, I do not know.

—Because I like it.

She kisses me and goes down to her children. And now I am ready to tell what she told me, the last thing—

When Daniel went again and again to Israel's grave, and other times when he went off, he was calling up ghosts, which did not come. He had sent them away for too long, he did not listen to them well enough, and none of them came anymore. He could not explain himself to them now, and he was sorry for that. So he said to Jemima those nights at the station when he wept and wept outside. What would it take to make them come back? Blood? Food? Air? The right words, the right song? He had no answer. He had thought they were powerful, but they are helpless. More helpless than we are.

So he thought.

When I am gone, Daniel, I will come back—

ACKNOWLEDGEMENTS

My brilliant editor, Anne Collins, the team at Penguin Random House Canada, and copy editor Tilman Lewis. My indefatigable agent, Denise Bukowski, and her staff.

Novelist friends Corinna Chong and Adam Lewis Schroeder for reading the draft, and Mary Ellen Holland for unfailing enthusiasm. Many other friends and readers for thoughts, questions, and interest.

Okanagan College and University of British Columbia Okanagan. The Canada Council for the Arts, the British Columbia Arts Council, CBC Books, and the Banff Centre for Arts and Creativity.

My family: Peter, Jocelyn, José, Carolyn, Dan, Laura, Jon, Marcela. And to Mike, Theo, and Kate, who have shared me with the Boones for a while now, much gratitude and love.

ALIX HAWLEY studied English Literature and Creative Writing at Oxford University, the University of East Anglia, and the University of British Columbia. She published a story collection, *The Old Familiar*, which was longlisted for the ReLit award, with Thistledown Press in 2008. Several of her stories have won accolades from the CBC, and in 2017 "Witching" won the CBC Short Story Prize. Her first novel, *All True Not a Lie in It*, was published by Knopf Canada as its New Face of Fiction pick for 2015, was longlisted for the Scotiabank Giller Prize, and won the Amazon.ca First Novel Award and the BC Book Prize for Fiction.